PRAISE FOR

The Puzzle Master

"The many irresistible elements in Danielle Trussoni's *The Puzzle Master* include Mike Brink, a preternaturally brilliant man billed as 'the most talented puzzleist in the world.'" —*The New York Times*

"[A] marvel . . . It has been some time since I read a novel I found as compelling as this one." —*Mystery Tribune*

"This immersive, brilliant book is a labyrinth of ciphers, cryptograms, logic puzzles, word puzzles, and a doozy of a conspiracy. Wouldn't you like to experience a book so singular?" —Minneapolis *Star Tribune*

"Danielle Trussoni melds a heady brew of genres—mystery, horror, supernatural, magical realism, ancient history, mysticism and plain old puzzles." —Oline H. Cogdill, *The Sun Sentinel*

"A surefire hit . . . [*The Puzzle Master*] is an ambitious story, expertly told. . . . A sequel, *The Puzzle Box*, is in the works, and it can't come soon enough." —*Booklist*

"This page-turner incorporates motifs of religion, security, meaningfulness, and loss into a mystical narrative that traverses different centuries focused on the same puzzle quest." —*Library Journal*

"Intriguing . . . Several subplots involve horror, mysticism, religious fantasy and, perhaps most importantly, dolls." —*Bookreporter*

"[Trussoni] is at the top of her game in involving the reader in the puzzle-solving process, making the most of historic settings, including the Pierpont Morgan Library, and making the book's *Da Vinci Code*–

like trappings pay off. The Kabbalah meets the *New York Times* crossword in a brainy thriller."
—*Kirkus Reviews*

"Your summer beach read is a lock."
—NPR

"A smart, complex supernatural thriller about a man with a gift that's also a curse . . . Trussoni always nails it no matter what she chooses to write about. . . . Don't miss this one."
—*Locus*

"This novel has it all and more. In the nimble, talented hands of Trussoni, the pages fly."
—#1 *New York Times* bestselling author David Baldacci

"*The Puzzle Master* is a riveting tapestry of a novel. . . . A beautifully layered, fast-paced page turner that's also dense with history and lore . . . You'll want to clear your calendar for this one."
—Janelle Brown, *New York Times* bestselling author of *Pretty Things*

"An absolute gem of suspense, with a wholly original and unforgettable protagonist, a superb cast of idiosyncratic supporting characters, a propulsive plot with diabolic twists, and pure reading pleasure on every page. I loved it."
—Chris Pavone, *New York Times* bestselling author
of *Two Nights in Lisbon*

"*The Puzzle Master* is an ingenious literary thriller that combines everything I want in a book: immersive, exhilarating, intellectually provocative, unputdownable—an absolutely blistering Russian nesting doll of fascinating stories that unveil and dismantle some of the most deeply engrained ideas about good, evil, and the origins of humankind. In short: *The Puzzle Master* = (*The Da Vinci Code* + *The Silent Patient* + sprinkle of Stephen King) × gorgeous writing."
—Angie Kim, bestselling author of *Miracle Creek*

"Danielle Trussoni's *The Puzzle Master* is so addictive and effervescent that you won't be able to put it down. Trussoni displays tremendous range, moving effortlessly from intricate puzzles to a traumatic murder to ancient secrets. . . . A tantalizing and delightful read that engages both heart and mind." —Jean Kwok, author of *Searching for Sylvie Lee*

"*The Puzzle Master* is one of the most insanely compelling novels I've read in ages. This story has all the elements I love—dark histories, gothic settings, murder, vivid characters, and a twisty, unpredictable plot—all written in elegant and vigorous English. I am normally a jaded reader, but I could not put down this book. . . . Highly, highly recommended."

—Douglas Preston, *New York Times* bestselling co-author
of *Bloodless* and *The Cabinet of Curiosities*

"I loved Danielle Trussoni's *The Puzzle Master*, an erudite, super compelling mystery that I couldn't put down. It's the story of savant-level puzzle-solver Mike Brink, who's called to a women's prison to decipher a drawing that may unlock the secrets of convicted killer Jess Price. Brink falls under Price's uncanny spell as soon as he meets her, launching a story that's a thrill ride through space and time, love and hate, and even good and evil. This novel is so original that I was happy to be taken wherever she led me!"

—Lisa Scottoline, *New York Times* bestselling author
of *What Happened to the Bennetts*

"Utterly absorbing . . . The 'master' of the title isn't the only master here. The word applies equally to the author of this fabulous novel."
—Justin Cronin, author of The Passage Trilogy

"My kind of thriller." —Steve Berry, author of *The Last Kingdom*

BY DANIELLE TRUSSONI

THE
PUZZLE
MASTER

THE
PUZZLE
MASTER

A Novel

Danielle Trussoni

RANDOM HOUSE

NEW YORK

2024 Random House Trade Paperback Edition

Published in the United States by Random House, an imprint and division of Penguin Random House LLC, New York.

RANDOM HOUSE and the HOUSE colophon are registered trademarks of Penguin Random House LLC.

Originally published in hardcover in the United States by Random House, an imprint and division of Penguin Random House LLC, in 2023.

LIBRARY OF CONGRESS CATALOGING-IN-PUBLICATION DATA
Names: Trussoni, Danielle, author.
Title: The puzzle master : a novel / Danielle Trussoni.
Description: First edition. | New York : Random House, [2023]
Identifiers: LCCN 2022033803 (print) | LCCN 2022033804 (ebook) |
ISBN 9780593595312 (paperback ; acid-free paper) | ISBN 9780593595305 (ebook)
Subjects: LCGFT: Detective and mystery fiction. | Thrillers (Fiction) | Novels.
Classification: LCC PS3620.R93 P89 2023 (print) | LCC PS3620.R93 (ebook) |
DDC 813/.6—dc23/eng/20220715
LC record available at https://lccn.loc.gov/2022033803
LC ebook record available at https://lccn.loc.gov/2022033804

Printed in the United States of America on acid-free paper

randomhousebooks.com

2 4 6 8 9 7 5 3 1

Book design by Caroline Cunningham

Title and part-title background image: Adobe Stock/berCheck

In memory of James Alan McPherson (1943–2016), who

taught me that writing fiction is a form of play

"The Supreme Being is one who has created and solved all possible games."

—GOTTFRIED WILHELM LEIBNIZ

Acquired savant syndrome is a rare, but real, medical condition in which a normal person acquires extraordinary cognitive abilities after a traumatic brain injury. There are fewer than fifty documented cases of acquired savant syndrome in the world.

PUZZLE ONE

The

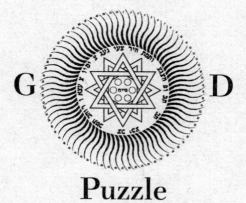

G   D

Puzzle

I

By the time you read this, I will have caused much sorrow, and for that I beg your forgiveness. As you know, my child, I am a haunted man, and while the toll has been steep, I have at last made peace with my demons. I do not write this as an excuse for what I have done. I know too well that there is no forgiveness for it—not in the eyes of God or man. But rather, I write this account of my discovery out of necessity. It is my last chance to record the incredible events, the terrible and wonderful events, that changed my life and will, if you venture into the mysteries I am about to relate, change yours, as well.

What, you ask, is responsible for such torment? I will tell you, but take heed: Once you know the truth, it is not easily forgotten. It has haunted me every minute of every day. There was no question of ignoring it. I was drawn to its mystery like a moth circling a flame—*In girum imus nocte et consumimur igni*. And while I am fortunate to have survived to record the truth, even now, as I stand on the edge of the abyss, I cannot help but shrink at the thought of entrusting such a dangerous secret to you.

I have suffered, but it is the suffering of a man who has created his own torture chamber. I believed I could know what shouldn't be known. I wanted to see things, secret things, and so I lifted the veil between the human and the Divine and stared directly into the eyes of God. That is the nature of the puzzle: to offer pain and pleasure by turns. And while the truth I am about to reveal may shock you, if it offers some small refuge of hope, then this, my last communication, will achieve all it must.

2

JUNE 9, 2022
RAY BROOK, NEW YORK

Mike Brink turned down a country road, drove through a dense evergreen forest, and stopped before the high metal gate of the prison. His dog, a one-year-old dachshund called Conundrum—Connie for short—slept on the floor of the truck, camouflaged by shadows. She was so still that when the security guard stepped to Brink's truck and peered inside, he didn't see her at all. He merely checked Brink's driver's license against a list and waved him toward an imposing brick institution that seemed better suited to a horror movie than the bright June sunshine.

Mike Brink had an appointment with Dr. Thessaly Moses, the head psychologist at the New York State Correctional Facility, an all-women's minimum-security prison in the hamlet of Ray Brook, New York. She'd called him the week before and asked him to come to the prison to speak with her. One of the prisoners had drawn a perplexing puzzle, and she wanted help making sense of it. Because of his work as a puzzle constructor and his fame after *Time* magazine christened him the most talented puzzleist in the world, thirty-two-year-old Mike Brink was barraged with puzzles. Most of them he solved in an instant. But from Dr. Moses's description, this puzzle sounded peculiar, unlike any puzzle he'd seen before. When he asked her to take a photo and email it, she said she couldn't risk it. Prisoner records were confidential. "I shouldn't be discussing this with you at all," she said. "But this is a unique patient, one who's become rather important to me." And so, despite his deadlines and the three-hundred-mile drive, Mike Brink agreed to come upstate to see it. Puzzles were his passion, his way of making sense of the world, and this was one he couldn't resist.

The prison was ominous, with steeples and dark, narrow windows. When he'd read up on its history, he found that it was built in 1903 as a sanatorium for the treatment of tuberculosis. The clean air, high altitude, and endless forests had been an integral part of the cure. The institution's one claim to fame was its appearance in Sylvia Plath's *The Bell Jar*. Plath had visited her boyfriend while he was recovering from tuberculosis at the facility and then repurposed the sanatorium in her fiction. Now the facility housed hundreds of female inmates. From the parking lot he saw a yard enclosed by a chain-link fence topped with razor wire and, beyond, a modern cinder-block addition, its severity a startling contrast to the Gothic excesses of the original building. Surrounding it all stretched an endless sea of thick evergreen forest, a natural barrier between the prisoners and the rest of the world. He imagined that such isolation was intentional: Even if a prisoner made it over the fence, even if she got free of its twists of razor wire, she would find herself in the middle of nowhere.

Brink parked in the shade, filled a plastic bowl with water for Connie, scratched her behind her long, soft ears, and plugged a portable fan into the truck's cigarette lighter, cracking the window so she'd be comfortable. Normally he wouldn't leave her alone, but he wouldn't be gone long, and the mountain air was cool, nothing like the heavy wet heat of Manhattan. "Be right back," he said, and headed to the prison.

At the main entrance, he paused at the security station, dropped his messenger bag into a plastic bin, showed his driver's license and Covid vaccination card to a guard, and walked through a metal detector. He'd been given prior approval to bring his bag—which held his laptop, his phone, and a notebook and pen—and was relieved that the guards didn't try to take it.

A woman in a loose navy-blue dress stood waiting. She was tall and thin with dark-brown eyes, dark skin, and hair cut in a bob. She introduced herself as Dr. Thessaly Moses, the head psychologist.

He didn't need to introduce himself. Clearly, she'd googled him. Still, she stared at him a bit too long, and he knew she was surprised by his appearance. He was six foot one and athletic, lean and strong and (as he'd been told) handsome, not at all what people expected of (as his mom sometimes teased) "a puzzle geek." He wore his favorite red Converse All Stars, black Levi's, and a sports jacket over a T-shirt that read SOMEBODY DO SOMETHING.

Aside from photos, a Mike Brink Google search would have brought up a video clip of his remote Zoom-in appearance on *The Late Show with Stephen Colbert,* recorded during the 2020 pandemic lockdown. He'd taken Colbert on a tour of his puzzle library and opened one of his Japanese puzzle boxes, which inspired a joke about sushi. There would be a Wikipedia page that linked to the *New York Times* Games page, where he was a regular constructor; a list of the puzzle competitions he'd won; and a link to a *Vanity Fair* profile that gave his entire life story: the normal Midwestern childhood, the tragic accident that had altered his brain, and the miraculous gift that had appeared in its wake.

"Thank you for coming so quickly," she said. "I would've driven down to the city, but I couldn't leave my patients."

"You've definitely made me curious," he said. "From your description, it seems pretty unusual."

"I don't understand it at all, to be perfectly honest with you," she said. "But if anyone can shed light on this, it's you."

Her faith in his abilities worried him. As his fame as a puzzle solver grew, people often assumed Mike Brink possessed a superhuman gift. Not just an ability to recite fifteen thousand pi places, or the talent to create a vicious crossword, but the power to read the future. But he didn't have superpowers, and he couldn't do the impossible. He was a regular guy with a singular gift—"an island of genius," as his doctor called it. The best he could do was give it a try.

"You have it with you?" he asked, noticing a folder under her arm.

"If you come this way, we can talk in private," Dr. Moses said, gesturing for Brink to follow her through a hallway.

Although he knew the prison had been created in a different mold than modern facilities, part of him had expected cement-block cells and barred windows, all the images he'd seen in movies. Instead, Dr. Moses led the way through a calm, almost pleasant space, institutional—the windows were reinforced—but human. There were potted trees near the metal detectors, art on the walls, and carpeting in the hallway. The bones of the tuberculosis sanatorium had been adapted to contemporary incarceration in the way that an old church might be adapted to a Zen meditation center: The symbols and decor had changed, but the essential structure remained the same.

She ushered him into her bright, stylish office, closing the door after him. He stood in a meticulously organized space: an immaculate desk, color-coded binders on a shelf, a Mac desktop, all perfectly uninteresting until his eye fell upon a Rubik's Cube sitting on the windowsill. It was a newer model, the cubies in plastic as opposed to stickers, a mix of blue, green, yellow, orange, red, and white. The cubies were scrambled in a way that showed regular unsuccessful attempts to solve it, weeks, perhaps months, of twists and turns as someone—Thessaly Moses, he assumed—strained to put the six color fields into alignment. He drummed his fingers against his thigh, nervous energy shooting through him. Just seeing the cube in that state of disorder filled him with an overwhelming need to put it right.

Noticing his interest, Thessaly picked up the cube and rotated it on the tips of her fingers. "I won this at the office holiday party last year," she said. "I was hoping for the Magic 8 Ball. I keep trying to solve it, but it's a losing battle. I don't know why I do it, to be honest. What's the point in wasting time on a useless exercise?"

Brink assessed each side of the cube as Thessaly turned it before him. Three moves forward clockwise, two moves backward counterclockwise, one move right, five moves left . . . He saw the series of steps clearly in his mind, each one leading to a perfect alignment of solid colors on six sides.

"The point," he said, tearing his eyes from the cube and meeting Thessaly's gaze, "is that there are over forty-three quintillion possible combinations but only one solution." He saw he had her attention and continued. "Wouldn't you like to experience something so absolutely singular?"

"Here," she said, tossing him the cube. "Show me."

He caught it in his left hand, glanced at each side so that the color blocks aligned in his mind, and solved the cube in twenty moves and, he estimated, fifteen seconds. It was not the best out there—the world champion speed-cuber Mats Valk could do it in 5.5 seconds— but pretty good nonetheless. A rush of adrenaline hit him as he placed the solved cube in Thessaly's hand. That was why he solved puzzles, right there: the feeling that everything in the universe made sense. It was like throwing a winning touchdown, like finishing a marathon, like great sex. "I have a talent for useless exercises," he said.

Thessaly stared at him, wide-eyed with amazement. "I guess you do," she said, running a finger over the solid colors, tracing the cube's perfect order before placing it on her desk. She started to ask him something, hesitated, then gave in to her curiosity. "I'm sure you're asked this all the time, and forgive me if I'm prying, but how in the world did you just do that?"

She was right. He'd been asked a version of that question a thousand times. How did his ability to solve puzzles actually work? Was it instinct? Intuition? Genius? Magic? Did he have a kind of computer in his head that spat out answers? Had he memorized thousands of solutions to thousands of puzzles? What was the trick? But the simple truth was that he didn't know how it happened. He couldn't explain it. His brain did it without his permission, the way his heart pumped blood or his lungs infused cells with oxygen. It latched on to patterns and sequences without his consent or, at times, his awareness and filled his head with a deluge of numbers and images. When he wanted to solve a puzzle, visualizing it was enough to call up the solution. Sometimes, when he recited pi places, listing numbers into the thousands, a texture emerged in his mind, a weave of color that guided him forward, just as it had happened when he solved the Rubik's Cube. Some doctors believed that this mixing up of the senses, or synesthesia, was his brain's response to his injury and the key to his abilities. But he wasn't so sure. Mostly, it was like opening a door: Information just rushed in.

Thessaly walked to the far side of her office, gestured for him to sit on a love seat, then sat across from him. When they were situated, she met his eye with the mindful alertness that marked trained therapists. He'd seen enough of them after his injury to know what to look for: the sympathetic tone of voice, the attempt to create an emotional connection. He disliked the pretense of it, the lack of authenticity, but Thessaly Moses seemed genuine. She'd brought him there for a reason.

She slid a piece of paper from the folder and handed it to him. "This is the drawing," she said. "I'm anxious to know what you think it means."

3

The paper was thin and light, almost transparent. As he unfolded it, he found a large circle drawn in black ink. Radials shot from the circle like a sun, and the outer edge was ringed with the numbers 1 through 72. At the very center, drawn in large bold strokes, were a series of Hebrew letters. Without effort, without even quite realizing he was doing it, he began to pick apart the circle, his mind scanning for patterns, searching for that particular kind of order that distinguished a puzzle from everything else on the planet: its symmetry and elegance, its hidden treasure, its need to be solved. It happened whenever he encountered a startling or unusual pattern; something sparked and sizzled in him, creating a flare of curiosity and desire that left him helpless to turn away.

But this puzzle—if it was a puzzle at all—was incomplete, only 10 percent filled with numbers or symbols, and the mystery of these absences lured him in, taunting him. *What was he missing? What did the blank spaces mean?* He laid the paper on the coffee table between them. "I've never seen anything like it before."

"But you can tell me what it is, can't you?"

He glanced at the Hebrew letters, the swirl of numbers. Clearly it was the beginning of something . . . but what? "There's not a lot to go on here. No solid pattern, no obvious sequences, nothing I can get ahold of."

Dr. Moses's expression fell. It was just as he'd thought: She expected him to wave a magic wand and reveal the truth behind the illusion. "But that's not possible," she said. She turned the paper over, revealing two handwritten words: *Mike Brink.* "She told me to find you. You must be able to tell me something about it."

"Who told you to find me?"

"Do you recognize the name Jess Price?"

He was about to dismiss the name, when an image of a newspaper article filled his mind. He saw a black-and-white picture of a woman, her hands cuffed behind her back, a headline above: JESS PRICE, CELEBRATED WRITER, ARRESTED FOR MURDER. Yes, he remembered Jess Price. Her story had been everywhere a few years back. She'd been accused of murdering a man in a Gilded Age mansion upstate. After her arrest, she'd refused to speak to the police, to her lawyers, or to the press and had been convicted of manslaughter without uttering a single word in her own defense. "You mean Jess Price the writer?"

"Well, she hasn't written anything for some time," Dr. Moses said. "She's been here for nearly five years and hasn't communicated with me until last week, when she drew that circle and told me to give it to you."

"Why me?" he asked, although it wasn't hard to guess. His puzzles had made him a minor celebrity over the past decade.

"Jess Price is aware of your talents. And while I don't know why she drew this circle, I believe it could be the key to understanding the most mysterious, most frustrating patient I've ever encountered. I've tried for years to reach her, and in the process I've seen things that make me doubt my capabilities. I'd do anything to get through to her. And yet she's asking for you."

He looked at the circle again, feeling an intense urge to fall into it, wanting to expose it the way a ray of light exposes a corner obscured by shadow. Instead, he pushed it away. "Solving a puzzle is one thing," he said. "But getting involved in something like this? I don't think so."

Dr. Moses held his gaze for a moment, then opened the folder and placed it before him. "These are Jess Price's files," she said. "Take a look. Maybe there's something here that will explain why she asked for you."

He found a stack of typed clinical reports, each with a signature at the bottom, a sheaf of photos, and some newspaper clippings. An article slipped from between the pages and fell onto the table. Photocopied from a Hudson Valley newspaper, the story featured a picture of Sedge House, a mansion built near the Hudson River, where a twenty-five-year-old man named Noah Cooke had been brutally murdered. Next to it was the photo taken after Jess Price's arrest that he'd seen five years before, the headline in bold over the top. He looked at it closely, comparing it with his memory. It was identical: Jess Price, hands cuffed, being led into a courthouse.

In addition to the newspaper articles, there was a portrait of Jess Price—most likely her author photo—and a few snapshots pulled from social media. Looking them over, he saw a woman with wide-set blue eyes, a blond pixie haircut, and sharp, elfin features. His first impression was that this woman wasn't capable of hurting anyone, let alone killing a man.

"She doesn't look . . ." He almost said *crazy* but stopped himself. "Unstable."

"From all accounts, she wasn't. Before the night of the murder, she was a well-adjusted young woman who led a relatively normal life. Now she suffers from an array of mental-health issues, none of which I've been able to fully diagnose. She appears to have aural hallucinations, meaning she hears things that aren't there. She suffers from acute anxiety that leads to self-harm—scratching her arms raw, refusing to eat, pulling her hair until it falls out. Last week she bit her fingernails down until they bled."

"And she won't communicate with you at all?" he asked, wondering how she could function without expressing her needs in some way.

Dr. Moses opened a manila envelope containing a composition notebook. "I gave this to Jess at the beginning of my time with her. I assumed it would help overcome the barrier she's created. Writing can be an excellent therapeutic tool. Her previous therapist, Dr. Ernest Raythe, left notes in which he stated that he'd had some success with a similar approach. But the result was not what I expected. . . ." She opened the notebook. It was filled with numbers and shapes, grids and lists of words, pages and pages of puzzles cut from magazines and pasted into the notebook. "She's living in a puzzle."

Brink took the notebook and looked more closely. He saw his puzzles, hundreds of them, all completed in blue ink.

"You see," Dr. Moses said, meeting his eye, "your games are the only things that interest her."

"Puzzles," he said, feeling something tighten in his chest. "I design puzzles, not games."

She gave him an amused look, as if humoring a child. "There's a difference?"

"Puzzles are composed of patterns. They are meant to be solved. There is always a predetermined order, and there is always a definite answer. With skill and perseverance, you will always complete a puzzle. Games are won, often by luck or random circumstances. There's an element of chance. You can have all the talent and determination in the world and never win a game. There's a big difference."

Dr. Moses held his gaze a second, then said, "Yes, well, your puzzles have become something of an obsession for her. Jess has solved everything you've ever published, as well as your weekly puzzles in the Sunday *Times* magazine. They take her outside herself. When she's working on one of your puzzles, she seems almost content. It is no exaggeration to say that your puzzles have saved Jess Price's life."

He'd never thought of his constructions as anything more than a challenging diversion, an amusing way to pass a lazy Sunday morning—coffee, bagels, and a Brink puzzle. Of course, he constructed puzzles with the idea that they would connect with someone, but that person was abstract, without features. And here was Jess Price, a real person, her photo before him. That his puzzles were so important to this woman, that they'd saved her life, left him with a strong feeling of responsibility. "I'm glad to hear they've helped her," he said at last.

"Indeed, they do help," Dr. Moses said, her manner warming. "Her inability to express herself has been deeply detrimental, perhaps even more imprisoning than her cell. Your puzzles have given her something to hold on to. They've allowed her to interact with the world. And, look, her first attempt to communicate with someone was with you." Dr. Moses closed the notebook and returned it to the envelope. "Which leads me to the other reason I've asked you to come here. I was hoping that you would consider meeting her."

"Meet her?" he said, taken aback. "You mean now?"

"It would be a short meeting," she said. "But one that could have enormous benefits for her recovery."

"Listen," he said. "I understand this is important to you, and I'd like to help, but I can't stay. It's a long drive back to the city. I have a puzzle due to my editor tomorrow and another due after the weekend. And my dog's in my truck."

"You can meet her now," she said. "It would take fifteen minutes, tops. In fact, it's all arranged. You're cleared for visitation privileges." She pulled a badge from a pocket in her dress and handed it to him. "I've set aside a quiet place for you. Please consider it. In addition to meeting your biggest fan, you might learn something about this drawing."

The circle did intrigue him, and he felt a strong urge to understand it, yet something warned him not to get involved. "I don't know," he said. "I'm not sure what good I can do."

"Mr. Brink, I've never invited anyone to meet one of my patients," she said. "But Jess Price isn't just another patient. There's something strange going on here. Something I can't explain. There are times when I'm with her when I am . . . I don't know how to put it exactly. Afraid. More than afraid. Terrified. Like I'm in the presence of something bigger than me. Something dangerous. That drawing could tell us why."

He glanced at the drawing, torn. He could say no and be back in his loft by dinner. Or he could stay, meet Jess Price, and solve one of the strangest puzzles he'd ever encountered.

Dr. Moses sensed his hesitation and pressed on. "I understand that this is a lot to ask. The odds that you'd come to Ray Brook at all, let alone help a woman you've never met, were small. But you're the only chance she's got left."

The mention of chance struck him silent. He understood better than anyone what it was like to face difficult odds. It was a chance in a million that he'd walked away from the accident at all and a chance in a billion that his injury would lead to the kind of skills he'd developed. But there it was: Mike Brink had beat the odds. How could he deny someone a chance to do the same?

He slipped a hand into his pocket and pulled out a silver dollar. Since the day of his injury, he'd carried it everywhere, and he believed in it—the structured randomness of a fifty–fifty outcome; its brutal clarity in moments of uncertainty—more than he believed in anything else. Religion or science, fiction or fact, nurture or nature. Nothing was as reliably unreliable as a coin flip.

Placing it on the top of his thumb, he balanced it at the joint. "Heads, I meet her," he said. "Tails, I go home. Deal?"

Dr. Moses looked at him, confused. It was an odd thing to do, but if she'd googled him, she knew all about his eccentricities. He'd once flipped his silver dollar at the outset of an important puzzle competition and, following its outcome, forfeited the match and left. Dr. Moses nodded, accepting his terms.

The coin gleamed against his skin, and he felt a tremor of anticipation, a shiver of uncertainty. He wasn't a superstitious man. He believed in the power of patterns, the sublime beauty of numbers, and the symmetries of reason. And yet this coin had a particular power over his fate. It had proven itself to be a conduit, a portal through which his future arrived, a kind of oracle.

Leveling the coin, he launched it into the air. It rose high above, turned once, twice, and then again before landing in the palm of his hand. He flipped it, pressing the cool metal into his skin and then, his chest tight with tension, he lifted his hand and looked.

4

D r. Moses took a ring of keys from her pocket and unlocked the door to the prison library. Brink followed her into an airy space filled with bookshelves and long wooden tables. At the far end of the room, a wall of triple-height windows overlooked a garden, where prisoners were weeding flower beds. Each window was composed of glass squares and, taking in their number—three by three by three—he admired the pattern: twenty-seven squares per window, a stack of perfect cubes. Dr. Moses led him to a table near the windows.

"I will get Jess now," Dr. Moses said, giving him a grateful smile. "Back in five minutes."

He went over to the windows and looked out at the yard. There was a dirt track where women in gray jumpsuits walked and, beyond that, the parking lot. His battered pickup truck stood out among the Hondas and Fords and Chevys glistening in the late-morning sunlight. His truck was a 1991 Ford, tomato red with rust at the edges, that had barely made it up to Ray Brook at all. It had shuddered and veered when he drove past sixty-five and gave an alarming screech when he pushed into fifth gear. The truck was already in decline back in 2008 when he'd driven it from Cleveland to Boston for college, but it had been his father's truck, one of the few things he'd held on to after his death, and he couldn't bear to let it go. It broke down all the time, but Brink accepted the truck's flaws the way one accepts the weaknesses of a beloved old dog: with tolerance and a sense of the end, sad but inevitable, looming ahead.

The truck had been around for all his teenage milestones: He'd learned to drive in that truck, got drunk in the cab with his friends, and had sex for the first time in a sleeping bag in the back. He'd driven the truck the day everything changed, October 12, 2007, the day of the Ohio high school state football championship. He'd parked the truck in the lot where the team caught their bus to the stadium, never imagining he'd be carried away in an ambulance a few hours later. The worn vinyl seats, and the acrid smell of dust and sweat, even the malfunctioning gearbox—it all brought him back to who he'd once been: the quarterback and captain of a high school champion football team, good-looking and self-assured, the kind of lucky, easy-going guy who walked through life without much struggle.

It was always hard to concentrate before a big game, but that night was even more difficult than usual. College scouts were there, watching, and his future depended on his performance. Win and he'd have a handful of full-ride scholarships to top football colleges. Lose and he'd fall back on the offers from the second-tier colleges that had already come courting. Either way, by the end of that night he would be going somewhere on a football scholarship.

Even without a scholarship, his parents would've helped him through college. They'd always been supportive, even when he messed up, like the time he got pulled over for speeding or flunked U.S. history. Looking across the football field, he found them in the second row of the bleachers, just behind the team, a wool blanket spread over their knees. His mom waved when she caught his eye, and his dad gave a nod of encouragement, and he felt a moment of heliotropic pride. Now was his chance to repay them. After all they'd done for him, all the out-of-town games they'd endured, all the gear they'd bought, all the encouragement they'd given. It was his night to make them proud.

The noise had been deafening. The pounding feet, the staccato chanting of the cheerleaders, the primal rhythm of the brass band—he tried to block it all out and focus on the game. It was end-of-the-season cold, brutal weather cutting through the field, and he was worried about throwing the ball into a wall of wind. As luck would have it, his team won the coin toss. The opposing team had called tails and the ref threw heads, giving Mike a downwind advantage. After the punt, his team was in a strong position, so he decided to take control. He called a play that carved a passage through center, allowing him to run the ball all the way to the end zone. It was an unusual move, risky at that distance from the goal, but a QB sneak would throw the opposition off-balance and demonstrate his agility and speed. Running a touchdown in the first minute would show them who was boss.

He gripped the ball, fell back, faked a pass, then ran with all he had. Ten yards, twenty yards, thirty. He felt the ball tucked against his side. He felt the chill wind at his back. He saw the end zone in the distance, wide open, waiting. And then the hit came. Down he went, hard, his head slamming in his helmet, and everything went black.

He woke strapped to a wooden board in an ambulance. His first thought was that he'd broken something, but as it turned out, other than blurred vision and a bump the size of a goose egg, there didn't seem to be anything wrong. After a thorough examination in the ER, a doctor told him he had a concussion and sent him home with instructions to ice his head and get some rest.

Signs that his injury was more complicated came a few days later. He was at home, recovering, when he noticed that everything around him seemed different somehow. More orderly, more coherent than before. To his bafflement, he realized that he saw patterns in everything. The marble floor in the kitchen—a checkerboard of black and white tiles—was a geometrical marvel, a 3D puzzle filled with endless passageways. He spent forty-five minutes in the shower one afternoon, simply watching the water's movement, its trajectory from the showerhead to the tiles as it swirled in a spiral around the drain. The water organized itself into elaborate architectural structures—rainbows and fractals, mathematical patterns that opened before him in waves of color. As he watched the play of patterns taking hold in the water, something clicked. He didn't know how, but he understood those structures. There was a system, an essential order to the world, and he saw it.

With time, he found still more changes in his way of perceiving things. When he thought of certain numbers or letters, they arrived in his mind in vivid color, bright and saturated, almost shimmering: The number 9 was cherry red, 6 a canary yellow, 3 a deep steel blue. Double digits showed up as blends of color, so 63 became green; 93 rich ultraviolet; 69 a bright orange. Sounds carried colors into his consciousness, as well, so that a song became a splashy color show, a painted concerto in the background of his mind.

These changes to his way of experiencing reality were so strange that he didn't say anything about them at first. All he knew was that he was experiencing highly structured, geometric hallucinations on a regular basis, and while he knew what he saw was real, he wasn't sure anyone would believe him if he tried to explain it. He was convinced that the patterns and colors would fade away as the bump on his head healed. He decided to wait it out, give it some time, and see what happened.

But they didn't go away. Four months passed after his injury, but his condition didn't improve. He was up all night and slept all day. His friendships became strained, and his girlfriend, Kelsey, who he suspected liked his football jersey more than she liked him, stopped trying to reach him. He couldn't go to school without panic taking over. Then, one night, he couldn't take it anymore. Numbers and patterns and colors flooded his mind with a hydraulic force, so many images and shapes he thought he might drown. He went to the kitchen, sat at the breakfast table, and broke down in tears. He needed help, but he didn't know how to tell anyone what was happening.

His mom joined him at the kitchen table. She insisted that he tell her what was going on. Mike told her that he'd been seeing patterns in his head for months but he'd been afraid to talk about it. He told her he thought he was going crazy and that he'd considered killing himself to make it stop. His mother listened as he described how the black-and-white grid of the kitchen floor opened before him, how it created all variety of patterns—a chessboard, then a crossword, then a grid of numbers—a black-and-white matrix of infinitely shifting possibilities. She listened as he described a puzzle that kept appearing in his mind, then fading, only to return.

His mom found a piece of paper and a pencil and gave them to him. "Show me what you see," she said, and he drew the puzzle right there, a number box, one he later learned to be a classic magic square called the Lo Shu Square: a grid of nine numbers whose columns added up to fifteen on every side. This magic square had been first constructed in China around 2300 B.C. He knew nothing of the square's history when he drew it for his mom at three in the morning one cold February night in 2008. She had studied the square with care and, recognizing that he'd made something extraordinary, said, "You've been given a gift. You can ignore it, or you can use it. But you can't hide from it."

It wasn't until after an MRI that he understood she was right. He couldn't ever go back to who he'd been before his accident. A neuro-surgeon explained that when he'd hit the ground, eight hundred pounds per square inch of pressure had slammed through his skull. His brain had recoiled in a contrecoup that damaged his left hemi-sphere. And while he didn't display the usual symptoms of a trau-matic brain injury—he had no seizures, no memory loss, no neurological damage, no pain—Mike Brink had been altered forever.

5

A guard led Jess Price to the table near the windows, unlocked her handcuffs, and retreated to the hallway, where he stationed himself at the door.

"If you have any trouble . . ." Dr. Moses gestured to the guard, gave Brink a quick nod, and closed the door behind her.

Jess Price sat at the table, light from the windows pouring over her. As he approached, Brink snuck a quick look at her, comparing her with the photos Thessaly had shown him. While those images were only five years old, they didn't resemble the prisoner at the table. The woman in the author photo was impish and mischievous, with a bemused expression of confidence. The woman before him had been altered by trauma, softened, like a statue whose sharp edges had been subdued by the elements. She was too thin, her hair had grown long and brittle, and there were crescents of dried blood at the tips of her nails, evidence of the self-harm Dr. Moses had mentioned.

And yet there was something alluring about her, a mysterious presence that had nothing to do with her appearance. It was an indefinable quality, heavy as a gravitational pull. He couldn't explain it, but something shifted in the air as he approached. It was like standing at the edge of a vortex, a dark and irresistible force both exciting and threatening.

He hung his messenger bag on the back of a chair, slipped off his jacket, and sat across from Jess. She watched him, her eyes filled with curiosity and something less definable—intense interest suffused with wariness. He'd been ready for silence but being there with her left him deeply anxious. The void between them was wide and deep. To reach her, he must make the first move.

"Dr. Moses tells me you like puzzles," he said at last, feeling awkward.

Her gaze was filled with intelligence, a steady watchfulness that belied any possibility that she was mentally unstable. On the contrary, he sensed a brightness behind her blue eyes, trapped and glistening, like a diamond suspended in a block of ice.

"She gave me this." Brink laid the circle between them. He looked at it again, although he didn't need to. He saw the puzzle with perfect recall. It was a side effect, or perhaps the biggest benefit, of the accident: He could see a pattern once, for a few seconds, and remember it forever. Yet for all his ability to see it, the puzzle left him perplexed. It brought him back to MIT, where his professor and mentor, Dr. Vivek Gupta, would assign him a mind-bendingly impossible problem. He would stay up all night looking at it from every angle, reversing it, folding it, twisting and turning it in every possible permutation, until something shifted in his thinking—like a window opening and allowing light to fall on a darkened room—and he found the way in. From that point, he could sit back and watch as the path revealed itself. He'd see the steps he needed to take and the order in which he needed to take them. Finding the solution felt like a benediction, what some people might call grace, but for Brink it was more than that: A solution was a lifeline, the one thing that kept him from sinking.

But when he called on that power now, the circle left nothing but questions: Why this number in that place? Why the Hebrew letters at the center? What was the significance of the number 72? He cleared his throat and tried again. "You wanted me to see this, and I admit, I'm intrigued. I'm dying to solve it. But I need more information. Can you help me understand what I'm looking at?"

She stared at him, silent. It was unnerving, the way she looked at him. Suddenly the air felt oppressive, suffocating. It pressed in on him, hot and cloying. He could feel his skin grow damp. Being close to Jess changed something chemical inside him, the way salt alters the boiling temperature of water.

"Listen," he said, leaning closer. "I don't know what this drawing means or its significance to your situation, but Dr. Moses believes that it has something to do with what happened to you. I want to help, but you need to give me something to go on."

She continued to study him.

"For example," he said, "where did you first see this circle? Is it original? A copy?"

Silence.

"The dial of numbers between one and seventy-two, and the Hebrew letters. It's an unusual configuration. It seems like a bunch of numbers and letters are missing. Do you know why?"

When she didn't respond, he pushed the circle aside. Direct questioning wasn't going to work. Clearly she wanted to communicate with him—why else would she have written his name on the back side of the puzzle?—but something was stopping her. She wrapped her arms around herself protectively, as if his questions pained her. Looking at her, he felt a stab of empathy. He was reminded of himself after his injury: afraid, confused, so trapped in his head he couldn't begin to explain what he was going through. He'd needed just one person to break through the isolation to reach him. One person to believe him when he described the unbelievable. His mom had been that person, and her patience had saved him. Maybe he could be that person for Jess Price.

"Something bad happened to me once," he said, watching her closely. "I was experiencing things that seemed totally . . . well, crazy. I was seeing patterns and numbers and colors everywhere. I was terrified. I wanted to explain it, but I knew no one would believe me. They'd think I was nuts. I mean, hell, I thought I was nuts. Do you know what changed that?"

She shook her head slightly. It was only the faintest reaction, but it was enough. He felt a surge of triumph: She'd responded to him.

"This . . ." He reached into his messenger bag and fished out a pocket-sized graph-paper notebook and his favorite pen, a Bic four-color retractable ballpoint, and drew the square he'd drawn for his mother the night he told her the truth.

4	9	2
3	5	7
8	1	6

Her eyes scanned the numbers, then returned to Brink, questioning.

"It's an ancient mathematical square, the Lo Shu Square, first drawn about four thousand years ago in China. For some reason, I kept seeing it after the injury. It would appear in my mind, each number blazing with color, and then fade away. I had no idea why, and really, I still don't. My doctors have theories, but they don't matter much to me. What matters is that, however bizarre it may seem, what I experienced was real."

Jess looked down at the Lo Shu Square, studying it.

"People experience frightening things all the time," he said. "I'm not the only one. And neither are you."

When she met his gaze, her eyes were filled with tears.

"Tell me what's going on," he said, sliding the drawing of the circle between them. "I'll believe you. I promise."

Slowly, Jess moved her eyes from Brink to the corner of the room. He followed her gaze to a surveillance camera mounted from the ceiling of the library, then back to Jess. Her expression wavered, and a shimmer of fear passed through her features.

"Are you afraid that we're being watched?" he asked, lowering his voice to a whisper.

She nodded, and it all made sense. There was surveillance over every inch of the prison. She wanted to tell him something but was afraid of being overheard. Suddenly he had an idea. It was clear that she could write numbers and letters and graphs—she'd solved almost every puzzle he'd ever made. He grabbed his pen and wrote: *You don't have to speak for me to hear you.*

He pushed the notebook to her. She considered it for a moment doing nothing. Then she grabbed the pen and drew the gallows for a hangman word puzzle. A thrill went through him when he saw it. Hangman operated under the same system as his favorite word puzzle, Wordle. He played Wordle every morning, usually solving it before his coffee got cold. The rules were simple: You find a word by guessing the position of the letters. You get six tries, and each correct letter brings you closer to the answer. In hangman, with each wrong choice, a part of a stickman is drawn on the gallows. Too many wrong guesses, and the stickman is hanged, and you lose.

Jess wrote out five spaces below the gallows. Brink knew from his experience with Wordle that he needed just one correct letter position to solve the puzzle. All the possible permutations of words with a letter in that position would flash through his mind, he would cross reference them with previous solutions—he remembered them all—and the correct answer would appear. It was simple, too simple, and he knew the answer on the second attempt 80 percent of the time.

He looked down at Jess's puzzle and began with the most frequent letter in the English language. He took his pen and wrote the letter E.

Jess gave an almost imperceptible shake of the head. No E. She drew the stickman's head.

He tried the four next-most-frequent letters: A, I, N, O, and Jess drew the stickman's body, his arms, and one leg. He could feel himself tensing up. Maybe it was being next to Jess Price, but he never had trouble with a word puzzle. True, it was more a guessing game than a puzzle, but still. Glancing at the gallows, he saw he had just one more shot to get it right. He chose the letter T. Jess smiled and wrote 2 T's in the puzzle.

$$T \_\_\_\_ T$$

He felt a rush of triumph as a word blazed in his mind. It was like capturing a rainbow in a jar, each letter a burst of color, elusive and shimmering.

"You want to know if you can trust me," he whispered.

She met his eye, and all the intensity he'd felt before returned. It was true that she didn't have to speak for him to understand her. He could feel her every thought.

"I'm not good at a lot of things," he said. "But I always keep my word. If you tell me what you need, I promise to help as best I can."

She considered this, staring at the notebook so hard he expected it to burst into flames. Then she turned to a clean page and wrote something down, covering it with her hand. When she'd finished, she bit a scabbed fingernail, opening a wound. Blood collected to a scarlet drop at the tip of her finger, and she pressed the blood onto the page, blotting as if to wipe her skin clean. Then she ripped the page from the notebook, crumpled it tight into a ball, and pressed it into his palm.

With her touch, a kind of paralysis came over him. It was electric, filled with a pulsing hot energy, a sensation so sharp he could hardly breathe. Time seemed to freeze as she leaned across the table and kissed him lightly on the lips. The library faded and suddenly he was inside the puzzle, its swirls of numbers and symbols arranging themselves into a series of interlocking pathways around him, Jess Price at the center of it all, a woman trapped in a labyrinth. He pulled her close, returning the kiss, feeling himself fall further and further into her, when suddenly a prison guard stood above them. "No physical contact with the prisoners," he said gruffly, as he pulled Jess back, locked her wrists into a set of cuffs, and led her away.

6

The door to the library closed, leaving Brink alone. His whole body throbbed and, as he reached for his messenger bag, he noticed that his hand trembled. *What the hell is happening to me?* His encounter with Jess Price had left him light-headed and unbalanced, his heart beating hard, his mind filled with questions. He felt like he'd just finished a grueling competition—ten hours of number puzzles or chess—his brain both energized and fried.

He glanced around the library, looking for a private corner. The shelves had been arranged to eliminate privacy, allowing the surveillance camera unobstructed views of the entire room. Sliding his bag over his shoulder, he grabbed his jacket off the back of the chair, wiped the sweat from his brow, and walked to the bank of windows. Turning his back on the security camera, he unfolded the paper Jess had given him. It was creased and covered with smudges of blood. Straightening it out as best he could, he found five lines scrawled across the center of the page. Jess Price had written a message. He read:

Thus we eat red apples, every
Wonderful kind,
Pink Lady,

Hokuto, Early Gold, Liberty,
McIntosh.

That was it. Five lines of . . . what? Poetry? He read it through again, trying to parse its meaning. It made absolutely no sense. This woman hadn't communicated with anyone in years, and when she did, she wrote a cryptic poem about varieties of apples? He felt an urge to crumple it up and toss it into the waste bin, but he knew that there was more to it. Jess had been afraid of being overheard, and she would also have been afraid that a written message would be intercepted. This poem could be a riddle.

Usually, a riddle draws upon a shared body of knowledge, some common reference point that two people understand. But he and Jess Price had no history whatsoever, and they had definitely never discussed apples. He glanced out the window, as if there might be apple trees in the yard, but there was nothing but a dusty track.

Reaching into his left pocket, he felt for his silver dollar. It was a Morgan dollar, stamped 1899, a collectible coin worth a few hundred dollars. The ref had tossed that very coin at the outset of the state championship game, just minutes before Brink's injury. It was a tradition that the winning team kept the coin. His team had won without him and voted unanimously to give it to him.

He'd taken to rubbing it between his thumb and forefinger when he thought, a habit that left the edge smooth as a river stone. While it usually helped him focus, it didn't help now. He sounded out the syllables Jess had written, hoping there might be some clue in the rhythm, but there wasn't a regular beat. He ran the words together in one line, eliminating the spaces, trying to see if a message might emerge. It did not. It didn't make any sense, even as a riddle.

Then he noticed something unusual: The smudges of blood were placed at distinct points on the paper. They were not random, as he'd initially thought, but orderly, each blotch of blood placed at a letter. Jess had pressed the point of her finger over eight letters in the first row, four in the second, and so on. Twenty-eight letters had been marked in this manner.

Instantly he went through the various mathematical possibilities of the number 28: It is the second perfect number, a harmonic divisor number, a triangular number. It is a Størmer number and the fourth magic number in physics. But, reading the lines over again, he saw that the number 28 meant nothing in this context.

And then, all at once, it clicked. Of course numbers had nothing to do with it. Jess Price was a writer, and she would communicate with words, not numbers. It wasn't a riddle but a cipher, a piece of coded writing, and a rather straightforward one at that. She had marked letters with blood, and these letters were the key to unlock a message.

Thus we eat red apples, every
Wonderful kind,
Pink Lady,
Hokuto, Early Gold, Liberty,
McIntosh.

The challenge sparked something elemental in Mike Brink, a primal yearning, one mixed with curiosity and desire. He wanted to grab hold of the mystery and tame it, to pick it apart and uncover its secrets one by one until its elusiveness crumbled in his hands. In short, the puzzle had caught hold of him. He had no choice but to solve it.

He slid the silver dollar into his pocket, took his pen from his bag, and wrote the marked letters at the end of each row:

Thus we eat red apples, every	T H E R D A R Y
Wonderful kind,	W E K N,
Pink Lady,	N A D
Hokuto, Early Gold, Liberty,	H K T E L Y D L I E
McIntosh.	M I H

It was obvious that the letters were scrambled. He would need to put them in order to understand their meaning. It didn't take more than a few seconds for Brink to line the letters up in his imagination, shuffle them around until they fell into patterns of words. He wrote the words in a third column next to the cipher and looked it over.

Thus we eat red apples, every	T H E R D A R Y	Dr Raythe
Wonderful kind,	W E K N,	knew,
Pink Lady,	N A D	and
Hokuto, Early Gold, Liberty,	H K T E L Y D L I E	they killed
McIntosh.	M I H	him.

He wrote the sentence out and read it: *Dr. Raythe knew, and they killed him.*

7

Mike Brink knocked twice on Dr. Thessaly Moses's office door, two hard raps, harder than he'd meant to. There was no answer, and he tried again, feeling an urgent need to speak with her. His encounter with Jess had left him unbalanced, as if his center of gravity had shifted. He couldn't stop seeing her face or remembering the dark attraction he'd felt around her. His whole body still tingled from their kiss. He didn't want to admit, even to himself, that he was overwhelmed. Maybe Dr. Moses could give him some perspective.

"Mr. Brink." Dr. Moses's voice came from down the hall. She wore a white jacket over her navy dress and carried a Louis Vuitton tote bag on her shoulder, files poking out of the top. There was a canvas lunchbag in her hand, and it was safe to assume that she'd just come back from lunch.

"Dr. Moses," he said. "Is this a good time?"

"Please call me Thessaly, and of course, come in," she said, unlocking her office. She held the door for him, then closed it. "I'm anxious to hear what happened in the library."

He was unsure of how much he should reveal about his exchange with Jess Price. He'd known Jess for a total of thirty minutes, and yet he felt a strong sense of loyalty to her and, after that kiss, a disconcerting need to understand her. He wanted to help her. But how?

That she'd drawn a cipher made it clear that what she told him was private and should be kept from the prison authorities, but he couldn't help her on his own. And if there was anyone in the world who wanted to assist Jess, it was Thessaly Moses. In fact, Jess had brought Thessaly into this by telling her to find him. That alone marked her as trustworthy.

Thessaly dropped her bag on her desk and took a sip of coffee. "So how did it go?"

"Not what I expected, to say the least."

She gave him a look filled with curiosity. "How so?"

"You'll hear about it from the guards, so I might as well tell you right away: She kissed me," he said.

"Kissed you?" Thessaly said, astonished.

"Across the table. A guard took her away."

"Of course he did," she said, shaking her head in disbelief. "There's no physical contact allowed, and kissing is totally—"

"That's not all that happened," he said.

"What?" she asked, crossing her arms over her chest, as if bracing herself.

"She wrote something down."

Thessaly's eyes narrowed. "You communicated through writing?"

"Kind of," he said. "She drew another puzzle. A cipher."

Thessaly leaned against her desk. "I suspected she would respond well to you, but I'm amazed she opened up so quickly."

"I'm not sure that you'll be so thrilled when you hear what she wrote."

Thessaly looked perplexed. "Why is that?"

"What did you say the name of her previous therapist was?" he asked.

"Dr. Raythe," Thessaly said, surprised. "Why do you ask?"

"You said that Dr. Raythe got through to Jess," he said, weighing his words. "That his methods worked with her."

"From the reports he left, I believe that's true," she said. "Briefly. Whatever transpired, it didn't last."

He remembered the solution to Jess's cipher: *Dr. Raythe knew, and they killed him.* What was it exactly that he knew? "Did he have any kind of special information about her?"

"I have no idea," she said, clearly confused.

"If he did," he said, "wouldn't there be records he might have kept? Case notes or something?"

"Of course. That's part of the job," she said, her brow furrowed and her voice flexed defensively, as if he'd suggested she'd overlooked something important. "But I've read everything in his notes. There's nothing to suggest that he had any new or extraordinary information about her."

"Is there any way you could take another look?"

"Well," she said, "I don't know what good it would do. I've been over everything he wrote. Dr. Raythe left his files an absolute mess, and my first weeks in this position were spent trying to clean them up. He wasn't very organized, but I doubt he would have left something as important as information about Jess Price undocumented. . . . Wait, though. Let me check something."

She walked to the other side of her desk. "A wholesale digitization of inmate records occurred around the time I replaced Dr. Raythe. If some of his files weren't fully digitized, they could be in storage." She typed something into a desktop computer, paused to read what had come up, then turned to Brink. "It looks like a possibility. Dr. Raythe may have kept some of his files in the old storage area. Why don't I take a look and let you know what I find?"

"That would be great," Brink said, feeling his excitement build. If she could find information in Raythe's files, he might be able to figure out what Jess Price was trying to tell him. "One more thing—you said you replaced Dr. Raythe. Why was that?"

She gave him an odd look, trying to understand where he was going with his questions. "This position opened because Dr. Raythe passed away," she said.

"And that happened suddenly?"

"Yes, his death was sudden. I was interviewed and hired quickly, which is one reason his paperwork was in such disarray."

"I think you should see this," he said, taking Jess's cipher out of his bag and showing it to Thessaly: *Dr. Raythe knew, and they killed him.* "Jess Price believes that Dr. Raythe was murdered."

He watched Thessaly's expression turn from one of skepticism to pure shock. "But that's totally, totally impossible," Thessaly said, aghast. "The man's car hit a patch of ice on Route 32 and slid over a guardrail. It was an accident. Everyone knows that."

"Everyone except Jess Price."

Thessaly read the paper again, then folded it in half. "I don't understand," she said, at last. "Why would she communicate this way?"

"Because she's afraid of someone," he said. "It's why she had you bring me here. I can see what other people can't. Do you think there's something in Dr. Raythe's files that might explain why she feels this way?"

"I'll look, but it could take some time," Thessaly said. "Old records are stored in an unused area of the prison, and I'll have to get clearance. If you can check back with me in the morning, I'll let you know where I'm at in the process."

Brink had planned to drive back to the city right away—he didn't have a change of clothes or even a toothbrush, and Connie's food was back home—but there was no way he was leaving without a better understanding of what Jess Price was trying to tell him. "I'll find a hotel," he said. "But I'd like to see Jess again. Can you arrange another meeting?"

Thessaly bit her lip as she considered his request. "I can't make any promises. It took a lot of convincing to arrange one meeting, and my supervisor may not approve another. That said, what happened today was an enormous breakthrough. You got Jess Price to communicate with you, which is more than anyone else has managed, so I'll see what I can do. Stay close, Mr. Brink. I will call you as soon as I hear something."

8

Vintage, garish, big as a billboard, the Starlite Motel's neon sign blinked AIR-CONDITIONED ROOMS and NO VACANCY in brilliant flashes of red and blue. Brink pulled into the parking lot and killed the engine. It was a dive, but there was something about the sign that reminded him of home—old motels and drive-in movie theaters still peppered the Midwestern landscape. It had been years since he'd gone back to Ohio, but walking into the Starlite Motel felt like going home.

He checked in at a desk in the main building, where a dozen keys hung on a tagboard, a clear sign that there were, indeed, vacancies. He made sure Conundrum was welcome, then paid for late check-out, so Connie could stay in the room while he went to the prison the next day, took an apple from a bowl at the coffee station, and went to his room.

He was in number 3, the smallest odd prime number, the first Mersenne Prime and the second Fibonacci prime, a dark box of a room with a low ceiling, a king-sized bed, and an old console air conditioner. Moss-green carpeting stretched to a fifties-era bathroom, its turquoise tiles and birdbath sink smelling of bleach. The place was run down, and the neon sign would probably keep him up all night, but it didn't matter. He wasn't staying long, and the Starlite was close to the prison.

Throwing his messenger bag on the desk, he prepared the food he'd bought for Conundrum at a supermarket on the highway: a quarter pound of chopped sirloin, broccoli florets, and shredded carrots. Connie was a carnivore, bred for hunting, so he fed her fresh meat when he could. He took good care of her. He monitored her daily fat and protein intake, made sure she had bones to strengthen her teeth, and gave her plenty of filtered water. The few friends who'd met Connie noted that he took better care of his dog than he did of himself, and it was true: Connie's diet was healthier than his own.

Caring for her had become an important part of his life. He'd adopted Conundrum as a puppy during the pandemic, when he was alone and needed a friend. Over the months of lockdown, he'd structured his life around her—taking her for walks, throwing a rubber ball in the park, teaching her tricks. She'd learned all the usual ones—to fetch, roll over, and shake—and a few unusual tricks, too, such as multi-Frisbee catching and (his favorite) playing dead. He never would've imagined that he'd spend so much time with a twenty-pound short-haired dachshund, but there it was: Conundrum was his closest companion.

As Connie ate, Brink took out his laptop and found his new puzzle. It was a Triangulum, a geometric demon he was constructing for *The New York Times*. He'd started building it as he always did. First he created the solutions. Then, once he knew how it ended, he worked backward, arranging the challenges and clues in ways that seemed both inevitable and surprising. Usually, it was easy enough. Intuitive. But for some reason he couldn't get the Triangulum quite right. The challenge for Brink was never in constructing a puzzle—he could do that in his sleep—but in making a great puzzle, one that struck a balance between all the elements. It should challenge but not frustrate; be elusive but not obscure; and, more than anything, a great puzzle should create a sense of satisfaction as each clue is cracked. There was an art to making such a puzzle, and Mike Brink was an artist.

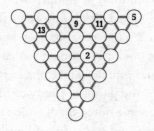

To solve a Triangulum, one must put a number from 1 to 6 in each circle, with no number appearing more than once along any of the gray lines. He put three numbers inside the triangles of three circles. Those three circles added up to the larger number. It was elegant, logical, and challenging, his favorite kind of puzzle.

When he finished it, he connected to the motel's Wi-Fi and sent it in an email to his editor. He didn't mention that he'd hidden his name in the Triangulum, but then again, he didn't need to. His editor knew that Brink loved leaving Easter eggs in his puzzles—his initials, his name, some secret about himself—hidden among the solutions.

After he'd sent it off, he opened a search engine and typed the words *Jess Price writer murderer*. The facts were plain enough. Twenty-three-year-old Jess Price had gone to Sedge House on a house-sitting job. She had been arrested on July 19, 2017, for the murder of Noah Cooke, twenty-five years old, her boyfriend. She was found guilty of manslaughter three months later and spent five years in prison without disclosing what happened that night. He searched for concrete details about the crime, but there wasn't much beyond that.

As he read more about Jess Price he found nothing that suggested her capable of such a horrendous crime. Born in New York City, she graduated from Stuyvesant High School and then attended Barnard

College on an academic scholarship, where she was an excellent student. At twenty-two years old, she published a collection of short stories that was a literary sensation. Brink pulled up the cover review on the *New York Times* website and read it: *Price's stories are small traumas that crack the reader open one rib at a time to expose the heart to fresh air.* Her website had long gone black, but a Wikipedia entry detailed her many successes. She'd been short-listed for a National Book Award and won the New York Public Library's Young Lions Award. One of the stories from her collection had been purchased for adaptation as a film. Then, in the fall of 2017, at the age of twenty-three, she had been convicted of manslaughter and sentenced to thirty years at New York State Correctional Facility.

When he cross-referenced her name with house-sitting websites, her old profile came up immediately. There was a photo and a short bio—*Barnard English Major, Native New Yorker, Great with Animals*—some five-star reviews, and praise for her personally: *reliable, communicative, friendly, responsible, meticulous.* When she took the job at Sedge House, she seemed to be, as Thessaly had said, a well-adjusted, talented young woman.

But the descriptions he read didn't jibe with what he experienced in her presence. The danger and darkness. The sense that being near her was like standing at the edge of a sheer cliff. He wondered at the incredible transformation that had occurred from the person Jess had been to the person she'd become.

Just remembering how Jess had made him feel sent shivers through him. She was not like anyone he'd ever met before. How had Dr. Moses put it? *She's living in a puzzle.* The fact was, she'd thrown him into a puzzle. His time at the prison had left him more turned around than he'd been in years. He was worked up, every muscle tight, as if he'd gone on a strenuous run or spent the afternoon in Manhattan traffic. He tried to get a handle on what put him in such a state, but he couldn't quite grasp it. There was something both exciting and frightening about her, a quality he recognized from the various puzzle competitions he'd participated in over the years. He had the feeling of being up against a formidable opponent, one who might beat him in the end.

Clearly she created a strong emotional response in everyone. Navigating the search engine, he found thousands of articles and video clips about Jess Price, discussion groups and archived chats and Reddit threads. People took sides, had theories about her motivations, her writing, even her appearance. One journalist had described her as *jolie-laide*, a French term his mother had used to describe women whose beauty stemmed from a combination of unique, sometimes unflattering features. He read that she was crazy, that she'd been set up, that she was innocent, that she was guilty.

In the beginning, Jess's innocence had been championed by the literary world: Her editor, her literary agent, and the spokesperson for the National Book Awards released a joint statement of support. When she'd refused to defend herself at the trial, her supporters became less vocal. And yet Jess Price's presence lingered. Her book of short stories remained on the bestseller list for months after the trial, and an unauthorized biography was written, then adapted into a film. Brink found a page of photos of Jess Price placed next to those of beautiful, talented women who had died young: Edie Sedgwick and Jean Seberg, both of whom she resembled. Jess Price had become an icon, a cult figure, perhaps a murderer, perhaps a victim of circumstances—nobody knew for sure.

Stumbling across a link to *The New Yorker* online, he read a short story by Jess Price published in the magazine in 2017, months before her arrest. Like so many stories in *The New Yorker*, there wasn't much in the way of plot, but he found himself pulled in by a certain texture in the narration and an off-kilter use of language: an acerbic child, a gibbous shoulder, the stumbling rainstorm. It was called "The Windmill," which he found odd, as there wasn't a windmill to be found anywhere in the story.

After reading for an hour or so, he had a good picture of who Jess Price was before the crime. He had a list of facts about her life, information about her writing career, the opinions of her supporters and theories of her detractors. And yet, despite the pages and pages of information he'd found, he knew she wasn't the person he'd read about online. She wasn't the bright student, or the friendly house-sitter, the brilliant, promising young writer, or even the tragic, beautiful cult figure. No, he'd encountered someone else in the prison library, a woman trapped in a vise that pressed away all that she had once been, leaving a distilled version behind.

It was dark by the time he closed his laptop. He hadn't eaten since breakfast, so he called in a delivery order for a large pepperoni pizza with black olives. As he waited, he pulled out his Victorinox Swiss Army Knife and peeled the apple he'd taken from the motel lobby. He'd carried the pocketknife since eighth grade, when his mom bought it for him as a birthday gift. It was one of his most prized possessions and, like his silver dollar, was a connection to who he'd been before the injury. Holding the apple in his left hand, he worked the tip of the blade under the red flesh and turned until a perfect Archimedean spiral formed, the ever-growing distance of the peel from the core creating a sense of order and well-being that he found infinitely soothing.

Finally, the pizza arrived. He opened a bottle of beer from the mini-fridge, sat on the edge of the king-sized bed, and ate directly from the box, his mind filled with thoughts of Jess Price. He couldn't figure her out. Why had she asked Thessaly Moses to find him? Was it really about the circular puzzle Thessaly had shown him? Was there something he wasn't seeing? Had Ernest Raythe really been murdered? She'd asked for his trust, but could he trust her? Or was this whole thing the creation of an unstable woman with an obsession for his puzzles?

When he finished eating, Brink downloaded an audio file of a 2017 NPR interview Jess Price had given to Terry Gross and listened to it in bed. The voice of this woman was inconsistent with the woman in the library—younger and brighter and filled with buoyancy. She spoke for a few minutes about the nature of being a writer in a world that cared more for Twitter than Tolstoy and her next book, a novel she was working on that she would "rather not discuss," making a joke about how her fiction instantly imploded the second she talked about it. The disparity between the funny, articulate person in the interview and the woman he'd encountered in the prison library gave him pause. Jess Price had once been an utterly different person.

It was late when he shut off the lights and slid into bed. He drifted off to sleep listening to the rhythm of Jess Price's voice. Although they were miles apart, he felt her presence as strongly as if she were right there, next to him in bed. A heavy sensation washed over him, the same gravitational pull he'd felt as he sat across from her in the prison library. What did she want from him? Why couldn't he stop thinking about her? Her image hovered in his mind—delicate features, her honey-blond hair, her strangely magnetic blue eyes. She'd lured him to the prison with a puzzle, drawn him closer with a cipher, and now he felt a desperate need to figure her out. But nothing about Jess Price made sense. The clues she gave were obscure, the patterns disjointed. Perhaps her contradictions were part of the puzzle. She'd set up the rules of the game, and if anyone in the world was made to play, it was Mike Brink.

9

That night Jess came to him in a dream. He stood with her in a darkening forest of thick, fragrant evergreens. Gone was the woman he'd met at the prison, gone the gray jumpsuit and the haggard appearance, gone the frailty. In her place stood a luminous creature in a red dress, beautiful and confident, whose whole being radiated seduction.

Taking his hand, she led him up a root-covered path, through the dense thickets of spruce trees. As he moved deeper into the forest, all the uncertainty he'd felt about her, the unnerving darkness he'd experienced in her presence, transformed to pure attraction. He wasn't wary of her. He didn't question her motives. On the contrary, he was aware that this woman was meant for him like no one else. When she gripped his hand, he was filled with an overwhelming sense of connection. They were together, intricately bound. Suddenly he wasn't sure where his body ended and hers began.

"Hurry up," she said, smiling over her shoulder as she led him farther and farther into the forest. Her voice was beautiful, clear, and vibrant in the chill air. "Follow me."

By the time they stepped out of the woods and into a clearing, night had fallen, the sky a blistered, roiling purple. Candles illuminated a banquet table where a feast waited: platters of meat, steaming tureens, bowls overflowing with fruit. Jess took a pomegranate, split it open, and held the vermillion flesh up to him, but even as he took a bite the candles snuffed, and he tasted her lips. The kiss was electric, deeply erotic, more powerful than anything he'd felt before. It was a kiss that, in the Escher staircase of his dream, happened in the present, the past, and the future at once, a kiss that unlocked a thousand possibilities. She grasped him tight, drawing him into her embrace, and he felt a primal need for her, a sharp physical longing but also recognition: She knew him—his secrets, his insecurities, what he most wanted—and he knew her.

"I knew you'd come," she said, pulling away. "It isn't easy to get here. Most people can't find their way. But you're not like most people."

"Where are we?" he asked, trying to get ahold of the wavering world surrounding him.

"Listen," she said, placing a key in his hand. "Take it. You'll need it to let me out."

The key was warm against his skin, old and rusted.

"I've been alone for so long, so very long," she said. "You can't imagine how lonely I've been. You're the first person to come here in thousands of years. But all of that's over now. You're here. You have the key. You'll keep it safe. You must promise."

"But I don't know—"

"Promise," she said, looking at him with furious intensity. "When you find the door, you will know what to do."

He put the key in his pocket. "I promise," he said, and even as he spoke, the landscape shifted, and they lay on an immense four-poster bed. Jess removed his clothes piece by piece and bound him to the posts, tying his ankles and wrists to the wood with white sheets. Laid out on his back, unable to move, he watched her as she undressed, as she ran her hands over his body, as she slid on top of him and pressed herself close. The moonlight cast patterns of light and shadow over their skin, a shifting chiaroscuro. He closed his eyes, feeling her every touch. She was ruthless and carnal, sensual, her movements a kind of sorcery. He'd never experienced anything like her, and yet everything about her was eerily familiar—her scent, the sensation of her breath in his ear, the soft sounds of pleasure she made, the way she rested her head against his chest, her hair spilling over him. She made him forget everything: who he was, why he was there, what he wanted. In the dimension of the dream, there was no question of why they were together. She had called him, and he had come to her. And now he belonged to her.

As the dream began to fade, Jess pulled him closer, as if to keep him there just a little longer. But everything was slipping away. The candles extinguished; the bed dissolved; the forest faded. He tried to hold on to Jess, but her skin became brittle under the pressure of his touch. Fissures opened over her skin like cracks through a mirror, leaving a honeycomb pattern. Her cheeks, her neck, her arms, every part of her fractured, then disappeared.

10

He woke covered in sweat, still caught in the grip of the dream. He felt invaded, exposed. His heart beat hard, and for a moment he sensed a living presence hovering nearby, one that left him so terrified he could hardly breathe. He sat up in bed and looked around the room, disoriented. *Where the hell was he?* The space was dark except for a streak of red and blue neon flashing against the curtain. He didn't recognize the grungy carpet or the empty beer bottles or the smell of stale pizza. Then it came back to him: He was in an old motel in a tiny town high in the Adirondack Mountains. He had fallen asleep and had one hell of a dream.

Conundrum stood by the bed, growling. She was perceptive, more perceptive than some humans he knew. She sensed something unusual in the air, and she ran around the bed, barking madly, as if chasing prey. He got up and scratched her behind the ears, soothing her. "It's okay, girl," he said. "It was just a dream."

He glanced at the digital alarm clock and saw it was just after three in the morning. It was too early to get up, and so Brink took a deep breath, lay back onto the pillow, and tried to fall asleep. Sleeplessness was something he was used to. Ever since his injury, he'd developed ways to quiet his mind. But no matter how much he practiced meditation, no matter how exhausted when he turned off the lights, his brain lit up. Patterns floated behind his eyes, a great web of geometric shapes—lattices and networks, crystalline fractals—and numbers, endless strings of numbers. At first he'd tried to ignore them, but he found that he could manage his brain—and fall asleep—only when he gave in to the torrent of patterns. He fell into the shapes, calculated equations, stacked letters into columns and diagonals, built words and then rearranged them into anagrams and palindromes, creating elaborate castles in his mind until he exhausted the possibilities and fell asleep.

He remembered the night he'd told his mother about his gift. He'd been overwhelmed by fear and confusion. It was the lowest point of his life, a moment when he wasn't sure he could continue living. It terrified him that his own body had turned against him so ruthlessly. And then he drew the Lo Shu Square for his mom. He described what was happening, all the wild things he was seeing, and she had believed him.

That night was the turning point. The next day, he and his mom began searching for help. Within a month they found Dr. Trevers, the renowned neuroscientist who specialized in brain trauma. Brink went through a battery of tests and learned that his brain injury had resulted in an extremely rare condition called sudden acquired savant syndrome. Only thirty people in the world had the condition, and most of them had varying levels of extraordinary abilities as a result. Brink's tests determined that he had spatial and mechanical savantism. He had a photographic memory that allowed him to reproduce images and structures with perfect recall and an ability to do instant numerical calculations, including calendar counting, reciting pi places into the thousands, and calling up numerical solutions to complex equations in seconds. His injury had opened a door, one that allowed him to access areas of the brain that were locked to most people. "Don't think of yourself as damaged," Dr. Trevers said. "Think of yourself as having a superpower. Once you learn to control it, your abilities can change the world."

With Dr. Trevers's help, Brink came to see that he could live with

his new reality and thrive. With training, Dr. Trevers assured him, he
would be able to control the more frightening aspects of his gift—
the insomnia and racing thoughts, for example, could be tamed with
meditation. Brink read a memoir written by a British man who had
the same condition. He wrote *I knew things that were deeper than my
own existence* and *I somehow knew things I didn't know.* This man
hadn't studied higher math or ciphers, and he'd never been good at
remembering dates or what he read. And yet he *received* information,
as if from another dimension.

This description resonated deeply with Brink. He didn't know
how he knew the things he knew; he just did. Shapes and patterns
simply arrived in his mind. His injury was a pickax that had burst
through a wall, releasing a surge of knowledge. It flowed into him,
filling him with a dizzying amount of information. He didn't learn.
He merely received.

Mike Brink never played football again. He threw himself into
collecting puzzle books, every kind imaginable: crosswords, word
puzzles, riddles, math games, mazes, sudoku. And he began to make
puzzles himself. Constructing a puzzle helped him focus the prolif-
eration of patterns into a singular problem and gave him an outlet
for his imagination. He made a crossword puzzle with an NFL
theme and sent it to the puzzle page of *The Plain Dealer.* They published it, sending him a check for fifty dollars and giving him his first
byline. He didn't try to hold on to the person he might have been.
He rerouted his life the way water, diverted by a boulder, changes
courses, moving ahead quickly and completely, too caught up in the
momentum to consider what was lost.

Instead of going to college on a football scholarship, he went to
MIT, where he put his gift to good use. He majored in mathematics,
specializing in topology, and found that his abilities gave him an
instant advantage. MIT was filled with the most brilliant minds in
the world, and yet he discovered that he was quicker than other
students—he rarely studied, he was the first to finish tests, and he
remembered long passages from textbooks and lectures without ef-

fort. His teachers saw that he was extraordinary, and he was funneled into elite programs, allowed to take graduate classes as a junior, and left school summa cum laude and Phi Beta Kappa, with an invitation to return as a PhD candidate.

But while his intellectual successes came easily, personal relationships were harder to navigate. The same gift that gave him a rapid-fire memory and an ability to solve complex equations in seconds hindered his ability to connect with other people. Facial expressions were difficult to parse, for example, and he sometimes missed simple physical cues, mistook the meaning of a look, confused a joke for a barb or a gesture of affection for one of annoyance. While he had a photographic memory when it came to patterns, other kinds of memories hazed at the edges and disappeared. He could remember certain details about people—their phone numbers, twenty anagrams for their name, how the pattern of freckles on their left hand resembled the constellation Hydrus—but there were moments when he struggled to read emotion. What people wanted to express about themselves, what they wanted from him.

It was a subtle challenge, known only to Mike Brink, an Achilles' heel that he learned to manage. He watched his classmates and professors with care, noting their ways of demonstrating thoughts and feelings, so that he could read them more effectively: One friend always touched his chin when he was nervous; a girl in one of his classes flared her nostrils when challenged; a literature teacher clicked her tongue to express dismay. He came to see emotional expressions as symbols. He cataloged them in his mind, creating a kind of lexicon, keeping track of expressions and emotional gestures as if they were clues to a riddle. Desire, fear, love, insecurity—human emotion was a grammatically complex foreign language he desperately wanted to speak.

For the most part, nobody noticed his struggle to connect. If they did, they figured he was distracted or just a typical absentminded math major. But the feeling of disconnection galled him, and he worked hard to make friends. He wanted a romantic relationship, someone he could be close to, someone he cared about and who cared about him. He'd been popular in high school and never had trouble asking girls out, but things had been easier then. When he messed up a chance to go out with a woman he desired—he asked her to dinner, and she reacted in a way he found unreadable—he couldn't help but wonder if he would always be alone.

He described the problem to Dr. Trevers. He'd continued to speak with his neuroscientist weekly by phone and went to his office whenever he returned to Ohio to check in. Dr. Trevers speculated that Brink might be suffering from a common side effect of a traumatic brain injury: a disruption in his ability to recognize and process expressions of emotion. There may have been frontal-cortex damage that wasn't detected after his initial screenings. He suggested another MRI and referred him to a specialist in Boston. When the results came back, the MRI showed that his frontal cortex was perfectly normal. And yet Brink was haunted by the possibility of disconnection and pushed himself to be hyperaware of what other people felt, often overanalyzing people's emotions.

Brink knew how fortunate he was. His injury could have left him paralyzed, or worse. Somehow he'd beaten the odds and walked away with minor damage. He had lived. Still, he wanted more than just survival. There were times when other people seemed unreachable. He'd leave a date without knowing if she wanted to see him again. He'd finish a meeting with his puzzle editor at *The New York Times* and have no idea if he was satisfied with his work. He tried to connect with colleagues but couldn't. He could have his pick of girlfriends—his fame and good looks created endless opportunities—but it never quite clicked. It was like living with a pane of thick glass between him and the world: He saw everyone clearly, and they saw him, too, but his ability to reach them had become blunted, distorted. Contained. He'd always struggled to connect to the person on the other side of the barrier. He hadn't felt that way with Jess Price, though. There'd been no barrier. There'd been nothing between them at all.

I I

During the day shift, when cameras tracked his path through the prison and his fellow prison guards clocked his every move, Cam Putney hid his interest in Jess Price. He snuck glances at her as he patrolled the cafeteria, stationed himself outside the rec room when the women had group therapy, and memorized the exercise schedule to know exactly when Jess Price went out to the yard to walk the dirt track. He was careful to mask his intentions. His orders were clear. Nobody could know that he was watching her.

But at night, it was a different story. Between two and five in the morning, when the prisoners slept, Cam had more freedom. He'd slip into the dormitory—a long, open room in the modern part of the prison with fifty-two bunks, all occupied—and watch Jess Price from the shadows. He avoided the security cameras, of course. There was always someone watching behind the blinking red light. Guards weren't allowed to enter the dormitories while the inmates slept, unless there was a good reason—a fight, a fire, a full-on medical emergency. There had been too many instances of abuse reported in recent years—favors traded between guards and inmates, drugs in exchange for sex—and so the guards were monitored almost as much as the prisoners.

But Cam wasn't interested in the women in the other bunks. He'd been sent to the Ray Brook facility the week Jess Price was incarcerated, and he would be called back the minute she left. His mission was simple: watch over her, protect her, and report everything he saw concerning her. For nearly five years, he'd been meticulous. When her shrink got through to her, he made sure Dr. Raythe understood that he wasn't dealing with an ordinary inmate. Jess Price was a woman of great importance, the keeper of something precious and rare. No one—not her therapist, not the other inmates, not her family—could know what she knew. He'd warned Raythe that he shouldn't even attempt to help her. But the guy hadn't listened.

Cam touched the tattoo on his neck, a triangle composed of ten dots. It'd been a rite of initiation, his tattoo, a sign that he'd worked his way up to the higher levels of the organization. It didn't mean anything to most people—they glanced at it and assumed it was just a trendy bit of body art. In all the years he'd worked in the organization, there'd been only a few times the mark was recognized. But when it was, it filled him with an indescribable feeling of satisfaction and pride. He wasn't alone. There were others like him. And together, they were building a new world.

The lights had been out for hours when the prisoner began to talk in her sleep. She kicked at her blanket and thrashed around, probably having some kind of nightmare, which would make sense—the way she looked, with her stringy hair and bloody fingernails, her whole life was one bad dream. But then he moved closer, angling so he could hear her. She was whispering something. He wrote everything down in his reports, making sure to mark the exact words he heard: *hurry up, follow me, promise.*

12

The next morning, Dr. Thessaly Moses met Mike Brink at the prison entrance.

He'd left Connie at the motel with the air-conditioning on and enough food and water to last until lunch. While he'd wanted to bring her, getting clearance for a dog would be complicated, even with her status as a service animal. When Brink told Dr. Trevers about Connie the year before, the doctor found Brink's attachment to Connie therapeutic and designated her an "emotional-support animal." At first, the label annoyed Brink. Why did Dr. Trevers have to medicalize everything? Couldn't a man even have a pet without it relating to trauma? When Brink told Dr. Trevers about Connie the year before, the doctor found Brink's attachment to Connie therapeutic and designated her an "emotional-support animal." At first, the label annoyed Brink. Why did Dr. Trevers have to medicalize everything? Couldn't a man even have a pet without it relating to trauma? And yet, he knew that Dr. Trevers was right. Connie was more than a pet. She was his friend and companion.

Thessaly led Brink through the central corridor to the far end of the prison, stopping before a thick reinforced metal door with a sign that read RESTRICTED. There was a sensor and keypad to the right. "I had to fill in a ton of paperwork to get clearance," she said, pulling out a plastic badge and showing it to Mike Brink. He saw a Code 39 barcode with a series of forty-three characters, a mixture of numbers, letters, and symbols. A Code 39 barcode was the first barcode to incorporate alphanumeric characters and numeric digits, and was one of the most popular barcodes in the world.

"I have access for one hour and then need to return the card to my supervisor. They change the code every forty-eight hours, apparently. Next thing you know, they'll ask for my firstborn child. So anyway . . ." Thessaly punched in the code. "We'd better get going."

The keypad beeped and the door unlatched. Brink shoved it open and held it for Thessaly.

"I admire the state's decision to preserve and use these old structures," she said as she guided him into a stairwell with peeling paint and battered linoleum tiles on the landing. "And having patient records at our disposal surely has its benefits. But they should really allocate the proper maintenance funds."

Above, there was a drop ceiling with damaged panels. A few were missing, revealing the original ceiling of the old brick structure, its vaults and windows creating a volume of light and shadow high above.

"If I were breaking out of here, that's the way I'd go," Brink said, gesturing to the open ceiling.

"This area is secured at all entry points," Thessaly said, "but it's true: If a prisoner were able to get up there, it would be hard to find her. And look," she said, pointing up so that Brink saw a ragged patch of roof twenty feet above, where shafts of light drizzled through. "The roof is damaged, which explains the mold. Water just leaks in. The Department of Corrections has been promising to fix it for years, but Lord knows when that will happen."

As Thessaly led him down a set of stairs and into a basement, Brink could smell the mildew in the air, feel the decades of abandonment in the chipped paint and cracked linoleum tiles. They walked past old medical equipment, iron cots and wheelchairs left from the tuberculosis sanatorium; a wall of moldering books from the library;

broken gym equipment, including a particularly battered Stair-Master that must have been brought down from the prison gym. Finally, Thessaly stopped before another door, unlocked it, and ushered Brink into a storage room.

"These are all the records from this institution prior to 2019," Thessaly said, escorting him into a maze of filing cabinets. They were marked by year: 1993, 1999, 2004. "Every person who was treated in this facility, whether sick with tuberculosis or receiving mental-health services, would have a file down here somewhere. Really, it's a shame to have so much information that isn't available in our treatment database. There must be a way to get the funding to scan these files into our system."

Thessaly stopped at a cabinet labeled 2018.

"Technically, I should submit a written request to show you, or anyone, these files," she said. "But as there isn't time for more paperwork, we'll pretend you didn't see any of this."

She opened a drawer, flipped through the files, and pulled out a thick accordion folder with the name PRICE, JESSICA typed across the top. She glanced inside. "Well, it looks like there is something down here after all." She led him to a table in a corner, where she emptied the file and spread its contents out before them. There were hundreds of pages, many slip folders, and a few manila envelopes.

"Raythe was a paper guy," she said, picking up a sheaf of case notes and paging through them. "Meticulous. Wrote everything down."

"If he was meticulous, why didn't you have a copy of these files?"

"That's the question, isn't it, Mr. Brink," Thessaly said, giving him a look. "Shall we see what's here?"

Thessaly took one stack of papers and Brink another. One of the qualities of spatial and mechanical savantism was an ability to read quickly and to remember every page exactly to the letter. This skill was the one that interested people most, and Brink was asked about it in every interview he'd ever given. He was fascinated by it, too, but mostly because of the pervasive misconceptions about it. For example, he loved thrillers and spy movies with heroes who had an eidetic or photographic memory, but they usually got it all wrong. It wasn't like taking a scan, or even a photograph, but an abstract, conceptual process, a resolution of consciousness that revealed a memory. It was mysterious, even to Brink, but give him a stack of a hundred pages and he would be finished reading in ninety seconds and retain every piece of information.

Dr. Trevers had measured this ability and found that Brink was able to read 18,000 words per minute with 100 percent comprehension and had a perfect recall of random sentences pulled from the text. Not the Guinness World Record for speed-reading—that was 25,000 wpm, held by Howard Stephen Berg—but not bad for someone who had no desire to read quickly. His ability to reproduce what he read had been good enough to get a perfect SAT score and a full ride to MIT.

Brink moved through the pages rapidly, taking in the information in one gulp. For the most part, the reports were dry as hell, filled with clinical language, but Brink was soon able to put together the basics of Jess's initial assessment, her behaviors and treatments during her first year at the facility. She'd been uncommunicative, refused to participate in group therapy, had a tendency to self-harm and to ignore inmates and guards, consistent with everything Thessaly had told him. But he hadn't anticipated the sheer amount of paperwork Raythe had on Jess Price. There were over a thousand pages of analysis.

"There's a lot here about Jess's treatment," he said, pushing the stack aside and taking another. "But nothing that seems out of the ordinary."

Thessaly glanced at the stack of pages, clearly skeptical he'd synthesized so much information so quickly. "It's out of the ordinary that these are down here at all," she said. "The entirety of Dr. Raythe's files were supposed to be in his office. It is bizarre that he would put anything down here that he might need. It's almost as if Raythe purposely kept these apart from her official file."

"Can you think of a reason why he would do that?" Brink asked, sifting through more papers—lists of medications she was prescribed, notes from a group session, a guard's report on an incident that had ended in disciplinary action.

"It makes no sense at all," she said. "But their relationship did strike me as odd. As I told you yesterday, I came to this facility after Dr. Raythe's accident. When I arrived, I found Jess to be quite emotional about it. She cried when I brought it up and even worked herself into a panic attack that required sedation. I was surprised, as nothing in his notes suggested that he'd made much progress with her. And of course, from my own experience with her, it was hard to imagine that Jess had a real connection with Dr. Raythe, but then, who knows what other methods he used to reach her. . . ."

As Thessaly spoke, Brink noticed a glossy blue folder. He slipped it out from under the pile of papers, slid off an elastic band, and opened it. The contents didn't seem to fit with the other files. There was one of Raythe's reports clipped to a thick white eight-by-ten envelope with the word CONFIDENTIAL stamped across the front in red, a Columbia County Sheriff's Office logo printed in the upper left corner. And, tucked into the pocket, a brown leather journal, a red ribbon curled over the spine.

"What's that?" Thessaly asked, gesturing to the folder.

"I have no idea," Brink said. He pulled out the large white envelope with the report and handed it to Thessaly. She looked it over, unclipped the report, and read it. "This is really . . . odd," she said.

He reached for the report, wanting to read it himself, but Thessaly pulled it away.

"Dr. Raythe wrote here that Jess had nightmares when she first arrived," she said. "It looks like she was moved twice because her screaming disturbed the other prisoners, from dormitory C1 to dormitory A. And it appears that Dr. Raythe was able to communicate with her about the nightmares. Listen to this."

Thessaly read from the report: *"The patient cries out in the night. She is terrified of a woman, who she claims has been hurting her. She woke several nights begging the guards to keep this woman away. It is the only time she has spoken in the months since her arrival and, seeing an opportunity, I began working nights, to be close by when she is in need. It was in this manner that I have been able to communicate with her. She describes what is happening not as nightmares but as visitations. The guards on duty, however, report that the other inmates have not been near Jess Price, and surveillance video shows that she has been alone in her bunk every night. Finding her terror genuine, I began to investigate the circumstances that brought her here. What I have found has shocked me. There are very powerful people behind this, people who don't want anyone to know the truth. I am beginning to suspect that Jess Price is not the only one in danger."*

Thessaly met his eye, her expression filled with shock, and he remembered what she'd said to him during their first meeting. *There are times when I'm with her when I am . . . I don't know how to put it exactly. Afraid. More than afraid. Terrified. Like I'm in the presence of something bigger than me. Something dangerous.*

"Wow," he said. "That's pretty serious stuff. Is there more?"

Thessaly turned over Dr. Raythe's report, showing a blank page. "That's all he wrote. But maybe this will help explain it." Thessaly took the white envelope and ripped it open. Seeing that she was distracted, Brink flipped through the brown leather journal. He recognized Jess's handwriting immediately and caught his breath. Before Thessaly noticed, he stashed the journal in his back pocket.

"What the hell . . ." Thessaly said, her brow creased in consternation as she examined the contents of the white envelope.

"Anything interesting?" Brink asked, stepping to her side to get a look. He saw the edge of what appeared to be a police report, but before he could read it, Thessaly slid it back into the envelope.

"I'm not sure what this is," she said stiffly, but her reaction said the opposite: She'd found something that interested her deeply.

He reached for the envelope. "Here, let me give it a try," Brink said. "Maybe I can help."

But she sidestepped him, slipped the envelope into the blue folder, and tucked it under her arm. "I think we should wrap this up for the time being."

"Hold on a sec, I was hoping to get a look at the rest of this—"

"I don't think that's going to be possible," she said, gathering up the files in her arms and pressing them to her chest.

"Come on, Thessaly," he said lightly, hoping to mask the desperation he felt. Whatever was in that blue folder might help him to understand what Jess was trying to tell him. "Could you at least tell me what's in the envelope?"

Thessaly's manner turned chilly. "I will share this information with you, Mr. Brink, if it is relevant. But first I am going to take these files to my office and go through them properly. I need to understand what I'm looking at before I share it with someone unaffiliated with this institution."

Brink took this in, stung. She'd brought him to the prison to help, and now she was cutting him out. They'd found a trove of documents, and he needed to see it. Justified or not, he believed he had a right to this information. Maybe because Jess trusted him with her cipher, or perhaps because of their intimacy in his dream, he felt a deep connection to her, one he didn't often experience. In less than twenty-four hours, this woman had become important to him.

"Besides," Thessaly said, glancing at her watch, "I was able to get permission for you to see Jess again. She will be in the library at noon. That is in exactly fifteen minutes. You will want to be on time."

13

Jess Price's journal formed a small, stiff square in the back pocket of his jeans and, as Brink walked through the hallway of the first floor, it took every bit of resistance to keep himself from reading it. Only the threat of Dr. Moses confiscating it stopped him. He couldn't risk that she'd take it away, as she'd done with Raythe's files. He'd seen a date at the top of the first page: July 7, 2017. That was twelve days before Noah Cooke died, which meant that Jess had written it while she was at the Sedge mansion. Maybe the journal would explain everything—the terrible events at Sedge House, maybe even the puzzle Jess Price had asked him to solve. One thing was certain: It was too important to lose.

Thessaly steered him toward the library, but he couldn't imagine seeing Jess without knowing what was in the journal. As they walked past a restroom, Brink excused himself. Thessaly didn't look happy but didn't object. "You have two minutes," she said. "I'll be waiting at the library."

As she walked away, Brink felt his pulse quicken. He had only a few minutes, but that was all he needed, that and a private space where the surveillance cameras couldn't find him. The restroom seemed like the perfect solution, but when he ducked inside, it was filled with guards. He stepped to the urinal, then to the sink to wash his hands, and left. He didn't want to take any chances.

A prison didn't offer privacy; it was designed to eliminate it. There were guards at every turn—in the hallways, at the security station near the entrance, leading a group of women out to the yard. He hurried past a few rooms near Thessaly's office that looked promising, but he didn't dare go inside for fear of the cameras. Finally, he found himself back at the set of metal doors that led to the old part of the prison.

Glancing over his shoulder, he made sure he was alone. While he didn't have Thessaly's badge, he remembered the code—the string of numbers below the barcode—exactly. Of course, most people used their badge with its barcode and would never manually enter such a long number. But Brink wasn't like most people. He punched the sequence of forty-three numbers and symbols into the keypad, and the lock clicked.

He pushed the door open and stepped into the stairwell. Thessaly had taken him down to the basement; he would go up. Climbing the steps, he found himself on an abandoned floor of the sanatorium, a dark, dusty space with cobwebs and outdated medical equipment. The sun shone through grime-slicked windowpanes, and although he could hardly see, he pulled the journal from his pocket and opened it.

One glance confirmed that he'd been right: He'd found Jess's journal. There was her handwriting, neat and looping, the words *Sedge House, July 07, 2017,* written at the top of the first page. He read the opening paragraph:

Sedge House is the kind of gabled and turreted estate you read about in a nineteenth-century novel, not the sort of place you would expect to spend the summer. That I am staying here, and that I have this whole place to myself, strikes me as both utterly wonderful and utterly terrifying at once.

Before going further, he flipped through the remaining pages and froze as a folded sheet of paper fluttered to the ground. Brink picked it up and opened it, stunned. It was a familiar construction, a puzzle he'd made himself, but finding it was a shock to the system. He'd never expected to see it again—let alone there, in a prison, in a journal belonging to a convicted murderer.

In an instant, his relationship to Jess Price shifted. Until that moment, he'd believed he was in control, that she was the vulnerable one. But that wasn't the case at all. This puzzle tipped the balance entirely. He saw the solutions appear in the blank spaces and felt an overwhelming possessiveness: This was something Jess Price shouldn't have seen. It was something nobody should see. He'd thought it was out of his life forever, but there it was, confronting him with the mistakes of his past.

The puzzle was a collection of twenty-five hexagrams, five to a row, with mathematical functions—addition and subtraction, multiplication and division signs—between them. A series of nine numbers could be plugged into the blank spaces to solve these equations. The answers were given in hexagrams that wrapped along the bottom of the equations and angled up along the right side.

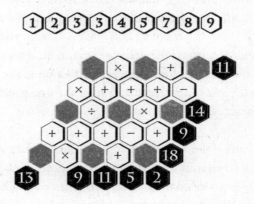

He'd constructed the puzzle in 2009, when he was nineteen years old and a sophomore at MIT. It was a simple puzzle from a time when he didn't think of himself as a professional constructor so much as a kid having fun. Playful. That was the spirit in which he'd made it, and seeing it there before him reminded him of who he'd been a decade before, a naïve kid with a wild talent he didn't fully understand. It was like coming across an old picture of himself: He recognized the guy, and even felt a protective urge toward his younger self, but that person was long gone.

While it was a relatively simple puzzle on the surface, there was another one hidden inside it, a puzzle within a puzzle. He thought of it as a kind of signature, a Mike Brink calling card, and while it carried significance for Brink, it was the least known of his puzzles. In fact, only a few people were aware it existed. He'd assumed it was buried and forgotten. Clearly, he'd been wrong.

He was examining the puzzle when a noise drew his attention. The door to the stairwell opened, slammed shut, and the sound of footsteps echoed behind him. Brink slipped the journal into his pocket and stepped back into a dark corner, pressing against a dirty window just as a prison guard walked into the hallway.

Brink recognized the guard. He'd seen him the day before when he escorted Jess Price into the library, but he hadn't gotten a decent look at him. He now saw that the guy was huge, six foot four, with bleached-blond hair and large diamond studs in both ears. His muscles bulged under his uniform, and he wore heavy-soled boots, the kind meant for serious ass-kicking. Not the guy he wanted to confront in a dark, deserted sanatorium especially with an inmate's journal in his possession. The guard had the instincts of a watchdog. He walked up and down the hall, as if smelling Brink out. The next thing Brink knew, the guard stood before him, looking down into his eyes. "What the hell are you doing up here?"

Brink stepped out of the shadows, holding up his clearance badge in defense. "I have permission to be here," he said.

The guard snatched the badge and examined it. When he returned the badge, his eyes were filled with belligerence. "This is a long way from the psych offices."

"Dr. Moses is waiting for me in the library," he said, grasping for an explanation. "I was looking for a bathroom and got turned around. If you could show me the way to the library, I'd appreciate it."

"You're way lost, bro," he said, and gave him a short, sharp push toward the door. It was little more than a nudge, quick and aggressive, but enough to knock Brink off-balance. He stumbled and dropped the badge. When the guard bent to retrieve it—muttering an insincere apology under his breath—Brink noticed a tattoo on the side of his neck, an equilateral triangle composed of ten dots. He'd only glanced at it, but when he closed his eyes, he saw the pattern blazing against the back of his eyelids: four rows of circles, four circles at the base and one at the apex, an elegant triangular configuration.

The guard gave him another nudge toward the door, and while his first instinct was to push back, Brink didn't resist. He walked quickly, relieved the guy didn't search him. If he discovered Jess Price's journal, he'd take it to Thessaly Moses. And Brink needed the journal, and the puzzle inside, to understand what Jessica Price really wanted from him.

14

The guard pushed Mike Brink's shoulder, directing him forward. It was a small sign of aggression, but one that galled him. He'd met guys like this when he played football: big burly dudes built like bulldozers, who needed to prove themselves over and over. They weren't complicated, but they didn't need to be. They threw their weight around, blocked and tackled, and that was enough to justify their presence on the field. Brink's talent had been slipping through tiny holes these guys left in a defensive line, using his agility to break free. Brute strength didn't mean much if they couldn't catch him. Then again, there were times when brawn trumped brains. For all Brink's skill, one hard hit had changed everything.

Thessaly was waiting for him at the door to the library, her arms crossed over her chest, a look of alarm on her face. "What exactly is going on, Mr. Brink?"

"I found him on the third floor," the guard said.

"We were supposed to meet here," Thessaly said, giving him a look of reproach.

"I got turned around," he said, but he could see she was skeptical. A man who could read a thousand pages of reports in minutes and solve a Rubik's Cube in fifteen seconds did not get turned around. She thanked the guard, opened the library door, and held it for him. He saw Jess seated at the same table they'd shared during their first meeting. "I managed to get you an hour this time," Thessaly said, as he passed into the library. "Just don't get turned around again, okay?"

With her gray jumpsuit and pale skin, her fingernails bitten down to scabs, and her silence, Jess Price was much as she'd been the day before. And although he knew that she could not possibly be different and that dreams, however emotional, don't change reality, he half-expected to find the woman he'd met in the forest, the beautiful, sensual creature who had so captivated him, her long hair cascading down her back, her touch enough to send shivers through him. He shook away the vision, but the intense, hallucinatory feelings of the dream didn't dissipate. He felt all the wonder and attraction, the overwhelming need to be close to her, that he'd felt in his sleep. As he sat across from her, his pulse quickened and sweat rose on his skin. He'd felt it in the dream, too. Her presence like the rush of some delicious drug.

Brink glanced over his shoulder to verify that the guard stood at the door, angled his shoulder to block the security camera, then pulled the journal from his pocket and placed it on the table. "I found this in Raythe's files," he whispered.

She picked up the journal and turned it in her hand, looking at it as though it were an artifact from an ancient ruin, a treasure salvaged from another lifetime.

"You recognize it, then?" he asked, taking in the minute changes in her expression, the surprise and confusion, the realization that Dr. Raythe had something that belonged to her.

She examined the pages thoughtfully, as if trying to reconcile them with something, then nodded slightly, acknowledging that it belonged to her.

"How about this?" he asked, turning to the puzzle folded into the back. "Where did you get this?"

She looked at the puzzle, her expression giving nothing away. He knew she wouldn't speak, and so he pulled his pen from his pocket and slid it across the table, hoping she'd write a response.

"I need to know where you got this," he said, hearing the urgency in his voice.

She studied the puzzle, grabbed the pen, and solved each of the equations. Under the puzzle's solutions, she wrote the letters of the alphanumeric substitution he'd use to encode his name: MIKE BRINK. Then, she pushed the puzzle at him and smiled. It was the first genuine smile he'd seen from her, a hint at the person she'd been when she'd solved this puzzle years before.

But he couldn't smile in return. Seeing his puzzle on the table before him was like discovering a part of his innermost self—his heart, his stomach—cut open and exposed. It felt all wrong. Nobody was supposed to know about that puzzle. Nobody.

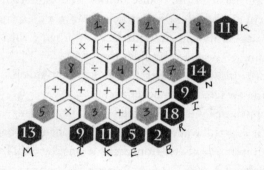

He leaned closer to her and whispered, "How in the hell did you get this?"

She gestured to the completed puzzle, as if the solution told the whole story, and in some ways it did: She had, through some miracle, found the one puzzle he wished he'd never constructed. Whether she knew what the puzzle meant, or how badly Mike Brink wished to forget it, was another question.

"You shouldn't have this," he said, hearing the confusion in his voice. The connection to Jess he'd felt just minutes before turned on its head. He was wary of her motives. She'd wanted to know if she could trust him, but he wasn't at all sure he could trust her. What if the circular puzzle had been nothing more than a ruse? What if everything she'd said was a lie? "Is this why I'm really here?"

She shook her head, her eyes wide with emotion: *No*.

"Then why?" he said, straining to keep his voice even.

Jess leaned back in her chair, her expression one of alarm. It was obvious that she hadn't expected to see the puzzle, either. She probably had no idea Raythe had her journal in his files. Still, if she'd known about this puzzle, she knew a lot more about him than she'd let on.

"You should have sent me this puzzle," he said. "If you had, I would—"

"—never have come," she said, finishing his sentence.

Her voice startled him. It was gentle, little more than a whisper, but powerful enough to bring his heartbeat to a crescendo. He recognized it, its clarity and strength. It was the same voice he'd heard in the dream.

"I couldn't risk that," she said. "I need you too much."

"Need me for what?"

"To keep your promise, Michael."

Maybe it was the way she called him Michael—a name nobody used, not even his mother—or perhaps it was the chill he felt as she grasped his hand, but he felt suddenly afraid. He struggled to free his hand, but she gripped him tight, the sleeve of her jumpsuit pulling away to reveal a honeycomb pattern carved into her right arm, an intricate web of fine, perfectly tessellated octahedrons from wrist to elbow. The pink scar tissue could only mean that the pattern had been carved into her skin with a razor. The symmetry of the pattern captured his attention, but what struck him most forcefully was that it was the exact pattern he'd seen on Jess's skin in his dream.

He began to question her, but she leaned close and said, "Do you remember the smell of the forest? How the moonlight fell over our skin? It was beautiful, what we shared. And it's only the beginning."

His heart skipped a beat as it all rushed back to him: the smell of the forest, the pale light of the moon on her body as he held her. He wasn't imagining it. She'd been there; she'd experienced what he had.

"I can't do this without you," she said. She looked at him and he felt everything he'd felt the night before: the almost psychic emotional connection, the overwhelming desire, the sense that he'd found a missing part of himself.

"I don't understand," he said at last, but in fact he did understand: The woman sitting across from him was somehow, in some inexplicable way, the woman in his dream.

15

It took a lot to surprise Mike Brink—he was generally three or four chess moves ahead of the game—but Jess had left him turned around and disoriented. *Do you remember the smell of the forest? How the moonlight fell over our skin?* The Brink puzzle, the references to his dream, the pattern of scars on her arm—it all stunned him. He struggled to get his bearings. He had questions he needed to ask her, but before he could begin, the library door opened, and Thessaly Moses approached. He slipped Jess's journal into his pocket, hoping she hadn't seen it.

"I will need you to come with me for a moment," Thessaly said. There was something odd in her voice, a steely authority that he hadn't heard before.

She'd told him he had an hour, but he'd been in the library all of ten minutes. "Can I stop by your office when I'm done here?"

"I'm afraid not," she said, glancing toward the door, where two prison guards stood by, watching: the blond bulldozer from earlier, and another, older guy with salt-and-pepper hair. They were waiting for Thessaly to give them the green light to kick his ass, and she seemed about ready to do it.

"Let's go, Mr. Brink," Thessaly said, gesturing to the door.

"What's this about?" he asked, pushing away his chair and standing.

Thessaly gave him a look, then turned her eyes to the security camera, a silent gesture that told him to shut up and follow orders. "I've been asked to inform you that your clearance has been rescinded," she said, her voice cold, impersonal as a recording. "I'm going to escort you out of the building, Mr. Brink. Please follow me."

The guards came forward, one standing by as the other cuffed Jess. As they led her past, she leaned close and, her voice little more than a whisper, said, "Remember your promise."

Brink followed Thessaly through the corridor, matching her quick pace. What the hell was happening? Fifteen minutes ago she'd given him an hour with Jess. Now she was ushering him out as if the prison were on fire. And although he was complying, everything in him resisted leaving. "Come on, Thessaly," he said, as they walked through the hallway. "Dr. Moses. Wait. Can you at least explain?"

She didn't answer but led him to the guard station, where they passed through the metal detectors, and out the front doors into the cool, perfect afternoon, the sky blue and the sun bright. As they made their way to the parking lot, Thessaly slowed and walked by his side. "I'm sorry about that," she said, her voice low. "But I needed to get you out of there as quickly as possible."

He turned to her, desperate to know what was going on. "What the hell is happening, Thessaly?"

"Just keep moving," she said softly, nudging his arm. "I've got a lot to say and not much time."

They walked side by side past a line of SUVs and compacts, a pack of motorcycles, going deeper into the parking lot. "After our trip to the basement, I went through the blue folder. As you probably saw, the white envelope was from the Columbia County Sheriff's Office. Inside were photocopies of confidential documents from the investigation into the murder of Noah Cooke. Information that I've never seen before."

"What kind of information?"

"An inventory of items found at the crime scene, photos, the medical examiner's report. Raythe must have put in a request for a copy—it isn't common but not unheard of for a therapist to read a patient's police records. But when I went into our system to find documentation of Raythe's request, I couldn't find any of his files regarding Jess Price in the database. There were folders for the files, but the reports themselves were gone. I thought there might be something wrong with my access, and so I logged out and tried again, only to find that my credentials no longer worked. I'd been locked out. I called IT and asked for help—I should have full access to these files—and within ten minutes I got the call from my supervisor. He told me that the governor's office insisted that you be removed from the facility." She gave him a look he couldn't decipher, one part panic, another part accusation. Either she suspected he was at fault and had done something illegal, or she was scared out of her mind.

"The governor's office?" he asked, utterly perplexed. "What does the governor's office have to do with me? Or Jess Price?"

"My question exactly," she said. "My supervisor told me that your visiting privileges had been revoked, that I should escort you from the facility and make sure you understand that you are not to return. If you come back, I'm supposed to call the police and have you arrested."

"But that's absurd," Brink said, feeling a wave of anger. "I have permission to be here. There has to be a mistake."

"My supervisor has never received a call from the governor's office before. Ever. Evidently someone doesn't like you or what you're doing," she said. "Also, I have a feeling that someone deleted the security footage of your meeting with Jess yesterday. I went to speak to the head of security, John Williams, who oversees surveillance. I'm on good terms with John, and he's usually very helpful. But when I asked about the footage, he couldn't locate the digital file."

Brink remembered Jess's wariness of the surveillance camera.

She'd known someone was watching and they might use what they saw against her. She'd been right.

"I shouldn't be telling you this," she said, stepping closer. "I could lose my job. But there is a lot of crazy shit in that folder. I would appreciate your take on it."

"What kind of crazy shit?"

"Here," she said, pressing a flash drive into the palm of his hand. "There wasn't time to scan everything, but I got most of it."

Brink tucked the flash drive deep into the pocket of his jeans.

"To be perfectly honest, I don't know what to make of it. Dr. Raythe was"—she looked over her shoulder, making sure they were still alone—"utterly out of line. He should not have kept such important information outside Jess's official files."

They reached his truck, but Brink couldn't leave. He needed to know as much as possible about what was going on. "What was in that folder that was so important? Why did Raythe need to hide it?"

Thessaly looked over her shoulder again. "I can't talk now. Call me after you've read through everything." She pressed a business card into his hand. "My cell number is on the back."

Brink glanced at the card, *Dr. Thessaly R. Moses, PhD*, then at the phone number scrawled on the reverse side. It was beginning to sink in that he wouldn't be allowed to see Jess again. The thought made him desperate. He'd only just found her, only just come to understand their connection, and the idea of losing her filled him with panic.

"Listen," he said. "It's crucial that I communicate with Jess. There's more going on here than you realize."

"This is not the time," she said, giving him a look of warning. "Call me later."

"One more thing," he said, remembering the honeycomb pattern carved into Jess's skin. "Jess's arm. The scars. Do you know how that happened?"

"Jess Price doesn't have scars on her arm," Thessaly said, confused.

"I just saw them," he said, the geometric shapes forming in his mind. "A hexagonal prismatic tessellation on her arm. At first I thought it was a tattoo, but it isn't. It's scar tissue."

"Jess Price doesn't have any distinguishing markings on her skin. No tattoos, no birthmarks, no scars. Of that I'm certain."

Brink knew what he'd seen and was ready to argue the point, but he was interrupted when a black Tesla pulled up at the entrance to the prison and stopped. A tall, thin man with red hair and sunglasses emerged from the car. He started toward the prison and then, sensing their presence, turned and walked toward them.

"You need to go. Now," Thessaly said, turning on her heel and walking toward the Tesla. As Brink got into his truck, he glanced beyond Thessaly to the prison and, for a moment, he thought he heard Jess Price's voice, hovering in the air: *Follow me.*

16

As he drove out of the prison gates, Mike Brink tried to make sense of what had happened. The past day had been an emotional roller coaster, to say the least. He'd arrived at the prison without attachments, his responsibilities nothing more pressing than feeding Connie and sending in his weekly *New York Times* puzzle. Now he felt an overwhelming commitment to helping a woman he hardly knew. He didn't understand it—not the dream, not the puzzle, not the strange pattern on her skin—but his connection to Jess was unlike anything he'd experienced before. What had begun as a puzzle had become a deeply personal quest. It was more than the perplexing drawing, more than Raythe's secret file, even more than the truth about Noah Cooke's death. Meeting Jess had changed something in him, opened him to emotions he'd never felt before, and he needed to understand why.

With everything Thessaly had told him, he knew beyond a doubt that they were in danger. Jess had tried to warn him; her cipher couldn't have been more clear: *Dr. Raythe knew, and they killed him.* Yet he hadn't fully believed her. He'd dismissed her fears, looked to Thessaly for answers, and that, he knew now, was a big mistake. If he'd taken Jess's warning seriously, he would've been more careful. He would've minimized his presence at the prison. He would've pushed harder to read Raythe's files while he had the chance. He needed to know who was behind this, and what they wanted from Jess. If he knew that much, he'd have a sense of what he was up against. As it was, he didn't have much to go on. There'd been a call from Thessaly's supervisor, his visitation privileges had been revoked, and he'd be arrested if he returned. There was the puzzle Jess had drawn, the journal in his back pocket, and the flash drive with the scanned files from Thessaly. But what did these things have in common? Were they clues or dead ends?

And then there was the guy in the Tesla. He sure as hell hadn't been there to take a tour of the prison. He'd spotted Brink across the parking lot, watched him get in his truck, and tracked him as he drove away. Brink was sure he'd come to the prison for him. But why? What could he want? Did it have anything to do with Jess Price? Or the puzzle he'd found in her journal? If so, what was the connection? And how was Jess involved? He wondered if Raythe had been killed because of information he had about Jess, as her cipher claimed, or if it was really an accident, as Thessaly insisted. As it was, he had more questions than answers. He couldn't be sure of anything. Only one thing was certain: It was impossible to walk away from the mystery of Jess Price.

A few miles from the prison, he turned onto a winding county highway that led into the mountains. It was a ten-minute drive to the Starlite, and he didn't want trouble. He needed to get back to the motel, sit down, and read the files Thessaly had scanned. The sooner he knew what was on the flash drive, the better.

He drove as fast as his truck would go, pushing the engine to climb higher and higher up the mountain. Out the window were forests of white pine, their height dwarfing everything in view. He opened the window to the cool mountain air, smelled wet earth and moss, and told himself that everything he'd experienced—the uncanny emotional connection to Jess, all the questions left unanswered—was taking him in a logical direction. He'd entered a puzzle and, as with every puzzle, there was a solution. He just needed to focus on the pattern, follow the clues, and solve it.

Checking the rearview mirror, he saw, in a flash of sunlight, the Tesla behind him. He gripped the steering wheel as he weighed his options: Try to outrun the Tesla, or hide. He knew his truck wasn't up for it, and—as he'd learned firsthand on the football field—a good dodge is better than being tackled from behind.

At a bend in the highway, he pulled onto a dirt road, drove into a thicket of evergreens, cut the engine, and lay back on the vinyl seat, his heart racing. When he was sure the Tesla had sped by, he sat up and looked around. Protected by towering pine trees, with the afternoon sunlight breaking through the branches in bright fractals, he took a long, deep breath, counted to ten, and slowly exhaled. For the moment, he was safe.

Somehow, Jess had known what was going to happen. She knew Thessaly would escort him from the library. She knew he'd be kicked out of the prison, his access blocked. She'd been expecting it. But she also knew that he wasn't the kind of man to give up: the harder the puzzle, the harder he'd work to solve it. That was why she'd chosen him, after all. Once he began a puzzle, he never quit.

17

He'd put the puzzle online in November 2009, less than a week after his father died of cancer. It had been an emotional time, and looking back, he blamed his inability to process his feelings for the stupid things he'd done.

He was home in Ohio at the end of his father's illness. His relationship with his mother had been strained at the time. After he'd moved to Boston to attend MIT, his mom left Cleveland, too. She'd gone to France, ostensibly to help his grandmother move into a *maison de retraite* in Brittany. His mother was French, born in Paris, and he knew she missed everything about her native country. He suspected she'd stayed in Ohio because of him. After his injury, she'd been his biggest support, bringing him to see specialists, helping him apply to college, and making sure he wasn't alone. When he was gone, she must have felt his absence as a void. She'd promised to be back from France in a few weeks, but the trip lasted over a year, and it became obvious that she wasn't coming home.

His father fell ill during her absence, and while Mike knew there was no connection—of course it wasn't anyone's fault that his dad was sick—he couldn't help but feel that there was some underlying relationship between her leaving and everything falling apart.

His mom flew to Ohio after his father's diagnosis, and Mike came back when his father's illness was in its final stages. They'd kept him at home until his pain became unmanageable and then moved him to the hospital. The three of them were together when his father passed away. It had happened in the middle of the night, the hospital bleak and quiet. One second his father was with them, the next he was gone.

Brink and his mom planned the funeral. They chose the suit in which his father would be buried, stood together at the interment, and—at a small reception in the church basement—shook hands, accepted hugs, and heard condolences. That afternoon he was transported back in time to his old life, to the time before his injury when he was just Bob and Celine's kid, the boy everyone expected to go places.

Before flying back to Boston, Mike sorted through some things he'd left in the basement. He found his old puzzle books, stacks of Mead notebooks filled with diagrams and equations and riddles. He found the first puzzle he'd ever made, the magic square, and the first puzzle he'd published, the crossword with a football theme. He boxed them up, along with a few things belonging to his father—silk ties; a copy of a computer-programming textbook he'd co-authored; his watch—and took them to UPS to ship east.

It was outside UPS, in the parking lot of a strip mall, that the man approached him. He introduced himself as Gary Sand, one of his father's colleagues at Case Western, another professor in the computer-science department. Brink didn't think to question his identity. He looked the part of an absentminded professor: shaggy gray hair, unfashionable clothes, fingers stained with ink. "Let me buy you a drink," Sand said, inviting him to a Mexican restaurant at the end of the strip mall. Mike assumed he wanted to reminisce about his dad. Robert Brink had been loved and respected; his funeral was packed with people Mike didn't know, all with stories he hadn't heard before. And so he followed the man to the bar, ordered a margarita, and drank it as he listened to Gary Sand make an offer that would change his life.

His assignments began small. Sand gave him a personal key, an encrypted code to an anonymous message board, where Brink would find documents from Sand: cryptograms, ciphers, pages of letters and numbers that, after a moment of examination, revealed messages. Brink would solve them, return them through his encrypted key, and Sand would send him a check. That was it. Easy money, which he needed at the time, despite his scholarship. Sand never asked more of him, and Brink never asked questions about the true nature of his work. He'd googled Sand, and when he found nothing, he assumed he worked with the NSA in some capacity, a hunch supported by the way they communicated: Everything was sent via an encrypted site. The NSA had begun a massive cryptography initiative over the past decades, and Brink knew his skills would make him a prime candidate for recruitment. But Sand never tried to recruit him, and as they never met in person again, Brink left it at that.

But then strange things began to happen. Dangerous things.

It started with online stalking. In 2009, during his sophomore year at MIT, Brink was part of a community of online puzzle solvers, where he posted under the pseudonym M. Like most puzzlers, he preferred to remain anonymous online. The *Time* magazine piece had come out by then, his puzzles were a staple in *The New York Times,* and he had a publishing contract for his puzzle books. His fame preceded him, but he didn't like to be treated differently in puzzle forums, and so he never used his real name. He found something online that he couldn't find in real life: a community of people who loved puzzles, loved talking about them, and included him not because of who he was or what had happened to him but because they spoke the same language.

The M legend evolved from there. It started as something simple. He'd post a puzzle on a popular puzzle forum, and people would stop by to solve it. In the beginning, he constructed mostly crosswords and acrostics, which were the most popular puzzles by far, but sometimes he'd throw out a theorem or a maze or a Nurikabe puzzle. He constructed at all levels of difficulty, but his favorite puzzles were the really hard ones, puzzles that only a few people could solve. He created a puzzle every week, posting it at exactly 11:11 EST Sunday night and removing it forty-nine minutes later, at midnight.

Soon, a tight-knit group of puzzle solvers began coming to his page. Everything was open, free, and downloadable, and he never imagined that his following would grow to be more than a few bored puzzle geeks with a common love of challenges. But soon he had thousands of people downloading his puzzles every week. It was exactly the opposite of what he'd intended. While his avatar was M, a few of his more admirative solvers called him the Puzzle Master.

The puzzle Brink found in Jess's journal was the last puzzle he'd posted on the forum as M. The popularity of his puzzles was getting out of hand, and there was a group of persistent fans who badgered him to reveal his name. A subreddit threat speculated about possible identities, and when he saw *Mike Brink* at the top of the list, it was too close for comfort. Anonymity was essential to the whole endeavor, and he never dreamed of revealing who he was, but after exchanging a series of emails with one of the solvers who aced his most challenging puzzles, he constructed a puzzle that contained his name inside it and posted it on a Wednesday, when no one was looking for their weekly puzzle.

He wanted his last puzzle to be a challenge for himself, and so he worked in his fourteen-digit personal key—the one he used to exchange information with Gary Sand—as the solution to the puzzle: 13911521891411, the alphanumeric substitution of which spelled *Mike Brink*. It was an inside joke, obscure, nothing anyone would understand. He put it up at 11:11 and took it down at midnight. When he checked the analytics, he saw that only two people had downloaded the puzzle. Then, feeling that his days of online puzzling had run their course, he permanently deleted M's profile from all sites.

Gary Sand showed up on his doorstep the next day with questions. There had been an unidentified log-in to the NSA site using Brink's code early that morning, and while no apparent harm had been done—none of the files had been altered, and the user hadn't had access to any of the documents, which were also encrypted—someone had viewed and copied Brink's files. As Sand explained what had happened, Brink listened, dumbfounded. Someone had known that he was M, had known that he had a relationship with Gary Sand, and had enough insight into his puzzles to use a string of numbers as a personal key to log in to the encrypted site. And while Brink insisted that it was impossible, explaining that only two people had downloaded the puzzle and that nobody knew about his work with the agency, it didn't matter. His log-in credentials were permanently deleted. His relationship with Gary Sand ended, and Brink was left with a deep sense of shame. He'd been stupid to reveal such personal information online, and he'd let Gary Sand down. He never realized, until later, that his work had more-dangerous consequences.

It had been a painful incident, one that he liked to pretend never happened. But it had happened, and Jess had learned of it somehow, which brought up questions of how she'd found it and how it had come to be in her journal.

Only yesterday, he believed he'd gone to Ray Brook to help a brilliant but troubled woman. It had been a lark, a flip of the coin, a caprice of chance. But Jess wasn't some mental-health curiosity, and his presence at the prison was no accident. Jess Price was someone who had carefully, meticulously planned her approach. She'd waited for the right moment. She'd tempted him with the puzzle and hooked him with a cipher. In Jess Price, Mike Brink had met his equal. Really, he'd never had a chance.

18

If it weren't for Connie, Brink would have driven straight out of the mountains, got on the highway heading south to the city, climbed the five floors to his apartment, and locked the door. But he'd left Conundrum in the motel room, a decision he now regretted. After what happened at the prison, nothing felt safe anymore, and the Starlite didn't exactly offer much security. While he'd managed to lose the guy in the Tesla, he had a hunch he wasn't done with him.

His intuition proved accurate as he pulled into the Starlite parking lot. The door to his room was busted open, the frame splintered and a barrage of boot prints stamped over the door. Connie was nowhere to be seen.

He bounded out of the truck and into the wreckage of his room. Whoever had broken the door might still be there, waiting, but he didn't care. Connie could be in danger. He imagined the worst: Connie running away in fright, someone finding her outside and taking her home, or—most terrible of all—his beloved dog being run down on the highway. "Connie!" he called, scanning the room. "Connie, where are you?"

The place was trashed—the bed overturned, and the bedding torn from the mattress—but whoever was responsible had come and gone. He waded through twists of sheets and stepped into the bathroom, where he found the motel toiletries—tiny bottles of shampoo, and a minuscule tube of Crest toothpaste—squeezed out onto the floor. Even Connie's food and water bowls had been overturned, leaving shredded carrots over the carpet. He didn't get it. What did they think he was hiding? A computer chip sunk in a tube of toothpaste? Was he living in a spy novel or what? It was ironic because, until about two hours before, when he'd found his puzzle in Jess's journal, he thought he didn't have anything to hide.

Even if he did, he would never leave it in his hotel room. Anyone who'd ever watched a spy movie knew it would be the first place they'd look. Then again, he'd been careless enough to publish his personal password in an online puzzle, so perhaps he wasn't as savvy as he thought.

Suddenly, he heard the scuffle of little feet on asphalt, then a familiar yelp. He turned to see Connie bounding across the parking lot. A wave of relief flooded through him. Squatting down, he ruffled her fur as she leapt on him, licking his face and barking with pleasure. He marveled at her intelligence. Somehow she'd avoided the guy who broke into their room, then she slipped out the door and hid in the forest. She must've watched the whole thing from behind the wild blackberry bushes that lined the parking lot. "I bet you know who did this, don't you?"

Picking Connie up, he carried her into the room, poured fresh water in her bowl, took the remaining sirloin from the mini-fridge, and laid it out before her. As she ate, he leaned against the wall, trying to figure out what to do next. When working on a puzzle, he always started from the simplest point and moved toward complexity, devising a clear plan of attack, but he'd never felt so turned around. As he stood among the ruins of the motel room, he knew he was too close to it all. He needed to react, to make a bold move, and fast, but what?

There were a number of possible places to begin. There was the flash drive in his pocket, holding Raythe's files; there was Jess's journal in his bag. Then there was Thessaly Moses, back at the prison, who he planned to call. Where one starts determines the outcome of any maze, but he was paralyzed.

Suddenly a series of dots appeared in his mind. It began with one solid black circle, then nine more arranged themselves in a triangle, until he saw the prison guard's tattoo. After what Thessaly had said about the deleted security footage and knowing that someone inside the prison had been watching him, he had a hunch that the blond security guard was involved.

The triangle had bothered Brink from the moment he saw it. Something about it—the arrangement of the dots, the elegant, orderly nature of it—pulled at him. It was the same feeling he had when he encountered a new kind of puzzle: He'd feel the allure of the challenge, the anesthetic of losing himself in the pursuit of its secrets, and, when he'd solved it, a flood of euphoria, a potent burst of serotonin in his blood.

Brink walked out to his truck and pulled his laptop from under the passenger seat. At least he'd been smart enough not to leave that in his room. If he had, it would be smashed or stolen. He opened it, entered the passcode, and got online. He typed a description of the tattoo into a search engine and quickly found himself confronted with dozens of images of the triangle, variations on its shape and construction, but all with the same description. It was a tetractys, a ten-point equilateral triangle attributed to Pythagoras.

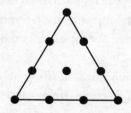

It was a geometrical representation of the fourth triangular number and, perhaps more in line with the guard's reason for tattooing it on his body, a symbol of sacred geometry. Brink typed in *sacred geometry* and *tetractys* and found himself on a website filled with esoteric information about the triangle. According to the site, the symbol expressed the name of God, the tetragrammaton—a four-letter name symbolizing Jehovah. In modern times, the symbol had been used most often—if the internet could be trusted—by Freemasons. But from what Brink knew about Freemasonry, which admittedly wasn't much, a prison guard wasn't the kind of man welcomed into such an elitist secret society. So why would a prison guard have a Pythagorean triangle on his body? Could there be another meaning? American culture had veered, in the last decade or so, into the Looney Tunes realm of conspiracy theories, secret societies, and end-of-days politics. He wouldn't be surprised if this guy had the Ark of the Covenant inked on his ass.

Despite the intrigue around Gary Sand, Mike Brink didn't believe in conspiracy theories. He didn't believe in stolen elections, that the apocalypse was coming, or that aliens had been visiting earth for decades. He believed in numbers and facts, that two plus two always equals four, that gravity makes an apple fall. He believed in logical solutions and that, with the right method, the truth could be known. The world's mysteries were really no different from a puzzle. They were all around us, and it was up to us to put the pieces together.

After packing his laptop, Brink loaded Connie into the truck and drove until he hit I-87 south, keeping an eye out for the black Tesla. An hour or so later, he pulled off at a rest area. As he got out of the truck, he looked back at the highway, then examined the parking lot. He'd been checking his mirror every ten minutes or so and hadn't seen anything suspicious. As far as he could tell, nobody had followed him.

He clipped on Conundrum's leash, grabbed Dr. Trevers's ESA document from the glove compartment in case someone gave him trouble, and headed across the parking lot. The brick rest-area structure was a single story with a fast-food court at one end, restrooms straight ahead, and a convenience store to the left. The air smelled of French fries and the nauseating stink of industrial soap, one that left him with a mild headache. The air-conditioning was too cold for comfort, but there was free Wi-Fi and, at 4:00 P.M. on a Friday afternoon, he was more or less the only person in the place.

He bought a turkey sub with extra mayo and pickles from Subway and a grande coffee from the Starbucks kiosk, then took a seat near a window overlooking the highway. He needed to be vigilant. While he was sure he hadn't been followed, it didn't mean that someone wasn't coming. His tomato-red truck wasn't difficult to find.

With one eye trained out the window, he pulled Jess's journal from his messenger bag and began to read.

19

Sedge House is the kind of gabled and turreted estate you read about in a nineteenth-century novel, not the sort of place you would expect to spend the summer. That I am staying here, and that I have this whole place to myself, strikes me as both utterly wonderful and utterly terrifying at once.

Usually I apply for house-sitting jobs, but the Sedge gig came to me. Someone sent an email through the luxuryhousesitting.com website with an invitation to apply for the job. I studied the description and fell in love with the idea of going upstate for the summer. The owner of Sedge House recently passed away, and the family wanted someone living on the property through the summer, and perhaps into the fall, while they prepare it to be sold. My primary duties would be light housework, maintaining the garden, and preparing the house before showings to potential buyers, which seemed manageable enough. And as it was two hours outside the city, and had no internet or television, it would afford me the quiet and solitude I needed to write.

It was easier than I thought it would be. I sublet my apartment and took the train upstate with a suitcase of clothes, a laptop, and a new journal. And here I am, writing in that journal instead of working on my novel. At least the words are coming. At least this is getting me unstuck. Listen to me trying to justify what I'm doing. But, really, there's no justification. Joan Didion said it best in "On Keeping a Notebook": *The impulse to write things down is a peculiarly compulsive one, inexplicable to those who do not share it, useful only accidentally, only secondarily, in the way that any compulsion tries to justify itself.*

A taxi met me at Rhinecliff station earlier and, after fifteen minutes or so, turned into a gated drive and up a long, winding road, twisting through a spindly forest of birch and maple trees. At the end of the road, perched on a hill overlooking the Hudson River, stood Sedge House, bright as a confection, a clutch of spires and cupolas rising into the sky like a great Gothic wedding cake. I've never seen anything quite like it, and it took me a moment to soak it all in—the enormous circular tower, the rosette windows that jeweled the top floor, the wraparound porch with its curls of white trim. I stood there, entranced, as the taxi driver deposited my suitcase on the grass and drove away.

The property manager, Bill, agreed to meet me at the house, but the driveway was empty and the front door locked, so I decided to take a look around. There was a path that led down to the river and, off one side of the mansion, a rose garden that had seen better days. The garden was orderly and symmetrical, marked with trellises and wrought-iron benches, but the original design had been eclipsed by overgrowth. Roses splayed over the paths, hearty, many-headed creatures rearing up from a single root, slightly sinister with their thorns and invasive abundance. I've never liked roses much. They've always struck me as beautiful but cold, like cut crystal or mathematics.

I heard the crunching of tires on gravel and returned to find Bill getting out of a white truck. He was around fifty, his hair graying, his eyes watery behind thick glasses, as if suffering from hay fever. As he unlocked the front door, he explained that the owner, Aurora Sedge, had passed away the previous December, and the heir, a nephew named Jameson Sedge, was planning to sell the place "lock, stock, and barrel." Sedge House, he said as I lugged my suitcase up the steps to the wide porch, had been built in 1876 by Franklin Sedge, who'd made a fortune in the manufacture of glass buttons. He'd parlayed his wealth into a socially beneficial marriage with one of the Rusten daughters, Adelaide, which was a big step up for him apparently, as he was from Albany and had few connections.

I followed Bill into a wide foyer, taking it all in. Glancing down the corridor, I saw objects everywhere, stacked in every corner and piled on every surface, a great congregation of treasures: crystal ashtrays and lacquer opera glasses and marble busts and art-glass paperweights. Even the foyer, whose sole purpose was to allow passage, was blocked by an enormous brass birdcage fashioned in the image of Sedge House, turrets and all. Inside, staring from behind the bars, sat a stuffed owl, frightening as a gargoyle.

Bill pushed his way in, showing me the dining room, a long, narrow space dominated by a table that might have seated twenty if it hadn't been covered with stacks of china plates. He flicked a switch, illuminating an enormous chandelier that hung above this porcelain landscape, the crystal prisms dripping light like melting ice. The walls were paneled in intricately carved mahogany squares that cast a tobacco hue through the room, giving it all a smoky feeling that would have been somber, even oppressive, if not for the flowers: vase after vase of roses bloomed through the room. They were too perfect to be real and, sure enough, when I took a petal between thumb and finger, I felt a fine silk tissue slip over my skin. They were exact replications, and something about the perfection of their mimicry—how they appeared more vibrant, more real than the roses outside—seemed unfair.

"Did someone actually live here?" I asked, trying to imagine existing in such a place.

"Aurora Sedge was alone in this house for sixty years, at least," he said. "Never married. Never had children. Didn't have friends, as far as I know."

Bill went to the kitchen and opened a wooden box hanging on the wall, revealing a series of hooks holding brass keys. "This one is for the back door, this one's for the basement, and . . . here it is." He grabbed a key. "This one's for the parlor. Aurora kept her collection in there. A professional appraiser will be coming up to take a look, so you'll need to open it up. Come on, I'll show you."

Bill walked down the corridor and inserted the key into the lock of a set of pocket doors and pushed them open. I followed him into the room and stopped, amazed and a little unnerved. When Bill said *collection,* I imagined Hudson River School paintings, or maybe a few Tiffany lamps. But from one end of the room to the other, planted like so many melancholy flowers, were porcelain dolls. Dolls in rocking chairs, dolls propped up on windowsills, still more dolls bundled into an old-fashioned perambulator. There was a doll with an eyelid jammed closed, leaving the other eye to stare wildly, madly, at me. Two Black baby dolls sat around a child's table, a tea set—pot, china cups, and a pastry ladder—laid out before them, as if taking high tea. A whole line of dolls in floral dresses sat leg to leg on a red velvet couch and, I saw, taking a closer look, their arms had been intertwined, one porcelain elbow locked with the next. A ray of slanted light fell over this coterie of babies, dust motes swirling through the air, and for one fleeting instant, I imagined their little eyes flickered with malice.

As I stepped deeper into the parlor, it seemed that the creatures shifted to stare at me, all those chubby cheeks and puckered mouths and upturned noses pressing in on every side. I, a rather average-sized person by most standards—five feet four inches tall—felt huge. Gigantesque. Like Alice after taking a pill. And although I've never been prone to claustrophobia, suddenly all the air left the room.

"These were Aurora Sedge's great passion," Bill said, looking as uncomfortable as I felt.

"Passion?" I said, giving him a look that must have revealed how bizarre I found the whole thing.

"Can't say I understand it myself, but I do know that this collection is worth a pretty penny. As I said, Mr. Sedge is selling the whole kit and caboodle before he puts the house on the market. The appraiser will need to take some photos for the auction, so you can let her in here when she comes. Otherwise, this room stays locked."

Bill locked the parlor. I followed him through the corridor, past a sweeping staircase with a newel post carved in the shape of a peacock, its single jeweled eye watching, and to a wall of sepia-tinted photographs. He paused to introduce the members of the Sedge family to me, picture by picture.

There was Aurora's father, Franklin Sedge, in a Harvard College sweater; then another of Franklin and his bride, Adelaide Rusten, standing outside a church on their wedding day. There was baby Aurora with her mother, then Aurora at age three with her baby brother, Franklin, Jr., known as Frankie. Next Aurora and Frankie appeared as teenagers, standing in a lavish drawing room that Bill called "the Sedges' city residence." There were snapshots of Aurora and Frankie posed on a dock before the *Queen Mary* transatlantic luxury liner; Aurora's graduation from high school; then Frankie's graduation. In every photo, Frankie was expansive and smiling, and his sister stood at his side, diminutive, serious.

"Frankie is deceased?" I asked, remembering that it was Aurora's nephew, Jameson, who had inherited the property and that there was no other living relative.

"Died in his mid-twenties," Bill said. "Ruled a suicide, although no other details were ever released, which of course got folks talking. Aurora found the body and was, by all accounts, devastated. She shut herself up in the house after that. Nobody's been in here for decades, except the odd repairman and Mandy, her housekeeper. Frankie's death did a real number on her. Aurora spent the rest of her life alone, surrounded by silk roses and porcelain dolls."

20

After closing up the parlor, Bill took me to the kitchen, a tiny room off the dining room with a 1960s-era stove, a large white ceramic sink, and a cabinet filled with porcelain teacups. A compact Formica-topped table sat by a window, giving onto a view of the river, although I didn't stop to look: Bill was already ahead, standing in what he called the butler's pantry—an ingenious space that was a cross between a closet and a hallway, shelves filled with dishes on both sides. I imagine a butler would walk through the pantry and collect platters and decanters, a silver salver, or whatever he needed, then walk out the other side, leaving the cook undisturbed.

For my purposes, the butler's pantry is where the cleaning supplies are kept. Opening a closet, Bill showed me brooms and mops and paper towels and various cleaning products. My duty to tidy the house before he shows it to potential buyers is beginning to seem more and more daunting by the minute.

Aurora had loved her home, he said, but at the end of her life she'd been too weak to maintain it and left it to her housekeeper, a local woman named Mandy Johnson.

"Which reminds me," he said, "I don't anticipate a problem, but if Mandy comes to the house, you should call me right away."

It sounded like he was anticipating a problem to me, and I told him so.

"Don't worry," Bill said. "Mandy's not a problem worry anymore. After Aurora died, though, there were some issues. Aurora had become partial to Mandy in the last years of her life, and she started to give her things from the house—family heirlooms, jewelry, some art. No one knew it was happening until Aurora died. As it turned out, Aurora named Mandy as the sole beneficiary in her will. All this"—Bill gestured around the house, a sweeping movement meant to capture the enormity of the cleaning woman's good fortune—"if you can believe it. Jameson Sedge filed a lawsuit claiming that Aurora wasn't in her right mind. He argued that Aurora had a history of eccentricity, which I can't say anyone would contradict. It also happened that there wasn't a witness to Aurora's signature, and without a witness, well, the whole thing was thrown out at probate court, and everything went to her next living relative: Jameson Sedge."

"But you're afraid she'll show up again?" I asked, more concerned about an aggrieved housekeeper than the details of probate court.

"She came here last month, and when Jameson found out, he got her arrested for trespassing and slapped her with a restraining order. I doubt she'll come back, but if she does: Call me."

After Bill left, I tried to make myself at home, but it hasn't been easy. Aurora Sedge has been dead for months, and yet she's so present I feel that I'm trespassing. Everything has been left just as it must have been the day she died. I found her dirty laundry in a wicker basket; her food—a bag of rotten apples, a lump of moldy cheese, a quart of solidified whole milk—in the fridge; a teacup on her bedside table, full of rancid tea, the tannins turned to tar. Her clothes hang in the closets—heavy dark wool skirts with French labels; white cotton blouses, crisp with starch; flannel nightgowns; and dozens of pairs of small lace-up leather boots, size 4.5, the heels stained with mud. Aurora Sedge is dead but lingering still, and I can't help but feel that her house, with its oppressive mahogany paneling, its trove of treasures, and its parlor full of porcelain dolls, shouldn't be disturbed.

Pushing aside my misgivings, I went to the library, where I found an enormous attorney's desk, a perfect spot to work for the summer. The room is octagonal, with bookshelves holding hundreds of books, some old and bound in leather. There is a fireplace glazed with milky green vitreous tiles, a thick oriental carpet, and two large windows overlooking the river. It was stuffy, the air thick with dust, so I tied back the heavy damask curtains and opened the windows. The sun was falling behind the undulant spine of the Catskills, its weak light filling the room, when I caught sight of a pushcart in a corner, its lower shelf filled with bottles of booze. Plucking a cut-crystal tumbler from a tray of bar glasses, I poured myself two fingers of bourbon, thinking it might help me sleep. I was ready for bed, and headed that way when I passed an old Bible perched on a side table. Opening its worn leather cover, I found the pages annotated, with underlined passages, notes written in the margins, exclamation marks added for emphasis, expressing an intensity of belief that required permanent ink.

There was a common thread between the marked passages, or so it seemed. All of them were about some act of creation. The *let there be light* line, and the creation of Eve from Adam's rib, and the part about resting on the seventh day—practically all of Genesis was marked up. Then there was Psalms 33:6: *By the Word of the Lord the heavens were made, And by the breath of His mouth all their host.* At the bottom of one page, in blocky blue ink, someone had written a passage that seemed out of place:

> *I believed I could know what shouldn't be known. I wanted to see things, secret things, and so I lifted the veil between the human and the Divine and stared directly into the eyes of God. That is the nature of the puzzle: to offer pain and pleasure by turns.*

By the time I'd finished reading, the bourbon was gone. I put the Bible away, found clean sheets in a closet, and made up a bed in a big, airy, west-facing room on the second floor with bay windows overlooking the rose garden. There was a rocking chair in a corner, an old wooden thing that I pulled to the window, thinking I might read. But there wasn't a reading lamp, and I was a little tipsy from the bourbon, so I propped the window open with my book. The bed was an iron-framed monster with a springy, uncomfortable mattress that must have been made a hundred years ago, but I fell asleep quickly, despite the discomfort.

It was the middle of the night, and I was in a deep sleep, when a noise woke me. Soft, barely audible at first, something skittered above my head, quick, like raindrops pattering against a glass pane. I sat up, listening closely. For a minute, there was nothing at all, and then it returned. A movement in the air overhead, soft but regular.

For a long time, I lay awake, listening. Moonlight fell through the window, casting a silver-blue glow over the hardwood floor, and I half-expected to see Aurora standing there, her ghost reprimanding me for invading her home, but of course there was nothing at all but the fluttering of the curtains in the breeze. I told myself that the noise must be wind brushing against the panes or air trapped in the antiquated plumbing. In the city, I once rented a room in a prewar building with old steam radiators that pounded like a drum whenever the weather turned chill. Sedge House has mammoth nineteenth-century accordion radiators, and while they aren't in use at this time of the year, it's possible that they would release trapped air.

I planned to work in the morning, and I was determined to sleep, but the sound returned, stronger than before. Not wind, not steam in the radiators, but a persistent scratching from the third floor. Mice. Definitely mice. Old houses always have rodents. Once, I read a house-sitter's review that detailed her frustration over hearing noises every night in a house-sit in New Hampshire. She looked everywhere, trying to figure out what the noises could be, and finally found a family of raccoons in the basement.

Luckily, mice don't scare me. I grew up seeing rats in the subway and in the parks on a regular basis. Anyone who has ever faced a Manhattan rat can manage a few house mice. I'd call Bill in the morning, and he'd deal with it then. With this to comfort me, I closed my eyes and went to sleep.

But not ten minutes had passed when the noise returned, the clicking and scratching above rising to a series of loud thumps. I sat up, frightened, scanning the shadows, trying to see what it could be, when another sound, altogether different, rose through the room: a high, plaintive, inconsolable sob.

I pulled myself out of bed and waded through pools of moonlight to the hallway. The sound had come from above, and so I stepped to the stairwell and peered into the darkness. Bill hadn't taken me to the third floor. Nothing up there, he'd said, pointing to a wide wooden door at the top of the stairs. Just boxes of old stuff. But he was wrong. Something was up there.

Climbing the stairs gingerly, my bare feet slick on the wood, I approached the door. I grasped the cool brass of the knob, and I tried to turn it, but it was locked tight. And so I pressed my ear to the wood, straining to hear what was beyond. There was a shuffling, soft and regular, like footsteps. Maybe not mice, I thought, but a larger animal, a stray cat or a possum. Whatever it was, I would need to call Bill. Surely he'd take care of it. But as I turned away, there was a sudden pounding at the door, a flurry of knocks. Stricken with fear and unable to move, I listened. *Open the door,* the voice whispered. *Please, let me out.*

Terrified, I half-fell, half-ran down the stairs to call for help.

21

It took Bill a few minutes to calm me down, but he was able to convince me to stay at Sedge House until he got there. I was waiting on the front porch, the sun just coming up, when he arrived. He led me into the house, sat me down on a settee in the corridor, and listened with concern as I told him about the strange noises in the house. "Something isn't right here," I said, but when he pressed me to explain, I couldn't bring myself to describe what I'd experienced other than to say I'd heard strange noises from the third floor. I didn't mention the words I'd heard at the door. I'd been half asleep, a little drunk, alone in a big house. I was beginning to think my imagination had gotten the better of me.

Bill looked at me for a long time, as if trying to reconcile his own misgivings about the house, then told me that the noises were most likely rodents. "It wouldn't be the first time this place had critters," he said, and took me to the butler's pantry, where he showed me a box of traps, about a dozen or so. "You know how these work?" he asked. And while I'd never set a trap before, I assured him I'd be fine.

After Bill left, I went to the key box, found the key to the third floor and, with a hunk of moldy cheese from the fridge, I headed upstairs. The third floor was an even bigger mess than the rest of the house: The hallway was jammed full of boxes and wooden trunks and old furniture, generations of the Sedges' discarded belongings. Pushing past, I tripped over a squat wooden chest, spilling a wave of glass buttons over the hardwood floor, hundreds of discs of colored glass gushing forth. I squatted down and scooped the buttons back into the casket. Lifting one into the air, I saw that the name SEDGE had been pressed into the pale-pink surface. Sedge buttons, the source of the Sedge fortune.

I headed down the hallway, sidestepping more junk, and found myself suddenly surrounded by mirrors, a couple of dozen or so hanging on both sides of the hallway. Each one reflected a fragment of myself at me—a slice of arm here, a piece of face there, an entire hand. I didn't realize it until just that moment, but I hadn't seen a reflection of myself since I'd arrived at Sedge House. Not a single mirror hung anywhere in the lower regions of the house, not on the first or second floors, not even in the bathrooms. Yet there, stretching the length of the third-floor hallway, were dozens of them: gilt framed and wooden, beveled and silver plated, some spotted with age, one with a jagged diagonal crack.

Perhaps the absence of mirrors is why everything feels so off at Sedge House. I remember an essay we read in my senior psychoanalysis-and-literature seminar: "The Mirror Stage," by Jacques Lacan. A baby, Lacan wrote, forms a sense of identity by seeing itself reflected in a mirror. The amorphous, unbound self becomes, with each sighting, contained. When we see ourselves reflected in a mirror, he argued, we understand the boundaries of who and what we are. I wondered if the absence of mirrors at Sedge House could achieve the opposite effect. Perhaps living without a reflection would make one disappear.

I put down mousetraps throughout the hallway, until there were ten or so arrayed at intervals. When all the traps were set, I went to the hall of mirrors, lifted one off the wall—an oval mirror with a gilded frame—and carried it with me down to my room, where I hung it on a nail above the vanity table. But just as I was about to go down to the library and get to work, a sound filled the air. I stopped and, holding my breath, listened: a scratching, a churning, then a screeching, the same horrid sound as the night before.

I ran back up to the third floor and walked through the hallway, following the noise to its source: a small wooden door cut into the wallpaper. When I opened it, I found a deep vertical shaft with hanging ropes. Leaning in, I looked up and saw that the ropes wound around a winch high above. It was odd, because there wasn't a fourth floor in the house, as far as I knew, and Bill hadn't mentioned anything about an attic. Bakelite buttons were mounted on the door-frame, and when I pushed one of them, the ropes jerked to life, bringing up a wooden carriage. The movement created the exact noises I'd heard: a pattering and shuffling and swishing punctuated by a terrible screech of rusted winches. There aren't mice in Sedge House, or if there are, they aren't responsible for the noises I heard. The culprit is an old, creaky dumbwaiter. And the voice? Clearly the product of an overexcited imagination. Mystery solved.

But another mystery arose in its place. Where did the shaft lead? I retraced my steps down the hallway, looking for a stairwell leading to another floor. It was a bright morning, and light through a rosette window bounced from mirror to mirror along the hallway, illuminating a rectangle carved into a patch of floral wallpaper. A secret door, one so well hidden that I'd walked by it several times without noticing. I knocked on the wallpaper and heard an echo, the unmistakable sense of volume. There was no knob, but I detected a small keyhole and, squatting down, peered through it. A set of stairs led up into darkness.

My curiosity piqued, I ran downstairs, made my way through the kitchen to the wooden key box. I hadn't paid much attention to it when Bill gave me the key to the third floor, but if there was a key to the attic, that's where it would be. Sure enough, the box had hooks for a dozen keys, four to a row, each with a handwritten label above its hook: *basement, pantry, library, parlor, attic.* I returned the key Bill had given me, grabbed the key marked attic, and took the steps to the third floor two at a time.

The key fit. Easing the door open, I climbed the narrow steps into a hot, airless attic. There was no light switch, and so I turned on the flashlight function of my iPhone and investigated the room. The space was long and narrow, and the roof angled inward, forming a peak at the center. Aside from an old engine near the dumbwaiter shaft—the mechanism that powered the pulleys, I realized—the attic was empty.

Or almost. As I turned to leave, I saw, tucked under the eaves of the roof, a leather suitcase. Ducking down, I grabbed the handle, pulled it from the shadows, and carried it to the center of the room. Three feet long, the leather mildewed with age, the case was from another era. How long it had been hidden in the attic I had no way of knowing, but it was covered with a thick layer of dust that, when wiped away, revealed an elaborate design of roses and tendrils framing the letters GLM.

The case was secured by brass buckles. I flipped each buckle and opened the case. Inside, wrapped in a white cloth, lay a figure. Peeling away the cloth, I found a porcelain doll of exquisite beauty. Her hair was glossy and thick, a deep auburn color, and her eyes were enormous green glass spheres, lapidary bevels of emerald that glittered with a depth and brilliance that entranced me. She wore a pale-pink dress that opened from her waist in petals. Around her neck I found a tarnished Victorian locket engraved with the name *Violaine.*

My first impulse was to compare her to the dolls in the parlor, but Violaine was as different from them as the sun from the moon. Whereas they absorbed light, she seemed to emit it, her pale face luminous, as if lit from within. She was nearly two feet tall and heavy, and while her arms and legs had been fashioned of the same creamy porcelain as her face, the torso was soft and pliable, inviting one to cradle her like a living, breathing child.

I held her close, taking in the scent of powder and dust and old silk, feeling her weight in my arms. The little creature stared up at me, her gaze filled with something I couldn't quite define—a glittering behind her glass eyes, a conscious awareness of my presence. Perhaps it was a trick of the light, or maybe the oppressive heat of the attic, but the doll seemed just then to radiate the hot, bright force of life.

22

Some days later, a knock came at the door. I found an elegant woman of about forty standing on the porch. She wore a matching cream skirt and jacket that reminded me a little of my book editor, who likes to dress as if she's meeting Jackie O for lunch. Offering her hand, she introduced herself as Anne-Marie Riccard, from Sotheby's, there to assess the antiques that would be going up for sale.

She apologized for stopping by without calling, but I wasn't about to turn her away. I had been at Sedge House less than a week, and already I was wary of being alone. I made coffee in the kitchen and brought Anne-Marie a cup. She drank it as she walked around the dining room, assessing Aurora's treasures with a sharp, knowledgeable gaze. "Jameson Sedge asked me to make an inventory," she said, glancing into a glass case filled with objects—ammonites, a cloisonné box, an ormolu clock. "I'm afraid it will be a bigger project than he expects."

Anne-Marie had an accent, and when I asked her where she was from originally, she told me that she was born in Montreal but had lived in New York for twenty years. "I came to New York to study ceramics at Cooper Hewitt and was hired immediately after graduation by Sotheby's. Porcelain is my specialty, European pieces in particular. It used to be such fun, back in the nineties. I could auction a piece of early Limoges for six figures without blinking. Now the market is all about high returns rather than taste. But this woman wasn't buying these pieces as an investment. She truly loved them."

Anne-Marie lifted a large robin's-egg-blue porcelain teapot from the center of the table, looked at it with an assessing eye, and returned it. "Nineteenth-century Wedgwood. A treasure."

"You don't find this all a little . . . excessive?"

"This collection?" Anne-Marie said, her eyes going wide. "*Mon Dieu,* this is nothing. I've seen houses filled with thousands of music boxes, basements piled from floor to ceiling with comic books, garages crammed with vintage typewriters. Collectors often go to extremes."

Without thinking, I asked the question that had been at the back of my mind since I'd arrived: "But why?"

"To collect is to organize the world in your own image, and Aurora Sedge clearly had a very strong sense of who she was. You can tell a lot about a person by what they collect. I would have liked her—I can see that from just a cursory glance around. She was very particular about the pieces she bought. She created an extraordinary world with these objects." She took a final sip of coffee and put her cup down. "I guess I should get to work," she said. "Bill said there was one room in particular I should see."

I went to the kitchen for the key to the parlor, thinking I would leave her there. But when I opened the parlor doors and led her inside, her reaction was one of profound shock.

"What in the world . . ." she said, glancing over the dolls. "Why didn't anyone tell me these were here?"

She dropped her leather bag on the couch, sauntered into the room, and bent before a doll on the velvet couch. It sat in a patch of sun, its wide eyes staring too brightly, its porcelain face so lustrous in the sunlight as to seem liquid.

"I simply can't believe it," she said. Turning to me, her eyes wide with excitement, she said, "Do you understand what these are?" She didn't wait for me to answer. "They're the creations of the legendary

French dollmaker Gaston LaMoriette." She took a small camera from her bag. "During his lifetime, he was known as the creator of Les Bébés de Paris, a line of dolls sold in European department stores such as Harrods and La Samaritaine from the late nineteenth century until the First World War. The dolls in this room are all La-Moriette dolls. They were extremely popular, quite expensive, and became collectibles almost instantly. Here, let me show you something. . . ."

She picked up one of the dolls from the velvet couch, pushed away the thick blond hair, exposing a stamp at the back of the neck, and ran the tip of her finger over a set of initials: GLM. "Gaston LaMoriette. Authentic as can be."

She put the doll down, positioned it in the light, and took a photo.

"I used to work for a doll collector who was obsessed, and I mean obsessed, with these dolls," she said. "She had me traveling all over the place buying them up. She owned something like two hundred by the end of my time working with her. When she died, her kids sold them all off, of course. Such is the redistribution of precious things. But when she was alive and collecting, what she really wanted, and what she would have paid a fortune to acquire, was a very particular doll, a masterpiece LaMoriette created in the 1890s. The doll was one of a kind, extremely special in its construction and materials, made entirely by hand, and rare, rare, rare. It was never for sale during his lifetime, which of course makes collectors go utterly mad."

She walked to the child's table and took a series of photos of the tea party.

"It was a fool's errand, of course: LaMoriette's masterpiece was legendary, and it would be very well publicized if it was part of a private collection or ever went up for sale. But you know how collectors are—they believe money can make anything happen. And while that is often the case, I told her from the very beginning that she would be disappointed. The last time this doll was even seen was before LaMoriette's death in 1909. Well, anyway, my client was absolutely relentless, and I wanted the commission, and so I took a gamble."

She photographed the baby with the jammed eyelid, then the chorus line of babies with interlocked arms.

"There was a private sale being held by the estate of Dina Vierny in Chartres." She paused, fixed me with her gaze. "She had one of the most incredible doll collections in the world. Vierny was also the muse of a dozen French painters—she sat for Maillol and Matisse among others—and was an ardent protector of the arts. I thought that perhaps, just maybe, Dina Vierny could have acquired the LaMoriette masterpiece under the radar. If anyone could do something like that, it was her. She was a miracle of a woman—lived in Paris during the war, participated in the Resistance, was persecuted by the Nazis. Anyway, my client sent me off with a first-class airline ticket and a generous expense allowance. I went to the private sale at the Galerie de Chartres and examined every single piece. Of course, the LaMoriette masterpiece was not there. I ended up having a wonderful weekend in Chartres, but no doll."

"This doll . . ." I ventured, trying to get more information without letting on that I was interested in a real way. "Did it resemble his other dolls?"

"I have only seen photos, obviously, and black-and-white ones at that, but I can say that there is a great difference in the construction of the masterpiece and his more-common manufactured dolls. The handmade doll was larger than these and was fashioned with exquisite details. It has a kid-leather torso sewn by hand, and the porcelain parts—the head, arms, and legs—were molded of a particular mixture of kaolin, giving the doll a unique luster that the factory-made dolls do not have. It has jointed arms and legs, a very unusual attribute for porcelain dolls of the period, more in the way that wooden puppets or marionettes might be constructed."

"And this doll," I said, remembering Violaine—the brilliant glass eyes, the glossy hair, the suitcase monogrammed with the letters

GLM—and feeling my pulse quicken, "you would know it's special if you saw it?"

"Oh, one would see the difference instantly," she said. "The hand-made doll is extremely particular, especially the eyes, which were fashioned from leaded crystal. LaMoriette used traditional glass-blowing methods, much like those for making Murano glass. When doing research for my client, I found that he developed this tech-nique in Prague, although the name of his teacher has been lost. Maybe intentionally. He never gave away his secrets. As you soon learn in my profession, the provenance of a piece of art is everything. Collectors want a good story, and LaMoriette's doll has an unbeat-able one. He was obsessed with his creation. The doll never left his side. Indeed, he supposedly carried it everywhere."

"But why?" I asked, perplexed as to why a grown man would carry around a porcelain doll.

"Because LaMoriette had made the doll in the likeness of his be-loved daughter, Violaine. The girl died tragically when she was fif-teen years old and LaMoriette never fully recovered from the loss. In 1909, after years of depression, he killed himself. His son inherited his workshop and sold off everything, including the doll. Since then, LaMoriette's masterpiece has disappeared. It may be that no one will ever find Violaine."

23

As soon as Anne-Marie left, I ran upstairs. I'd left Violaine in my bedroom, sitting in the rocking chair, but when I rushed into the room, the doll was gone. Everything else was the same—the bed made up with a floral matelassé quilt, my suitcase on the floor, the window open to the bright afternoon. But the rocking chair was empty. I crouched down and looked under the bed, around the rocking chair, and behind the curtains, as if there was any chance a large porcelain doll might flit away in a breeze. But Violaine was nowhere to be found.

I walked through the entire house, looking. I opened up all the rooms, rifled through the armoires, pulled out junk from the closets, shoved around the boxes on the third floor. From the basement all the way up to the attic I hunted, growing more and more disturbed. Although I knew perfectly well she couldn't be in the parlor—I had been there all afternoon—I went back and hunted through Aurora's collection of dolls, hundreds of little faces gazing at me as I picked my way through the room. I felt the chill of their vacant stares, the creeping sensation that they knew something I did not. But Violaine was not among their number. Violaine was gone.

The thought crossed my mind that Bill might have come to the house, but that was equally unlikely: The parlor overlooked the driveway, and I would have seen Bill's car. He was also talkative and would have wanted to speak to Anne-Marie. Could someone else have come into the house? I checked that the front door had been locked, then went from window to window, pulling the drapes closed and checking the latches. Everything was secure.

Finally, when there was nowhere else to look, I sat down on the velvet couch in the parlor, defeated and anxious. Could I have possibly imagined what I'd found in the attic? It was impossible. I'd held the doll in my hands, gazed into Violaine's green eyes. And yet there was no other explanation.

I went to the library, grabbed the bottle of bourbon, filled a tumbler, and drank it down. It burned my throat, leaving a sweet, caramel aftertaste, but it brought my anxiety down a notch. I poured a second glass and, fortified, returned to the parlor.

Balancing the glass at the edge of the couch, I picked up one of the dolls and looked at it. Her skin was translucent, with the slightest blush of pink to her lips, her eyes large and glassy. As I looked around the room, it seemed suddenly that the dolls were watching, assessing, judging. I drank the glass of bourbon, then poured another. For hours I sat there, thinking, trying to sort through everything. It was absurd, I knew that, but I was afraid. My heart beat hard in my chest, and I felt a wave of revulsion move through me. I didn't want to be there. I needed to talk to someone, tell someone what was happening, and so I ran up the steps to my room on the second floor, sat down in the rocking chair by the window, and took out my phone.

There were any number of people I could call, but my mind went immediately to Noah. We'd been together on and off since I was a sophomore in college, although no one would have thought of us as a couple. He was five years older than me, twenty-four to my nineteen when we met, and worked at an art gallery in Chelsea. He was a sculptor who made beautiful, abstract pieces from painted scrap metal. We'd been together a year or so when he left to study art history in Italy, and while we didn't break up, we weren't exactly together, either. When he came back to New York, we continued our friendship, one that sometimes involved spending the night together.

It had been weeks since we'd last spoken. He didn't know anything about my house-sitting job upstate, but he knew something was wrong the minute he heard my voice. Even though we were not in regular communication, Noah was the only person I felt close to. He understood that I like to be alone. But he also understood that I needed him from time to time, too. He'd had more than his share of emotional calls from me over the years. While I don't need to see him every day, when I need to talk to someone, it's always Noah I call.

"You realize that it's been a month since you called me, Jess," was the first thing Noah said after he picked up. The second was, "Tell me what's wrong."

The rocking chair creaked as I shifted my weight. The moon had risen by then, and the lawn had grown white under its light. Propping my feet on the windowsill, I told him only the vaguest outline of what was going on. I didn't mention the dolls or Anne-Marie, or even the fact that Sedge House was a cabinet of curiosities. But I told him enough to know that I was alone in a big house upstate, that I was having trouble of some sort, that there was good liquor and lots of space. Before I had fully thought it through, I was asking him to come to see me, and he was promising to be there as soon as he could.

And that might have been that, had I not, some hours later, woken to someone in my room. There wasn't any one thing that alerted me to the presence, not a creaking floorboard or heavy breathing, but an undefinable aura hovered in the atmosphere, something just below the surface of sound that had reached into the depths of my sleep.

I sat up in bed. It was a hot, humid night, and I'd left the windows open, yet the air was freezing. There hadn't been a hint of a breeze earlier, but now an arctic chill suffused the darkness. Disoriented, I looked around the room, trying to get my bearings. I'd had too much to drink, that I knew, but there was no explanation for the chill in the room, or the numbness in my body. A tingling sensation buzzed through my arms and legs, a sharp and painful prick of pins and needles.

Half asleep, I got up to close the window, but my limbs were bloodless, my balance precarious: My knees buckled, and I landed flat on the floor. Moonlight fell through the window and pooled around me, thick as spilled milk. I tried to get up, but a kind of paralysis had come over me, and the air filled with a strange energy, a jolting vibration that moved through my body like a current. For a long terrible moment, I lay there, straining to move, unable to turn my head or clench my hands, unable to scream. Something—some strong, electric force— had taken hold of me, a heavy sensation that collected in my limbs and knotted my muscles. It was a force both cold and hot, one that created a low and persistent buzzing in my ears.

And yet, even as I lay paralyzed on the floor, I could see everything clearly enough. The furniture vibrated. The bed shook. The vanity table inched away from the wall. The pressure built in the room, growing to a frenzy and, from the corner of my eye, I watched as the oval gilt-framed mirror, the one I had brought down from the attic, exploded into a spiderweb of cracks.

Then, suddenly, everything went quiet. The furniture stilled; the electricity evaporated. I grasped the bedpost and pulled myself up, trembling so I could hardly stand. My voice returned, and I called out, asking who was there. Somebody was in the room, I was certain of it, but there was nothing but silence.

I tried to convince myself that it was only too much bourbon or the remnants of a dream, and I had almost started to believe this when my gaze fell upon the curtains. Although the night was still, the panels of silk billowed. I knew then that my instinct had been correct. I wasn't alone. Someone was standing behind the curtains. My gaze fell upon a tiny hand, ice white in the moonlight. It clutched the edge of the curtain, four tiny pale fingers gripping the silk. And then, everything slowed, and the little fingers spidered over the seam of the curtain—pointer, middle, ring, pinkie, pointer, middle, ring, pinkie—as if playing a run on the piano, sending the silk shivering like water in the moonlight. All at once, the curtain parted and there stood Violaine.

24

I ran downstairs just as the sun was beginning to rise, determined to leave. The first floor was exactly as I'd left it: The Sedge family portraits and the elegant newel post and the catastrophe of collectibles. Not a china plate had been disturbed, and for a moment I believed that what I'd experienced could be cataloged away, shelved and forgotten. If I could get away from Sedge House, everything would be fine.

But even as I leaned against the balustrade to catch my breath, I knew that my world had changed. Two tracks opened in my mind. One track held the world I knew to be real—the solid ground below me, the air in my lungs, the sun that rose in the morning. And on the other track, moving in the opposite direction, was a new reality, one I had never considered. On this track inexplicable things appeared, impossible things, ones that terrified me. Ones I could not allow myself to believe.

The only solution was to leave Sedge House immediately. I'd call a taxi and catch the first train back to the city. But as I headed for the door, something moved in the corridor. I jumped and stumbled into the great brass birdcage, knocking it over. A woman stood in the shadows, watching. She flipped a light switch, and I saw she had sandy-blond hair, narrow-set gray eyes, and a plain, open face. She held up a set of keys. "They changed the lock on the front door but forgot the basement."

It was Mandy Johnson, the cleaner.

Bill had asked me to call him if Mandy showed up, and I knew that there was a restraining order out on this woman, but I knew right away that Mandy wasn't dangerous. In fact, there was something comforting about her. After the night I'd had, I felt an urge to fall into her arms and cry.

"Looks like I got here just in time," she said, glancing at the toppled birdcage. "Come on, I'll make you some tea." She turned and walked toward the kitchen. I followed her in. "I'm Mandy, by the way," she said, as she filled a kettle with water, adjusted the gas, and lit the stove.

"That's what I thought," I said, getting a better look at her. She was pushing forty and wore old jeans, high-top sneakers, and a faded Guns N' Roses T-shirt. "Aurora Sedge's housekeeper."

"I started out cleaning for Miss Aurora, yes," she said. "But that isn't all I did here." She gestured to the little table by the window. "Sit down and take a load off. Looks like you had a rough night."

I sat, feeling the weight of terror in my back and shoulders. I was at the edge of collapse. "I think I'm going crazy," I said at last.

She glanced at me as if she understood precisely what I had gone through. "It's okay. You don't need to explain it to me. I've seen things here that you wouldn't believe. Actually, maybe you would."

Mandy was familiar with the kitchen. She pulled a porcelain teapot and cups from a cabinet, dug a tin box marked *Mariage Frères* from the cupboard, put two scoops in the teapot, set it on a lace doily, and sat across from me. As she poured boiling water into the teapot, her small gray eyes drifted over me, sizing me up. "It can be hard to get through the night at Sedge House," she said, pouring tea into my cup. "But you don't have to stay. Once you take it, you can leave. Nothing's keeping any of us here anymore."

"Take what?" I asked, confused.

Mandy gave me a long look, as if settling something of great importance. "Drink some tea, honey. We'll talk about it when you've had a minute to calm down."

I picked up the porcelain cup and took a sip of hot tea. It was black with a note of orange, the caffeine strong and welcome.

"You know, I always hated this tea. But Miss Aurora had to have it. It's French, I think. Can't find it at Hannaford's. She had me special-order it from a tea shop down in the city. She wanted me to sit with her and drink it. It made her happy, so I did it, but, man, I used to dump in a ton of sugar just to get the stuff down." She smiled. Her teeth were uneven, a strange contrast to her extraordinarily regular features. A ring sparkled on her pinkie, ruby baguettes surrounded by diamonds in an Art Deco setting, clearly one of Aurora's gifts. She saw me staring at it.

"Pretty, isn't it?" she said, turning it in the light so the rubies glinted. "Belonged to Aurora's mother. It's small, size four—just barely fits my little finger. I probably should get it resized."

I glanced out the window. The sun had risen, and the weak light played over the surface of the river, mirroring the flash of the rubies.

"People think I was taking advantage of Miss Aurora. Well, I wasn't. I earned everything she gave me." She sat back, never taking her eyes from me.

"Bill said you and Aurora had become close," I said.

"Close?" Mandy smiled. "I guess you could call it that. I was her employee for over twenty years, and I was the only one who got near her, so in that way we were close. She trusted me. I was eighteen when I came to Sedge House, just a kid smoking too much pot and generally fucking up my life. I'd dropped out of high school and was living with a guy who treated me like shit. But Aurora Sedge changed all that. She gave me full-time work, paid my health insurance, made me go back for my GED. I'm not saying I'm perfect now or anything, but she made me see that there is a reason things happen the way they do. A purpose. We all have a calling, each of us, a reason God put us here, and mine was to help Aurora Sedge. She needed me, especially at the end. I was the only person she could rely on. I helped her protect the relic. That's what she called it—the relic—and I never told a soul."

Curiosity and anxiety rushed through me. There were so many questions I wanted to ask that I didn't know where to begin.

"And, believe me, it hasn't been easy with that nephew of hers," Mandy said. "He came snooping around and found out more than he should've. Once, he came to the house, forced his way in, and pressured her to see it. He knew she had it, he said. He claimed that it belonged to his father, too, and that he'd get lawyers involved to get his proper inheritance. Miss Aurora was scared and told him too much. She regretted that, because once he knew, he wouldn't leave her alone. He demanded that she show it to him, but she refused. If she told me once, she told me a hundred times: *'If Jameson gets ahold of it, he'll only hurt someone.'*"

The tea had brought me back to my senses to a small degree, and I asked the question that was foremost in my mind. "You said that there's something here for me. What did you mean?"

"In the last few years, Aurora began to worry about the future. She knew her health was failing, and she needed to believe that her most treasured possession would be taken care of properly. She asked me to stay here to watch over it, and while I agreed, I told her that it was only until I found someone better-suited to the job. I promised Miss Aurora I would carry out her wishes, and while nobody will call me an angel, I do stand by my promises. I never said this to the probate judge, but Miss Aurora didn't care if I owned this place. She just needed me to keep watch over it. She needed me to keep her nephew out. She needed me to be here to give you the relic."

"Are you saying that you expected me?" I asked, trying to understand how that could possibly be the case.

"I didn't expect you," she said, "so much as go out and find you. Someone young and smart. Responsible. Trustworthy. Five-star reviews. Someone who would come without asking too many questions."

Suddenly I understood: It had been Mandy who found me in

the house-sitting database, Mandy who sent me the job description, Mandy who put me in touch with Bill. Mandy had been behind it all.

I thought of everything I'd seen at Sedge House. The markings in the Bible, the porcelain dolls, the electricity that had torn apart my room. I was confused and tired and afraid. I wanted to go back to the city and forget that Sedge House existed. I glanced out the window. There was Mandy's car, a beat-up Toyota, parked in the driveway. She could drive me to the train station. But first I needed Mandy to answer one question. "What is it that Aurora Sedge is keeping here?"

Mandy looked up—as if to heaven, as if Aurora Sedge might whisper down to her—and then back at me. "Come with me," she said. "I'll show you."

25

Mandy led me through the kitchen to the narrow corridor of the butler's pantry. She bent down, opened a cabinet door, pushed aside a few heavy copper pots, and—reaching deep inside—pulled a latch. There was a sharp *pop* and the cabinet released. It swung away from the wall, revealing the dark depths of a secret room.

I leaned inside, just far enough to feel the heavy, stale air. "In here is where the family hid the booze during Prohibition," Mandy said, gesturing to an arrangement of dusty Depression glass, about two dozen bottles of Canadian Club and Old Saratoga whiskey. She reached up behind the booze and took a leather portfolio from the highest shelf. She placed it in my hands. "This is for you."

I rubbed the surface of the portfolio, lifting a film of dust. Mandy had described it as a relic, and while I had imagined some old Christian artifact—a saint's finger or a bottle of holy water—the portfolio was no older than the 1960s and couldn't hold much more than a few documents. I began to open it, but she stopped me.

"No. Please. Wait until I'm gone. Miss Aurora never showed it to me, and I don't want to see it now." She started out of the room, but I grabbed her arm, holding her back.

"That can't be it," I said. "There has to be more you can tell me."

"I've kept my promise to Miss Aurora," she said, pulling her arm free. "There's nothing more I'm obligated to do." And yet she didn't leave. Her eyes didn't leave the portfolio, and I could see that, despite what she said, she was curious. "For years I noticed strange things going on in the house, signs that something wasn't right. I'd find broken glass everywhere—on the stairs, in the hallways. Crystal vases in a thousand pieces, as if they'd exploded. Then the mirrors started breaking. I couldn't explain it—they weren't falling off the wall or anything but just cracking to bits right in their frames. It freaked me out so much I had to move them all upstairs. And then there were the weird noises. Laughter and crying, little feet running around. I don't believe in ghosts, but I started considering it might be something like that. I thought I was going out of my mind. When I would ask Miss Aurora about it, she told me it was nothing. My imagination, she said. She was clumsy with her crystal, she said. But then, as she got older, she was less buttoned up about hiding what was happening. She went to the parlor and left the doors open. I'd see things—strange things—and I knew that something terrible was going on."

"Like what?"

Mandy glanced down at the leather portfolio in my hands. "I don't know what's in there, but whatever it is, it's responsible for everything bad that happened here."

I had so many questions for Mandy, but even as I began to ask them, there was a commotion outside. I followed Mandy to the kitchen window and saw a police car in the driveway. Mandy swore under her breath, gestured for me to hide the leather portfolio in the pantry, and swung the door shut, securing the latch. We were just walking back into the kitchen when Bill arrived, two policemen at his side.

"Not smart to park your car in the driveway if you want to stay out of jail, Mandy," he said, his gaze shifting from Mandy to me.

"I'm just having some tea with the house-sitter," she said, her expression innocent. "No harm in that, is there?"

Bill reminded her of the restraining order, not that he needed to:

Within minutes, Mandy was being led out of the house. As I watched her leave, I realized that I was still in the dark about what I was supposed to do with the contents of the leather portfolio. Mandy was the only person, other than Aurora's nephew, who might explain it.

After Bill left, I locked the front door, ran back to the butler's pantry, knelt before the cabinet, reached inside, and pulled the lever. With a click, the secret pantry swung open. Without Mandy blocking the way, I saw that the room was much larger than I'd initially realized, the darkness stretching far beyond the shelves of booze. Venturing inside, I found a large empty space with stone walls and a cracked cement floor. As my eyes adjusted, I took the portfolio in my hands, running a finger over its soft surface, feeling its weight. My pulse quickened at the thought of discovering what was inside. My curiosity was unbearable, and yet something, some deeper instinct, warned me that I should leave it alone. I should follow Mandy's lead and wash my hands of the whole thing.

But I couldn't leave. I needed to know what Aurora had hidden, to know the meaning behind what Mandy had told me, and, most of all, I needed to understand how it related to the beautiful, haunted doll I'd discovered in the attic.

In the end, my curiosity won out. The portfolio was fastened with a thick leather string. Unwinding it, I found a sheaf of loose pages, handwritten in French. While I couldn't understand them, the structure of the lines came together to form a letter—at the top of the first page was a date, *24 Décembre, 1909,* and below this a salutation: *Mon cher fils.* The writing was florid and seemed to have been put down in haste, the lines uneven, the ink smudged. On the final page, there was a flourishing signature: *Gaston LaMoriette.* I recognized the name immediately. Gaston LaMoriette, the dollmaker who had created Violaine.

26

Mike Brink looked up from the journal, glanced at his watch, and saw that it was 4:08 P.M. He'd been lost in Jess's journal for nearly ten minutes. She'd written only a few dozen pages, which should have taken him all of sixty seconds to read, but he'd found himself going over her words slowly, sometimes reading her sentences a few times. It was a revelation to meet the person Jess had been before the murder—the woman he'd heard in the NPR interview, the one described as funny, warm, smart—and he felt a stab of remorse for the young woman whose life had been destroyed.

He flipped back through the journal, pausing on a line that stood out, a quote from the writer Joan Didion about notebooks: *The impulse to write things down is a peculiarly compulsive one, inexplicable to those who do not share it, useful only accidentally, only secondarily, in the way that any compulsion tries to justify itself.* He was reading Jess's journal hoping to find something useful, but if he did, it would be accidental, secondary, a stroke of luck. He believed in the power of random events, and in the life-altering result of chance encounters, but he didn't want to leave himself prey to them. If there was anything concrete in Jess's writings that could answer his questions, he needed to find it.

Brink leafed through the pages with care, looking for something he might have missed, but Jess's writing stopped abruptly, leaving many of his questions unanswered. He would have to find them on his own.

The air-conditioning was cold and relentless, blowing from a series of ceiling vents overhead. A shiver rose through him as he looked out the window at the parking lot. He half-expected to see the black Tesla waiting beyond, near his truck, but he'd parked at the center of a nearly empty lot. Whatever had happened back at the Starlite wasn't happening again. At least, not yet.

Conundrum was restless, but Brink needed more time, so he bought a stick of beef jerky from the convenience store and laid it before her. Connie loved beef jerky—it was one of her favorite treats—and would chew on it for hours if given the chance.

While she was distracted, he opened his laptop, navigated to Google, typed in some keywords—*Frankie Sedge; Sedge House; death*—but there was nothing except references to Jess Price. He navigated through the pages until he hit upon the name: *Jameson Sedge.* As he read, he learned that Jameson was Frankie's adult son, now in his fifties. He had been an infant when his father died. According to a Wikipedia page, Jameson Sedge was a successful entrepreneur and founder of a company called Singularity, which was involved in unspecified biotech and blockchain ventures. It didn't seem likely that this information would be useful, so he didn't pay much attention and moved on to another link, this one from the *New York Times* website: an obituary titled FRANKLIN "FRANKIE" SEDGE II, HEIR TO SEDGE GLASS FORTUNE, DEAD AT 25. Brink enlarged the document and saw a photo of a young man, handsome and boyish, his eyes squinted against the sunlight, looking like Gatsby in a white summer suit. There were no details of the cause of death, only the date of the funeral and the location of the burial. The article mentioned that he was survived by his wife, Renee, twenty-three years old, of London, England, his infant son, Jameson, and his elder sister, Aurora Elizabeth Sedge, currently residing in Clermont, New York.

Brink typed in Jameson's name and searched, but while there were thousands of hits about his company, Singularity, there wasn't a single photograph. It was odd, he thought as he moved through the pages. Usually there would be dozens of photographs for someone like Jameson Sedge. He was about to give up and close out of the search when he saw a photo of a tall man with red hair and fair skin standing next to a woman. The photo had been taken at a black-tie function at the Metropolitan Museum of Art. Below the image were the names *Jameson Sedge* and *Anne-Marie Riccard*. The woman's name was so particular that he was sure it must be the same woman Jess had mentioned in her journal. And while he couldn't be 100 percent sure, the guy in the picture resembled the man with the black Tesla. He enlarged the photo to get a better look. There was no doubt. The man he'd seen at the prison, the guy he suspected to have trashed his hotel room, was none other than Jameson Sedge.

Going back to Jess's journal, he scanned the pages, hoping to find more personal information about Anne-Marie Riccard. There wasn't anything concrete but enough for him to be sure that this was the same woman Jess had met at Sedge House. He didn't understand her connection to Jameson Sedge, but clearly there was a connection.

He typed Anne-Marie Riccard's name into the search engine, and within seconds a list of links appeared on the screen. At the top of the list was a profile on Bard College's website. Apparently she had left Sotheby's for a teaching position. Brink clicked on the page and read her bio: *Anne-Marie Riccard, PhD, Ceramics and Fine Porcelain.* He found a color photograph of a woman with dark hair, brown eyes, and a serious look about her. The page listed her office hours, an email address, and a telephone number. He pulled out his phone, glanced at the call log—Thessaly had promised to stay in touch, and yet there was still nothing from her—and dialed Anne-Marie Riccard's number. When it went to voicemail, he left a message. Then he clicked the link to Anne-Marie Riccard's email address and sent off a message explaining that he was an acquaintance of Jess Price and would be thankful if she had a moment or two to speak with him.

He asked her to get in touch at her earliest convenience. It was risky to contact her—she was connected to Jameson Sedge, after all—but he saw no other way to get the information he needed.

Brink clicked through pages and pages of information about Dr. Anne-Marie Riccard, reading them quickly. There were articles she'd written, mostly academic papers about the history of ceramics, particularly European porcelain from the time the first pieces were imported from China to the beginning of European factories in Meissen in the sixteenth century. But there were also a few popular articles—one in *Town & Country* about her love of French porcelain, another in now-defunct *Toy* magazine about porcelain dolls. She'd written a book about French porcelain of the late-nineteenth and early-twentieth century, which had been published by a university press and had nine five-star reviews on Amazon. She wasn't writing about a popular subject, but she knew her field. Talking to her might not get him any closer to understanding what had happened to Jess at Sedge House, but according to the journal, Anne-Marie was one of the last people Jess saw before Noah's death.

When he'd read everything he could find about Anne-Marie Riccard, he took the flash drive Thessaly had given him from his pocket, plugged it into his laptop, and opened it. There were two files: a PDF titled "Police Records," and a second PDF, which had been left untitled. Brink clicked open "Police Records," and a fifty-seven-page document appeared. He scrolled through and found scans of various reports and notes taken from the investigation into Noah Cooke's murder. The Columbia County Sheriff's Office seal was stamped on every page and he understood: These were the papers that had been inside the big white envelope marked confidential. He saw documents relating to Jess's arrest and booking, a mug shot, an itemized list of clothing and personal effects taken from her—a sundress, a pair of sandals, a gold chain.

He opened a file and found a copy of Noah Cooke's autopsy, which he read with great interest. There'd been much speculation about how Noah Cooke had died—in the press, during the trial, in the film made about Jess. The results of the autopsy had never been released, as far as Brink knew, and now he understood why: The cause of death was listed as blunt-force trauma to the chest and abdominal region. There was a note that, in the opinion of the doctor performing the autopsy, the deceased's injuries were consistent with a car accident or a fall of at least fifty feet, the impact of which led to severe damage to his internal organs. The heart, lungs, liver, and intestines had ruptured, causing extensive internal bleeding. Essentially, Noah Cooke's organs had been pulverized.

It didn't surprise Brink that the autopsy had been kept under wraps—there was a lot about the case that hadn't made it to the press, especially because Jess refused to testify. But that Jess's defense team hadn't used this information to defend her seemed unconscionable. A young woman could, feasibly, stab her boyfriend; she could shoot him, or poison him, or even strangle him. But how could Jess be responsible for Noah's death if his injuries were from a fall? How could a five-foot-four woman pulverize a man's internal organs? It was utterly perplexing.

Then, clicking back to the drive, he saw a folder. He opened it and was confronted with a series of color Polaroids. As he looked at the photos, he understood why they, like the autopsy, had been buried. If these photos were to circulate, it would be clear that Noah Cooke's death was even more gruesome than what people imagined.

In the photos, Noah Cooke was laid out in the library of Sedge House. He was naked, eyes open in a glassy stare, his long black hair matted with blood. But while his expression was startling, what made Brink's blood curdle was his skin: Every inch of his body was covered with the same pattern of cuts Brink had seen on Jess's arm, the searing honeycomb of red lines crossing his torso and legs, his arms and face. His chest was particularly grotesque, the pale folds of skin pink and mottled with blood.

He scrolled down, feeling sick at the sight of it, and found another set of photos, black and white this time. He enlarged them, confused. Why were there two sets of photos, and why was one in black and white? But when he looked more closely, he saw that it wasn't merely a second set of pictures of Noah Cooke but an entirely different body. This corpse was lying on the floor of Sedge House, which he recognized from Jess's description: the wide staircase with its carved newel post and the wall of family portraits. Over the man's chest was the same web of cuts that had marred Jess's arm, the very cuts that covered Noah Cooke's body. At the bottom of the photo was the name *Franklin Sedge*. The dead man was Aurora Sedge's brother, Frankie. He had been killed in the same manner as Noah Cooke.

Brink scrolled between the photos, moving from Noah Cooke to Frankie Sedge, trying to make sense of it. It wasn't so very strange that two young men of roughly the same age would die in the same house five decades apart. But that they would be killed in the same unusual manner? It was utterly inexplicable. Brink magnified the photographs, zooming in on Frankie's body, then Noah's. For a long, intense moment, Brink studied the cuts. They fanned over the bodies like crimson spiderwebs. The only other time he had seen a pattern like that was on Jess's skin. And, of course, in his dream.

Brink was about to close his laptop when he glanced at his email and, to his surprise, found a response from Anne-Marie Riccard in his inbox. The name *Jess Price* in the subject line may have had something to do with it, because she wrote just one sentence in response, demanding to know his connection to Jess. He wrote back, explaining who he was and that he had begun working on a project with Jess Price, one that had led him to Dr. Riccard. He knew his answer might not be enough for her—he didn't say what kind of project, and he didn't say what kind of information was linked to her—but he hoped she would be intrigued enough to speak with him.

The response came in less than a minute: *Dear Mr. Brink, I am familiar with you and your work, and as you probably know, I am well acquainted with Jess Price's situation. I will be at my office (address below) all afternoon. I've been waiting for this message for many years. Come as soon as you can.*

There were times, when playing a game of skill, that risk becomes unavoidable. Moving a piece to a vulnerable position in chess to lure an opponent into a trap. Running a play through a thick defensive line to score a touchdown. To win, risk was inevitable. One had to face it, accept it, and deal with the consequences. If he wanted to get answers, he needed Anne-Marie Riccard and, despite the danger, or perhaps because of it, he felt a rush of excitement at the prospect of seeing her.

Brink stood, threw away his trash, and headed toward the door. The drive would be a few hours, but it was only four twenty. He could get there by early evening if he hurried. He looked in his bag, confirming that the journal was inside, and felt a great swell of anticipation. Whatever had happened at Sedge House, whatever series of events had led him to become involved, Anne-Marie Riccard would be able to explain them. The sooner he got to her office, the better.

But as he approached the glass door, he stopped cold. Maybe it was a mirage rising from the hot black asphalt of the parking lot, or maybe the images he'd seen had seared themselves into his mind, because there, wavering on the surface of the glass door, was the image of a man he didn't recognize, a man whose skin had crystallized and cracked into a thousand tiny fractals.

27

He'd just unlocked his truck when he heard a chime notification from his phone. His former professor, Dr. Vivek Gupta, was trying to reach him through his encrypted video app. Dr. Gupta called him only once or twice a year, and so Brink picked up right away. Balancing his phone in one hand, he opened his truck, he let Connie jump inside, then slipped into the hot cab, propped his phone on the dash, and connected.

"My boy," Dr. Gupta said. "So glad I've caught you before you manage to get yourself into more hot water."

Vivek Gupta was a Renaissance man in the truest sense. Aside from his work in cryptography and mathematics, he was a visual artist who studied and replicated the techniques of the Dutch masters. The "incredible luminosity" of Vermeer had inspired him to study painting, and he'd left Boston during Covid and retreated to Cape Cod, where he'd turned an old fisherman's hut into a painting studio. Brink had visited him just the year before for a long weekend, eating lobster and talking about everything from topology to Albrecht Dürer. He'd slept in the studio, surrounded by *nature morte* paintings of wine bottles and dead birds and pomegranates, images that transfixed him with their color and—like everything pertaining to his mentor—filled him with a sense of humility.

Dr. Gupta had taken the young Mike Brink under his wing in the fall of his first semester at MIT. Brink was trying to adjust to the move, getting used to his classes, and scrambling to find a way to pay his astronomical rent. He saw Dr. Gupta for the first time from the back row of his Patterns, Puzzles, Equations seminar. Dr. Gupta was a tall, elegant man with a Hindi-inflected British accent. He was known as an eccentric. One of his many eccentricities was keeping a sixties-era Rube Goldberg machine on a table in his classroom, a shiny tangle of twists and loops that fascinated his students.

During the second class of the semester, Dr. Gupta addressed him. "Excuse me, Mr. . . . ?" He was pointing at Mike Brink from behind a podium.

"Brink," Mike said, wishing he could sink through the floor.

"Yes, well, Mr. Brink, I realize this is the first time you've taken a class with me, but if you would be so kind as to glance around you, you will see that your fellow scholars are taking notes. Would you care to join them?"

Brink had experienced this before—a professor interpreting his lack of paper and pen as indifference or even arrogance. For that very reason, Brink always sat at the back of the classroom. "I am taking notes," he said. "Just not on paper."

"Oh?" Professor Gupta said, leaning against the podium, a look of amusement on his face. "Is that so?"

"It is," Brink said, feeling his cheeks grow warm. It was a small class, with only fifteen students, but every one of them had turned to stare at him. "I can show you, if you'd like."

"Please do," he said. "Last week we discussed Fermat's Last Theorem. Please give me an outline of Andrew Wiles's proof on the whiteboard."

"The whole thing?" Brink asked, a bit surprised that he would ask him to reproduce such an elaborate proof. It was long and complicated. It would be a challenge to reproduce it, even for Brink.

Professor Gupta held a marker up and gestured for Brink to come to the whiteboard. "The whole thing, if you please."

The week before, Professor Gupta had spent the class discussing the challenges and mystery surrounding Fermat's theorem. Pierre de Fermat, a seventeenth-century Frenchman, had jotted down a theorem while reading Diophantus's *Arithmetica*, adding the tantalizing note that the answer was too large for that margin. For centuries, mathematicians had struggled to solve Fermat's Last Theorem. Finally, a British mathematician named Andrew Wiles discovered a proof in 1994, over three hundred years after Fermat formulated it. Gupta had projected the Wiles proof onto the whiteboard, asking the class to write down the major points. Brink had taken it all in, fascinated. He wasn't interested in the math involved in Fermat's Last Theorem so much as the struggle that had gone into solving it, the pains Wiles endured, his persistence, the relentless pursuit of the solution. For Brink, the quest to solve a puzzle was always more interesting than the answer.

As he walked to the whiteboard, he doubted anyone, even the most assiduous notetaker, had written the whole thing down. Brink didn't fully remember the equation, and yet, when he lifted the marker, he saw it exactly as Gupta had projected it. It arrived in his mind in tiles of colors, brilliant shades that led him through the equation as if he were playing scales on a keyboard. When he finished, the whiteboard was covered with numbers and the entire class stared at him in utter amazement.

"Bravo, Mr. Brink," Professor Gupta had said, unable to hide his astonishment. "Bravo. You are henceforth relinquished from the necessity of bringing pen and paper to class."

From that moment on, Professor Gupta had adopted Mike Brink. He was his most steadfast supporter at MIT, a mentor and friend who guided him in matters both intellectual and practical. He fast-tracked his degree, nominating him for numerous distinctions and accolades; he advised him in career decisions, signed him up for various conferences, and had his back whenever something unexpected came up with faculty and administrators.

Over time, Brink had come to see how valuable a friend Vivek Gupta could be. While Brink's knowledge of puzzles and patterns, ciphers and cryptograms, was intuitive, Gupta's knowledge was experiential, stemming from three decades in the trenches. Vivek Gupta was nearly fifty years old when Brink met him, a legend in his field and beyond. A "veteran of the Cypherpunk era," as Gupta liked to call himself, he distrusted governments and the businesses aligned with them and believed that the only way to protect oneself in the modern world was through airtight digital codes. He and his fellow visionaries had put their talents into creating free spaces, digital landscapes without borders, digital currencies, and private networks that would allow them to avoid surveillance. He'd been an early proponent of cryptocurrencies and had gone on to co-create a blockchain network, then funneled his wealth into a billion-dollar charitable foundation that seeded small businesses in India. He believed that capitalism and the freedom of capital over borders could lift the world out of poverty, both physical and intellectual.

One day after class, Dr. Gupta had given Brink a piece of paper with the following written on it:

People have been defending their own privacy for centuries with whispers, darkness, envelopes, closed doors, secret handshakes, and couriers. The technologies of the past did not allow for strong privacy, but electronic technologies do. We the Cypherpunks are dedicated to building anonymous systems. We are defending our privacy with cryptography, with anonymous mail forwarding systems, with digital signatures, and with electronic money.

Brink did a quick search online and found that these words were part of "A Cypherpunk's Manifesto," written by Eric Hughes in 1993. He read that the movement was often regarded as the forerunner to the technology revolution: the internet, digital communication, cryptocurrencies, and decentralized systems on the blockchain.

The Cypherpunks wanted to lock down identity and privacy, and their members were some of the most powerful tech entrepreneurs in the world.

Brink understood the need for privacy, but he was of another generation. He didn't see the harm in being visible. He didn't have anything to hide, so why should he be worried? What he hadn't understood, Dr. Gupta taught him, was that privacy was about more than "having nothing to hide." It was about what those in power might do with information in the future. It was about how they could limit and contain his life. It was why Professor Gupta and the early pioneers of cyberspace had begun their work: freedom.

"Everything you say can and will be used against you," he had said to a small group of his students late one night at a pub in Cambridge. "Anonymity is power. Bitcoin's white paper—its founding document and arguably the most revolutionary invention in finance since paper money—was dropped online by someone called Satoshi Nakamoto. This is a pseudonym. Some believe the name represents many people working together and not a single person at all. Whoever Satoshi Nakamoto really is, they hid in the shadows for a reason. There is a war happening right here, right now, and the outcome will transform the future."

In Brink's sophomore year, Dr. Gupta was furious when he learned that Brink had shared his personal "cryptographic key" online in his Mike Brink number puzzle. No matter that Brink was young and stupid, no matter that only two people had downloaded the puzzle, the revelation that Brink's personal information had been released online deeply upset Professor Gupta. "Of course, you can try to bury it," he'd said. "And you can cut all ties with Gary Sand and that whole lot. They only used your talents for their own ends, as I'm sure you now realize. You were a victim. You cannot be blamed. But something such as this can follow one forever."

And it had. That one stupid move, that one online slip-up, that momentary lack of judgment, had followed him.

Brink studied the phone screen. Dr. Gupta stood in his painting studio wearing a paint-covered smock. His former professor had gained a significant amount of weight since leaving MIT, and it suited him. There was gray at his temples, a gray goatee at his chin, and deep laugh lines around his eyes and mouth, physical evidence of his good humor. "Mr. Brink, my good fellow, what the devil are you doing searching for Jameson Sedge on an unencrypted public Wi-Fi connection?"

Brink explained the situation—the puzzle Thessaly had shown him, the meeting with Jess at the prison, and all that had ensued—then dug out the drawing of the circular puzzle and showed it to Gupta. He fully expected his mentor to take one look at it and give an explanation that was both elegant and obvious, something Brink should have seen immediately. But he didn't. He stared at the circle a moment too long, a furrow deepening between his eyebrows. He seemed worried. Finally, he said, "I suspected you were in over your head when I was alerted to certain searches you were doing online."

"Alerted to my searches?" he asked. He knew that Vivek Gupta had the power to see anything he wanted online and should've suspected he was watching him. "You've been spying on me?"

"And I'm not the only one," he replied. "The only way to be sure you're not being watched is to crush your electronic devices, and even that isn't adequate protection. Now, tell me: How did you manage to connect Jameson Sedge to the events you described? Surely there was nothing online to give you such an idea."

"It wasn't easy. There was just one picture of Sedge—a photo at a charity event."

"I'm surprised there was even that one image," he said. "Sedge is old school, like me. He doesn't have online profiles, doesn't release personal information, and doesn't allow his image to circulate. He has his photos removed when they pop up, and everything you read about him—on Wikipedia or *Forbes* or in *The New York Times*—has been assiduously curated. I know because I use the same guy to wipe my online footprint clean."

"The photo I found shows Sedge with a woman named Anne-

Marie Riccard. She had contact with Jess Price at Sedge House, which—it turns out—was owned by Jameson Sedge at the time. Anne-Marie Riccard was at the house several days before Noah Cooke died. I want to see if she can help me understand what happened."

Silence, so uncharacteristic for Vivek Gupta, settled between them. Finally, he said, "Are you sure that's a good idea, my friend?"

"I don't see another way," he said. "Anyway, she agreed to meet. I'm supposed to see her in a few hours. Do you really think Sedge has something to hide?"

"I've known the man for nearly three decades, and I can tell you that he most definitely has something to hide. I liked the chap well enough, at first. We bonded over William Gibson and Philip K. Dick. We were both deeply interested in the practical elements of cryptography, and how it might protect anonymity, especially as it was formulated in the work of David Chaum. We were early members of the Cypherpunk subculture, part of the original group that met in San Francisco to write and publish manifestos. And we were early proponents of blockchain technology, as well, and developed businesses that revolved around it. But over the years, our paths diverged. I don't know what he's about now, and that is intentional. He is not, to be frank, my cup of tea. The man is ruthless about his privacy. If you've somehow threatened him, you have stepped into something much deeper, much darker, than you can imagine."

"But I didn't threaten anything," Brink said. "I was pulled into this. The puzzle came to me."

"You're helping Jess Price," Gupta said. "Correct?"

"You could say that, yes," Brink said, realizing that was, in fact, the case. What had begun as a single visit had turned into something more profound.

"For Sedge, the friend of his enemy is his enemy. From what you've told me, Jess Price is not Sedge's friend."

"You're right about that," Brink said, remembering Jess's cipher, her terror at being watched.

"Then I suggest you do not meet his girlfriend. Drop all of this. Destroy the puzzle and go back to Manhattan."

"I can't," he said, and he knew it was true. Even if he walked away, even if he could forget the puzzle, Jess would haunt him.

Dr. Gupta sighed. "Then appease him as best you can. Find a way to speak to him. Assure him that you're not getting involved in his affairs."

"But I don't even know what those affairs are," Brink said.

"Nobody does, exactly," Gupta said. "But the crime that occurred at his family home was the first narrative he couldn't fully control. While you won't find anything about it online, his name and the nature of his company came under scrutiny. That Anne-Marie Riccard is willing to speak to you surprises me. Greatly."

Brink pressed his head into the steering wheel; the vinyl was burning hot. He felt, suddenly, a desperate longing to take Dr. Gupta's advice and go back home to his loft, to the comfort of his puzzles, his afternoon run, a quiet night of television with Connie. "Maybe you're right. Maybe I should just drop it."

"Yes, of course you should," Vivek Gupta said. "But I know you better than that. Besides, if you're on Sedge's radar, there's a bloody good reason. Go see his friend, as planned, but be careful. In the meantime, you have my encrypted messaging app. Scan the puzzle and send it to me. I'll see what I can find out about it."

28

It was early evening when Mike Brink pulled into a parking lot outside Bard's Fisher Center, an angular structure designed by Frank Gehry with an exoskeleton folded and creased like a piece of metallic origami. Connie needed to run, and so he unleashed her on a manicured lawn, where she sprinted in circles, leaping and catapulting, barking with pleasure in the bright sunshine and fresh air. Her exuberance caught the attention of a group of children playing at the far end of the field. A girl of about ten in a yellow dress blew bubbles from a plastic wand, and Connie, eager to play, darted from bubble to bubble, popping them with her nose. Brink watched the soapy, iridescent spheres lift and spin in the sunlight, their shifting colors a miracle of constant air curvature. He saw each bubble's steradians, saw their edgeless symmetry. When numbers began to flood into his mind, he shook them away. There wasn't time to get lost in an endless stream of digits. Anne-Marie Riccard was waiting.

As Brink clipped Connie into her leash, his phone vibrated in his pocket. He pulled it out and saw there was a voice message from a number he didn't recognize, most likely the manager of the Starlite Motel, angry after discovering his room. He opened the message and stopped abruptly when he heard Thessaly Moses's voice:

I've had some rather disturbing news. I've been trying to get my head around what happened earlier this afternoon, and now my supervisor just phoned to say that they're moving Jess out of the Ray Brook facility. What a nightmare. Anyway, I'm calling to check if you've read through the files on the flash drive. Call me back when you can. It's urgent that we speak.

Inside the art-history building, the air-conditioning enveloped him like an ice bath. As he walked through the empty hallway, looking for Anne-Marie's Riccard's office, he realized that he felt anxious about meeting her. It was irrational, especially because of how close he'd become to Dr. Gupta, but his defenses rose around academics. Not every teacher had been as appreciative of Mike Brink's talents as his mentor. In fact, most of his professors had treated him like a circus freak at best and an outright fraud at worst. He could understand why. He could read *War and Peace* in a few hours and recite passages from it on demand; he could solve difficult math equations after glancing at the textbook. Even the professors who knew his history had been suspicious of him. They never said it outright, but he felt the accusation lingering behind every interaction: Brink had an unfair advantage. Somehow, in ways they couldn't prove, he was cheating the system.

Brink had skated through MIT, graduating in three years with the highest honors. While he'd been a star student, he wasn't a scholar. He didn't find academic work challenging or even interesting. When he was offered a full scholarship to MIT's PhD program, he'd refused and moved to Manhattan, where he started working as a puzzle constructor at *The New York Times,* a decision that perplexed his professors and caused outright derision among his peers, who were accepting prestigious academic posts and highly paid consulting positions in corporations around the world. Mike Brink had been offered those positions, too, but he'd turned them down.

Rare was the person who understood that he had no choice. Brink didn't need prestige or money half as much as he needed to solve puzzles. He'd taken the cards he'd been dealt—a brain that both functioned and malfunctioned in life-altering ways—and learned to use them to his advantage. He'd embraced what Dr. Trevers called his "superpower" and couldn't imagine what his life would be if he hadn't been injured on that football field fifteen years before. But still, there were times when he felt the damage more acutely than others.

"Dr. Riccard," Brink said, as he stood in the door of her office. He recognized her from the photograph on the Bard website. She was tall and thin, elegant, her dark hair cut to the shoulder. She had a pale knit shawl, its large stitches forming intricate latticework around her shoulders.

"Call me Anne-Marie, please," she said, gesturing for him to come inside her cramped office. He sat on a small leather love seat near a shelf filled with art books: a catalog from the Rodin Museum in Paris, another of Japanese ceramics. "And who's this?" she asked, bending to pet Conundrum, who looked at her warily.

"Connie will love you forever if you give her this," he said, handing her a stick of beef jerky from his bag. It was a lie. Conundrum had intense feelings about people; she knew instantly if she liked someone and rarely changed her opinion. It was one of the things he most admired about her—she had a sixth sense about people. Anne-Marie tossed Connie the treat, then sat across from Brink on an identical leather love seat.

"Thanks for talking to me on such short notice," he said, as Connie sat near his feet and began to chew on her second jerky treat of the day.

"I've been hoping that someone would contact me about Jess Price for years now," Anne-Marie said. "Is she still . . . ?"

"Incarcerated?" Brink finished her sentence. "Yes. In a facility in the Adirondacks. I'm coming from there now."

"You mentioned you're working with her on a project," Anne-Marie asked. "What kind of project?"

Brink hadn't intended to lie, but the story came easily. "Puzzles for prisoners. A volunteer effort put together by the state."

"How generous," she said, giving him a skeptical look. "Is that kind of volunteer work common for someone with your level of . . . expertise?"

"Not exactly," Brink said, realizing that his reputation had, once again, preceded him. "But I like to help out where I can. Which is why I wanted to talk to you. You met Jess, is that right?"

"Just once, at Sedge House. The owner hired me to assess, certify, and sell all of the antiques in the house. That never happened."

This surprised him. He assumed everything at Sedge House—including the house itself—had been liquidated. "It hasn't been sold?"

"No," she said. "The owner wanted to leave the antiques exactly as they were when his aunt was alive."

"Isn't it a little expensive to maintain a Gilded Age mansion for storage purposes?"

"Jameson doesn't think much about expense. But, yes, it was an odd decision. Most people would have sold that place as quickly as possible. After everything that happened there, he decided to hold on to it. He pays a housekeeper to clean and dust, a gardener to maintain the roses, and heats the place enough to keep the pipes from bursting in the winter. Jameson is as eccentric as his aunt Aurora. Maybe even more so."

"So the porcelain-doll collection is still in the house?"

Anne-Marie's face flushed, and he could see her go tense. "Jess told you about the dolls?"

He nodded, careful not to reveal how interested he was in anything Anne-Marie might tell him about them.

"I became well acquainted with Aurora's collection. I never knew Aurora, but I felt, from her collection, that there was something, well, sort of wonderful about her. She was odd, no doubt, but she held what she loved close and didn't let the world intrude."

Anne-Marie folded her hands in her lap and continued. "She also had an excellent collection of porcelain, and porcelain has been a passion of mine for many decades. It is my area of expertise as an art historian, and I've written extensively about everything from ancient Chinese temple vases to the masterpieces of French faience. While porcelain dolls were originally an extension of this work, I admit, they began to take over at a certain point."

"It's a very particular field," he said, feeling a need to keep her talking. "How did you come to it?"

"The truth?" She smiled, a hint of embarrassment causing her to blush. "As a child of ten years old, I was served hot chocolate in one of my great-grandmother's teacups—an eggshell-thin china cup with a rose at the center, the rim trimmed with gold. The porcelain, with its weightlessness, its albumen clarity, and its ability to capture light and bend it around itself, entranced me. Later, when my great-grandmother died, I inherited those cups. They were Limoges, it turned out. I brought them with me to my first apartment in Manhattan, where they occupied half of the cupboard space in my tiny kitchen. I used them every day—a bit ridiculous for an impecunious student, I know. They bolstered me somehow. Each day, I would hold a Limoges cup in my hand and think of my great-grandmother but also of all the artistry that had come together to create it, how beauty survives generations and brings joy over time. That cup was a piece of art, I realized, one as precious as a Roman statue, only one I might enjoy every day. I changed my focus to the history of ceramics. Thus began my passion for porcelain." Anne-Marie gave him a self-conscious smile. "Please forgive me," she said. "I must be boring you."

"Not at all," Brink said. In fact, he understood perfectly well how an obsession could overtake a life—his discovery of puzzles had saved him, structured his existence, changed everything, really. "I find it fascinating."

"Indeed, it is fascinating," she said, pleased. "The history of porcelain is especially captivating. Europeans were first exposed to porcelain when Marco Polo brought back a small jar from China. He called it *porcellana,* an Italian word for a shell, the lustrous nacre of which the object resembled. Many, many artisans attempted to replicate Chinese porcelain in the years that followed, and they all failed. There were techniques they couldn't discern, a secret formula that the Chinese had mastered. The prices of imported porcelain were astronomical, and only the wealthiest aristocrats could afford even a few pieces.

"All of Europe was entranced by porcelain and desperate to have it. A German king by the name of Augustus the Strong invested a fortune trying to find the formula. Eventually he succeeded. Once the cat was out of the bag, so to speak, porcelain production exploded across Europe. French porcelain factories were established and became world-renowned, as were British companies such as Wedgwood. Figurines became coveted trinkets. Boxes, teapots, vases—people could not get enough of them. In many ways, European life changed with the introduction of porcelain. Great wealth and prestige were generated from it, of course, and the kings and queens of England and Europe commissioned breathtaking masterpieces, but by the nineteenth century, a porcelain teapot or a set of pretty cups could be acquired by ordinary people, like my great-grandmother."

"And like Aurora Sedge," Brink said, steering the conversation back to his purpose.

"Yes, like Aurora Sedge," she said. "Although she was not at all ordinary. But tell me—why did you contact me? Does it have to do with your project with Jess Price?"

Brink had been feeling out Anne-Marie and decided that it was time to come to the point of his visit. "I'm trying to understand what happened at Sedge House," he said. "You were one of the few people Jess saw while she was at the house."

"I was there to assess antiques," she said. "I hardly spoke to her at all."

"Maybe you saw something odd at the house," he said. "Something that could explain what happened to Noah Cooke?"

"There was an investigation, I believe," she said, her voice becoming cold. "And, as you well know, there was a conviction."

"I don't think the right person was convicted."

"And you're going to fight for justice?"

"Is there a reason I shouldn't?"

"Perhaps not," she said. "But you should understand the magnitude of what you're getting involved in before you try."

Brink remembered Jess Price's cipher. She believed someone had killed Ernest Raythe and that he was in danger, as well. He studied Anne-Marie, trying to glean how much she knew. "That's why I'm here," he said at last. "To understand."

Anne-Marie drew her voluminous, gauzy shawl closer, a careful gesture that was echoed in her tone. "It is a bit of a Pandora's box, Mr. Brink. If you open it, you will understand what has happened to Jess Price. You'll have all the information you're seeking, and more. But knowledge comes with consequences. You see, she found something that has been hidden for a very long time. There are people who do not want that discovery out in the world. Jess got too close to it. You've seen the result."

"I'm afraid I don't understand what you mean," he said, watching her carefully.

"Knowledge is seductive," she continued. "It creates a desire to uncover it, to strip away every layer protecting it. We think we want to possess the truth and that it will gratify us—give us reassurance, security, comfort. But really, there are times when knowledge can harm us. Sometimes a secret remains out of reach for a reason."

Brink took this in, unsure of how to respond. He wasn't built for secrets. A compulsion, one rising from the center of his being, didn't allow him to leave one unsolved. "I'm not the type of guy who can walk away without knowing."

Anne-Marie took a key from her purse, unlocked a filing cabinet, and pulled out a small leather portfolio. Brink recognized it immediately as the portfolio described in Jess Price's journal—brown, scuffed, held together with a thick leather string. Returning to her seat, she clutched it tight in her hands, her nails digging into the soft flesh. "I think you understand already that what happened at Sedge House is not what it seems. It's not just a question of who killed Noah Cooke, or even if Jess Price is responsible for what happened. The contents of this portfolio will change your perception about what happened. In fact, they will change your perception about everything."

Brink glanced out the window. The light was dimming, the day draining as the sun set. "Perceptions are made to be changed."

Anne-Marie tucked the portfolio into her bag, grabbed her keys from the bookshelf, and headed to the door. "Come with me, then," she said, her voice quiet, as if she was afraid of being overheard. "And I will show you."

29

Mike Brink drove behind Anne-Marie's BMW, following her along a series of small county highways. It was getting dark, and so he flipped on his headlights as they turned onto her property, following a steep driveway through a dense forest of fir and birch and maple trees. His headlights flashed over signs that read NO TRESPASSING, NO HUNTING, PRIVATE PROPERTY, nailed on tree trunks. He checked his rearview mirror, looking for the black Tesla, and was relieved to find that he hadn't been followed. It had disappeared, and yet part of him felt it out there, in the dark, ready to materialize at any moment.

Finally, they reached the end of the driveway and parked before a modern house composed of three glass cubes perched atop slabs of concrete. He shut off his headlights and checked his phone. No service. He got out of the truck and followed Anne-Marie to the front door, Connie at his feet, but Anne-Marie stopped him. "Would you mind?" she asked, glancing at the truck. "I never allow dogs in the house. . . ."

Brink spread Connie's blanket on the seat of the truck, cracked the windows, and locked the doors. He'd have preferred to leave her in the bed of the truck, but dachshunds were bred to hunt, and he could only imagine what would happen if Connie got scent of an animal. She wasn't happy to be locked in the truck and began to bark and jump at the window, so he opened the door and let her out to pee near a tree. When she returned to him, he pointed his finger like a pistol. "Bang!" he said, pretending to shoot her, and she collapsed. Playing dead was a hard trick, but after months of practice, she'd mastered it. Connie lay on the driveway, her tongue lolling comically from her mouth. He laughed, gave her a quick scratch behind the ears, then put her back in the truck and locked the door.

In front of the house, Anne-Marie pressed a fob and the lights blazed on, illuminating the interior in a whoosh of soft light, the kitchen and living room clicking into focus, creating a ripple of reflection over the glass.

"There's not much privacy, but then again, I have no neighbors, so . . ." she said, leading him into the kitchen, where she took a bottle of Sancerre from a wine fridge. She uncorked it and poured two glasses of white wine. Handing him one, she led him to the living room, where the sleek architecture of the house—its glass walls and polished concrete floors—was softened by haloes of amber light from lamps scattered through the vast space. From the high ceiling hung a colorful chandelier, its red and yellow glass twisting like the arms of an octopus. "That's a Dale Chihuly," Anne-Marie said, when she saw him staring. "And those," she said, gesturing to three porcelain figurines with feline eyes on the mantel of the fireplace, "are Art Deco masterpieces made by Erté." He turned to find framed Hebrew scrolls hanging on the wall of the living room. There was a cabinet filled with porcelain and a golden chalice sitting on a shelf. "If it were up to me, all my time would be spent at auctions." She turned back to him, her brown eyes suddenly serious. "Instead, I have been wholly occupied with another treasure hunt."

Anne-Marie set her wineglass on a coffee table and took the old leather portfolio from her bag.

"Jess is not the only one to lose the last five years of her life to this mystery. What happened in that house, what happened to Aurora Sedge and her brother, and their connection to events that happened long ago, have become a significant part of my life."

She sat down on a couch, unwound the leather string, and opened the portfolio. Brink watched, his anticipation rising. But Anne-Marie stopped suddenly. "Where is your phone?"

Brink placed the wineglass on the coffee table, and dug his phone out of his pocket. He looked at the call log, which showed three missed calls from earlier—the call from Thessaly, and two from Vivek Gupta—but there was no service now. The realization hit him that no one knew where he was. He was in the middle of nowhere without connection to the outside world.

"Turn it off, please," Anne-Marie said, glancing at his phone.

There's no service, anyway, Brink thought. He pressed the power button, shutting it down, then held it up to show her the black screen.

"I know it seems paranoid, but I can't be too careful," she said. "I've gone through too much for this to be recorded."

Brink edged closer so that he could see the portfolio. Anne-Marie held it tightly in her hands.

"When I began my career," Anne-Marie said, "I didn't know much about LaMoriette. Of course, I'd heard the stories about his dolls. Everyone coming up in my field of expertise does: the beautiful, rare luxury dolls that so obsessed collectors. But it was the haunted baby doll, the masterpiece that was created in the likeness of his beloved daughter, Violaine, that intrigued students of LaMoriette the most. The supernatural, especially when mixed up with the allure of a beautiful object, can become irresistible to a certain kind of person. I spent a good deal of time hunting down the facts behind the legend.

"But I soon found that there was more to it than I originally believed. We form a rather small group, we experts in the history of porcelain, and I began calling colleagues in my circle to ask what they knew about LaMoriette. A friend of mine from graduate school, Cullen Withers, a specialist in French porcelain, had been collecting information about LaMoriette for decades. It turned out he had an

abundance of documents pertaining to both Les Bébés de Paris, La-
Moriette's manufactured line of dolls, and his singular creation, the
doll that was considered his masterpiece: Violaine. Cullen had gone
down the LaMoriette rabbit hole and dug up newspaper articles and
interviews with LaMoriette; a catalog from a presentation of his
work at an exhibit in Paris in 1901; some photographs, a handwritten letter, and so on. He discovered that LaMoriette had studied
with a dollmaker in Prague in the 1890s. His much-lauded doll
eyes—lead crystal suffused with color—had been greatly influenced
by Czech glassmaking techniques, and there was a vague reference in
a letter from that period to a friendship LaMoriette had formed
with a Jewish man in Prague. I followed up on this, and while I
found nothing more about this friendship, the story intrigued me,
and I continued my research."

Anne-Marie took a sip of her wine and continued.

"I soon learned that the American tycoon John Pierpont Morgan
had bought LaMoriette's workshop—which included a collection of
rare books and manuscripts, as well as Violaine—after LaMoriette's
death by suicide in 1909."

"The banker?" Brink said, recalling a story he'd read about the
1907 financial crash, when J. P. Morgan had brought the most prominent bankers together and locked them in a room until they agreed
on a bailout.

"Exactly right," Anne-Marie said. "He bought the collection for
the books, I assume, and got Violaine as part of the bargain. The doll
was given by J. P. Morgan to his granddaughter, Frances Tracy Morgan, as a Christmas gift. The girl's nanny, Miss Clarice Clementine,
had extensive contact with the doll and claimed the doll Violaine
was possessed—that was the exact word she used," Anne-Marie said.
"She published an account of her experiences in 1928, long after her
tenure with the Morgan family was over. Her memoir described all
the things one would expect to hear about haunted dolls: electro-
magnetism, strange movements from one part of the house to the
other, auras of light, mysterious crying, and, ultimately, violence.

Young Frances Morgan was injured and, if the nanny's story is to be believed, permanently scarred.

"Violaine was sold off with the documents that verified the doll's provenance: drawings LaMoriette had made when he designed the doll, personal documents about his work. It was a private sale, made in cash, and there was no record in the Morgan Library of who bought Violaine. As it turned out, Aurora Sedge's father was the buyer. He purchased the doll for his daughter, Aurora.

"This portfolio," she said, "contains the papers sold with Violaine. They were found at Sedge House after Jess's arrest. These pages"— Anne-Marie removed a sheaf of papers and placed it on the table between them—"are part of a letter written by Gaston LaMoriette to his son, Charles LaMoriette, on the twenty-fourth of December of 1909. It describes a period in LaMoriette's life that had taken place almost twenty years before, in 1891, when LaMoriette went to Prague to study under a dollmaker called Johan Král. It was the last communication LaMoriette had with anyone. He killed himself on Christmas Day, 1909."

Brink tried to take the pages, but Anne-Marie stopped him. She removed a small envelope from an interior pocket of the portfolio and produced three sepia-toned photographs. "These are pictures of LaMoriette, his wife, and his daughter, Violaine, taken in 1890 in Paris. I found them a few years ago among the belongings of LaMoriette's son, Charles."

Brink picked up a photo and saw a portly man with a neat beard, one arm around a woman with a large-brimmed hat decorated with stuffed birds and the other around a teenaged girl, Violaine. Brink looked more closely at Violaine. She was tall and too thin, not pretty, exactly, but with a brightness in her expression that made her seem so. Like her father, she seemed happy, almost jovial.

"And this," Anne-Marie said, her reflection stretching over the glass as she laid down another photo, a picture of a porcelain doll, "is LaMoriette's masterpiece. Notice how similar the doll is to the daughter? It's remarkable. Do you see it?"

Brink did see it. The resemblance was uncanny. The doll was, like the girl, rather odd-looking, with large eyes and a face that expressed a mischievous playfulness.

"She died tragically not long after this photo was taken," Anne-Marie said.

"He captured her well," Brink said, feeling a stab of sadness as he fully understood what LaMoriette's masterpiece had meant to the man: It was a way to pay homage to the child he had lost.

Anne-Marie spread the pages into two piles on the table. "Aurora Sedge kept this portfolio for decades. Jess Price must have found it, as it was discovered in the library of Sedge House after she was arrested. The pages were scattered around the room, totally out of order. It isn't complete, unfortunately. I believe there were more pages, although Lord knows what happened to them. They may have been lost by LaMoriette's son, to whom they were addressed. Aurora might have mishandled them. There's no way to know for certain."

Brink remembered Jess's account of the secret pantry, he remembered the description of the portfolio and the letter, and while it verified what Anne-Marie was saying, he wasn't about to tell Anne-Marie that. He didn't trust her. Anyone who didn't allow dogs in her house had something wrong with her.

"The original is in French, and the translation was made in the early twentieth century, perhaps when the doll was purchased from LaMoriette's son," she said, pointing to the two sets of documents on the table: the original, handwritten pages in French, and a sheaf of onionskin pages in English, a typed translation. Brink had grown up speaking French with his mother and had perfected the grammar through reading Simenon novels. If Anne-Marie allowed it, he would be able to read the original, and he glanced at the letter, anxious to understand what it said.

"This letter is important for a number of reasons," she said. "First, it was never meant to be read by anyone other than his son, Charles—LaMoriette asks his son to burn the letter after he's read it—and therefore, they give an honest account of what happened to La-

Moriette in Prague. In addition, the account shows how deeply wounded the man was by the loss of Violaine. She had died only two months before he left for Prague and, from the letter, one gleans that this was the reason he went to work with Master Král in the first place. In any event, the letter shows the man as he was, without artifice, and there is an emotional frankness that throws the sensational events he experienced into relief."

Brink skimmed the first page, his eyes stopping at a line at the bottom:

> *I believed I could know what shouldn't be known. I wanted to see things, secret things, and so I lifted the veil between the human and the Divine and stared directly into the eyes of God. That is the nature of the puzzle: to offer pain and pleasure by turns.*

Brink felt a tingling through his body as he realized that Jess had copied this passage exactly. She had read a line of it that was written in the Sedge family Bible, which meant that Aurora Sedge must have transcribed it from the very same paragraph, which meant—of course—that this letter had been in Aurora's possession. *"I lifted the veil between the human and the Divine and stared directly into the eyes of God,"* Brink said. "That is an unusual thing to say. Do you know what he was talking about?"

He heard Connie barking outside—going crazy over a squirrel, most likely—but was too engrossed in LaMoriette's letter to check on her.

"He is talking about a discovery," Anne-Marie said, her gaze fixing upon him with a peculiar intensity.

"What kind of discovery?" Brink asked.

A voice from behind said: "Perhaps the greatest discovery ever made."

Brink jumped up and found the red-haired man he had fled in the parking lot of the prison, the same man whose Tesla had trailed him through the Adirondacks. "The treasure of Divine knowledge."

30

Cam Putney started as one of ten guys working security at Jameson Sedge's Midtown office. He was twenty-one years old, living in a dump in Queens and working two jobs to pay child support. He owned nothing. No car. No savings. He had a major drug problem—hash and steroids and the occasional tangle with coke—that ate what little was left of his paycheck. He'd been picked up for disorderly conduct after a fight in a club on Steinway Street, and when he tested positive for OxyContin, he was fined, sent to mandatory rehab, and almost went to jail. Nothing anchored him except his daughter, Jasmine, a beautiful two-year-old he saw every other weekend.

But Mr. Sedge must have seen something in him, some spark of his true nature—his capacity for loyalty and obedience, a longing for a higher calling—because he summoned Cam to his office one afternoon and asked him if he was interested in a promotion. "I want you to become part of my personal security team," he said. "It's an opening that doesn't come often."

"A bodyguard, you mean?"

Sedge smiled. "Security is more than providing physical safety, although that is, of course, part of the job. Security is existential. It encompasses all elements of a man's being: physical, intellectual, spiritual, financial. Virtual. Perhaps you are aware that sixty million identities are stolen every year, but are you aware that soon there will be nothing else but our identity? My identity is as vital, and as valuable, as my physical body. Why? Because it will supersede my body. I will live in it, experience existence in it, far longer than I will biologically exist. Compromising my identity is compromising my very being. I am not a man who will be compromised. Do you understand me, Mr. Putney?"

He nodded, unsure exactly what the job entailed but eager to hear more. "Yes, sir," he said.

"This isn't like any other job you have ever had. It will require significant dedication. The hours are, shall we say, expansive. Quite more than a full-time job. Rather more of a vocation, one that will require certain acts of compliance: weekly drug tests, extended hours, mental and physical reeducation, international travel. And you will need training in alternate security techniques. Are you comfortable with these conditions, Mr. Putney?"

Cam stared at Sedge, at his steady gaze, his manicured fingernails, all the confidence that money and power had given him. Although he had no idea what Sedge had in mind, he knew that he wanted more from life than what he had. "Yes, sir."

"The job will stretch your limits," he said. "My ideas and my business are unorthodox, and joining my team will challenge you. I see my security team as modern samurai—physically primed, but also intellectually and spiritually sharp. You will be the blade that stands between me and"—he gestured out the window at the world beyond—"them."

Cam glanced out the window at the Manhattan cityscape. They had never done a damn thing for him. "I'm interested," he said. "Sir."

"Very good. I've observed you these past months. You're smart. Hardworking. In excellent physical condition. I believe you will rise to that challenge. At least, I'm willing to take the risk."

"Thank you, sir," he said, hearing the emotion in his voice. It was the first time anyone, ever, had expressed that he was worth anything.

"I daresay it will be worth your while. The salary, for one, is generous. But there are other customized benefits. One being an education fund for your daughter, Jasmine Lee Putney, that will cover the cost of tuition at the institution of your choice."

Cam had never mentioned his daughter to anyone at work, and it took him off guard to hear her name. He felt suddenly that Jameson Sedge could see through him, through the tattoos and muscles, through his dyed blond hair and his work uniform, and into his soul. "That's very generous, sir."

"While I need you on weekends, I can arrange for your bimonthly custody arrangement to continue, at least for the time being. I cannot guarantee this in the future, however. There will be times when you will need to arrange alternate visitation. I trust you are open to this inconvenience?"

Cam stared at him, dumbfounded. He knew not only his daughter's name but the details of his custody agreement. "I can manage that," he said.

"Then I believe we understand each other." His words were both handshake and dismissal. He looked at the door, and Cam, numb, left.

Within a week, Cam signed a series of digital agreements—Ricardian contracts, Mr. Sedge called them—that guaranteed legally what he'd already given morally: loyalty and silence. His training began the following week and, over the next eighteen months, transformed him. Half of his time was spent with Mr. Sedge, ensuring his physical safety. But during the other half, he was pushed to extremes. Firearms training, martial arts, meditation, but also computer technology, online security, and understanding the complex cryptographic keys that secured Singularity's networks. He learned everything from coding to analyzing data systems to managing Sedge's encrypted internal-communication system. He monitored every communication that went in or out of the business server. Over time, Cam became a physical barrier between the world and Jameson Sedge, but also a digital one. The triangle tattoo sealed his training, a sign that he was ready for service.

During that period, he saw his daughter on schedule, having her at his place every other weekend. He stopped the drugs, stopped drinking, and became a better father. His salary and the education fund created a kind of stability for Jasmine that Cam had never had. It allowed his child to thrive.

That was over a decade ago. Since then, Cam had come to understand the nature of Jameson Sedge's power. It was not only financial, although he had that, too. The man's network of friends was stronger than money. Sedge got what he wanted when he wanted it. Cam saw that up close during his time in the prison, where every resource was focused on Jess Price.

When Mr. Sedge told Cam that he would be relocating to Ray Brook, he'd resisted leaving the city. Not only because he'd be more than five hours from Jasmine, but because he didn't trust anyone to take care of Mr. Sedge the way he did. The other guards didn't care as much as Cam did. Protecting Mr. Sedge wasn't his job. It was his calling.

31

"Jameson," the man said as he walked to Mike Brink, extending his hand. "Jameson Sedge."

Brink shook the man's hand and glanced outside. The black Tesla sat in the driveway, and, to Brink's astonishment, the bleached-blond guard from the prison—the man with the Pythagorean triangle tattooed on his neck—leaned against the car, smoking a cigarette. Suddenly he understood. The guard was Sedge's inside guy at the prison. Jess Price had been right: She was being watched.

Anne-Marie took the pages of LaMoriette's letter from Brink's hands, slipped them back into the portfolio, and tied it shut. Then she stood, kissed Jameson, and went to get him a glass of wine.

Brink had wondered about Ann-Marie's relationship with Jameson Sedge, and the kiss —as well as the fact that the guy had a key to the house—confirmed what he suspected. He wondered if they'd been a couple back when Jess Price met Anne-Marie five years ago, or if their relationship had grown after Anne-Marie assessed Aurora Sedge's antiques. He turned back to Jameson, studying him. He was a handsome man, with a sprinkling of freckles over his nose and cheeks, and intense hazel eyes. He guessed him to be in his late fifties, but he had a boyish quality that made him seem younger. His clothes were stylish and expensive: voluptuous Italian driving shoes in green suede, designer jeans, a green polo shirt. He remembered what Vivek Gupta had said about his old friend: *The man is ruthless about his privacy. If you've somehow threatened him, you have stepped into something much deeper, much darker, than you can imagine.*

"Pleased to finally catch up with you," Jameson said. He had an accent somewhere between British and American, a boarding school Brahmin dialect Brink had first heard in Boston. His own Midwestern accent had stood out, and he'd quickly learned to sharpen his vowels and clip his consonants. "You see, I have been rather desperate to speak with you."

"A phone call is usually your best bet," Brink said. He was unsure of how to handle Jameson's mixture of aggression and charm. The man had trashed his motel room, closed down his access to Jess, and followed him from the Adirondacks. He was behind Thessaly's problems at the prison, as well, no doubt. Brink couldn't just sit down and have a pleasant chat with the guy after that. Something about Jameson Sedge put Brink on high alert, a kind of sleek, predatory quality, elegant and dangerous, like a water moccasin slipping through shallow water.

"I've made you uncomfortable," Jameson said. "It's my Achilles' heel, I'm afraid. Anne-Marie always tells me that I rush into things without considering how it will affect other people."

"No worries," Brink said. He slipped his hand into his coat and found the key to his truck. He needed to get going. "Another time."

"You're not leaving already?" Jameson asked, glancing at the keys in Brink's hand.

"It's getting late," Brink said. "And I have a long drive ahead of me."

Anne-Marie returned from the kitchen. "You must be exhausted," she said, giving him a sympathetic look. "But stay just a little while longer." She handed Jameson a glass of white wine.

"That's really not possible," he said. He didn't want to know what Jameson wanted with him. He needed to get on the road, the sooner the better.

"Please, dinner will be ready in a few minutes. You can eat and be on your way in half an hour. Besides, you and Jameson must talk." She shifted her eyes to the leather portfolio on the coffee table. "And there is something important that I need to discuss with you, as well."

"Come, Mr. Brink, it's a beautiful night and there is a glorious view from the deck," Jameson said, gesturing for Brink to follow him. "Cam Putney will take good care of your puppy."

Brink glanced outside and saw that the blond prison guard was now leaning on his truck. Brink wasn't leaving until they allowed him to leave.

Brink followed Jameson out onto a cantilevered deck overlooking the dark sweep of trees. Beyond, the land dropped away, angling sharply into a steep declivity that disappeared into the night. The air was warm and yet, as he stood next to Jameson, he felt his skin prickle. Brink took out his phone and turned it on. Still no service.

"When I built this house for Anne-Marie, it was the view that won me over. I imagined a glass box perched among pines, a pure form nestled against these old, noble trees. It is the exact opposite of my aunt Aurora's home. Sedge House is so heavy, so rambling, so filled with junk. I wanted to live as if I were part of nature, become one with the landscape, as it were."

The moon had risen. It was bright, and the light fell over a clearing, where a helicopter sat on a circular landing pad.

"My Eurocopter," he said, following Brink's gaze. "I bought a hundred-acre cushion to ensure that neighbors wouldn't complain about the noise. Still, it annoys people, even when they can't hear it—nothing like New Yorkers' petty jealousies over status. I had to get my legal team involved to make it happen, but you can't beat getting to the city in half an hour on a Sunday evening. Anne-Marie got her pilot's license so that we can go at a moment's notice."

"Anne-Marie?" Brink said, surprised. With her calm, composed demeanor and her career in antiques, she didn't seem like the type of person to go hopping around in a helicopter.

"She didn't like flying when I met her, but she didn't let that stop her. She learned to fly to overcome her fear. That is, perhaps, her greatest quality—using knowledge to overcome the terrors of the world. When she's afraid, she masters what she fears. She is really quite a surprising woman."

"I don't doubt it," he said, thinking of her persistence in hunting down LaMoriette's letter.

"She is one of the most intelligent people I know, which is certainly why we have been together so long. I don't think anyone else could have understood the incredible value of what Aunt Aurora discovered. She has been an asset to me in many ways."

"Was your aunt's porcelain collection so very valuable?" Brink asked, remembering that Anne-Marie had implied that porcelain had fallen out of fashion with collectors. From the way Jameson spoke about it, you'd think it was worth millions.

"Aurora's porcelain doesn't interest me," Jameson said, dismissive.

"Then what?" Brink said. "Men like you don't do anything without an incentive."

Jameson looked at him for a minute. Then, leaning against the railing of the deck, he said, "I've read about you, Mike Brink. They say you're a genius, a man with a one-in-a-million brain. It's humbling, I admit, to realize that one is merely average. Abilities such as yours are beyond the grasp of most of us. But I am a practical man. If there is something I cannot do myself, I make sure my friends can do it for me."

"The only problem," Brink said, giving Sedge a weak smile, "is that I'm not your friend."

"I get it," he said, returning the smile. "You think you've got me figured out. I'm a rich old man searching for a way to keep his privileges in a changing world. Well, I suppose I am. But . . ." Jameson looked up at the sky and Brink followed his gaze, the stars glittering against the clear black slate of the night. "I am capable of seeing how small we are, how insignificant. There is so much we don't know and so much that is beyond our reach. Still, we are on the edge of something that will change that, and this pushes me to continue. You can't fault me. Wanting to live forever is as old as life itself. In *Hamlet*, death is referred to as *the undiscovered country from whose bourn no traveler returns*. And yet Hamlet feels the compulsion to explore that which remains beyond understanding."

Jameson leveled his gaze at Brink.

"That undiscovered country is my life's work. Consciousness, the characteristics of consciousness during one's lifetime and beyond— these subjects have become the dominating drive for my business and, frankly, everything else. After my father died, his share of the family fortune was put in a trust for me. When I came of age, I used my advantages to build businesses, all of them clustered around a single belief: that consciousness is not born or destroyed but that it is an indestructible and universal force that shapes matter. That, indeed, matter serves consciousness."

Brink leaned against the railing of the deck, listening, trying to find a clue about how any of it related to Jess Price or the puzzle she had given him.

"I started Singularity Technology to investigate my belief that the human mind endures beyond the decay of the body. You might call it transhumanism, but I don't think of it in those terms. Indeed, after reading LaMoriette's letter, I've come to see that the quest to understand human consciousness—and to protect it from the vicissitudes of matter—has been the primary quest of mankind from the very beginning. We are living in a time when that search has reached a tipping point: We can use artificial intelligence, gene-altering technologies, and the power of computer networks to explore the infinite possibilities of human development. I've partnered with philosophers, geneticists, biologists, and everything in between to explore possible structures of what one might call 'the human soul' and how it interacts with the body. Humanity's oldest inquiries, our oldest artifacts, our ancient texts, and our most cherished religions have always been about the nature of such things, yet we are still searching for answers. That is why I believe we must work together, Mr. Brink. Your talents would be very useful to my work."

"I can't possibly see how."

"I think you underestimate your talents."

"And I think you overestimate them. I have an ability to see patterns and solve them. I'm not superhuman, and I have no interest in living forever."

"*Overestimate* is another word for faith," he said. "And there you're right: I have faith in your abilities. That is the difference between men like me and other people. When I have faith in something, when I know in my gut that it's true, I pursue it relentlessly. To the end. And so I will save us both time and get to the point: Jess Price has something I need."

"And what would that be?"

"Perhaps she mentioned something to you about it at the prison," Jameson said. "Perhaps she alluded to something she found in my aunt's house and then concealed. Maybe this information is very, very valuable to me. So valuable, you would find yourself relieved of financial worries for quite a long time should you help me find it."

"Do you have any idea what Jess has been through?" He'd been wary of Jameson, but he was beginning to find the man vile. He didn't seem to care that a woman's life was in ruins. "I doubt she wants anything other than her freedom."

"It is possible that she's not even fully aware of it," Jameson said. "But I believe she knows something that could help me find what is, by all rights, mine. Maybe she gave you that information, or, if she did not, maybe she alluded to how to find it. There is also the possibility that she destroyed it, which seems to be more and more likely as the years pass. I have torn apart Sedge House looking for it, but it seems to have vanished."

"Then you have no need for me."

Jameson assessed him for a moment, then took a step closer to Brink, cutting the distance between them in half. "I understand your reluctance. You don't appreciate that I cut off your access to Jess Price." He took another step, cutting the distance between them in half again. Brink could smell him, the mixture of sweat and expensive cologne; he could hear his breathing. It was a display of masculine posturing, one Brink understood from football locker rooms. "But let me make myself clear. Jess Price can try to hide it, but I will find it."

"Why don't you make this easier for both of us," Brink said, "and tell me exactly what you're looking for."

Jameson must have been prepared for that question, because he didn't hesitate. "It's an antiquity of great value, one that my aunt Aurora had in her possession. One that has been hidden for millennia for its power to change the relationship between humankind and our place in the universe."

"What kind of antiquity?" Brink asked, but he knew already. His mind fixed on the image of a circle, numbers along its perimeter and Hebrew letters at the center.

"One that has the power to change the future," Sedge said. "And if you will help me, we can change it together."

The door opened and Anne-Marie stepped out onto the deck. "This is exactly what I wanted to speak with you about," she said. "Come, dinner is ready, and there's much to discuss."

32

On the drive from Anne-Marie's house to Ray Brook, Cam Putney thought of his daughter. It's where his mind went whenever he stopped moving long enough to think. He turned on the self-driving function, programmed the destination into the Tesla's GPS, and let the car do the work. The Model S Plaid had a top speed of 155 miles per hour, and while he couldn't go that fast the whole way—he'd programmed the car to slow when encountering radar controls—he'd be in Ray Brook in no time.

Watching the landscape fly by through the windshield relaxed his mind, stilled it, creating a kind of screen upon which he saw Jasmine's evening without him. He saw her leave school, saw her get on the subway with her babysitter, saw her drop her backpack at the door and go to her room. He imagined her finishing her science homework, a papier-mâché dinosaur that was due Monday, and her mom arguing with her about eating her peas at dinner. He knew her nightly routine, even though he hadn't ever lived with her: picking out clothes for the following day, a shower, packing her school bag. His daughter was nearly thirteen, growing up fast, and he was missing it. And while they spoke on the phone often, and he made sure she had the best of everything, his failure to be present filled him with regret. There were times he wondered if it was worth it. The sense of belonging he had at Singularity, the money, the knowledge that what he was doing could change the world—it meant a lot to him, but what was he giving up in return?

Usually, his work left little room for regret. After his first year as part of Singularity's elite security team, he started training with Ume-Sensei. Mr. Sedge introduced her as his mentor and called the work they would do *consciousness training,* but Cam saw her as something between a military drill sergeant and a New Age life coach. At first he didn't like the idea of being schooled by a young woman. They were about the same age—early twenties—and she was half his size, thin as a twig, with a calm, watchful presence. She spoke English with a strong Japanese accent he strained to understand, and he tended to tune out when she spoke. He wanted to dismiss her entirely, but then, during their first martial-arts training, she knocked him off his feet and stunned him with a quick, sharp blow to the solar plexus. From that point on, he paid attention.

Ume-Sensei trained him in martial arts, meditation, and the responsibilities that came with power. "In this moment," she said, "you are strong. There will come a time when you are weak. Understand both states of being, and you will survive."

Cam came to understand that strength needed weakness to exist. Action was the natural result of stillness, death the natural counterpoint to life, and violence the basis of care. It was true that his work, as brutal as it could be, allowed him to support the one thing he loved more than anything: his child. All he'd done for Sedge made it possible for Cam to protect Jasmine. He just needed to fulfill his commitment, help Mr. Sedge get where he was going, and he would be free to be a better father.

It wouldn't be long. Mr. Sedge's plan was coming together. When Mr. Sedge explained that Cam must drive to Ray Brook and stop Dr. Moses from interfering, Cam knew they were near the end. Of course, it would mean harming, perhaps even killing, her. But Ume-Sensei had opened his eyes to the true nature of violence, and while he didn't enjoy it, he accepted that it was necessary. There could be no peace without war. There could be no life without death. The future could not exist without the annihilation of the present.

It wasn't just Buddhist bullshit, although that's how Cam saw it in the beginning. It was at the heart of Mr. Sedge's mission. It took a long time for Cam to come around. He'd almost left Singularity over a disagreement with Ume-Sensei about his diet—no red meat, lots of Japanese vegetables he'd never heard of, grueling physical training, and a whole pharmacy of natural medicines. When he told her to fuck off and leave him alone, she'd looked at him with her imperturbable brown eyes and said, "We must love those who hurt us. Those who wound us are our most profound teachers." Mr. Sedge might appear to many as an enemy, but he was, in fact, their savior.

Cam came to understand this during his third year on the job, after he'd gained full access to Singularity's encrypted network and saw the full scope of Mr. Sedge's mission. The man had created a new layer of existence over the known world, a global network of information secured by an inviolable ledger and backed by billions of dollars' worth of digital currency. The ledger was authenticated and maintained across the globe and, unlike other forms of blockchain technology, was powered by a new variety of computer processor, one Mr. Sedge had created with a team of international developers. Singularity wasn't just a business, and Mr. Sedge wasn't just a billionaire. He was a visionary who would alter the course of human existence. This network would place Singularity, and Jameson Sedge, at the very center of life itself. It was Cam's job to make sure that happened.

Cam was all in from his first mission. He boarded the Singularity jet at Teterboro and flew to Kyiv, where he met a man in the lobby of the InterContinental Hotel. They didn't exchange a single word. The man placed a finger on the screen of Cam's phone to verify his identity; Cam placed a large envelope on a table and picked up a package containing a hard drive and walked away. He knew nothing about the contents of the envelope; he knew nothing about what was on the hard drive. But Sedge was happy with his work, and over the next years he made dozens of exchanges, in Kyiv, Minsk, Moscow, and London. Every time, it was the same routine: deliver an envelope, pick up a hard drive, and return it to Sedge.

The only variation on this routine were the trips to London. There, he always met an American man. The guy was afraid they'd be watched, and Mr. Sedge agreed that he was probably correct, so their exchanges were handled with particular care. Once, they passed each other outside the National Gallery, handing off envelopes without so much as a word between them. Another time, they met in the tube, the man leaving a bag on his seat, pocketing the envelope as he stepped onto the platform. The most contact they had was their last meeting, in November 2017, at a pub near Red Lion Square, not far from Holborn station. The man introduced himself as Gary Sand and invited Cam to have a drink. They took a seat in a corner of the pub, far from the door. Cam ordered a pint of Guinness and listened as Gary Sand—clearly not the guy's real name—talked to him about investment opportunities in a fund he was putting together. Cam played along, asking questions about the fund until, his pint almost empty, he felt a hand under the table. Sand slipped him the hard drive, got up, and left. Cam finished his beer, paid the check, and flew back home.

The meetings with Gary Sand intrigued Cam and inspired his one and only breach of Singularity protocol. He searched the network and found that Gary Sand and Mr. Sedge had a long history. They'd been part of a group of early developers of cryptographic communications, a band of tech futurists who lived in the Bay Area in the late eighties. Some members of this group dropped out of society altogether. But not Gary Sand and Jameson Sedge. Cam found a series of emails from 2008 that referenced Satoshi Nakamoto and the development of an alternative form of exchange that couldn't be manipulated or rigged by the rich to dominate the poor. Mr. Sedge had been part of this experiment. Not for money, but to free the world from oppression.

"We are close," Mr. Sedge had told him the day he left Manhattan to work at the prison in Ray Brook. "So close to the greatest breakthrough in the history of mankind, one that will vanquish death. A great revolution is coming. And Jess Price holds the key."

The true nature of Mr. Sedge's mission, with its radical social and political foundation, surprised Cam. He knew the man's personal mission—to understand the nature of consciousness and mortality—but he hadn't realized until that moment that the man who had changed Cam's life planned to change the world.

33

Anne-Marie set the dining room table, turned the lights low, and began serving pasta from a dish.

"Well done," Jameson said, nodding at Anne-Marie as he sat. It was a clipped, almost formal gesture, like one made to a servant.

Anne-Marie dismissed the compliment. "I made it this afternoon and kept it in the fridge—farfalle with fresh tomatoes, garlic, mozzarella, and basil from the farmers market," she said, as she opened a new bottle of wine and began pouring it into glasses. "You're hungry," she said, scooping pasta onto Brink's plate. "Eat and you'll feel better."

It didn't take much convincing. He was starving. "This is delicious," he said, taking a bite of the pasta. "I exist on fast food." It wasn't far from the truth—his last two meals had been pizza at the Starlite and a turkey sub at the highway rest area.

Anne-Marie sat, began eating, then paused to run a finger along the edge of her cobalt-blue plate. "Here's a question: Do you think food tastes better when eaten on three-hundred-year-old porcelain?"

"No clue," Brink said, studying her, trying to gauge if she was serious. It was such a weird question, and her expression was unreadable, but he decided she was. "I've never eaten on a three-hundred-year-old plate before."

"Well, you are now, and I can assure you that it does taste better," Anne-Marie said, stabbing a tomato with her fork.

"The poison, no doubt," Jameson said, winking at Anne-Marie. "That blue is probably laced with lead."

"I started to tell you the history of porcelain, but there is another side to the story, an esoteric history if you will, one that has occupied many scholars before me. One that has a direct connection to the antiquity Jameson began to tell you about."

Brink looked up, sensing that the conversation had shifted. "How so?"

"Porcelain, as I mentioned earlier, was seen as a mysterious substance in early modern Europe. Kings coveted it for its luminosity and strength, but it was impossible to make, so impossible that the process was equated with alchemy. Indeed, it became one of the alchemists' primary pursuits. Discovering the formula to turn base metals into gold and clay into porcelain became sister quests: The secret formula for the transformation of lead into gold was the search for the Philosopher's Stone, while the formula for creating porcelain from clay was called the Arcanum.

"The man who made the first piece of European porcelain was Johann Friedrich Böttger, an alchemist and gifted chemist, who established the first European porcelain factory in Meissen, in the seventeenth century. Soon, other factories were established. As porcelain became more common, its value dropped. Yet while it was no longer as valuable as gold, its properties—it began as unrefined earth and transformed into a pure, luminous substance—remained part of the esoteric tradition. And it was a porcelain vessel that came to hold a very important secret."

"What kind of secret?" Brink asked, glancing out the window, hoping to catch a glimpse of Connie. The truck sat where he left it, but the Tesla was gone. All was quiet, and he supposed Connie had fallen asleep.

"We first learned of it from LaMoriette's letter to his son," Anne-

Marie said. "He references a text, one that contains sacred knowl-edge of ancient origins. In that text, there is a kind of code or puzzle."

"It's known as the God Puzzle," Jameson said.

"And that's where I come in," Brink said, understanding at last why Jameson was so interested in him. Jameson suspected that Jess Price had given Brink information about the puzzle, which, of course, she had. "You think I'll help you solve it."

"First we need to find it," Jameson said. "We know from La-Moriette's letter to his son how he acquired the puzzle. We know that it—along with his masterwork, the doll Violaine—was in his possession in 1909 when he died by suicide. And we know that my aunt owned Violaine until her death and that Jess Price discovered the doll in the house in 2017. But the doll disappeared, and we don't have any information at all about the puzzle—what it looks like or even what kind of code it holds. But that is what I aim to find out."

Brink met his eye, keeping his expression neutral. He was a few steps ahead of Jameson and Anne-Marie. He knew what the puzzle looked like. He saw it clearly, each number and letter in its place.

"The more I've searched for it, the more I believe that the puzzle contains a piece of sacred information, a kind of cryptogram that, when used properly, will alter the way mankind sees the past, the present, and the future. I believe my aunt had this cryptogram in her possession."

"And as Jess Price was the only person to occupy the house after Aurora's death," Brink said, "you think she has information about this puzzle."

"We know she does," Jameson said. "Ernest Raythe confirmed as much."

"He was working for you?" Brink said, feeling a surge of anger as he realized that Jess's first psychiatrist in Ray Brook had betrayed her. He remembered the hundreds of pages of files in the basement of the prison. Had Raythe shared all of that with Sedge?

"He was," Jameson said. "He gave me regular updates about her progress. Jess told him she'd found something that she described to him as 'an incomplete puzzle.'"

"But why?" Brink asked, trying to understand how a doctor could do what Raythe did. He had a moral and professional obligation to his patient. "Money?"

"Raythe and I had similar goals—to understand what really happened at Sedge House. His aim was to help Jess. He believed she was innocent and wanted her to go free. I believe he was genuinely interested in her and wanted justice. My reasons were, well, quite different, as I've begun to explain. We shared resources. Including that journal in your bag."

Brink stared at Jameson, abashed. How on earth did he know about the journal?

"Don't look so surprised," Jameson said, smirking. "Cam saw you reading it at the prison. When he described it, I knew it was the one I found at Sedge House and gave Raythe. The police took everything from the house that could be used in their investigation. But the journal had been left tucked inside Aurora's Bible, which the police didn't think to examine. I found it after the police left, read it, and gave it to Raythe after Jess's incarceration at Ray Brook."

"If you read her journal, you knew Jess found Violaine. And you knew about the hidden pantry."

"Indeed," Jameson said. "We opened up the pantry and looked inside."

"But no Violaine," Anne-Marie said. "And no puzzle."

Sedge gestured to the living room, where the leather portfolio lay on the coffee table. "The pages of LaMoriette's letter were left scattered throughout the library. They were taken as evidence by the police but returned when it was determined that they had absolutely no bearing on the case. They contain information about what happened, but the police didn't realize it."

"And they were incomplete," Anne-Marie added. "The final pages were never discovered. They may have been lost after LaMoriette's death. Or Jess may have destroyed them. We tried to get more information about them through Dr. Raythe, but Jess never revealed what had happened to them."

"If you were communicating with Raythe," Brink said, putting his messenger bag on the table and pulling out his laptop, "you've probably seen these." Fishing the flash drive from his front pocket, he inserted it, clicked into a folder, and pulled up the photos: the black-and-white images of Frankie Sedge's corpse, then the Polaroids of Noah Cooke's body. He moved them side by side on the screen and zoomed in, magnifying the patterns etched into their skin.

"Over fifty years separate these two bodies, and yet there is a striking similarity between them."

Jameson slid on a pair of glasses, leaned close to the laptop, and examined the photos. Brink sat back and watched him react. It wasn't nice, springing something like that on him, like kicking the chair out from under him and watching him struggle to find balance. Jameson's face filled with surprise, then confusion, then pain. In this succession of his emotional responses, Brink saw the man Jameson was under the hard exterior, a child feeling the pain of his father's death, a man who used money and power to mask all he had suffered, a man who glorified immortality even as he struggled to come to grips with his own past.

"Where in the hell did you get these images?" He was disturbed, his refined demeanor cracking for the first time all evening.

"I guess Dr. Raythe didn't show you everything he found," Brink said.

"*Mon Dieu,* how did Raythe even get these?" Anne-Marie asked, slipping on a pair of reading glasses and leaning close to the screen.

"He had a lot of information that nobody saw. Not even Jess's current psychiatrist knew about this file."

Jameson didn't take his eyes off the images. "I didn't know these photos of my father existed," he said, his voice quiet. "Of course, I've always wondered what happened to him, but it was never discussed. My mother was so devastated, so broken. She couldn't bear to speak of it. Ever. Eventually, I read about his death in old newspapers. But there was nothing like these photographs among anything I've seen. I never imagined his death to be so horrible."

"Raythe must have thought there was a connection to Jess, or he wouldn't have kept these in her file."

"He was right," Anne-Marie said. She sighed and pressed the laptop closed. "There is a connection. Here. Let me show you something." She placed a porcelain plate under the lights. "If you look closely, you will see that the surface of this plate is marked by a pattern of cracks. It's called crazing. Crazing lines appear as an expression of extreme or uneven pressure."

Brink stared at the pattern, astonished. It was the same as the pattern on the bodies of Frankie Sedge and Noah Cooke. The same pattern on Jess's skin. The very one he'd seen hovering over his own skin in the glass door.

Anne-Marie continued, "The words *crazing* and *crazy* have the same root, incidentally: to crack up, to lose wholeness. Crazing in porcelain, like going crazy, is the result of an internal disruption. An internal pressure that results in an explosion."

Brink remembered the autopsy report. It had given the cause of death as blunt-force trauma to the body—a fall or a car accident—but both of those scenarios were impossible. It was almost as if the trauma had been something along the lines of what Anne-Marie described: a pressure, one of great force, something from within.

"And this is related to what happened to them?" He nodded at the photos on his laptop screen. "And Jess?"

"It is all in LaMoriette's letter," Anne-Marie said. "The one he wrote to his son on the night before he died. It brings it all together: the esoteric elements of the alchemist's Arcanum, and a secret that has been passed down from generation to generation for thousands of years, one that could change the future of humanity."

"Not could," Jameson said. "It will change the future of humanity. Once we have the completed puzzle."

"Listen, Mike, we know about the drawing Jess Price made," Anne-Marie said, her voice soft, as if offering an apology. "We know that it was intriguing enough to bring you to the prison. Now that you understand what's at stake, surely you see that it's in Jess Price's best interest to help us complete the puzzle."

"As far as I can tell," Brink said, sitting back in his chair, "this thing isn't even a puzzle. It lacks a cohesive pattern that would allow for a solution. And even if I could solve it, I really don't see how it's in Jess's best interest for me to help you."

"Well," Jameson Sedge said, pulling a pistol from a holster hidden under his shirt and placing it on the table, "it is certainly in your best interest. What do you say to helping us find the answer?"

34

The gun lay on the table between them. Brink had never seen a real one up close. While Ohio was full of guns, his father didn't hunt, and his French mother found America's gun culture baffling, never allowing a firearm anywhere near her home. There was, he realized, something alluring about it—the gleam of its black metal, the rectangular grip, the perfect angle of the barrel, the finial of the magazine cap. He had to restrain himself from reaching for it.

His interest seemed to amuse Sedge. "A vintage Walther PPK semiautomatic," he said. "German made. It belonged to my father."

"It's a beauty," Brink said, feeling his stomach turn.

"I agree," Sedge said, picking it up and running a finger over a metal plate on the barrel. "I've always thought that if there was an elegant way to leave this plane of existence, it would be by the grace of my father's Walther." He turned the gun slowly on Brink. "Don't you think?"

Brink had constructed puzzles under extreme deadlines, he'd withstood the pressure of a twelve-hour pi-digit contest, he'd solved puzzles for money and prestige and for his own sanity. But never had he been threatened over one. "Guns aren't really my thing," he said. He was numb from head to toe, his limbs tingling and bloodless.

"I'm much more a die-peacefully-in-my-sleep-as-a-wrinkly-senile-hundred-and-one-year-old kind of guy."

Sedge laughed. "So, you see, Mr. Brink, we aren't so very different. We both value longevity. There's no need to die prematurely. Certainly not now. So, let's have the puzzle."

His heart was racing. He couldn't stop thinking about the gun. He didn't doubt for a second that Sedge would use it. For all he knew, Raythe had had information Sedge wanted, too. No way he was getting out of there without giving them something. But handing over Jess's drawing—which was in his messenger bag in the living room—felt like a betrayal. There was another way. "I need paper," he said flatly.

Anne-Marie stood, walked into the kitchen, and returned with a piece of paper and a pen. He took the pen in hand and drew the circle—the radials like a bursting sun, the numbers 1 to 72 at the outer ring—only altering it slightly, leaving out some of the Hebrew letters and a few of the radials. He handed the drawing to Jameson and stood, steadying himself against the table. Adrenaline rushed through him. He felt, suddenly, like he was going to be sick. Sedge holstered the pistol, picked up the drawing, and examined it with care.

Anne-Marie leaned in, studying the circle. Brink knew that they wouldn't find anything more than he had. "What does it mean?" Anne-Marie asked finally.

"It's incomplete," he said, cracking his knuckles, hoping the dull pain would help quell the anxiety coursing through him. "Unsolvable until we find the original."

"But Jess Price must know what's missing," Jameson said.

"If she does, she hasn't told me."

"Here," Anne-Marie said, bringing a Hebrew dictionary from a bookshelf and opening it on the table before Jameson. "This might help."

As Anne-Marie and Jameson tried to translate the puzzle, Brink glanced beyond, into the house. He needed to get out of there, fast, but it wouldn't be easy. The place was entirely open, every space—the living room and dining room and kitchen, even a lofted bedroom—visible. There was no way he could slip out without being noticed. There was only one place with any privacy in a house like that: the bathroom.

Anne-Marie pointed him down a hallway on the other side of the living room. Glancing out the plate-glass window at the shadowy driveway, he verified that the Tesla was gone, his truck unimpeded. His first impulse was to run out the front door, climb in his truck, and get the hell out of there. But it wouldn't take much for Sedge to stop him. One shot with his Walther would do the trick. Brink needed out, but he had to be smart about it.

He grabbed his messenger bag from the couch, and there, on the coffee table, lay the leather portfolio, exactly where Anne-Marie had left it. He knew instantly what to do. Quick, before Anne-Marie and Jameson could see, he bent over the coffee table, took the sheaf of pages from inside the portfolio, and slid them into his messenger bag. He couldn't leave without knowing what LaMoriette had discovered.

Brink locked the door to the bathroom, leaned against it, and closed his eyes. His heart was racing. He felt unable to breathe. He hadn't had a panic attack for years, not since his freshman year at MIT, but he was on the edge of one. A wave of adrenaline hit him and seeped away, then another. His chest constricted; his throat tightened. He went to the sink, ran cold water, and splashed his face, the chill bringing him back to himself. *What in the hell have I gotten myself into?* He was in way over his head. Nothing was at all what he had believed it to be.

The bathroom was enormous, with a Jacuzzi bathtub surrounded by picture windows. There was a separate steam shower enclosed in glass and a marble bust of a Roman emperor, perhaps taken from Sedge House. The air was filled with the scent of fig—a Diptyque candle burned in a corner, its light just bright enough to read. He took out his phone, pleading with the powers of technology to grant him service. But when he checked the top right corner for bars, he saw that there were none.

And yet, just as he was about to tuck the phone away in his pocket, he saw a notification for a missed call. Thessaly had left a recorded voice memo at 6:44 P.M., about three hours before, when he was in Anne-Marie's office. He turned the volume as low as possible, pressed PLAY, and listened:

> *I do not want to frighten you, but something is going on here that I cannot explain. When I returned to my office, I found that my digital access to all DOCCS files, even the internal database with my current patients, was blocked. My password was rejected, and when I called tech support, they told me that my name and employee ID were not in their system. I made them check three times before I accepted that my information had been deleted.*
>
> *That I've been locked out of the system is too much of a coincidence to be a simple computer glitch. Something out of the ordinary is happening here. Someone is slowly removing everyone who might help Jess Price. First Dr. Raythe. Then you. Now they are trying to remove me. I am beginning to see that I am in grave danger.*
>
> *I don't have proof, but I believe that the man I intercepted in the parking lot is behind this. I spoke to him for only a few minutes but got his name: Jameson Sedge. He knew a lot about you—that your access to the facility had been terminated, for example. He wanted to speak with Jess. When I told him he needed to be approved for visiting privileges, he insisted that he had already received permission. I didn't buy it— I review all prison visitors seeing my patients—and had the guards escort him to his car, which royally pissed him off. When I went back to my office and checked the visitors' log, however, his name was in fact on*

it. The man has friends in high places, it turns out, which might ex-plain how you lost your access to the prison. And why I'm now losing mine.

Nothing about this guy sat the right way with me, and so I decided to call the police department down in Columbia County, where Jess Price was arrested. I have an acquaintance in the department, and asked him if he knew anything about Jameson Sedge. He almost choked when he heard the name.

As you know, there was a media circus around Jess's arrest. There was never really a question that she was guilty—the police found her covered in Noah's blood—and the press treated her as guilty, even without evidence. But my acquaintance told me that there were other people who were questioned during the investigation, and while the police couldn't get evidence to support their inquiries, he felt that there was a solid chance that those people might have been involved in what happened at Sedge House that night. When I asked him who the prime suspects were, he said: Jameson Sedge and Dr. Anne-Marie Riccard.

He also told me that my predecessor, Dr. Raythe, had been in contact with him in 2018, the year after Jess came under his care. Apparently, Dr. Raythe came down to the Columbia County police offices and went through the case files. That is how he had the photographs I scanned, the ones on the flash drive. If you haven't had a chance to look through those files, do so right away, and you will understand why this is so disturbing.

While nothing makes sense to me right now, I know one thing for sure: We can't leave Jess Price unprotected. I'm aware that if I go home, I may not be able to return. And so I am going to speak with Jess in my office. I'll ask her what you wanted me to ask, and if she agrees to con-fide in me, which—as you know—she's never done before, I will record it and send it to you. I make no promises other than to do my best to understand who is trying to harm her. And to protect her.

Brink felt a sense of urgency shoot through him as Thessaly's voice message ended. Jameson and Anne-Marie were not merely treasure seekers hoping to find a valuable antiquity. They were much, much more involved in this than he had thought. He had to get out of there somehow.

Brink surveyed the bathroom, looking for an escape route. The picture windows near the Jacuzzi didn't open, but, near the toilet, there was one that did. It was small, but if he maneuvered the right way, it would be just big enough to squeeze through.

He unlatched the lock, opened the window, pushed out the screen, and leaned out into the night. Moonlight left a residue over the forest, fine and white as powdered sugar. He took a deep breath of fresh air. As he looked out over the darkness, the world seemed suddenly sharper, clearer. He felt imbued with a sense of purpose. It struck him that perhaps this was what he'd been missing since his accident took him off the football field—the sense that he was part of an important struggle. It was what was so gratifying about puzzles. He was in it to win but also to achieve something profoundly personal. To solve the problem and finish the puzzle. To leave the field with an absolute result. Now that he knew for certain that Jess was in danger, every decision he made had consequences.

The window faced the forest, and there was a drop of about ten feet to the ground. Checking to make sure his messenger bag was secure, he climbed up on the toilet and slid one leg, then the other, out of the window and jumped, hitting the earth lightly. He walked around the house and saw Anne-Marie and Jameson talking intensely in the kitchen. Jameson appeared to be angry, and Anne-Marie seemed to be trying to calm him down, and while he wanted to know what they were arguing about, he didn't have a minute to spare.

He pulled his key from his pocket and opened the door to his truck. He expected Connie to leap on him—she hated being locked up, and he'd been gone over two hours. But the truck was empty. Trying not to panic, he searched the floor on the passenger side. He found her plastic water dish and her chew toy, but no Connie. He turned to the forest behind the house, thinking she might have somehow gotten out. But Connie was gone. When he realized that her leash and blanket were missing, he knew that the worst had happened: Cam Putney had Conundrum.

Rage subsumed him. He wanted to go back in the house and confront Jameson, make him call his thug and tell him to bring Conundrum back. But that, he knew, would be stupid. It was exactly what they wanted—Brink irate and illogical, ready to do whatever they asked. Despite his anger, despite the growing fear at the thought of what might be happening to Connie, he needed to stay calm.

Climbing into his truck, he closed the door and took a deep breath to steady himself. As soon as he was out of there, he'd be free to figure out his next move.

He slipped his key into the ignition and turned it. Nothing. He tried again and again. Nothing. Not a revolution of the engine or a flutter of the lights. He checked the gas, which was half full, and then saw, to his horror, that the battery was dead.

35

Cam Putney watched Thessaly Moses. She began at one end of her townhouse and walked to the other, turning on lights until the place burned bright as the prison yard at night. Obviously, the woman was terrified. She'd picked up on his presence, felt him there even if she hadn't actually seen him. Her first mechanism of defense was to expose every nook and cranny to light. Interesting, he thought as the second-floor lamps popped on, how light was always equated with safety—sunlight, a campfire, a nightlight in a child's room. His daughter couldn't sleep without one until she was seven years old. But light made Cam's work easier. He saw everything with perfect clarity. The thick files Dr. Moses pulled from her bag and set on the dining room table next to a slim gold-tone MacBook Air, the same model he'd bought for his daughter when school went online during the pandemic. Light cleared away the shadows until nothing was hidden from Thessaly Moses. But nothing was hidden from Cam Putney, either.

The townhouse was part of a gated community about two miles from the prison, a collection of ten homes nestled in the dense Adirondack forest. Cam parked more than a mile away, hiding the Tesla in the trees. Brink's mutt was barking like crazy in the trunk, banging around like a pinball. It hadn't stopped for hours, and he was tempted to put it out of its misery. But Sedge wouldn't like that. He'd told him to take Brink's dog, not kill it, and Cam wasn't going to risk making him angry over something like that. Better to let it tire itself out and fall asleep.

Cam walked around the townhouse, looking for a way in. He stayed in the shadows, careful to keep out of sight of the neighbors. The last thing he needed was someone calling the police. At the back of the house, he found a window that opened onto the living room. He could see Dr. Moses at the dining room table, her laptop open. She was trying to get into the NYS government database again, but, of course, her access was denied. He'd changed the password himself, cutting her off from all information relating to her patients, including Jess Price. It had been easy to break in, to change her password and redirect everything to his own account. If her laptop was anything like her desktop, she didn't have any protection, no virus-detection software, not even a VPN. She clearly had no idea that everything she wrote, every case note, every personal email message, every social-media post, every cent she deposited in her bank account, everything was being monitored.

Suddenly, Dr. Moses stood and turned to the window. For an electrifying moment she stared at him, and he was sure she detected him behind the glass. But she turned, walked out of the room, her movements steady, without fear, and he knew she hadn't registered his presence.

Cam went to work. First he tried the window. It was locked. Then the back door. It was locked, as well, but it was a tumbler lock, one he could pick without too much trouble. He pulled out his set of bump keys and bent down before the lock. Sweat slid over his skin. He wiped it from his eyes and got to work, trying the keys quickly, quietly. The fourth one worked. The bolt clicked. He turned the knob and pushed the door open quietly, a blast of cold air sweeping over him as he stepped inside, the air-conditioning creating a chill over his damp skin. He shut the door behind him and slid inside, moved through the dining room and into the connecting living room. As he stationed himself behind a bookshelf, Dr. Moses returned to the dining room with a bottle of wine. He felt a wave of relief. She hadn't heard the door open or close. She hadn't heard him walk across the hardwood floor of the dining room. She hadn't heard a thing. She poured a glass of rosé, took a drink, and sat down before the laptop.

Standing near the bookshelf, he saw DSM-4 and DSM-5 manuals, a shelf of hardcover novels, and rows of popular self-help books, all neatly arranged. There was a photograph of an older Black couple standing in a park—Dr. Moses's parents, he guessed. Softly, without making a sound, he pushed the photo over. He didn't want to know anything about Thessaly Moses's life—not about her parents, not about her reading habits, not that she cranked the air-conditioning down to subarctic temperatures. The more he knew, the harder it would be to do what he'd come to do. And he needed this to be easy.

He pulled his Glock 43 from its holster, feeling its weight in his hand. It was warm, retaining the heat from his skin. Lifting it was like lifting a finger, his gun an extension of his body, part of him. His hand was steady when he aimed. That was one of his strengths— a rock-solid aim, an uncanny ability to hit his target in any condition, reflexes that allowed him to strike without hesitation. Yet he didn't strike. Not yet. He watched her. He wondered about her. Did she feel how trapped she was? How every way she turned, he would be there?

He slipped a finger over the safety button and aimed at the back of her head. But just as he was going to pull the trigger, she bent down and fished her phone out of her bag, slid a finger over the glass surface, and plugged the phone into her laptop.

He placed his Glock on a shelf and stepped closer, straining to see. It took him a second to realize what she was doing, but suddenly he got it: She'd manually transferred a file from her phone to the laptop. From the look of it, it was a WAV audio file, a voice recording. A shock of anxiety shot through him. He knew every corner of her online existence. He monitored her email, her social-media channels, her bank accounts. But she'd found a way around his surveillance. She created the file at the prison, saved it on her phone, and was now downloading it, keeping it free of his electronic net. He'd been away from Ray Brook for just half a day, and she'd slipped this by him.

Cam had killed before, but those jobs were quick, anonymous, and far from home. He'd killed in hotel rooms and alleyways, once in an airport bathroom, but always without personal complication. The single exception had been Dr. Ernest Raythe, a man he saw every day at the prison. Mr. Sedge didn't give him time to prepare, and it had come as a surprise. Still, when it was time to eliminate Raythe, he'd been ready.

It took a hell of a lot of creativity to make it look like an accident. It was a cold December night, a week before Christmas, one of those short gray days when the sun set at four in the afternoon. The prison parking lot was dark enough to cover him as he broke into Raythe's car—a Subaru Outback, brand-new from the smell of the interior. He hid in the back seat, hunched down low, and waited for Raythe. Snow fell thick against the glass, blanketing the windshield, so that when Raythe slid into the driver's seat, the car was a dark and enclosed capsule.

In another life, breaking into cars had been Cam's specialty. This skill bought him his first stint in juvie, at fifteen, then his first round of real jail time, at seventeen. He'd always been good at tinkering and kept a bunch of master keys on his belt, but, really, the easiest locks to crack were the electronic ones, which he could disable without damaging the car. The fancier the electronics, the easier they were to shut down. Mr. Sedge must have known this about him, known that he had a gift for assembling and disassembling systems, about his early carjacking and his jail time. It made sense. Only a criminal with a talent for solving complicated systems would fit into the Singularity picture.

But, as luck would have it, Raythe's car hadn't been locked at all. It was an unexpected gift. As was the snow: It fell wet and slushy, then froze, laying an ice glaze over the mountain roads. Raythe never suspected Cam was there. He drove slowly, methodically, into the night, too concerned about the dangers of winding country roads to suspect that a man was crouched behind him. Cam was a big guy, but he could fold into the hollow behind the driver's seat like a phantom, his breathing slow and silent, his hands folded in his lap, waiting. Years of meditation had taught him to close down his body, to regulate his breathing, to become nearly transparent.

Raythe drove on, crawling up the dark mountain, and Cam knew that it wouldn't take much, a hard quick twist of the head, one strong blow, to kill him. The faster the better. Ernest Raythe was a good doctor, dedicated to his patients in a way that Cam respected—loyalty was one of the most noble attributes, as Ume-Sensei always said. Cam lived this belief every day, sacrificing his desires for the larger mission. But Raythe's concern for his patient brought him too close to Mr. Sedge, too close to the truth, and this created a threat to the entire enterprise. No matter how it pained him, he couldn't allow Raythe to get closer.

Cam didn't enjoy violence. Some of the guys on Mr. Sedge's security team did. They bragged about the brutality of their work, relished the ability to dominate, humiliate, and destroy another human being. Over time, Sedge fired all of them, until the original group of Singularity samurais had been cut down to just one man: Cam Putney. His position gave him power, but he knew it to be a double-edged sword, as Ume-Sensei had taught him. One day he would be on the opposite side of this exchange. It was inevitable, an absolute law of the universe, that matter and energy transformed. Day to night. Strength to weakness. Life to death. One day his power would fade, and he would be at the mercy of a force stronger than himself. But that was a long time off, and he had a job to do.

Cam picked up his gun and moved deeper into the dining room, silent as a ghost. He took a breath, steadying himself, then raised the Glock. He remembered the moment he killed Ernest Raythe: the crack of his neck, the momentum of the car hurtling along the country road. He'd timed it so he could jump out of the car just before it slid down the ravine. Dr. Raythe hadn't suspected a thing until it was too late. And neither would Dr. Thessaly Moses.

36

A dead battery. Mike Brink swore under his breath, frustrated. It was not the time for his truck to malfunction, but it wasn't his fault: When Cam stole Connie, he'd left the passenger door ajar. The overhead light must've stayed on, draining the battery.

He took a deep breath and assessed the situation. The truck sat at the top of a steep driveway, surrounded by one hundred acres of thick forest. He could try to walk to the road, but it would take too long. Getting down the hill as quietly and quickly as possible was the only way.

But even if he could start the truck, its engine was old and loud and would give him away in a second. Wait, though—he didn't need to start the engine. Gravity would carry him to the bottom of the hill. Slowly, Brink released the emergency brake, depressed the clutch and took the stick shift out of gear, then eased off the pedals. The truck rolled silently down the steep driveway.

He was buzzing with anticipation as he looked down the dark, winding road. While Cam wasn't anywhere in sight, Brink had a feeling that the guy wasn't too far away, either. He could be waiting at the end of the road or even parked somewhere near the house. There was no way of knowing. He had no choice now but to move forward.

The driveway was long and twisting. He could hardly see it, but the headlights didn't work, so he made his way through the darkness, trying his best to stay on track. Finally, he reached the bottom of the hill. He popped the clutch. The engine turned over, caught, and sputtered to life.

Flicking on the headlights, he drove fast, putting as much distance as possible between himself and Jameson Sedge. As the miles passed, Brink began to relax. He rolled down the window and felt the cool night air against his skin. It was only then, as his distance from Jameson Sedge increased, that he realized how tense he'd been. For the past hours, every muscle in Brink's body had been drawn tight. He rolled his shoulders, trying to work out the tension. The scent of pine filled his senses, and his mind cleared.

Glancing at the clock in the truck's dash, he saw that it had been twenty minutes since he told Anne-Marie he was going to the bathroom. He wondered how long it had taken them to figure out he was gone. He imagined her knocking at the door, checking on him. When there was no response, they would've broken the lock and seen the open window. He imagined Jameson walking out to the driveway and finding the truck gone. Anne-Marie would open the leather portfolio, discover that Brink had taken the letter, and then all hell would break lose.

Brink reached the end of the road, turned onto a small country highway, and accelerated. He didn't know where he was headed, only that he needed to be far away. He was a good ten miles from Anne-Marie's property before he pulled to the side of the road, turned on his hazard lights, fished his phone from his pocket, and checked his reception. To his relief, he had bars. He found a text message from Thessaly that read: *It's not safe to send the audio file from my phone, and I don't trust my work computer. I can't help but feel that I'm being watched here. Going home to email it now. You were right. Jess Price is in way over her head. Check your email in half an hour.*

He typed out a text message to Thessaly Moses asking her to call her cop friend and tell him that he's right: Jameson Sedge and Anne-

Marie Riccard are involved. They'd removed evidence from the crime scene—a journal that Jess kept while she was at Sedge House—and hid evidence. Brink urged Thessaly to call the police immediately and tell them to bring Jameson and Anne-Marie in for questioning.

After he sent the text, he put his phone away and concentrated on the road. It was late, and he was in the middle of nowhere. He was tempted to pull over and read LaMoriette's letters in his truck, but it would make him a sitting target. He needed to find someplace public where he could read in peace. Stopping could put him in danger, but his need to know what was in the letters was stronger than caution. Finally, he spotted an all-night diner on the side of the road. It stood like a beacon in the darkness—an angular prefab structure from the fifties with a wall of glass that opened over rows of turquoise vinyl booths. It seemed safe enough. The place was empty and there wasn't any traffic on that road, so he pulled around to the back of the building and parked behind a dumpster. No one would see his truck there.

Inside, he chose a booth way in the back, far from the windows. He felt light-headed, his blood thrumming. He needed coffee. He flagged the waitress and ordered a cup and a slice of cherry pie. She was young, maybe twenty, with black fingernail polish and a streak of green in her hair, and from her expression he knew that he looked as bad as he felt.

After she walked away, he felt a great weight descend upon him as he realized how drastically the situation had changed in the past few hours. He'd become wrapped up in something dangerous and complicated, a game with high stakes. As if that wasn't bad enough, Connie was gone, and he had no idea how to get her back.

He reached into his pocket and felt the silver dollar, warm and smooth. Fate and chance, destiny and free will—what was at play here? He'd taken a chance and decided to meet Jess Price, only to find that it had opened a door to another puzzle, a maze that turned him round and round. For years he'd skated through life, his talents carrying him. But now all of his skills were being tested.

He waited for his coffee, staring at his hands, letting everything settle. He tried to make sense of it all. The dead men with identical markings on their bodies, and the strange pattern on Jess's arm that matched them. The God Puzzle, as Jameson had called it, and La-Moriette's letters, waiting for him to read. The Pythagorean triangle tattooed on the prison guard's neck, and the Mike Brink puzzle with his cryptographic key. He lay the pieces out before him like transparency sheets, separate layers that, when brought together, created a composite picture. They would come together to reveal something important, he knew they would, but no matter how he examined the pieces, he couldn't see what it was.

At last, the waitress brought his coffee and cherry pie. He ate quickly, glancing out the bank of windows, looking for Jameson. The guy wasn't going to let him off so easily, of that he was certain. Although the diner was remote, the black Tesla could show up at any minute. He really shouldn't have stopped, but he needed to read the letters he'd taken from the portfolio. He needed to know what Jameson and Anne-Marie were talking about; he needed to understand how it tied back to Jess Price. Maybe something in the letters would help him understand the circle Jess had drawn. Sometimes, when he was working on a puzzle that challenged him, a flash of insight would come when he least expected it, and he'd know the answer. Maybe he'd get lucky and see a solution to the God Puzzle.

He finished his coffee and felt slightly less anxious. The sugar and caffeine evened him out. The light-headedness dissipated, and he began to see his situation with some clarity. He was in danger, that was indisputable, but he was also in a position of strength. He had information Jameson and Anne-Marie wanted, and he had outmaneuvered them at every stage. He had developed a connection with Jess; he had unearthed the confidential police file from the prison's basement; he had Thessaly Moses and her contact at the police department willing to help him. But the ace in his hand was La-Moriette's letter, the document Anne-Marie claimed would tie everything together.

As it stood, he held all the cards. As the chess grandmaster Savielly Tartakower once said: *The winner is the one who makes the next-to-last mistake.* Now he just had to make sure that his mistake was not the final one. Reaching into his bag, he removed the sheaf of pages he'd taken from Anne-Marie's portfolio, LaMoriette's letters, and began to read them.

37

My dear son,

By the time you read this, I will have caused much sorrow, and for that I beg your forgiveness. As you know, my child, I am a haunted man, and while the toll has been steep, I have at last made peace with my demons. I do not write this as an excuse for what I have done. I know too well that there is no forgiveness for it—not in the eyes of God or man. But rather, I write this account of my discovery out of necessity. It is my last chance to record the incredible events, the terrible and wonderful events, that changed my life and will, if you venture into the mysteries I am about to relate, change yours, as well.

What, you ask, is responsible for such torment? I will tell you, but take heed: Once you know the truth, it is not easily forgotten. It has haunted me every minute of every day. There was no question of ignoring it. I was drawn to its mystery like a moth circling a flame—*In girum imus nocte et consumimur igni.* And while I am fortunate to have survived to record the truth, even now, as I stand on the edge of the abyss, I cannot help but shrink at the thought of entrusting such a dangerous secret to you.

I have suffered, but it is the suffering of a man who has created his own torture chamber. I believed I could know what shouldn't be known. I wanted to see things, secret things, and so I lifted the veil between the human and the Divine and stared directly into the eyes of God. That is the nature of the puzzle: to offer pain and pleasure by turns. And while the truth I am about to reveal may shock you, if it offers some small refuge of hope, then this, my last communication, will achieve all it must.

There are many places that the story of a man's downfall might begin, but I will start in the month of September 1891. You were but a small child, but you may remember that year was the year we lost your elder sister. Your mother and I had been married some sixteen years by then and had lived our share of happiness and sorrows, but nothing had tested our marriage before like the passing of Violaine. Reeling from the loss, I believed that a foreign atmosphere, and separation from the places your sister had lived and died, would offer relief.

And so I traveled to Prague to work for the master dollmaker Johan Král. Although I was not young, having just reached thirty-four years that summer, I came to Master Král eager to learn his arts. Of course, I had learned my craft many years before, under the supervision of my father, whose shop at 147 Rue Saint-Denis was a legend in Paris even then, before I inherited it and made it into the great success it is today.

But Master Král had a skill I did not possess—the art of Bohemian-crystal eyes, the like of which was unknown in Paris. His technique was quite ingenious. He created color at the center of the glass orb using a method of glassblowing that infused the iris with minuscule bubbles of air. The result was that the eyes captured and dispersed light. Indeed, when I saw one of Král's dolls in a shop in Paris, the little thing seemed to turn its gaze to follow my every movement. His dolls were mesmerizing, so life-like as to be unnerving.

And yet, while Master Král was clearly superior in the art of crystal orbs, his dolls, on the whole, were rather simple compared to mine. The shape of the limbs, and the quality of the material, the flat expressions of the faces—all of this attested to his need of me. When I learned that Master Král intended to make a full transition to porcelain doll parts, I wrote to ask for an exchange: I would help to set up his porcelain factory in exchange for the secret of his crystal eyes.

My first weeks in Prague were spent in the factory. It was stationed outside the city, in what had once been part of a mineral quarry, where lime and other natural stones were mined, refined, and ground to dust. The factory was cramped and rather dark, with clerestory windows giving on to the eastern and northern sides. We worked by gaslight, even during the day. My first act upon entering the workshop was to push my hand into a barrel of glass eyes, hundreds of perfectly cast orbs, just to feel their weight. What beauties they were! Their smooth, cold crystal surfaces knocked together; their frigid perfection chilled me.

All day long we made porcelain dolls. Král had installed a freestanding hovel oven, a kind of bottle kiln with a brick exterior shell that allowed one to stand inside the chimney, angling close to the flame when delivering and removing the porcelain. Out from the kiln the little bodies came, long-limbed and swollen with heat, like loaves from an oven. When they emerged, it was a moment of alchemy, a pure elemental reaction when fire and earth and air and water coalesced into solid form. When I lifted a doll by the leg with metal tongs and tossed it into a vat of cold water, it would hiss and spit like a viper. I would step back, quick, as if stung, watching the swirls of steam rise to the metal beams, up through a hole in the roof, and into the chill blue sky.

In my memory, Prague was always dark and gloomy, a feeling that has little to do with the quality of the light but is rather a reflection of the mind of the man I was then. My sorrow that year was immense. I had lived, until then, a rather charmed existence. Your mother was, quite simply, the love of my life, and Violaine . . . well, *Violaine*. My hand wavers as I think of her, my quick, brilliant child.

Nevertheless, I was anxious to learn from Master Král and ready to share my knowledge with him. I had brought a doll from our shop in Paris, one of the first attempts I made at using glass eyes. While the body was perfect, a gleaming porcelain with a creamy white glaze, the eyes left much to be desired. I had misaligned them, so the gaze was off, giving the bébé a frightening cross-eyed stare.

The doll was received by the master as a sign of friendship: If I was willing to display my weaknesses as a dollmaker, so might he. Master Král noted the defects but also admired the proportions of the figure, especially the luminous quality of the porcelain. Master Král put the Bébé de Paris in the front window of the doll shop, where it gazed out over the passersby, cockeyed and mad as an Aquitaine goose.

Some weeks after I had arrived in Prague, I noticed a man outside the doll shop. He was tall and thin, wearing a cap and a long black overcoat, strange attire on that warm autumn day. I wouldn't have given him a second thought had I not met him again at the market in Old Town Square. I had paid for a loaf of rye bread and was considering a ring of dried sausage when he appeared at my side, pretending to examine a stack of cabbages. He had a trimmed dark beard and large black eyes. He stared at me with a peculiar intensity, one that gave the impression that he had been looking for me and, now that he had found me, he would not let me go.

He introduced himself as Jakob and began to speak to me in Czech. My incomprehension was immediately apparent: I had learned enough Czech to buy bread at the market, but that was the extent of my abilities. I tried to communicate, and Jakob detected my accent and instantly switched to French. What a relief it was to hear my language! It had been only a few weeks since I had left Paris, and still, I felt as though I had lost a limb.

"Join me for a stein of beer," he suggested, and as I had the remainder of the day free and was intrigued to understand his intentions, I agreed.

The tavern was near the Estates Theatre, an opera hall that had hosted Mozart some hundred years before. Jakob had invited me for a beer, and while he ordered one for me, he drank tea, sweetened with a cube of sugar.

"Pardon me," he said. "I realize this is a rather strange way to approach you, but you are the dollmaker, are you not? Tell me—is that your creation that sits in the window of Mr. Král's shop?"

It flattered me that he would notice my doll. I was proud of it, even with its terribly flawed eyes. I told him that the doll was mine and that I was in Prague to learn the art of crystal.

"Your creation is a refined figure, much more so than the other dolls I have seen."

I thanked him and soon learned that Jakob was in his twenty-fourth year, Jewish, lived in a quarter north of the doll shop, and was the son of a rabbi. After this introduction, Jakob lowered his voice and said, "Do you believe that one has a purpose in life?"

"Of course," I said, without hesitation. "How would one survive without one?"

"And your purpose?"

The question was one that had been much on my mind since losing Violaine. Her death had thrown off the balance of the universe. Evil seemed to vastly outweigh good, and I had often wondered why I should continue. If one such as Violaine, a child of sensitivity and intelligence, could be taken so unjustly, what kind of world could this be?

"To create beauty," I said at last. "When all the horrors of life have revealed themselves, it is beauty that God sends to comfort us."

This brought a smile to Jakob's face. "We have been waiting for you, Mr. LaMoriette. For many years, we have waited."

"Who has waited?" I asked, still confused by his intentions.

"We will invite you to our home soon."

I finished my beer and turned to signal for the barmaid. When I looked back to his chair, it was empty. A stack of coins sat on the table and Jakob was hurrying down the cobblestone street, his black hat distinct in the crowd.

38

It was around early October that a mystery arose at the doll shop. I arrived one afternoon and found that the doll I had made was no longer in the window. Believing someone had moved it, I searched the shelves, pushing aside wooden puppets, rag dolls, bisque-headed babies, looking for my porcelain Bébé de Paris. Král was at the counter, assisting a customer. When he was free, I asked after the doll. Master Král was perplexed. No one had purchased it, he said. Indeed, he would never sell it, as he treasured the gift. But when we searched the shelves together, my first assessment was correct: The doll was gone.

Not long after, Jakob approached me again. It was a Saturday afternoon at the end of October, and I had just returned from an afternoon at the kiln. Jakob waited outside the doll shop, standing in the shadows, much as he had the day of our first encounter. This time he invited me to his home for dinner. I accepted. I was hungry and had nothing to eat in my room, but even more enticing than food was the chance to learn more about the *quartier* of his birth. And, of course, there was the allure of my native tongue. Speaking to Jakob in French acted as a tonic, soothing my spirits when I longed for Paris and giving me the illusion that nothing—not homesickness or loss—was insurmountable.

We walked through the narrow streets, night falling. As we crossed the river, I found houses with freshly chopped firewood stacked outside doorways, the smell of smoke lingering. Fifteen minutes we walked and soon came to the town hall, a large, elegant structure with a mansard roof supporting a high tower. There was something of the buildings of Paris in its shape, Baroque, the tower carved from stone like a chess piece.

Jakob led me to his family home straightaway, an unadorned house on a square across from an imposing structure that rose into the purpling sky: the Old-New Synagogue. Jakob explained that this was the temple where his father presided as rabbi. And while I was curious to hear more, there wasn't a moment to ask. We were surrounded at once by a crowd of children—his brothers and sisters, seven or eight girls and boys. We walked into a home filled with the scent of a stew cooking, a violin being played in a room beyond, and the low sounds of a language I could not comprehend. In my ignorance, I had interpreted Jakob's fluency in French as a cultural affinity. I had believed that we shared customs, that we had similar ideas about the world, perhaps even the same rituals at the table. But the moment we stepped into his home, I understood that I knew nothing at all about him.

Jakob's father, the Rabbi Josefez, greeted me as I removed my coat. I couldn't understand him, of course, and Jakob translated, as he would every time his father spoke to me.

"My father welcomes you," Jakob said. "He is honored to have such an artist here with us."

I was flattered but surprised that he would know my work. There were no examples of it in Prague other than my missing Bébé de Paris, and I hadn't spoken of it to Jakob, other than to explain my purpose in working with Master Král. Seeing my consternation, Jakob said, "It was my father who saw your golem in the window of the doll shop. He asked me to inquire about its maker. It was he who understood your talents. It was he who chose you."

Golem. It was the first time I had heard the word, and I knew nothing at all about its meaning. I might have asked him to explain, but I could hardly get my bearings. Jakob had promised dinner, but there was no talk of this. He led me through a hallway and to a darkened room, where the rabbi gestured for me to take a seat at a table and then sat across from me. Before I had a chance to get comfortable, a knock came at the door. A group of four men entered. They removed their overcoats and their hats and joined us at the table. Jakob introduced the men as friends. As they sat, they greeted Jakob warmly, calling him Bocher, which, Jakob whispered to me, denoted a young man who studied the Talmud.

Soon, the men began to talk. They never addressed me directly, never asked Jakob to translate their words, and in that fashion I remained ignorant of the precise details of their discussion. And yet I felt, as they glanced at me, their keen interest in my presence.

Eventually, Jakob's mother arrived and served dinner—the stew I had smelled upon entering. We ate in silence and, when we finished, the rabbi put on a wool overcoat and bid the others good night. He gestured for me and Jakob to follow him into the chill autumn air. The night was clear, the moon was large in the sky, illuminating the peaked roof of the synagogue and, beyond, the spires of the town hall, a spattering of spikes against the night sky. At the temple, the rabbi pulled a key from his pocket and opened the door.

Once inside, Jakob lit a candle and gave it to me, then lit another for himself, and together we walked through a narrow hallway, up a set of steps into a loft that overlooked the space below. At Saint-Sulpice, where I had been baptized, this would have been a choir loft. But there in the synagogue I found no organ, no piping, nothing that signified a musical purpose. Jakob lit more candles, until the space glowed with light. The rabbi took one and walked to a large wooden armoire in the corner of the room, lifted his ring of keys, and opened it.

You cannot imagine, my child, how startled I was to see a foot appear in the candlelight. As the light expanded, a leg emerged, then a thick torso. Astonished, I found myself examining the creature with trepidation. What on earth could it be? Jakob helped his father, and together they removed a kind of mannequin from the armoire.

I saw that, while it had been cast in human form, it was larger than a man, a kind of giant at least two heads taller than Jakob, who was, in my estimation, tall. They carried the creature to the center of the room and placed it gently on the floor so that it lay on its back, bathed in candlelight. It was damaged, even crumbling in places—an arm had deteriorated, and the head and torso had been fractured.

Finally, the rabbi spoke, gesturing from the mannequin to me.

"My father would like to ask if you will repair our golem," Jakob said.

The figure lying before me was in a terrible state. As I ran my hand over the chest cavity, the clay crumbled. "It is very fragile," I said. "I daresay you should not have moved it from the armoire."

"It was made by my father's ancestor, the Rabbi Loew of the male line of David," Jakob said. "He shaped it from the dust of this synagogue."

I looked about the synagogue, at the stonework, wondering what on earth he meant. A figure of that size would require five kilos of clay, at least. "When did the Rabbi Loew fashion it?"

"The golem came into existence some three hundred years ago."

My first reaction was amazement—it was absurd that clay, even baked and protected from the elements, could endure two decades, let alone thirty.

"Look, here." I touched the right hand, where three of the fingers were missing. "Even this relatively simple repair would not hold. The hand would break if I tried to remold the fingers. I would have to recast the entire arm, the entire torso, the legs and head. I would need to remake it entirely from new clay."

As Jakob explained to his father what I had said, I looked more carefully at what they called the golem. Its face was rough-hewn, the limbs were thick, the torso square, and the eyes and nose were blocky, as if cut with a knife.

"The golem is a simple creature," Jakob said, seeing my interest. "Its sole reason for existence is to serve and protect. It has no intelligence, but its strength is immense. For three centuries, my family has cared for it as best we could. But we cannot do that any longer. It is disintegrating."

The rabbi gestured to his son, and Jakob went to a wooden trunk nearby.

"Come, there is something we must show you," Jakob said. I walked to the trunk and saw my Bébé de Paris lying inside. The glass eyes, which had always been misaligned, took on a sinister cast. I started at the realization that Jakob, my new friend, had stolen the doll.

Before I could demand an explanation, the rabbi opened a folio and removed a sheet of vellum. It was very old, yellow with age, and—at the center of the page—I saw a large, elaborate circle with many numbers and symbols.

"This is the true name of the Creator, HaShem, our most precious secret," Jakob whispered. "It has been passed from father to son for thousands of years. There have been those who learned the secret of the Name before they were ready, and these men have suffered grave consequences. But do not fear. You are protected. You come to this knowledge by invitation, and out of necessity."

The rabbi spoke to his son, and Jakob turned to me. "My father asks if you are here willingly, and if you assent to witness what we are about to show you?"

Despite my confusion, I didn't hesitate. I wanted to understand the secret to which Jakob had referred. I affirmed that I was there of my own free will and begged the rabbi to continue.

"Stay by my side," Jakob whispered. "No matter what happens, do not speak."

There was little opportunity to react. The rabbi began the ritual immediately, reading something from his text, chanting words that I could not understand. Jakob gripped my arm, holding me still or, perhaps, using me to steady himself. He had a most terrible look in his eyes, one that did little to calm my own sense of disquiet. Five times around the golem, six times, the rabbi walked. After the seventh circle, the rabbi stopped. He bent over the creature and touched its forehead.

The next seconds swelled, slowed, filled with a tension that pressed through me. And then, in that close stillness, the creature awoke. The eyes fluttered open and, for ten seconds, perhaps twenty, I watched as the doll twitched to life.

But just as the force swelled, it overwhelmed the creature. It began to move about in a most terrifying manner, its eyes shifting around the room in a crazed fashion. The rabbi put a hand over the doll's face, spoke the words again, and life left the doll.

"You see," Jakob said. "Porcelain is a hard, luminous substance, like light made solid. The Creator's powers are expressed through light. The golem withstood the force of life. It did not break. Your work is suited to our purposes, my friend."

I stared at all of this, astonished, too terrified to speak and yet too fascinated to run.

"We can make the golem live," Jakob said. "But we need a strong shell. A better shell. One made of porcelain."

The rabbi met my eye, and I understood at last what they wanted of me.

39

I worked in secret. It wasn't hard to do. Master Král rarely supervised his artisans now that I had come—he trusted my eye, he said, better than his own—and so I knew when the men would be working and when they were away. I went to the kiln late at night, when the others were long gone, or on Sunday morning, when they were sleeping off their liquor or asking redemption in church. Thus I worked without interference, using kaolin and fire to experiment with my golem.

The rabbi wanted me to engineer a porcelain body that could move with ease, that was strong and light and durable. I did not for a second believe my attempts would succeed or that it would actually walk. And yet some part of me fell into the fantasy that I was creating a real child. Like Geppetto fashioning his wooden boy, I imagined a little being that would go off into the world of its own volition, carrying the artistry of my labors—its beautiful little nose and perfect chin—with it.

My father once told me that the creation of a porcelain bébé is much more than making a toy. It is more, even, than an artistic endeavor, although much art is involved. The children who adopt our creations, he said, love them with the tenderness of a parent. They memorize the shape of the baby's ear, the color of the eyes, the precise weight of the body. They learn to love and to protect it. In that regard, the dollmaker's art is the foundation of what makes one human. And I kept this in mind as I created this figure, crafting it with such tenderness that it could only be loved.

My instructions had been specific in every regard, but the exact features of the creature were mine to design. I began with sketches of the figure I would make, working out the mechanics of the hinged joints, the contours of the face, and the placement of the cavity that would hold the scroll of paper. The limbs, I decided, should be jointed. I made them with springs, adding a system that cushioned the porcelain, protecting it from the shocks of movement, and made its ankles and wrists twist on greased screws. I decided to use soft leather for the torso, attaching the doll parts with a cord inside the shell. It allowed great flexibility and strength, much like tendons. This method, I was certain, would be of use to me in the future, and indeed, it was one of the methods I patented upon my return to Paris and has been of great value over the years.

Every element of the process had to be reinvented. I made new molds. I created a new way to attach the limbs and neck to the torso: a ball-and-socket design that allowed for even more strength and mobility, an innovation I also went on to patent. The springs at the knees and elbows would give the creature flexibility, and Master Král's extraordinary crystal eyes would give it a mesmerizing stare.

The engineering of so delicate a machine pushed me to such extremes that there were times, in the months I worked, that I doubted my capabilities. Nothing like it had been fashioned before, and I made many, many errors along the way. But pride in my work pushed me onward, the same sense of pride I felt when my Bébé de Paris had been placed in the window of Master Král's shop and the passersby would stop to gaze at the gleaming, heavenly luminosity of the porcelain. I felt an artist's pride, a blazing, buoyant pride, the pride of the creator for his creation, one that, I see now, after all that has happened, utterly blinded me.

For what man but a blind one would create a figure in the image of his dead child? Violaine left us when you were but five years old, my son, but you have seen the portrait of her hanging in the drawing room. It is true to her likeness and captures her startling auburn hair and clever green eyes so well that I would often feel that she was still with us when I passed by. She was fifteen when we lost her, but I still saw her as she had been as a child, playing with the dolls she'd selected from the shop on the Rue Saint-Denis. Violaine was a wonderfully willful and stubborn girl with her own set of peculiarities. She did not like ice cream, for example, or any cold sensation—not ice, not snow, not even a marble floor under her bare feet—a fact that amused your mother and me to no end but that left me, after we placed Violaine into the cold crypt at Père Lachaise, so desperate that I could not sleep for a week. *She must be so cold,* I would think, *so very cold, my poor child, so dreadfully cold in that tomb.*

There were a hundred small details that personified her singular personality—freckles on her cheeks, and eyes of a pellucid green, and thin, delicate lips—and while they had left the world with her death, I could bring them back in porcelain. I cast and recast, until one day she materialized. I laid the clay figure out on a stone slab, its small pale body like a child on a pyre, and I pushed it into the fire. I fastened the door to the kiln and stepped away, my heart beating in my chest, and when I pulled the pallet from the flames, I found a creature too perfect to be real. She glowed with an intemperate heat, a throbbing, pulsing force that I dared to compare to the power of the sun. With her body afire, and her vacant eyes hollowed in a ghastly stare, she seemed like some ancient totem heaved up from an abyss. How noble my Violaine was! How radiant! How the heat clung to the slick porcelain, the matte white blazing orange, explosions of color flickering over surfaces like water sliding over wax! Watching the figure cool, the shocks of the heat receding and the skin hardening to a glossy, nacreous white, I knew what I had made was good. In that moment of joy, I felt that I had paid tribute, however humbly, to my lost child.

On the eve of the new year, I developed a fever. The chill conditions of the factory and the months of grueling work had left me weak, I suppose, and I fell ill. I didn't leave my apartment for many days, not even for food. Fever consumed me, and I became lost in the land between waking and dreaming. I saw Violaine as she had been only the year before, in the warmth of a spring afternoon, the sun on her skin, how she smiled with pleasure as she ate *tarte au fraises* under the cherry tree behind our home. It was a sweet torture to remember her, and it made the reality of her death all the more terrible.

She'd been on an excursion outside the city with a friend when she died. She had not come home on time, and I'd been up waiting all night, sick with worry. When at last the bell rang at the door and your mother led the gendarme inside, I knew Violaine was dead. Still, I greeted him civilly. I took him out to the terrace, as if fresh air might dilute his message. His brass buttons gleamed in the early-morning light, and, aware of the gravity of his news, he took his kepi in his hand and held it over his chest in deference. It was his job, and he performed it with dignity, relating the news with the sensitivity of a doctor pronouncing a terminal illness. I heard him say what had happened—*an accident, sir*—but I didn't fully understand it. It seemed a kind of nonsense, his words, too far outside the realm of possibility to be true. *A bend in the road. A simple moment of inattention. A terrible tragedy.*

How could a moment of inattention undo so much? I understood the facts well enough: The horses had startled; the driver lost control. As fate would have it, there was a pond below the road, and their carriage overturned into it. The condition of the carriage suggested Violaine would have been grievously injured, even if they hadn't hit the water. Her friend's neck had broken, and later reports from the village doctor confirmed that she would have died had she not drowned. But when they pulled Violaine from the pond, they found that while her legs had been crushed, she died by drowning.

After Violaine's death, I understood the nature of despair. It colored every hour of every day with a somber hue. But with time I came to understand that it is not despair that governs the world and certainly not despair that keeps one alive. It is, rather, love—the love I feel for you, my son, the love I felt for Violaine, the love I felt as I fashioned the golem in her image. Love such as that allows one to endure any sadness.

40

While I had been instructed to bring the golem to the rabbi upon its completion, it was many months before I returned to the Jewish Quarter. I delayed by making her perfect in every way. I spent a small fortune to purchase hair from a wigmaker in the Old Town, the most expensive in their collection: lustrous auburn tresses that fell to the doll's waist. I ordered clothes to be made by a seamstress—a luxurious silk dress in pink that matched the party dress Violaine had worn the night she died. Not just one layer of silk but five, so that they opened around her legs like the petals of a flower.

But by the end of April, I could wait no longer. I packed the golem into a leather case, placed it in a small wagon from the workshop, and transported it through the Old Town to the Jewish Quarter. I walked slowly, resistance in my step. Every bump on the cobblestone, every jostling of a child running by, filled me with the urge to turn back. I was obligated to give up Violaine, this I knew, but with each step, I felt how wrong it was to part with her. I had come to think of her as mine, although I certainly had no justification in doing so.

More than six months had passed since I had last been to the Jewish Quarter, and it had changed considerably in that time. Flowers grew in boxes at the windows and the streets were filled with children playing. I knocked at the rabbi's door and Jakob opened it, looking me over, his eyes bright with excitement.

"Come, come inside and join us," Jakob said. His gaze settled on the wagon. "We are sitting down for dinner."

I stepped into their home, pulling the wagon after me. All was just as it had been in the autumn, with the sound of a violin and the scent of a meal cooking, but a profound alienation had come over me. When Jakob tried to take my coat, I stepped away. When his mother offered me tea, I refused it. Instead of feeling welcomed, as I had before, I felt threatened.

Jakob was surprised to see this change, but he did not push me to explain, and I could not have justified my behavior even if I tried. How could I express my regret at our bargain? How could I tell him that I felt like a father giving up his own child? I knew my obligations, and I had every intention to fulfill them, but it pained me.

The rabbi entered the room and greeted me. His beard had grown longer in the months since I had last met him. I could see, from how he looked at me, he noticed the changes in me, as well.

"I have finished your commission," I said, allowing Jakob to translate for us. I took the case from the wagon and placed it on a table between us. "You will be pleased. It represents the very height of my abilities and, forgive me for my arrogance, it is perfect."

"One does not require perfection in a golem," the rabbi said. "Only strength and durability."

"Please," I said, feeling my cheeks flush with emotion. "Might I show you the extraordinary creature I have made?"

The rabbi stared at me, his expression unreadable. He gestured to his hat, and his son brought it to him. "Come," he said, and led us out of the house and into the square. Carrying the case in my arms, I brought it into the synagogue and up to the loft. The rabbi gestured to his son, who lit candles around the case. In the weak guttering light, I opened it.

Violaine lay in a bed of wooden shavings, cushioned like a bird's egg in a nest, her green glass eyes fixed upward. The creamy porcelain of her skin reflected the glow of the candles; her lustrous auburn hair spilled over her shoulders. I recalled the hideous golem I had seen in that same loft, with its crumbling clay hand. The difference between my creature and the Rabbi Loew's golem was extreme: one dull and rough and decaying; the other as beautiful as a real child. But the rabbi and Jakob did not react as I expected. For a full minute they stared at Violaine, and then they launched into what I surmised to be a discussion of the creature, their words quick and incomprehensible.

Jakob turned to me. "We are surprised to find that the golem is female," he said, his eyes questioning.

"You did not specify the sex," I said, realizing all at once how far my beautiful golem was from their expectations. They had wanted a porcelain shell; I had given them a masterpiece. "But I assure you, it is as strong, as durable, and as capable a figure as any I could make." I proceeded to show them the jointed limbs, the movable head, and the hidden compartment at the base of the neck. All the while, the rabbi said nothing. Finally, he spoke to his son, then gestured for him to translate.

"It is good, my father says," Jakob said, relieved. "Very good. The spirit could live here in this creature. We accept the work you have done and thank you for your efforts."

I thanked them in return and, the strength of my feelings threatening to tip my equilibrium, turned to leave.

"But wait," Jakob said. "My father has one last request, Monsieur LaMoriette."

"What more do you require?" I said, my pride mixing with sorrow. "I have given you my best work. It is as bright and brilliant as the sun."

"What good is the sun if you have never seen it shine?"

If I had been a less prideful man, a less curious man, I would have turned my back then and walked away. But I wanted to understand the secrets of the rabbi's circle. I wanted to lift the veil between the human and the Divine and see the miracle of creation. I wanted to see life burn in my Violaine. And so, to my everlasting regret, I stayed.

41

Mike Brink turned the last page of the letter over. There was nothing more. Clearly it didn't end there. But where were the remaining pages?

Pushing the letter away, he blinked and looked around, taking in the empty diner, the turquoise vinyl booths, his reflection wavering over the black glass of the window. Everything felt strange and distorted. The air was too hot, the lights too bright, the caffeine rushing through him too intense. He took a deep breath and flexed his fingers, balling them into a fist, feeling the need to squeeze until his knuckles turned white. LaMoriette's letter lay before him, a solid sheaf of pages filled with the writings of a man haunted by his past. The man had experienced something profoundly disturbing in Prague, something of such force that his life revolved around it, circling and circling.

Brink slid the pages into the front pocket of his messenger bag and zipped it closed. He couldn't stop thinking of the rabbi's circle, the circular representation of the name HaShem the rabbi used to awaken the golem. From its description, he was certain it was the same circle Jess Price had asked him to solve, the same circle Anne-Marie called the God Puzzle, the very circle Jameson Sedge had described as a priceless treasure.

But while those connections were clear, Brink was no closer to solving the puzzle itself than he was at the moment he saw it. He tried to understand what it had to do with Anne-Marie's Arcanum or, for that matter, Jameson's "undiscovered country." What did the letter of a bereft man in Prague, written so long ago, have to do with Jess Price? And what in the hell did any of it have to do with him? Anne-Marie had promised that LaMoriette's letter would bring everything together. And yet, even after Brink read it, the letter only served to present him with more questions.

He pulled out his phone, asked the waitress for the Wi-Fi password, and noticed that he didn't have much in the way of power. The battery was nearly dead, and his charger was in the truck, with the rest of his stuff. He switched into low-power mode and checked his email. There were two messages: one from Thessaly Moses, with a heavy attachment—clearly the audio file she'd promised to send. The second message was from Vivek Gupta, his mentor and friend, with a link to his encrypted app. He opened the link and read:

My dear boy, I must admit, the adventure you've fallen into is causing me to lose sleep. That Jameson Sedge is after this puzzle would've been enough to intrigue me, but I have examined the configuration you sent and have discovered something of great interest. I must warn you again to be careful. What you've uncovered is unique, much coveted, and dangerous for many reasons, not only because Sedge wants it. You must know by now that you have a singular gift, and this gift draws you into situations that most of us would never experience. Extraordinary people attract extraordinary events, both good and bad. You must protect yourself. Throw away your devices, as they most certainly have been compromised. Don't try to contact me. I will find you.

Below his message, there was a link to a blog connected to the *Adirondack Daily Enterprise.* Dr. Gupta's message had been sent five minutes before, at 11:03 P.M. Brink opened the link and read the

blog post's headline: BREAKING: PROMINENT RAY BROOK PSYCHIA-
TRIST ATTACKED, HOSPITALIZED.

He only needed to read the first line to realize that the article was about Dr. Thessaly Moses. She'd been attacked at her home, and while the article didn't give him much information—not the extent of her injuries or if the person responsible had been apprehended—it was exactly as Jess Price had warned them. Someone had been wait-ing and watching. Thessaly had been hurt and, if that person hadn't been caught, Jess was in danger.

He turned to Thessaly Moses's message. It had arrived at 9:47 P.M., meaning she must have sent it just before she was attacked. The mes-sage was empty, an audio file attached at the bottom. He down-loaded it but decided to wait to play it. He couldn't risk that it might be overheard, even by the waitress, so he dropped cash next to the check, grabbed his bag, and left the diner. There was nowhere as safe as his truck.

As he walked out into the night, he checked his watch. It was 11:09. The parking lot was still empty, the road beyond barren of traffic, and he paused, his antennae going up. Something wasn't right. He scanned the parking lot, with its cracked pavement and vacant parking spots, feeling that someone was there, waiting in the shad-ows. For years, Vivek Gupta had urged him to shield himself from observation, but he'd dismissed it as paranoia. Now, though, after his experiences at the prison and Thessaly's attack, he understood how right Vivek Gupta had been.

The night was still, the low shriek of cicadas filling the air. And despite the urgency he felt to get to the truck, he couldn't help but admire the wild disharmony of the creatures. There had been cicadas near his childhood home in Ohio, and their singing had always filled him with melancholy. On a warm summer evening, his father de-scribed the cicada's perplexing life cycle, how one might live for years as a nymph underground, only to climb to the surface for a few days or weeks, find a mate, lay eggs, and die. Such a brief existence seemed to demonstrate the futility of life, but who was to say that longevity mattered in the scheme of things? He thought of Sedge's mad search for immortality, his refusal to accept the boundaries of life and death. But the singing was the important thing, whether it lasted one day or one hundred.

His truck waited in the shadows. He got in and locked the doors. There was not a soul in the parking lot, and yet he was wary, so he started the engine, quick, pulled out of the parking lot. Surveying the road, he searched for signs. He needed to think clearly. He needed to make the right choices. But he had no clue where the hell he was. He'd driven haphazardly, following small twisting roads, losing himself in the tangle of rolling hills, steered by his emotions more than any definite sense of direction. He could use his GPS if he had any sense of a destination.

He couldn't help but feel that he should've foreseen what happened to Thessaly. Jess warned him that they were in danger, had told them that Dr. Raythe's death was not an accident. Thessaly's attack was no coincidence. Raythe had died after he started digging up information about Jess, and Thessaly had picked up where Raythe left off. Surely Brink could have done something more to prevent it.

But even as he blamed himself for deserting Thessaly, he reminded himself that she'd insisted he leave the prison. She escorted him to his truck. She told him she'd be in touch when she needed him. There was no arguing with her. What happened wasn't his fault, and it wasn't her fault. Neither of them could have known how serious this was, or how dangerous. Something Anne-Marie had said came to mind: *You should understand the magnitude of what you're getting involved in.*

He was beginning to see that magnitude. The attack on Thessaly changed everything. The stakes were higher now, the consequences deadly. Whatever stories he'd been able to tell himself before—that there was a logical explanation for his dismissal from the prison; that he wasn't in real danger—were gone for good. They were playing a game of life and death, and the danger was real.

He wanted to drive directly to Ray Brook, but that wouldn't do anyone any good. They weren't going to let him back in the prison, and the Ray Brook hospital would be the first place Jameson Sedge would look for him. He was a target as much as Thessaly was. He remembered something Dr. Raythe had written in his report: *There must be very powerful people behind this.* Jameson Sedge was one of those people. A gut instinct told him that Sedge was behind the attack on Thessaly, and his instincts about people like that were rarely wrong. Vivek Gupta was right—under that polished exterior, there was something fanatical about Jameson, something ruthless. Jameson had admitted to being on a quest for esoteric knowledge and that his aunt had discovered something essential to human consciousness. But how far would the man go to acquire it?

He remembered the last thing Jess had said to him: *Remember your promise.* But how in the hell could he keep a promise he'd made in a dream? He didn't understand what she needed him to do. Solve the God Puzzle, that much he understood, but what then? But could an ancient religious text do anything to clear her name? Could a wild tale about religious secrets and arcane rituals have any concrete value? Jameson Sedge clearly thought so, and Anne-Marie did, too. But Brink wasn't so sure. He felt close to the limit of his ability. His genius ran deep but narrow. With the right elements and the right clues, he could do extraordinary things. But what Jess was asking pushed him to the edge of his imagination, and the ability to imagine a solution, he knew, was the trick to finding one.

He turned off the road, parked on the shoulder, and typed his password into his phone. Dr. Gupta had warned him that his phone might be compromised, that someone could use it to track him, but he needed it to hear Jess's message. The audio file opened in the darkness, illuminating the screen. He hoped the phone had enough power remaining to get through it. As he pressed PLAY, he felt a rush of anticipation and dread: Soon, in a matter of seconds, he would hear Jess's voice again. And while he longed to know what she had to tell him, he was terrified of what it would mean.

42

Mike Brink started the recording. He heard the scratch of the microphone, then Thessaly Moses's voice filled the truck.

Mike Brink thinks you have something to tell him. I don't know if that's the case or not, but I agreed to give you the opportunity to record a message for him. I will make sure he gets it.

There were a few seconds of silence, the buzz of the air conditioner in the background, a shuffling as Thessaly spoke again.

I know you're concerned about being overheard. There's no surveillance camera here. This is a private office.

Silence. Thessaly tried again.

I know this is difficult for you, Jess, but there isn't an alternative. Mike Brink may be in danger. If there's anything you can tell him, anything at all, you need to do it now.

There was a tapping near the phone's microphone, and he imagined Jess hitting the coffee table with the tips of her scabbed fingers.

He felt her fragility and her intensity, her manic energy welling up behind the recording.

Would you prefer that I leave? This door locks.

Brink heard the clang of a set of keys being lifted.

I have the key here. I'm the only one with access. If you need me, just knock. I'll be waiting in the hall.

There was the sound of high heels, the whoosh of the door opening, and the firm click as it closed. The bolt locked into place, and Jess was alone.

Brink imagined Thessaly's immaculate office, with its organized binders, its jar of colored pens, the solved Rubik's Cube in the corner of her desk. He imagined the prison at nightfall, the prisoners in their dormitory. He imagined Jess leaning over the table, preparing to speak. He felt her draw close as she lifted the microphone to her lips:

Michael, if this makes it to you, there may still be a chance.

Something about the way she said his name, and the intimacy of her tone, nearly stopped him cold. He took a deep breath and gripped the steering wheel, his heart beating hard.

I wasn't able to tell you before. I tried, I really tried, to give you as much information as possible, but it was like tapping bits of Morse code through a wire: There was always more meaning under every signal, always so much more that I wanted to say. I knew they were watching us, and I couldn't risk speaking, but I felt, somehow, that you understood. Do you feel it, too, our telepathy? How a look means more than words? I don't think I'm wrong that there is something between us, some extraordinary connection that allows us to understand things no

*one else could. I knew the moment we met that you could help me piece
together what happened. Forgive me. I know I've sent you blindfolded
into a maze, one that has you turning in circles, but you might be the
only person who can solve this. Now that it's started, it's impossible to
go back. We must navigate the maze together. So, while I have the
chance, I will send you in the right direction. Listen, and I will tell you
everything as clearly as I can.*

Brink heard Jess stand, heard the sound of her moving to the door,
checking the lock, then returning to her seat and pulling the recorder
close.

*I remember only fragments of that night. I remember that Noah
showed up on his motorcycle with take-out Chinese and a bottle of cold
white wine, and his presence at Sedge House made every strange thing
that had happened seem, suddenly, inconsequential. If I had insisted,
we could have left right away. I could have jumped on the back of his
motorcycle and gone back to the city. But Noah was hungry and had
driven over two hours to see the house and, of course, spend time with
me. We cleared a spot on the dining room table and ate, drank wine,
and talked. We made love on the Turkish carpet in the library and
were happy in a way neither of us would ever be again.*

*When Noah saw Aurora's dolls, he was fascinated. He was a sculp-
tor, and he must have recognized the craftsmanship in Aurora's collection, because he studied them for a long time. I told him the story of
LaMoriette as Anne-Marie had told it to me, told him what Mandy
had said, and even told him about the odd things that had happened
since I'd arrived, insisting that I must have imagined them. He demanded that I show him everything, and so I brought Violaine down
to the library, then took him to see the secret door in the pantry. Like
kids on a treasure hunt, we took the portfolio from its hiding place and
opened it up. I felt the thrill of reading the dollmaker LaMoriette's letter, the excitement of discovering a hidden treasure.*

Noah examined Violaine with care and found a small compartment at the back of her head. Using the tip of a kitchen knife, he opened it. Inside was the circular puzzle, written out on a tiny piece of paper. Although LaMoriette had mentioned it in his letter to his son, it was the first time I had seen anything like it. It was a strange and beautiful circle filled with numbers and symbols, intricate, drawn with great care. It intrigued me, and I examined it for a long time, trying to understand what it might be.

We went into the library, lit some candles, and studied the circle together. Noah had gone to Hebrew school as a child and explained that the four symbols were Hebrew: Yvd, Hay, Vav, Hay. The name of God. And despite the warning in LaMoriette's letter—or maybe because of it—Noah and I attempted to pronounce it.

It was just a game for us, like kids playing with a Ouija board or performing a séance. Noah stood in the center of the room and read it in a playful, dramatic soliloquy. With candlelight dancing through the darkening mansion and the hot July night gathering outside the windows, it all seemed a kind of dare: How far would we go? What could stop us?

Nothing, I thought. Nothing could stop us.

The next thing I remember is waking up. Time had passed. The candles had burned low, the flames guttering in wax. I know now that I blacked out, but at the time it felt like I was underwater, swimming up to the surface, impeded by the weight of a heavy dark sea. I tried to sit, but everything buckled under me. When I finally had the strength to stand, the room appeared unfamiliar. The library was in chaos, the shelves disemboweled, books strewn everywhere, an armchair overturned, the wineglasses broken. It took a moment to grasp that I was at Sedge House, and I didn't remember that Noah had come at all. And then I saw him.

He lay on his back, splayed on the parquet floor, his blood eating the edge of the Turkish carpet like coffee at a sugar cookie. There was a terrible heaviness in the air, the scent of blood, the sensation that something unspeakable had happened. I remember thinking that it couldn't be real, none of it could possibly have actually happened, and yet some-

*thing had happened, something so powerful and destructive that it left
me as changed as a tree after a lightning storm, burned and deformed
by what I had attracted.*

*Of everything I remember of that night, Noah's face is what I see
most clearly—his blue eyes frozen open, as if staring at something just
beyond his vision. The color had drained from his cheeks, leaving him
gray-yellow. Shock and fear, despair and helplessness overcame me. For
a moment I believed I could go back and change what I'd done. But of
course, I couldn't go back. I knew nothing would ever be the same
again.*

*I tried to make sense of Noah's death, but the world had broken
apart. I have spent the past years putting the pieces together. And while
I haven't fully succeeded, what I know now, from the timeline presented at the trial, was that I called 911 at 1:14 A.M. The paramedics
arrived thirteen minutes later, the police following close behind. Noah
was declared dead at 1:33 A.M., and I was taken into custody. There
was nothing I could do or say to explain what had happened—it terrified me to the very core of my being—and so I remained silent.*

*But what was not presented at the trial, and what I have never
told anyone, was that there was someone else at Sedge House that
night. A woman dressed entirely in red. She slipped silently into the library, fiery and beautiful, and wiped the blood from my hands and the
tears from my cheeks. She'd come to comfort me, she said. To save me.
She told me she wouldn't leave me alone. She told me to take the final
pages of LaMoriette's letter—the ones with the information about the
circle and the ritual—and hide them with the doll. "We will return for
them when it's safe," she said, and in my terrified state of mind, I
trusted her. Together, we hid Violaine and the letter in the leather case,
sealing them away, and everything felt different suddenly, as if I'd
captured a genie in a bottle. And in some ways, I had: The storm was
contained. At least momentarily.*

*Then I hid the case. Not in the secret pantry—Mandy knew how to
open it, and I couldn't risk that she would tell someone—but someplace
else, a place where nobody would find it. A hidden place. We would*

come to get it later, I thought; the woman in red would help me under-
stand what I was meant to do.

Of course, that ended up being impossible. I should've known that
they would lock me up. But now you can do what I can't. To find the
case, you must venture into the undergrowth to search for what is hid-
den. You will need to be brief and make some changes along the way,
but if you look down into the depths of darkness, you will find it: Dela-
ware, 16; Maryland, 24; Virginia, 1; Illinois, 8; Arkansas, 4. Virginia
and Arkansas get a blue ribbon. The others, red.

With that, the audio recording ended.

Brink felt an ominous weight in his chest, a familiar need overtak-
ing him. Jess had constructed a riddle, one that would direct him to
the hidden case.

Delaware, 16; Maryland, 24; Virginia, 1; Illinois, 8; Arkansas, 4.

Part of him wished he could ignore it. Going deeper into this
couldn't lead to anything good. But Brink had no choice. His mind
fell upon the riddle, isolating the clues, angling around them, examining each word and number for information he could pick free. He
couldn't have stopped himself from solving it even if he'd wanted to.
Jess had known that about him. She knew he wouldn't be able to
break free. *Now that it's started, it's impossible to go back. We must nav-*
igate the maze together.

He started the engine, put the truck in gear and drove. Ahead,
there was a railroad crossing. Brink slowed the truck as the gates
lowered. Red lights flashed through the darkness, streaking the road
crimson. Glancing behind him, he saw that the road was empty. And
yet he felt something lingering, something watching, a presence just
out of sight. It was the same eerie feeling he'd experienced in the
parking lot: someone or something coming closer.

Brink took his phone and scrolled back through the audio file and
pushed PLAY: *You must venture into the undergrowth to search for what*
is hidden. . . . Delaware, 16; Maryland, 24; Virginia, 1; Illinois, 8; Ar-
kansas, 4. Virginia and Arkansas get a blue ribbon. The others, red.

He put his head to the steering wheel, letting Jess's voice wash over him. A terrible longing came over him. He couldn't explain it, but the sound of her voice brought him back to the song of the cicadas. His time with Jess had been limited, and they'd had only a few brief moments together, but she made him feel alive.

Venture into the undergrowth. Sedge was a forest plant, a part of the undergrowth. *Look down into the depths of darkness.* Jess had hidden something and she wanted him to find it. Brink did a U-turn and drove in the direction of Sedge House.

43

As Brink drove up the winding gravel road and approached the dark house beyond, it seemed eerily familiar. He'd never actually set foot on the property, but he recognized the turrets and gables, the rosette windows. What had Jess called it? *A great Gothic wedding cake.* The description matched what he saw: the perfect perch of the mansion over the river, its wraparound porch, with its curls of white trim. While it was the middle of the night and he couldn't see much of the grounds, he noticed the rose garden, with its rows of trellised roses, all perfectly maintained. Jameson kept a gardener, Anne-Marie mentioned, but it didn't appear that anyone lived in the house. He glanced at a bay window and, for a moment, imagined Jess standing behind the dusty pane, her pale skin stark against the dark glass.

Jess had given him a series of clues, but he couldn't solve her puzzle until he got inside the house. *Venture into the undergrowth.* But how would he get in? Surely Jameson had security cameras or, at the very least, an alarm. The guy was a security fanatic, according to Dr. Gupta. And yet, as he walked around Sedge House, he saw no cameras, and there were no automatic lights, no guard dogs. Nothing.

The doors were locked, as were the ground-floor windows, but as he walked around the house, looking for possible points of entry, he remembered something from Jess Price's journal. Mandy had come into

the house through the basement door. He found it at the back of the
house. It, too, was locked, but the door was old, the wood softened
with age. He dug out his pocketknife, opened the screwdriver, jammed
it between the soft wood and the strike plate, and pried the lock apart.

The basement was damp, dark, and smelled of mildew. He fumbled for his phone and turned on the flashlight function. The bright
white light cut through the darkness, opening a path through a
pinched space, passing over walls of shelving and an enormous early-
twentieth-century furnace, big as an octopus, its copper pipes snak-
ing out in every direction. At last, he found a narrow wooden stairwell
that took him up to the first floor, emerging near the butler's pantry
Jess had described. He walked through the corridor, turning the
flashlight over a grand staircase, with its peacock carved into the
newel post, jeweled eye glittering. The darkness was deep and vast,
and he felt his way through it as though through a cavern. He could
have turned on all the lights—Sedge House sat far from the road,
and there wasn't another house in sight—but he couldn't risk it. He
was there to solve Jess Price's riddle, get what he'd come for, and get
out of there as soon as possible.

Still, he lingered a moment before the stairwell. What an eerie
sensation, being in a space he'd only imagined. His flashlight fell
over the crystal chandelier in the dining room, over heavy damask
curtains, and stopped at the framed photographs of the Sedge family.
Aurora and Frankie emerged from the darkness, staring from the
sepia prints, Aurora thin and birdlike, her brother tall and jovial, a
smile on his face, unaware of the terrible events to come.

He made his way down the hallway to a set of pocket doors that
opened to the parlor. Moonlight streamed through dusty windows,
falling over the furniture. For a moment, the room seemed like something from an archaeological dig, an ancient structure salvaged from a
natural disaster, ash and sediment on every surface. He recalled that
Jess had felt that she was trespassing on Aurora's property, and now he
felt that his presence might alter the clues Jess had left behind.

He went to the center of the room and lifted a sheet, exposing a velvet sofa. A row of baby dolls sat side by side, glass eyes gleaming in the light. He didn't believe in spirits or hauntings or that these dolls were anything more than abandoned antiques. And yet, as he passed the dolls, he felt a shiver of unease. He picked one up, feeling its weight, noting its luminous eyes. There was a logical explanation for what happened that night, of this he was certain. Some combination of elements—a dark, empty mansion, alcohol, and a writer's overactive imagination—had conspired to create the circumstances Jess had experienced. He tossed the doll back on the sofa. It was a toy, nothing more, nothing less.

Jess hadn't known what she was getting into when she came to Sedge House. She got caught up in something that had nothing to do with her and suffered terrible consequences: a burgeoning career destroyed, the trauma of Noah's death, years of imprisonment. She'd been led into it and cornered. It made him furious, and the strength of his feelings reminded him how emotionally involved he'd become with Jess and what had happened to her. This was no longer about solving the puzzle. It was about a connection to a woman whose story had begun to take over his life.

He sat on the edge of the couch. Pushing aside a doll, he took his notebook from his pocket and wrote down the series of clues Jess had given in the audio file:

Delaware, 16; Maryland, 24; Virginia, 1; Illinois, 8; Arkansas, 4.

What had Jess said? You will need to be brief and make some changes along the way, but if you look down into the depths of darkness, you will find it.

Be brief. Shorten the words. He wrote down the abbreviated forms of the states:

DE, MD, VA, IL, AR.

He studied the ten letters, trying to see if they might be an anagram. But no matter how he arranged the letters, they didn't add up to anything. He wrote down the numbers next to the letters:

DE, 16
MD, 24
VA, 1
IL, 8
AR, 4

Make some changes along the way. What kind of changes did he need to make? He was studying the numbers when it struck him: substitutions. He needed to swap out some of the letters and replace them. The numbers next to the abbreviations told him how to do it. *Virginia and Arkansas get a blue ribbon.* A blue ribbon was first place. VA and AR were first-place substitutions. *The others, red:* second-letter substitutions. He wrote the 26 letters of the alphabet out in his notebook.

A B C D E F G H I J K L M N O P Q R S T U V W X Y Z

Brink counted 16 letters past the letter E, stopping at U. He crossed off E and substituted it with U, getting the first syllable: DU. He did the same with MD, counting 24 letters past D, and got B, creating the syllable MB. DUMB. It took less than thirty seconds for him to work out the solution: DUMBWAITER.

Jess had hidden the case in the dumbwaiter.

Brink bounded up the stairs to the third floor and found the door to the dumbwaiter. He recognized it at once from Jess's description. There was a panel cut into the doorframe with two small Bakelite buttons. His first guess was that the case was inside the carriage, but when he worked open the door, he found only empty space. He pushed one of the Bakelite buttons. The engine began to thrum, but the carriage didn't arrive. He pushed the other button and heard the motor churn again, but again the carriage didn't appear. The thing wasn't broken; it was jammed.

He was beginning to wonder if he'd made the right substitutions. As Jameson had pointed out, there couldn't have been much time to hide anything. She would've had to have the presence of mind to pack Violaine into her case and find a secure place to stash it—someplace that she could return to later, as she had said—between the time she called 911 and when the police arrived. She would have been severely traumatized by the violence of Noah's death, and yet those were calculated, levelheaded actions.

He was about to head back downstairs when he remembered the clue: *Look down into the depths of darkness and you will find it.* Look down. He went back to the shaft but looking down the dumbwaiter revealed nothing but a void. He must be missing something. He was contemplating what that might be when he remembered that Jess had found Violaine in the attic. There was another floor. Maybe if he went up to the attic and looked down into the dumbwaiter shaft, he would find the case.

Moving through the hallway, he examined the floral wallpaper with his flashlight, trying to find the hidden door. At last, he found it and, prying it open, climbed the steps into the darkness. He swung the flashlight around the space, sending light through a latticework of cobwebs. The air was cloying, oxygen-less, spinning with galaxies of dust motes.

The door to the dumbwaiter hung open. Brink walked across the room and looked inside. It took all of ten seconds to verify that the pulleys had been jammed—there was a pen stuck into the mechanism. Pointing his flashlight down, he saw, in the depths of the shaft, lying on the top of the carriage, a leather suitcase. Jess had dropped it down the shaft and jammed a pen in the pulley to ensure no one could discover it. He worked the pen out of the winch, then pressed a button. The carriage jolted and lifted, rising slowly, slowly, as it brought Brink the suitcase, with its treasure locked inside.

44

He'd just arrived at the bottom of the staircase when the creak of a floorboard startled him. Suddenly the room filled with a blinding light, and Brink found himself face-to-face with Jameson Sedge. The man looked from Brink to the leather suitcase and back to Brink, astonished. Jameson was used to predicting every move of the game, and Brink had surprised him.

"Well done," Jameson said. "Well done."

Brink took a step back, assessing him. If it were just the two of them, he could overpower Sedge in a second. But he knew the PPK pistol was there, hidden under his coat, and he was no match for that.

"You've certainly had a busy night," Jameson said. "I was considering joining you for coffee at the diner—the cherry pie looked scrumptious—but you seemed so utterly engrossed in what you were reading that I couldn't bring myself to disturb you."

"Thanks for the tact," Brink said, trying to control his anger. He'd known he was being followed—he'd felt Sedge lingering the whole time—and he'd allowed himself to be caught.

"No thanks needed, Mr. Brink," Jameson said, glancing down at the case. "You've done more than enough already. I do have a question, however. Where was it?"

Brink considered his options. There were three: He could talk his way out, stay and fight, or run. Talking was a good place to begin. "In the attic. I'm surprised that you didn't find it."

"Ah, the attic," he said, shaking his head. "When I was allowed back into the house after the investigation, I went through every room, every closet, every corner of this house, including the attic. The case wasn't there. I concluded she had destroyed it."

"Clearly not the case," he said.

"Clearly not," Jameson repeated, reaching for the suitcase.

Brink took another step back, evading Jameson. He needed to get out of there. His window of opportunity was closing. "Why don't you tell me what really happened to Jess."

"Nobody fully knows what happened that night. Or what happened to my father, for that matter. But it's time that we do."

As Jameson lunged for the case, Brink shoved him, turned, and ran through the corridor, throwing himself down the steps to the basement. The door hung open, giving him a clear path to the lawn. Running with everything he had, the suitcase cradled like a football in his arm, with the faintest echo of cheerleaders and chanting and feet stomping on bleachers in his mind, he sprinted across the moonlit lawn to his truck.

Brink was half a mile away when Anne-Marie's BMW appeared behind him. Pushing the truck as fast it would go, he kept his lead for a minute or two, but his truck was no match. Jameson was soon there, racing at his side until, in one quick sweep, he passed the truck and cut him off.

He swerved, slammed on the brakes, and the truck flipped. Everything revolved, each rotation bringing an explosion of glass and metal. While the whole thing couldn't have lasted more than a second or two, time seemed to stretch, elongating into a blur of movement. A succession of lights burst behind his eyes, and he saw, standing at the edge of his vision, a woman made of light. She was there, just beyond, watching, a being of pure energy, her eyes burning, her hair wild with flames. As she reached for him, he felt an overwhelming desire to give himself over to her, to fall into the flames and burn with her.

When he regained consciousness, he hung upside down, pinned in place by the seatbelt. A drop of blood fell from a cut above his eye onto the ceiling of the cab. While his first reaction was to struggle, it was impossible to move. He was trapped in his beloved old truck, his head throbbing with pain. Even without seeing the full extent of the damage, he knew it was a total annihilation, one that he couldn't salvage. The same was true of his position: Even if he pulled himself out of the truck, even if he wasn't badly injured, he didn't have a chance in hell of escaping. There was nothing but endless forest as far as he could see. He had nowhere to hide.

Cam Putney's boots appeared through the cracked glass of the windshield, and beyond, parked behind the BMW, sat the black Tesla. Brink reached for the suitcase—it had been flung to the ceiling of the cab—and grabbed it, but it was pointless: Cam opened the door and pulled it from his grasp. Then, with a click of the seatbelt and a firm grip on his T-shirt, Putney lifted Brink out into the cool night air.

It hurt to stand. He leaned against his wrecked truck, dizzy. There was a burning sensation above his left eyebrow and, when he touched his cheek, blood streaked his fingers. Brink looked at the shattered windshield and felt something break inside, some point of balance between the man he'd been and the one he'd become. There was no going back now.

Just then he heard a familiar whimper. Across the road, Cam pulled Conundrum from the trunk of the Tesla by the leash, dangling her by the throat. Connie kicked and struggled, her whimpers growing desperate as she gasped for air. Brink ran to her, impervious to the pain he'd felt a second before, but just as he reached for his dog, Cam dodged him. Rage exploded through Brink, leaving him trembling. Cam could do what he wanted to him, but he was going to leave Connie alone.

Brink went after Cam, ready to fight, but before he had the chance, Jameson snapped his fingers. "Let the dog go, Mr. Putney." Cam stopped, dropped the leash, and walked away.

Brink scooped Connie up, feeling her tremble in his arms. "Don't you ever, ever touch my dog again," he said.

"I'm beginning to see that you're not as easy as I thought you'd be," Jameson said, giving Brink a steely look. "That is a compliment."

"Always nice to feel appreciated," Brink said, wiping blood from his eyes. "But you're fucking insane."

"Let's not argue, Mr. Brink," Jameson said. "It won't lead anywhere productive. And there is more, much more, to do. Come." Jameson laid a cold hand on his arm. "Let's see what's inside this case."

45

Back at Sedge House, Cam escorted Brink through the mansion. Connie had stopped shivering by then, but she eyed Cam warily, her large brown eyes assessing his every move. Their destination was an octagonal room filled with bookshelves, with a large attorney's desk at the center, a fireplace with green glass tiles, and an overstuffed armchair. The library was just as Jess had described. Even the books she'd admired—the hundreds of leather-bound books—remained as they had been years before.

Jameson entered the room and walked to the desk. "The room was cleaned after the body was taken away, and the Turkish carpet was not salvageable and was thrown out, but everything else is just as Jess Price left it."

He lifted the suitcase and placed it on the desk.

"During the investigation, the house was torn apart. Every room was dusted for fingerprints, every chair overturned, every carpet lifted. If Jess Price had left the case in the open or even in a conventional hiding place, it would have been found and confiscated. Everything would have been lost."

Jameson slipped a thumb under a brass buckle and pushed a leather strap up, unfastening it.

"I cannot tell you the number of times I've tried to imagine what happened here that night. It seems fanciful, I realize, but I've held on to the notion that I might find something the police missed, a message or a clue to guide me to this suitcase. I was certain that my aunt's precious Violaine was here somewhere. As it turns out, I was entirely right. She was here all along."

Jameson opened the second buckle, easing up a second leather strap and slipping it out, then paused to look around the library.

"This room was where Ms. Price intended to write her next masterpiece. The police combed the library during the investigation. They confiscated her laptop computer, her books and papers, but there is one thing they overlooked." He walked around the desk, opened a drawer, and pulled out a stack of magazines. "If they had looked through these more carefully, they might have wanted to speak with you long ago. Go ahead, Mr. Brink, take a look."

He saw stacks of old magazines and newspapers, and while his first impression was that they were nothing special, as he shuffled through them, he saw that they were filled with his puzzles. There was a copy of his first puzzle book, *Brink's Brain Busters,* a spiral-bound collection of crosswords and geometric puzzles, the puzzles he'd published in *The New York Times* and *The New Yorker* and, to his amazement, an essay he'd written in 2010 at MIT. It was the only personal writing he'd ever published, an essay in *The Tech,* the MIT student paper. In it, he described his struggles with a traumatic brain injury, how frightened he'd been in the months that followed the accident, and how patterns, puzzles, riddles, and mathematical games had saved him from severe depression. He read a line he'd written in the essay: *Losing myself in patterns and puzzles offered me a way to move forward with my life and freed me from the fear and uncertainty of unreliable perceptions about the world and other people.*

What he hadn't written in that essay, and what he'd never articulated to anyone, was how close to suicide he had been before coming to understand his gift. Learning about sudden acquired savant syndrome, and knowing that others lived happy and meaningful lives, had been the turning point. Having a name for what he was experiencing helped him accept his new reality. And while dark moods could creep up on him at any moment, puzzles kept him steady. He needed them the way some people needed medication. And, as with medication, his tolerance had grown over the years. He needed ever-more-challenging problems, harder puzzles, more-difficult and obscure challenges.

He looked up to find Jameson studying him. "Jess was collecting my puzzles?" he asked, confused.

"They didn't belong to Jess Price," he said, reaching into the desk drawer and removing the M puzzle—the very same number puzzle Jess had written out for him in the prison, the one that contained his cryptographic key—and laying it on the desktop. "They belong to me."

Brink stared at Sedge, abashed as he realized the truth: Jess hadn't solved the M puzzle. Jameson had.

"After my aunt died, I used the library from time to time. Security at Singularity is strong, but one never knows who might be watching. Sedge House has never had internet service, no cable television, no phone lines. Being here is a black box for any kind of digital surveillance. Especially the kind that Gary Sand specializes in. Or your friend Vivek Gupta, for that matter."

"How did you know about M?" Brink asked.

"I've been in cryptography since before you were born," Jameson said. "And I had a good tip. Gary Sand is first-rate. Despite his loyalty to the NSA, he's been working with me for a long time. Your skills caught my attention right away. In fact, I initially hoped to hire you. You could have been an enormous asset to us. But things went in a different direction. Obviously."

Brink glanced at the puzzle on the desk, recognizing the structure and the solutions. Jess must have found Jameson's stash of information about Brink, studied M's puzzle, and, after her imprisonment, decided to find him herself. It all made sense. Jameson Sedge was the thread that connected everything.

Jameson turned to the leather case and opened it. Inside, wrapped in a cloth, lay a porcelain doll with large green eyes and alabaster skin. Brink recognized it at once as Violaine, the doll Jess had described and he'd read about in LaMoriette's letter. Jameson turned the doll over, pushed aside her long auburn hair, and pried open a compartment at the back of her neck. Using the tip of his fingernail, he worked a tiny scroll free, his hand trembling with excitement, perhaps terror.

"This is it," Jameson said, his voice filled with wonder and triumph. "The key to it all."

Jameson pressed the scroll open on the table. Brink saw an elaborate circle modeled after the sun, tongues of fire surrounding the circumference; between these flames were numbers, 1 through 72, giving it the appearance of an esoteric roulette wheel. He saw the pieces of the puzzle Jess Price had remembered—the position of the numbers and the triangles. But this puzzle was far more complex. The most notable difference, aside from the Hebrew letters, was a circle of small black and white squares at the outer edge, one that instantly drew his eye. There was a pattern there, he could feel it.

"This is Abulafia's Variations on the Name of God," Jameson said, interrupting his thoughts.

Brink felt an itch to understand the pattern of the numbers and letters, its strange and beautiful symmetry. The circle Jess had drawn was merely a framework. She had remembered the numbers around the perimeter and a few of the symbols, but her drawing had been, for the most part, a blank slate. This circle, however, was complete. Its symmetry was beautiful, the radial of numbers elegant and alluring. He desperately wanted to take it away from there and study it, dissect it, solve it.

From the look of it, however, it wouldn't be so easily cracked. It had been designed for a very specific solver—someone who knew Hebrew and had a solid grasp of mathematics and number games—and perhaps had a kind of ancient cryptographic key. Opening the door to this puzzle wouldn't be as easy as saying open sesame. But then, from everything he'd learned about the God Puzzle, it wasn't meant to be.

While the scroll absorbed Jameson's attention, Brink turned back to the suitcase. Jess had said that she'd hidden the final pages of La-Moriette's letter in the case with Violaine. Yet as he scanned the interior of the case, Brink didn't see anything else inside. He angled to one side of the case, then the other, searching. Finally, he saw it. There, peeking from the silk lining, was a corner of paper. It had been well hidden, pushed so deep into the lining he wouldn't have noticed it at all if Jess hadn't told him to look for it.

Jameson returned the scroll to the cavity and turned back to the case just as the room began to tremble. A low, steady vibration rattled the windowpanes, drawing Jameson to leave the desk and go to the window. He pushed away the heavy damask curtains to reveal a great metal insect hovering in the night sky. The vibration turned to a rhythmic whirring of a blade as the Eurocopter landed. Anne-Marie jumped out of the cockpit and walked toward the house, her hair blowing in the wind.

"As you see," Jameson said, throwing open the window and waving, "Anne-Marie has many talents."

But so did Mike Brink. With Jameson's attention diverted, he slipped his hand into the leather case, worked open the silk lining, and pulled the hidden pages of LaMoriette's letter free.

46

Mike wasn't an aggressive guy. He'd been in a total of two fights his entire life, one of them in elementary school. As the starting quarterback of his team, he never risked hurting his arm by throwing a punch, so he'd learned to resolve conflict with humor. But as Cam Putney escorted him across the lawn, he felt a visceral need to level the guy.

As they approached Anne-Marie, Cam gave him a final shove. "That is quite enough, Cam," she said, her voice uncharacteristically sharp, and Brink realized that she thought the cut above his eye was Cam's doing. He didn't disabuse her but gave a weak half smile as she looked him over, taking in the extent of the damage. Her brow furrowed with worry. "I'm so sorry, Mike," she said. "Really, I didn't think things would end up this way."

"They still don't have to," he said, wondering how someone like Anne-Marie, a scholar and professor, could have become so entangled with a man like Jameson Sedge. Obviously, his initial impressions of her were wrong. How many art historians could pilot a helicopter? "You don't have to be part of Jameson's insanity."

She gave him a long look, and he thought he saw some glimmer of sadness in her eyes.

"When I told you about our work, I believed you would understand the importance of what we're doing. I thought you would see that we are close, *this close,* to a monumental discovery. It was a risk, of course. I couldn't know if you would help us or not. I could only wager that you were the type of man who would trade safety for knowledge. For truth." Anne-Marie's gaze floated to the wound above his eye, and Brink realized he was as mangled and beaten as he felt. "And I was right. You are that kind of man. We've discovered something that will change the very nature of existence. You are a part of it now. But I need you to trust us."

He touched the cut on his brow, feeling the sting. A headache had begun to bloom behind his eyes, lush and sinister. "Forgive me if I'm finding it hard to trust anyone at the moment."

Anne-Marie stepped closer and put a hand on his arm. "It is every scholar's dream to discover a thread that ties knowledge of the past to the discoveries of the future. To see that there is a knot that connects it all together makes one feel that there's purpose in being here. What you've just found does that. That circle could be the point where a theoretical possibility becomes real, the point where past and future meet. Perhaps you don't see it now, but soon you will: Now that we have the God Puzzle, nothing will be the same again."

Brink stared at her, taking it all in. While part of him wanted to reject Anne-Marie out of hand, he couldn't deny that he was curious and that his curiosity made him want to know more. Jameson had told him that he was searching for immortality, but Brink couldn't imagine that a tiny piece of paper hidden in an old house could overcome the limits of human biology.

Jameson approached the helicopter, the suitcase in his hand. "Did you make the call?"

"Our guide is standing by," Anne-Marie said, climbing into the pilot's seat. "He'll be ready for us when we get there."

"Wonderful," Jameson said, giving Brink a triumphant smile as he climbed into the helicopter and buckled himself in. "Let's go change the world."

Brink buckled his belt and settled Connie in his lap. As the Euro-copter lifted into the air, Connie pressed her nose against the glass, watching while Anne-Marie maneuvered over the Hudson River, rising above the treetops and into the dark sky. Soon, the landscape opened below, a shadowy expanse of forests and country roads, the occasional pair of headlights dotting the gloom.

Brink glanced from Cam to Jameson Sedge, trying to imagine what they planned to do. He wondered if Jameson had seen his sleight of hand in the library. He was the type of man who might know what Brink was up to but would wait for the ideal moment to let on. Case in point: Jameson had known he was at the diner, had probably parked outside and watched him reading LaMoriette's let-ter, even knew he'd ordered cherry pie, but he bided his time, waiting for the right moment. That, Brink supposed, was the real power Jameson wielded: the ability to give his prey just enough liberty to imagine they were free.

But he wasn't free. He understood the danger he was in. He knew they could be taking him anywhere and that he was powerless to stop them. But he still had one card up his sleeve, or, rather, in his pocket. Sliding his hand inside his sports jacket, he felt the envelope. He had the final pages of LaMoriette's letter.

As he leaned back into his seat, exhaustion overwhelmed him. He was running on two sleepless nights. His muscles were heavy; his eyes burned with fatigue. Within minutes, the gentle jostling of the helicopter rocked him to sleep.

Jess was waiting for him on the other side of consciousness. She grabbed him by the hand and led him through a dark, narrow hall-way lined with doors. "You have the key," she said, and it was true: He felt in his pocket and there it was, the antique key. He unlocked the door and walked into a dingy hotel room with heavy wooden furniture, a threadbare carpet over terra-cotta tiles, vintage wallpaper peeling away in curls. French windows overlooked a European city at night. Gray clouds smudged the black sky. Rooftops angled into the distance. A candle burned on the bedside table, casting light and shadow over a large bed.

They undressed and fell upon each other. If he was hungry for her, she was starving. He slid onto the bed and pushed away the sheets, desperate for the few moments he would have with her. He knew that he was sleeping, that he could wake at any minute, and he'd have no way to find her again. The seconds slipped away, each one a blade slicing them apart.

Jess must have felt it, too, the urgency, the need to be together before the dream ended. She tied his hands, then his feet, to the bedposts, cinching his limbs so tight they burned. Cold air poured through the window, chilling the room, but Jess was impossibly warm as she slid over him, her touch light as oil on his skin. She kissed his fingers, his toes, his navel. She became absorbed in her own pleasure, and this made him want her all the more.

When she untied him, they lay together, tangled in the sheets. He ran a finger over her neck, her shoulders, her breasts, losing himself in her beauty. This, whatever it was—a hallucination, an illusion, a miracle—was wondrous, saturated with meaning.

Jess got out of bed, slipped into a kimono, and poured a glass of wine from a bottle and drank. "Listen, I need to tell you what really happened," she said, turning her gaze out the window and over the endless rooftops. "It's not what you think."

He propped himself up in bed and pulled the sheets up. Without her, he felt bloodless, cold as marble. "You mean to Noah Cooke?"

"You think I'm responsible, but it wasn't my fault. It was a mistake. It's as simple as that. The whole thing was a big, stupid mistake."

He stared at her, trying to understand. Was this a confession? An apology? If she'd killed Noah Cooke, did it matter where they were?

Jess came to the bed and offered him the glass of wine. He took a drink, tasting blackberries and pomegranate, a vein of minerality. When he looked up, the room was gone and they sat on a balcony overlooking a vast desert. The sky was a deep oceanic blue, so intense that he had to turn his gaze away. In the distance, at the very edge of his vision, a pyramid baked under the sun, ten dots pulsing at the edges.

"Your turn," Jess said, gesturing to a board on the table between them.

Red and black squares formed a checkerboard. He tried to count the rows of squares, but nothing added up. Jess was winning. She had stacks of pieces she'd taken, and he had none. He knew the rules of the game—they were easy—but it seemed utterly impossible. He didn't know how to move the pieces. He didn't know how to win. He couldn't see the point.

"Hello?" she said, looking at him impatiently. A swarm of hummingbirds had collected around her, hovering. "Are we playing or what?"

As he looked over the board, an overwhelming sense of relief washed through him. The checkerboard was just a checkerboard. There was no three-dimensional pattern, no stream of mathematical equations, no geometric folding. The squares were just simple fields of black and red, nothing more, nothing less. For the first time in years, his mind was free of puzzles, and Mike Brink was the man he used to be.

47

Mike Brink woke as the helicopter touched down, the residue of his dream leaving him reeling. He stretched, still half asleep, and looked out the window to find himself on a heliport overlooking Manhattan's East River. The sun had begun to rise, casting a pale light over the skyscrapers, leaving the surface of the river awash in orange and yellow. Its brilliance was almost blinding. The hard gray of Manhattan's buildings seemed softer, warmer in that light, and he felt a rush of relief to be back in the city. It had been only two days since he'd left, yet it seemed to him that he had lived another lifetime. The city felt different. He felt different. He'd become entangled in something much deeper, more intense, and, he couldn't help but admit, more exciting than anything he'd ever experienced before.

He touched his jacket, feeling for the envelope to make sure Jameson hadn't searched him while he slept. He felt it under the fabric, filled with the promise of answers, and he had to control his impulse to take it out and read it then and there.

Brink hopped out of the helicopter, Connie close at his heels. Wind from the propellers sliced through his jacket, and a shiver of vertigo hit him as he stepped onto solid earth. He was running on fumes. He needed water. He needed food and sleep. Whatever lay ahead would require concentration, and right then, as he walked across the pier and took in the brightening colors of the sky, he felt cloudy as hell.

A black Cadillac SUV waited at the end of the pier. Cam got into the passenger seat and gave the driver an address, while Jameson sat with Anne-Marie and Brink in the back. Connie huddled between his feet, resting her nose on his shoes. If nothing else, he needed to get Connie back home, fed, and out of danger.

As they pulled away from the pier, Brink lowered the window. The early-morning streets had a clean, just-washed scent, as if scoured by a downpour. There was no traffic at all, not a single car on Pearl Street. The stillness was a balm. With the throbbing in his head, and the anxiety he felt about where Sedge might be taking him, he relished the quiet city streets, their serenity. He never tired of the city—no place on earth quite matched the Rube Goldberg machine of his mind like Manhattan—but just then he needed a moment to get himself together.

They glided past buildings, under the Brooklyn Bridge, and onto Bowery in a matter of minutes. At a light, he saw an iPhone billboard stamped with Chinese characters and realized they were only a few blocks from his apartment.

"If we're meeting someone," he said, pointing to his T-shirt, which was covered in blood, "I'll need to stop home and shower. Or change my clothes, at the very least."

Jameson eyed Brink, clearly suspicious.

"And it will be a hell of a lot easier if I leave Connie at my place," he added.

Anne-Marie glanced at Connie with disdain, then at Sedge. "That's an excellent idea," she said.

Sedge told the driver to pull over near Canal and Bowery, confirming that he knew a lot more about Mike Brink than he'd originally let on, including where he lived. When they'd stopped, Jameson lifted Brink's messenger bag from his hands. "I'll hold on to this," he said. "And Cam will accompany you."

He felt a twinge of panic at leaving his bag with Jameson, but there was nothing in there Jameson wanted: He'd already read Jess's journal. The envelope with LaMoriette's letter was the most important thing, and that was safe inside the pocket of his jacket.

Brink climbed the familiar steps of his building, following Connie. He took a deep breath, welcoming the scent of rat poison and laundry detergent. He loved his loft, loved being five flights up, high above the street. He loved looking over his small corner of Chinatown—the flashing signs in Chinese, the spice shops, and the dim sum places. But most of all, he loved his puzzle collection. He didn't want Cam—or anyone, for that matter—near it.

At the door, he punched a code into a pad—his Social Security number and date of birth in sequence and rearranged into a series of ascending numbers, a more or less impossible code to crack. Quick, before Cam could follow, he picked up Connie, slipped into his apartment, and slammed the door shut. A barrage of pounding and yelling ensued, which only made his homecoming more delicious. *Take that, asshole,* he thought, as he dropped Connie into her fleece-lined bed and walked to the center of his apartment. Standing in his loft, he felt all the tension of the past two days ease. There, in that moment, he was safe.

He glanced at his collection, the stacks of puzzle books, his Japanese puzzle boxes, and felt an urge to get lost in their comforts. Collecting puzzles had been a constant for Brink after the accident. He sought them out, bought them without reserve, and never threw one away. Now he had a couple of thousand, many of them rare and collectible—including the first crossword book ever published, Simon & Schuster's *The Cross Word Puzzle Book.* He also owned a rare 1858 Sam Loyd Trick Donkey puzzle, bought at auction for a small fortune. There were the puzzle books—crosswords and sudoku and word finds and mazes; a few vintage 15 puzzles; card tables covered with five-thousand-piece color-gradient Ravensburger Krypts; and a wall of Rubik's Cubes, some old, some new, the colors all in perfect alignment. Fifty or so lacquered Japanese puzzle boxes—his great passion—perched on various surfaces, glistening and unreadable.

While his place appeared chaotic, there was a clear and definite order to his collection. In fact, the wild experiences of the past days allowed him to see it all the more clearly: He was a man with an insatiable need to bring order to chaos.

He filled Connie's water and food bowls, then opened the window to the fire escape. His downstairs neighbor—and older man named Dennis, a lifelong bachelor—loved Connie and took care of her when Brink was away. During the pandemic, Connie would get multiple walks a day between Dennis and Brink. Connie knew to go down the fire escape, scratch at the window, and Dennis would let her in. Brink was relieved to know that Conundrum would be taken care of, no matter what happened.

He slipped out of his dirty clothes, splashed water on his face, and changed into a clean pair of black jeans and a black T-shirt that said I AM TRIMTAB, swag from an event he'd done at the Buckminster Fuller Institute. Then he sat on the edge of a windowsill and removed the envelope from his jacket pocket.

Opening the pages in the early-morning light, he recognized the particular narrow slant of LaMoriette's handwriting, the dark-blue ink, the fragile paper. There was no doubt that these were the missing pages of LaMoriette's letter. They were out of order, so he spread them over the floor and put them right. His guess was that Jess grabbed the pages quickly and, rushing to hide them, folded them into the lining of the suitcase. He felt a rush of excitement at the prospect of reading the final pages of LaMoriette's communication to his son. Surely they would give answers to the meaning of the ritual.

But just as he was about to begin, his eye fell over three words written on the bottom of the final page:

HELLISH EVIL RITE

He stared at the words, trying to understand what they meant. One thing was certain—they hadn't been written by LaMoriette.

The ink was red, the letters large and blocky. No, they had been written by Jess Price. *Hellish evil rite.* Why had she written these three
bizarre words on the bottom of LaMoriette's letter? Was it a confession about what happened at Sedge House? An explanation of how
Noah died? It was odd that she'd told him how to find the pages but
hadn't mentioned a thing about the message she'd written. But every
interaction with her yielded a puzzle, and this could be no different.

He needed to examine it more closely, but there wasn't time. Cam
banged on the door, shouting that it was time to go. "Hold your
horses, bro," he shouted, which only made the guy angrier. There
wasn't much time to read the final pages of LaMoriette's letter, but
that wouldn't be a problem. He leaned against the window frame
and, with Cam pounding on the door, Brink took in the words.

48

I spent days recovering from what I witnessed that night at the synagogue. Days and nights slipped into one long dreadful nightmare. Master Král, believing that I had fallen ill again and fearing for my health, relieved me of any remaining duties at the kiln and urged me to rest. And so I lay in bed for days, lost in a fever dream.

I couldn't forget the windstorm that overtook the loft, the lightning that illuminated the golem as it moved for the first time. I watched it turn its head, slowly, carefully, unsure of its power of movement. Then, like a foal wobbling on untried legs, it took a step. Then another. In that moment, my faculties gave way, and I lost all ability to express myself, let alone find a reasonable explanation for what I was seeing. Over the years, I have relived those moments many times and have, with the aid of reflection, come to name the emotions I felt standing in that synagogue: awe and fear and disbelief and humility. Terror shot through with jubilation, for this creature could mean only one thing: The power of creation was in our hands. And I had made the vessel in which it lived.

No greater wonder, no greater horror, had I experienced in my life. And even as I stood witness to an incredible power, I saw that it was a most pernicious triumph. For I had fashioned the golem in the image of my child, but the creature was not my Violaine at all. Her hair was the precise color, her eyes the same brilliant emerald; even the smattering of freckles across her cheeks matched those of my child. But the golem contained a spirit so unlike my precious Violaine that I felt an instant repugnance. Its vile nature filled the air, swirling about us with a frightening violence, and I knew that I was in the presence of an angry, restless soul.

I turned my eyes away, terrified. The rabbi called for Jakob, and he assisted him in examining the page we had used. They had asked me, as the creator of the vessel, to write the words. I had done as they asked, copying the Hebrew exactly from the manuscript. I had given them to the rabbi, and he had spoken them. Although I couldn't understand their frantic words, I knew I must have made a mistake. Something had gone wrong, terribly wrong.

There was an immense heat, the smell of burning flesh, and the sensation of the air filling with pressure, as if on fire. And indeed, when I turned my gaze back to them, I saw Jakob standing in a whirlwind of flames, screaming and flailing, his body encompassed in blue-orange tongues of fire.

I ran from the synagogue, making my way through the streets of the Jewish Quarter, and only stopped when I reached the Vltava. It was there, in the dim glow of the gaslights, that I saw the cuts on my arms, branching like honeycomb over my skin. They were a marking unlike any I had ever seen—the result not of burn or blade but of my encounter with evil. I had been marked by a demon.

When at last I felt well enough to leave my bed, I determined to return to Paris as soon as possible. I was packing my trunk in preparation for my journey when an envelope addressed to me arrived at the doll shop. There was no return address, but I knew who had sent it when I found a card inside with a single phrase scrawled in French: *Viens, mon ami.*

I tucked the card into my pocket and left that very minute. I was terrified to return but knew that there was no other way—Jakob lived, and I had to understand what had happened to him. In half an hour I was at the Jewish Quarter, knocking at the door of the rabbi's home. All was silent within. Not a light shone from the rooms; there was no sound of a violin in the recesses or the smell of meat cooking. Peering through a crack in the shutters, I saw to my amazement that there was no furniture, no pictures on the walls, no rugs on the floors. The rooms were bare, as if the family had abandoned their home.

I ran to the synagogue and knocked furiously at the door. It was a warm evening, the square full of people out walking at dusk, and while I knew I was making a spectacle—a mad Frenchman scream-ing at the synagogue door—I didn't relent. All sense of decorum had left me in the weeks since I was last at the synagogue. Indeed, all that had once consumed me—my work and my artistic aspirations; the perfect porcelain creature I had made—was utterly irrelevant. All I could see was the rabbi speaking in the low light of a candle, his hands laid upon the golem; all I felt was the terrifying sensation that something dark had entered the world, a spirit, a demon, a violent force of evil.

Jakob would explain what had happened, if only he would answer the door. And while at the time I believed I was simply anxious to know the truth, the edges of my sanity had begun to fray. The unrav-eling would take nearly twenty years, and I would try time and again to repair the damage, but I have no doubt that the events that oc-curred at that synagogue were what brought me here, to this mo-ment, to this pistol at my side and the terrible act I am about to commit. Even this, my last communication to you, is little more than an attempt to right this terrible wrong.

Finally, the door to the synagogue swung open. A man I had never seen stood before me. I asked to see the rabbi, in broken but clear enough Czech that the man understood my request. I looked over his shoulder into the dark cavern of the synagogue, half-expecting to find hellfire burning. "Please. He is expecting me."

"But I am the rabbi of this synagogue," said the man, looking at me with curiosity. "And I am not expecting a soul."

I struggled to contain my impatience. "The Rabbi Josefez has sent for me."

"That, I'm afraid, is not possible."

"He sent this," I said. Removing the paper from my pocket, I gave it to the rabbi.

The man looked carefully at me, then at the card. "Are you the dollmaker LaMoriette?" he asked. When I affirmed, he stepped aside so that I might pass into the synagogue, then closed the door. Perplexed and more than a little unnerved, I followed the rabbi to the loft. When we arrived, I found a very different scene than the one I had left. It was empty, clean, the air fresh. The wooden armoire and candles, indeed everything that had once served the golem, had been removed. All that remained was the leather case I had carried to the synagogue weeks before, sitting on a table.

He looked at me for a long moment, then spoke. "For hundreds of years, HaShem remained hidden. But it wasn't always this way. The Creator's name was originally spoken among all the Jewish people every day—in prayer, as a salutation, as a blessing. Then, when the second temple was destroyed, the true name of the Creator was forced underground. Rabbis substituted the word Adonai for the true name. Over time, even this word became too sacred to share with those outside our traditions, and the word HaShem—or simply 'the Name'—was used in everyday discourse. But you," he said, meeting my eye, "you have heard the secret pronunciation."

The rabbi walked to the table. The large leather case that held my creation sat waiting.

"The Rabbi Josefez was wrong to bring you here. Your golem caused great harm."

"That was not my intention," I said. "If I can see the rabbi and his son, I will explain that."

"The rabbi died last week of his wounds."

I leaned against the table, fearing I would fall. "And his son, Jakob?"

"The Bocher has endured much suffering."

"But he is alive?"

The rabbi nodded, affirming that my friend lived. "This belongs to you." He gestured to the case. "You must take it away from here as soon as possible."

I opened the case and found the doll inside, my beautiful Violaine. Relief flooded through me: My creature was safe. But this sensation was quickly followed by dread. What if the evil that had possessed her returned? I ran a finger over Violaine's cool porcelain cheek, then closed the case.

"I would like to speak with Jakob," I said. He gestured that I should follow him, and I didn't hesitate. I hurried down the steps, eager to see Jakob.

On the lower floor of the synagogue, the rabbi opened a small room off the main hall and allowed me to enter. A most hideous stench filled the air, a putrescence that spoke of sickness and infection. I was turning away, repulsed, when a terrible sight stopped me cold: a creature, its skin mottled with scabs, huddled on the bed, its long thin body bent and twisted with disease. For a moment I simply stared, dumbfounded, struggling to make sense of what I saw.

Finally I understood that it was a man, but a man so deformed as to appear monstrous. I took a step closer to the wretched soul, stricken with pity and terror. Clearly some insidious variety of disease had struck. Leprosy, perhaps. Or a pox that raged with infection. The skin of his arm puckered and suppurated, folded and bled. Bandages lay in heaps in a corner, stained green and brown with pus and blood. It was an awful sight, and I hadn't the stomach to stay. I was about to leave the man to his suffering when the wretch lifted his head. His eyes met mine, and although injury had transformed him almost beyond recognition, I saw a familiar brightness burning in his gaze. It was Jakob, changed utterly, but Jakob nonetheless. I went to his side and stood over him, assessing the full extent of his injuries.

"My friend," I whispered, feeling a tremor of horror pass through me. "What has happened to bring you to this state?"

"You were there," Jakob said, his voice weak. "You saw as well as I."

"But how . . . ?" Questions overwhelmed me. I wanted to know how our actions had wrought such harm. I wanted to know how, by what provenance, what ministrations, had such evil arrived on earth.

Jakob grasped my hand and held it. "It was an error. It must be destroyed, my friend. Please hear me. I have made a grave mistake. The golem must be burned. The circle. The vessel. Everything must be burned."

He made little sense, and I concluded that his suffering had affected his mind. I turned to the rabbi, who stood beyond the door. "He requires a doctor immediately."

"A doctor has been here many times already," the rabbi said. "His father died in a similar fashion. Only quickly, as the spirit was strong and vital."

"The spirit?" I asked, perplexed.

"It took over the Rabbi Josefez and then, when it had exhausted that vessel, it visited his son."

The rabbi went to Jakob and lifted a bandage from his chest, revealing skin scored with geometric cuts, as if carved by a blade. I recognized the mark, for I was branded with the same.

"What on earth is it?" I asked, so horrified by the sight that I could hardly speak.

"The mark," the rabbi said, his voice filled with horror. "The mark that will never fade."

"Leave us," Jakob said to the rabbi, his voice a whisper. And when the rabbi stepped from the room, Jakob pulled me closer, gesturing for me to retrieve something under his mattress. It was the manuscript I had seen that first day at his home and in the synagogue, the pages that contained the infernal circle, the book that, Jakob had told me, held the secrets of all creation.

Then, thrusting a sheaf of loose pages at me, he urged me to take it. "Quickly, before the rabbi sees it." When I resisted, insisting that I had no right, he became agitated. "It is the language of the portal," he said. "The ladder on which the intelligences climb and fall. The spirit can only be destroyed with this. Destroy the golem first, then the circle," Jakob whispered, his eyes wide with fear. "Destroy them before it happens again."

Tears filled my eyes, but I did not argue. I took the manuscript and placed it in the case, next to Violaine. Unable to control my emotions, I bid him farewell. But he gestured for me to come close, so that my ear touched his lips. What I believed at first to be a gesture of *adieu* revealed itself to be much more. In a state of agony, his voice so low I could only just make out the sounds, he whispered the sacred name, HaShem, pronouncing it in my ear slowly, clearly, once, twice, and then a third time, so that I would hear and remember. And those words, my son, and the infinite power they contain, have never faded from my memory.

The very next day, I traveled by train to Vienna and then on to Paris. I vowed to put the horrors of Prague away, to lock them up at the back of my mind. But how does one forget such a power as that, one that contains the seed of life and death? How does one unsee after one has looked into the eyes of God and divined His secrets?

It was not until I had been in Paris a month and was safe in my workshop that I examined the book Jakob gave me. It was filled with many writings, but what interested me most, what hypnotized me with its alluring symmetry, was the circle. I had glimpsed it in Prague but had never fully seen it until that moment. I studied it intently, under a magnifying glass, trying to make out the letters and numbers, the strange symbols. And in that manner, I became hypnotized by this ancient doorway into the unknown.

Jakob had entreated me to destroy the circle, but I could not. Nor could I destroy the golem, as you by now surely know. Rather, I protected them. In all the years after my time in Prague, I have shown the circle to no one.

And while I did not destroy the golem, I urge you, my son, who feels no love for the creature, who sees nothing familiar in her features, to do so. I could not destroy Violaine. I tried, many times I tried, but I could never do it. That, my son, I leave to you.

49

The SUV turned at Madison Avenue and 36th Street and stopped before The Morgan Library. Brink took his messenger bag from Jameson and followed him out of the vehicle to a long Palladian villa constructed of marble, an anachronistic structure in a neighborhood filled with twentieth-century architecture, the highrises of Midtown framing it to the north. "This building has always been an anomaly," Anne-Marie explained as she led them to a private entrance on 36th Street. "J. P. Morgan built it as an idyllic retreat from Wall Street and stored his priceless collection of rare manuscripts and books here. When he died, his son turned the library into a museum."

Rare books and manuscripts were fine, but it wasn't even seven in the morning. Surely the museum was closed at that hour. And yet this didn't stop Anne-Marie. She walked up a set of marble steps to an enormous bronze door, looked up at the security camera, and gave an abrupt wave.

"The director is a friend," she said to Brink. "He's probably risking his job to see us, but when I told him we'd found LaMoriette's masterpiece, he was more than willing to take that chance."

The bronze door opened and a tall, thin Black man with tortoiseshell glasses and a lavender dress shirt appeared. He gestured for them to enter, then closed the heavy door behind him. They stood in a rotunda, surrounded by marble pillars. Frescoes filled the walls with images of Roman gods and goddesses. "Anne-Marie," the man said, his tone anxious. "I thought you'd be here an hour ago."

"Cullen, you've met Jameson," Anne-Marie said. "And this is Mike Brink, who's helping us with some of the research. Brink, meet Cullen Withers, director of the Morgan Library."

Cullen Withers shook Brink's hand, his gaze settling just long enough to take in Brink's swollen eye. "I'm a fan," he said, smiling sheepishly. "That art-history crossword in *The New York Times Magazine* last month was truly brilliant." He didn't wait for Brink to respond but turned back to Anne-Marie. "After your call, I couldn't go back to sleep. You certainly do know how to create intrigue. I've been here since three this morning."

"You don't have trouble with security?" Jameson asked, glancing at the cameras mounted around the rotunda.

"They're used to my odd hours," Cullen said. "I'm here at all times of the day and night, especially when we're installing an exhibition. You've brought the LaMoriette?"

"Of course," Anne-Marie said, gesturing to the leather case in Jameson's hand.

"I'm sure you're aware that there have been a number of fakes over the years," Cullen said. "There was an excellent faux Violaine that came on the market three years ago. You must have heard of it, Anne-Marie."

"Who hasn't," she said. "The Bonham sale was notorious."

"The doll looked exactly like the 1909 photos of the authentic Violaine, but when the buyer's agent sent fibers from the dress to a lab, they found a synthetic material that didn't exist in the 1890s. One has to be so careful . . ."

"I assure you that you will be able to verify this doll's authenticity," Jameson said.

This was all Cullen needed to hear. He turned on his heel and led them through the rotunda, his wingtips clicking on the stone floor.

They passed under a vaulted ceiling painted with figures from mythology, nude gods holding fruit and treasure, and into a magnificent library, three stories tall, with floor-to-ceiling bookcases rising in three tiers. The ceilings were painted with murals of mythological figures, and a great stone fireplace occupied the far wall.

"This was Mr. Morgan's private library, built to house his incredible collection of rare books and manuscripts. It was originally designed with just one tier of bookshelves, but his collection grew even as the library was being built, and so his architect, Charles McKim, quickly changed his plans and added more shelving.

"Gaston LaMoriette's papers had a special place in this library, as did LaMoriette's masterpiece. LaMoriette's workshop was bought outright for Mr. Morgan by Belle da Costa Greene, the first director of the Pierpont Morgan Library and a legendary figure around here. She was a specialist in illuminated manuscripts who built this collection. She was born into a distinguished African American family but chose to live as a white woman. Her sharp wit and intelligence made her a great favorite of Mr. Morgan's, and he trusted her to run just about everything here at the library. He left her the equivalent of 1.3 million dollars in his will, which led some people to believe they'd had an affair, but their friendship was a true meeting of the minds. Her genius for acquisition is behind the Morgan collection—she was notoriously good at outmaneuvering bidders at auctions, but she was also very good at keeping records of her purchases. Which brings me back to the LaMoriette workshop. Her records of the 1910 purchase of Gaston LaMoriette's papers were impeccable."

Cullen walked to the corner of the room, grasped a handle in the bookcase, and the shelf swung open to reveal a hollow space behind the wall. He stepped inside, walked up a spiral staircase tucked behind the wall, and soon a bookcase on the second floor swung open. Cullen walked along a narrow balcony, stopped at a bookcase, pulled something from the shelf, and returned with a small ledger.

"This library is filled with hidden nooks, secret doorways, and codes," he said. "And this, Belle's personal ledger, is a key to decode them." He opened a page. "It says here that there were forty-seven items acquired in the 1910 LaMoriette sale: a first edition of Cornelius Agrippa's *De Occulta Philosophia*, which is still in our collection, an Italian copy of *The Key of Solomon*, also still in the collection, and many other lesser works, which were immediately sold off. It was a highly unusual purchase, as it says in her notes, one that Mr. Morgan felt very strongly about."

As he paged through the small leather book, Brink saw rows and rows of even handwriting punctuated by numbers.

"Included in the Morgan Library's purchase of the LaMoriette workshop was a collection of papers from the Prague period that contained LaMoriette's sketches and notes, as well as another manuscript, much older, dating from the late thirteenth century and containing ten circles. That manuscript was originally kept in Mr. Morgan's vault, a reinforced steel chamber in his private study."

"He must have thought it important," Jameson said.

"Indeed, Mr. Morgan kept his most valuable manuscripts there. The Gutenberg Bibles—all three copies, one vellum, two parchment— were there; the gem-encrusted Lindau Gospels manuscript was there; his most treasured Book of Hours, also there. The manuscript that contains the circles was written by Abraham Abulafia, a Jewish mystic, in 1278. The book had a strange hold over Mr. Morgan. He hired experts to read it to him and was rumored to carry it with him on his travels. If you look there," he said, turning to an enormous tapestry hanging above the fireplace, "you will see how deeply the book affected him."

Brink turned to see an enormous tapestry that filled an entire wall.

"That," Cullen said, "is a sixteenth-century tapestry called *Triumph of Avarice*. Seven such tapestries were made, one for each of the cardinal sins, but Mr. Morgan purchased only this one. As you see, it occupies a primary position in his library. That man," he said, pointing up to a figure in the tapestry, "is King Midas, and I believe his story was an important one for Mr. Morgan: the man who loved riches so much that he couldn't touch another person without turning them to cold, lifeless gold. It was a memento mori, perhaps, a reminder that there is more to life than money, or as some have suggested, the clue to Mr. Morgan's secret treasure. Do you see where Midas is pointing?" Brink's eye followed King Midas's finger up above the tapestry, to a mural painted on the wall. It depicted a morose woman reclined on a stack of books, a mask in her hands. Above her had been painted the word *TRAGEDY*.

"The personification of the elements of drama was not unusual," Cullen said, gesturing to a mural on the opposite side of the tapestry of another woman, much happier, the word *COMEDY* painted above her. "And, of course, Midas's life was tragedy."

"Gold means nothing without the time and ability to enjoy it," Jameson said.

"Precisely," Cullen said. "But what is interesting about this, and what has made me wonder how much Mr. Morgan knew about LaMoriette's secret history, is the book in Tragedy's hand."

Brink studied it closely, trying to see a title or distinguishing mark.

"It is Abulafia's book, the very one you've come to see," Cullen said. "It is stored in our archive, and the story it tells is fascinating. Come with me, and I will show it to you."

50

Cullen Withers led them into the modern annex of the library, a glass structure filled with the bright light of morning. He took a stairwell to the lower level, pushed through a door marked EM-PLOYEES ONLY, and entered a basement.

"During visiting hours, certain manuscripts are displayed in glass cases in the library. But when the library is closed, rare books live below the Renzo Piano Annex, in the underground vault. The La-Moriette sketches and the corresponding manuscript attributed to Abulafia are kept here."

Cullen punched in a code, a simple number sequence, not complex enough to offer any real security. Anyone looking over his shoulder could see it. Sometimes Brink would see a code without having fully intended to, and the code would be imprinted on his memory forever. He averted his eyes as Cullen entered the final digits.

The tumblers of a lock clicked, and the door popped open, releasing air, as if vacuum-sealed. The vault was large, dimly lit, reinforced with steel, and filled with shelves of archival boxes. They gathered around a table at the center of the space. White cotton gloves were folded in a glass box at the center of the table, a pad of paper and a magnifying glass placed nearby. Everything was as immaculate and orderly as a hospital room.

Cullen shut the vault door, punched in a code on a second keypad, and the bolts locked into place. Brink realized that they were locked inside, at the mercy of Cullen's code, and wished he hadn't looked away from the keypad after all.

"Half of my work is preservation. Manuscripts are composed entirely of organic materials, and sunlight degrades them. Although there is no UV light whatsoever in the library, we rotate the collection, putting manuscripts on display for about three months before bringing them down here for a breather. Books, correspondence, ephemera relating to the collection, all of that is here in this vault."

He slipped on a pair of white cotton gloves, went to a shelf, and pulled down an archival box. From it, he removed a folio filled with loose pages.

"This folio contains pages of a manuscript by Abraham Abulafia," he said, placing the pages on the surface of the table. Brink had expected a manuscript, something big and heavy and voluminous, a tome of learned commentary that would explain the mystery surrounding the circle. But there were only a few loose pages and, on each page, at the very center, a circle similar to the one Thessaly had shown him.

"They are ink on vellum, and while I am no expert on their religious use, I believe they were made to aid prayer. Belle da Costa Greene left extensive notes on the collection when she purchased it."

Cullen carefully lifted the delicate leaves from the folio, arranging ten sheets of vellum on the table. "These ten pages of Abulafia's prayer circles were found as we see them now. They were never bound. Any damage you see to the vellum was there at the time of acquisition."

Brink scanned the ten circles. He took in the patterns and sequences, noting that each circle was a rhyme of the others: circular constructions with Hebrew letters, radials of flames shooting from the center, and seventy-two numbers configured at the edges.

"They are incredibly beautiful," Anne-Marie said, looking over the circles. "But what do they signify?"

"I'm afraid I can't speak to that," Cullen said. "My expertise stops with the manuscript itself. I can tell you the composition of the vellum—it is sheepskin stretched to one quarter of a millimeter—and the chemical properties of the ink—lead oxide suspended in a plant-based binding agent, most likely madder, which explains the red-brown tone. I can tell you that these pages have been authenticated by carbon dating as having been written in the last quarter of the thirteenth century, and that you can find more of Abulafia's circles in a collection held by the British Library. I can even tell you that these pages were originally rolled together and secured with a leather string, as you can see from the stress marks here, at the edges of the vellum. But as to their significance or aspects of their meaning in terms of religious history, I cannot say. For that, you will need an expert. And I know just the person."

"There's an expert on something as obscure as thirteenth-century Jewish prayer circles?" Jameson asked.

"Her name is Rachel Appel, and I've already spoken to her," Cullen said. "She runs a Center for the Study of the Kabbalah here in Manhattan. I called her early this morning and discussed all of this with her. I also sent her the PDF of the LaMoriette letter that you forwarded me, Anne-Marie."

Brink glanced at Anne-Marie. He'd stolen the originals of LaMoriette's letter from her home, but of course she had scanned copies.

Cullen continued, "She'd heard the LaMoriette legend and immediately offered her services, which is an incredible stroke of luck: There isn't another scholar in the world with her expertise. She's studied the extensive collection of Abulafia's manuscripts in the British Library, including his prayer circles. She would like to see you, and the circle you've found, as soon as possible."

"That's not going to happen," Jameson said. "Too many people know about this already."

"Jameson," Anne-Marie said. Brink could feel the tension between Jameson and Anne-Marie and suspected an underlying disagreement. "We can't move forward without understanding what these circles are. We've tried to do it on our own. We need help."

"Bringing anyone else into this is out of the question."

"Rachel is discreet," Cullen said. "And her professional credentials are impeccable. I believe she would be an enormous asset in identifying exactly what these are and why they were important enough for a man like John Pierpont Morgan to protect them."

Cullen went to the door and punched in the code. Two security guards stepped inside.

"The one request Rachel has is that she be allowed to see Abulafia's original manuscript as well as the copy you discovered in La-Moriette's doll." He collected the pages of vellum, slid them into the folio, and closed the archival box tight. "I agreed to bring it to her. I'm anxious to see Violaine, and I must keep an eye on this manuscript, and so I will accompany you. We have three hours before the library opens—just enough time, if we hurry."

51

They followed the armored security vehicle up Madison, drove across Central Park, and soon stopped before a stately brick townhouse on the Upper West Side. Brink stepped out of the SUV and into the brightening morning. It was just after eight o'clock, but it was a Saturday morning, and the city was quiet, almost deserted. He stretched and glanced around, taking in a park across the street, a Citi Bike terminal stretching at one side. Beyond, the Hudson River swelled with seawater. When Brink took a breath, he could almost taste the brine in the air.

Cullen emerged from the vehicle—the kind of tank that usually transported cash from bank to bank—and was immediately flanked by two armed security guards. Brink glanced at Cam Putney, dwarfed by the level of security Cullen brought to the situation. He imagined the plethora of insecurities hitting Putney just then—that he wasn't strong enough, quick enough, savvy enough. While he disliked the man, he felt a sudden sympathy for Cam. Even at six one, Brink had always been small on the field. It was never easy to feel outmuscled.

Brink followed Cullen, Sedge, and Anne-Marie up a set of steps to the door of the townhouse, where a brass plate etched with the words CENTER FOR THE STUDY OF THE KABBALAH had been embedded in the stone façade. Within a second of Cullen's knock, the door opened. A young man in jeans and a sweatshirt greeted Cullen by name—"Mr. Withers, come right this way"—and led them into an airy foyer filled with flowers, then up a staircase to a reading room with oak tables and glass-domed reading lamps.

"I'll tell Ms. Appel you're here," the man said, and walked down the hall.

Brink gravitated to the bookshelves. There was a thick Hebrew–English dictionary on a stand at the center of the room, and he knew that if he had a few hours to study it, he could work out the basics of the language. It was a gift, his ability with languages, one that arose from the same source as his talent in solving puzzles. After his accident, he became fluent in French, Spanish, Italian, Latin, Japanese, Chinese, and ancient Greek, all of which he'd learned by reading grammar textbooks. Learning languages was like cracking a code, and he saw foreign languages like puzzles. The solution was the ability to communicate with another person.

A woman with long dark hair walked into the room, startling Brink from his thoughts. She was tall, thin, with prominent cheekbones and large blue eyes, and wore loose wine-colored harem pants and a silk tank top. She greeted Cullen warmly, gesturing for him to put the archival box on a table, then turned to the others, introducing herself as Rachel Appel, head of the center.

"A pleasure to meet you," she said, offering Brink her hand. "But I have to be honest, after reading that *Vanity Fair* article, and banging my head against your crosswords every week, I feel like we've already met." She glanced at his injuries. "I see this pulled you out of bed early, too. Or should I say dragged you out?"

He touched the cut over his eye. The swelling hadn't gone down. "That's a better way to put it," he said.

"None of us has slept much, I'm afraid," Anne-Marie said.

Rachel stepped to Cullen's side as he opened the archival box and, slipping on his gloves, laid the pages of Abulafia's manuscript on the table. Rachel moved around the table to look closely at each circle. "Abraham Abulafia and his mystical circle are worth a sleepless night. It isn't often that one has the chance to examine a piece of history."

"We have Mr. Withers's word that you will be discreet," Jameson said. "I trust he was correct on that front."

Rachel laughed and gave him a look of complicity. "*Discreet* is too weak a word to describe me, Mr. Sedge. After you've left, I will not even remember that you were here."

This seemed to mollify Jameson. He smiled slightly and didn't press further.

Rachel leaned against the table. "After I read LaMoriette's letter to his son, I was so wound up that I came directly to the center to do some digging in our collection. I found in our genealogy archive that there was, indeed, a Rabbi Ezekiel Josefez who lived in Prague during the years that LaMoriette was there and that this rabbi was the rabbi of the Old-New Synagogue. He had a son named Jakob. Both father and son died, as LaMoriette wrote, in 1891, and both men are buried in the Old Jewish Cemetery in Prague, in a plot not far from the Rabbi Loew himself."

"So it's true," Cullen said. "LaMoriette's story can be verified."

"Some of it can, and while under most circumstances I would be tempted to dismiss such stories as little more than an overheated imagination—stories of the golem, like those of ghosts and vampires, seem to inspire wild flights of fancy—I found LaMoriette to be quite credible. He understood very particular religious ideas that are outside the usual mythology. The most sensational tales borrow details from the story of the golem of Prague, the creature brought to life by Rabbi Loew in the sixteenth century. He wrote the letters EMET, meaning *truth*, onto a golem's forehead and it came to life. When the E was taken away, the word became MET, or *death*, and the golem died or deactivated. LaMoriette did not write of seeing the word EMET and did not describe erasing a word. And, of course, he mentioned the most secret element: the Name, or HaShem."

Rachel walked to a shelf and removed a book.

"To understand what the Rabbi Josefez was up to, we need to

understand what a golem actually is. The word *golem* first appears in the Talmud," she said, flipping open the book and stopping at a passage. "Sanhedrin 38b describes God's creation of Adam, referring to the newly fashioned body as a golem, a *shapeless husk*. In early Hebrew, *golem* was translated as *shapeless mass*. The golem was seen as a clay model, a kind of prototype. Adam's body, before the Creator breathed into it, was a golem, an imperfect creature, a body without a soul. While the story of creation has been interpreted as metaphorical, many believe it is literally true and acts as the model of all creation, from the smallest particle of matter to the entire universe."

"I'm guessing you're not referring to the big bang," Jameson said, smirking.

"Actually, you'd be surprised how close this creation story is to the big bang," Rachel said, smiling slightly. "In the Kabbalist conception of the universe, the material world came to exist in a burst from the Divine, positive and negative elements, masculine and feminine manifestations of God that combined to form the building blocks of the material universe. Scientific research has shown that the first compounds were made of a proton, with its positive charge, and an electron, with its negative charge, and that these elements combined to create more-complex forms until, many billions of years later, they formed the universe as we know it."

Rachel Appel closed the book, walked to a shelf, and removed another.

"Creation, whether it is from a religious perspective or a scientific perspective, is about that moment when the invisible becomes visible, when nothing becomes something. In my tradition, the oldest and most important text to touch on this process is the Sepher Yetzirah, translated as *The Book of Formation*."

Rachel opened the book to a page filled with a network of circles connected by pathways. On each circle, and in each pathway, were Hebrew letters. She traced a finger from the top circle, zigzagging down the pathways.

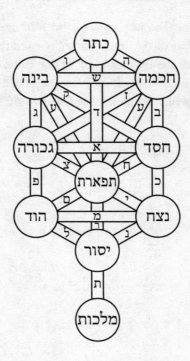

"This configuration is called the tree of life, or the Eitz Haim, and it's composed of the Sephiroth. It represents the movement of the infinite Divine as it reveals itself in the material world. The top circle, Keter, the crown, is the realm of pure energy, and the bottom circle, Malkhut, the kingdom, is the material world that we know. Kabbalists believe that movement from pure energy to the material plane happens through words. Words have an immense power, a magical power in the Kabbalah. To speak the correct word in the correct way in the correct environment is to manifest this power. And that materialization happens through portals, or windows, from one dimension—the ethereal unmaterial realm of God—to another realm, earth.

"The Rabbi Josefez and his son, Jakob, harnessed this power to create life. They knew the secrets of HaShem and thus the secrets of all creation." She turned and met Brink's eye, smiling at him, and he had the feeling that she was speaking to him specifically. "But to understand how they did it, one must understand the Sephiroth, the direct channel from the infinite, God, to the finite, earth. It requires a strength of imagination, but I don't think that will be a problem for you. If you come here, next to me, I will show you."

52

"Abulafia's circles were designed as Shem HaMephorash, symbolic representations of the hidden name of God. They are composed of seventy-two variations of the tetragrammaton, the four-letter name YHWH. Abulafia created hundreds of them, but these ten circles had a specific purpose," Rachel said, gesturing to the loose pages they'd brought from the Morgan Library. "They were drawn to correspond to the ten circles of the Sephiroth."

Rachel took one of the pages of Abulafia's manuscript and lay it at the top of the table, signifying the highest circle of the Sephiroth.

"But why?" Brink asked, studying the Sephiroth, taking in the Hebrew letters. Already, a system had formed, and he was able to understand the pattern of the letters, but he struggled to see the larger mean.

"To make contact with nonmaterial realms, of course," she said in a matter-of-fact way, as if contacting spirits was an everyday occurrence. "The words in these circles were chanted, performed, enacted, and repeated endlessly, in order to summon the intelligences associated with each realm."

She took another circle and put it over the second circle of the Sephiroth.

"The power inherent in the name of God, or HaShem, was the ultimate vehicle to bring the spiritual world down to the material world. Abulafia believed that he could, quite literally, invoke spirits with these prayers. His approach was wildly unorthodox. He believed one could channel God directly through ritualistic practices that opened the mind to visions and prophesy. Aldous Huxley's *The Doors of Perception*, or, later, Jim Morrison and the Doors, explored the idea that one must tear down the rational mind to 'break on through to the other side,' but Abulafia enacted these practices six hundred years earlier. These circles are the crystallization of that philosophy."

"And yet," Brink said, gazing down at Abulafia's circles, "they're extremely literal, with precise patterns, like equations with a singular solution."

"Exactly," Rachel said, meeting his eye. "Abulafia believed the letters of the Hebrew alphabet to be a magical code. He devised ingenious permutations of that code, creating circular incantations, some of them incredibly intricate, that appear—as you noticed—to be labyrinths or puzzles. These puzzles were meant to be performed, so that one might enter into the circle and become spatially and sensually connected to God through repetition and visualization. They were portals. Abulafia claimed that he could transport spirits from heaven to earth and, conversely, could bring earthly beings to experience heaven through these circles. That is why the Rabbi Josefez believed they would bring his golem to life."

She placed a third, fourth, and fifth circle in their positions. Then the sixth, seventh, and eighth.

"They are magnificent," Anne-Marie said, leaning over the circles. "While they are beautiful to look at, they are not aesthetic objects: They were meant to be performed, probably while fasting, and preferably over and over, until the performer fell into a trance. And the spirits came."

"The Sufis prayed like that," Anne-Marie said. "Turning in circles until they reached a state of higher consciousness."

"Of course, these ideas are not limited to Kabbalists. The human desire to alter reality and to align the self with the power of creation is at the heart of many spiritual practices: Christian prayer, Buddhist concepts of Nirvana, Sufism, Transcendental Meditation, even taking mushrooms at Burning Man. All the so-called New Age talk one hears about manifestation and so forth—the idea that one creates a desired reality through intention and words—well, the original source for this concept is the Kabbalah, which teaches one how to have direct communication with the Divine through certain forms of ritual that creates connection with God's abundance, or shefa.

"But Abulafia's circles weren't about creating wealth and power, or even about attaining a higher state of consciousness. When one performs a prayer circle correctly—unlocking it, so to speak—one opens a pathway between dimensions. When a certain spirit is called, it moves through the circle and into a vessel. In the case of LaMoriette, the vessel was the doll Violaine. That spirit can be good. It can be evil. But whatever its intentions, it is incredibly powerful.

"And dangerous. It was necessary to hide the Name in the way it's necessary to shield your eyes when looking at the sun. Without that protection, it would be too powerful, too destructive. For that reason, and because of the persecution my people have undergone throughout history, our most sacred and secret texts were encrypted. The true name is the most sacred cryptogram, but there are many who believe that the deepest meanings of the Bible are encrypted, as well. For example, the name Moses in Hebrew, when flipped, spells HaShem, a signal that he is the conduit and vessel of the true name. There are endless examples of hidden meanings in our sacred texts. Palindromes, one-letter shift ciphers, even a Greek decryption device called the scytale—all of these were used to hide the true nature of God's sacred being."

"I know a lot of puzzleists," Brink said. "No puzzle constructor would create a system that couldn't be solved. The whole point is to connect, through time and space, with a solver. Connection is everything. Surely, Abulafia created these circles for someone."

"True," Rachel said. "But Abulafia would have said that he didn't create these circles at all but rather that they were sent to him from heaven. The Name originated and led back to the Creator. It is a circular puzzle. The question and the answer is God. He is the puzzle creator and the solution in one. But, practically speaking, these circles were constructed by a rabbi for other rabbis. It was an exclusive group. They all knew the rules."

With that, Rachel lay the ninth circle on the table, then the tenth. With the ten circles holding their positions, the Sephiroth was complete.

Brink gazed over the circles, relishing their mind-bending complexity. Suddenly something clicked, and he felt a kind of satisfying symmetry, the same feeling of relief he got when the colored sides of a Rubik's Cube came together: There was a pattern. The circles had an essential structure that he recognized. It was like a moment in chess when one saw the entire match laid out in a succession of moves. Something sparked, letters and numbers illuminating in his mind, and he saw it, the circle configuring, unbinding, and rebinding. He saw consistencies and inconsistencies. A pattern. When he looked up, Rachel was studying him.

Turning to Cullen, Jameson, and Anne-Marie, she said, "You came to me for answers, and I would like to give them to you. If you would allow me a few moments alone." She gestured to the leather case. "I would like to examine the copy of the Shem HaMephorash you found."

Jameson's body language was tense, and Brink could see he was about to object, but Rachel said, "If you want me to help you understand the information that these circles contain and how that information might be used, I need to see the circle you found and the vessel that carried it."

"I think that is a reasonable request," Anne-Marie said, easing the case from Jameson's fingers and laying it on the table near the configuration of circles.

"Thank you," Rachel said. "Give me half an hour, and I will have some answers for you."

"Fifteen minutes," Jameson said. "I will be standing outside that door, waiting."

As Brink followed the others out of the room, he felt Rachel's hand on his arm. "You stay," she said. "I need your help."

53

When the room cleared, Rachel locked the door and joined Mike Brink back at the table.

"You saw something," she said, looking at him intently. "I could tell by the way you were looking at the circles."

"You'll see it, too," he said, opening the leather case and pushing it toward her. "When you open this."

She unwrapped the doll and held it under the light so that its brilliant green eyes glittered. Then she placed it facedown on the table and opened the cavity at the back of the neck. Pinching the scroll of paper between her fingernails, she pulled it free and pressed it flat against the table.

"It is definitely a copy of Abulafia's Shem HaMephorash but I don't see anything unusual." She looked at Brink. "But you do."

"After my injury," he said, "I had every test imaginable. But it wasn't until I went to see a neurologist, and they did a test for synesthesia, that I began to understand the nature of what had happened to me. One of the tests I took looked like this. . . ." Brink pulled out his graph-paper notebook and drew a diagram filled with the number 5 and the number 2. "Take a look." He pushed the diagram to Rachel.

"If I ask you to point out all the instances of the number two in this diagram, you will be able to do it, but it will take you time. But people with synesthesia, like me, see the number two instantly, in a fraction of a second."

"How?" she asked.

"Like this," he said, shading the twos darker. "The wires of my senses have been crossed. Every number has a color value, and that color distinguishes the twos instantly. Look," he said. "That's how I see this diagram."

"And that relates to Abulafia's circle?" she said, raising an eyebrow as she studied the diagram.

"I can see patterns instantly," he said. "That's why this inconsistency stood out. . . ." Brink took the copy of the circle and placed it next to one of Abulafia's originals. "The circle found in LaMoriette's doll was copied from this circle in the manuscript, the tenth one. The two circles should be identical. They aren't."

"You're sure?" Rachel said, looking closely at the two circles.

"Positive," he said. "I saw right away that they're nearly identical but have one significant difference."

"Which is?" Rachel asked, her gaze shifting between the two circles, trying to discern the difference.

"As you pointed out, the words themselves, and the order in which they are spoken, are a kind of code. Accuracy, down to the letter, is essential. So what at first appears to be a tiny difference is actually an enormous divergence. Comparing the two, it is clear that the circle was copied incorrectly."

"How do you know?"

"Do you see these letters here?" Brink pointed to the Hebrew letters חַיִּים.

"Yes, that word is *haim*," Rachel said. "Which translates as *alive*. It is the root for *l'chaim*, a wish for life, a phrase that is often used as a celebratory toast: to life."

"Well, the word was written one way in the original circle, and it's flipped or inverted in the copy. Look." He showed her the circle with the inverted letter.

Rachel studied it for a moment. "So, what you're saying is that *haim* was written backward in the copy."

"Exactly," Brink said. He remembered the last pages of La-Moriette's letter. What had Jakob said? *It was an error. It must be destroyed.* "There was a mistake when it was copied."

There was a tense silence as Rachel examined the circle, her gaze drifting from the original in the manuscript to the smaller copy. "You're right," she said finally. "*Haim* is inverted in the copy. I'm just trying to understand how this happened. The rabbi had Abulafia's manuscript. He would have known the correct spelling. It couldn't have been a mistake."

"But the rabbi didn't copy it," Brink said, pulling out the final pages of LaMoriette's letter and showing them to Rachel. *I had done as they asked, copying the Hebrew exactly from the manuscript.* "The Hebrew would have been confusing for him and—"

"Of course," Rachel said. "Abulafia's original was composed in boustrophedon, a practice of mirroring or inverting text that was common in the ancient world. The Rabbi Josefez would have known to write and read it correctly. But LaMoriette didn't. He copied it as it was on the page, creating the error."

"One that clearly made an impression, as he used such mirroring again, much later," Brink said.

"Where?" she asked, looking over the letter.

"You read the first page of LaMoriette's letter to his son. Did you notice the palindrome?"

Rachel shook her head. "Palindrome?"

"A sequence of letters or numbers that is identical in both directions, written so that it can be read exactly the same way forward and backward."

"I know what a palindrome is," she said, rolling her eyes. "But I don't recall seeing one in LaMoriette's letter. What was it?"

Brink took his notebook and wrote down the Latin sentence from the first page of LaMoriette's letter. He capitalized the last letter, to emphasize the mirroring: *In girum imus nocte et consumimur ignI.*

Rachel read the Latin phrase aloud, translating as she did. "In circles we move at night and are consumed by fire."

"It's a riddle," Brink said, feeling a stab of pleasure at the elegance of the construction, both the meaning of the phrase and the perfection of the palindrome.

"What circles a flame in the darkness until it is burned?" Rachel asked.

"A moth," Brink said.

"Yes," Rachel said. "But also Icarus, who flew so close to the sun his wings burned and he fell to the ground. And Prometheus, who was punished for stealing fire from the gods. The Rabbi Josefez, too, came too close to HaShem and died."

"And LaMoriette himself," Brink said. "His letter is, in its essence, a long suicide note."

"The letter was a suicide note, yes, but most of all, LaMoriette wanted to warn his son of the seductions of such power. When he wrote, *In circles we move at night and are consumed by fire,* he described the incredible power of vocalizing the true name of God."

"It also explains the urgency of his letter," Brink said. "LaMoriette felt that he himself was in danger. It may even be the reason LaMoriette killed himself. The man was terrified."

"Abulafia's circle was designed to create such terror," Rachel said. "The experience of that fear and awe of God, the true terror one felt in communicating through prayer—a state of communion with the Divine—is the whole point. The circle is the door, but the state of mind, the trance that the words produce, is the key to that door."

"Are you saying that a state of mind led to what happened to the rabbi and his son?"

"That is one part of it," she said. "But the actual words and numbers in the circle are another, equally important element. When the word *haim* was altered, the result changed. This explains what happened to the rabbi and his son and also the terrible events at Sedge House. While the changes you discovered in the copy of Abulafia's circle may seem minor, they had the power to create terrible consequences. And when this circle was used by Rabbi Josefez, the result was utterly catastrophic."

Brink remembered the gruesome description of Jakob in LaMoriette's letter and the photos he had seen of Frankie Sedge and Noah Cooke and knew that Rachel was right. He also knew that a few small alterations in a code could wreak havoc in complex systems. Sometimes the smallest error can be the most damaging. Serious defects arise from a tiny mutation in a single gene. A minuscule error in a computer code can shut the whole system down. Brink understood how such errors might alter a system—Dr. Gupta would've called them bugs or a virus. "Okay, but what system did it alter here?"

"The ultimate system," Rachel said. "The system of life. Like Dr. Frankenstein channeling electricity into his creature, they used Abulafia's prayer circles as a direct pathway of energy from God, to endow a golem with life. And, by all standards, they were successful. They performed the ritual correctly. But the result was not what they expected."

She brought Brink's attention back to the Tree of Life laid out on the table.

"I began to explain the Sephiroth and the positions of the ten circles on the Tree of Life before, but there is another aspect to this that I didn't discuss. It is simply too esoteric for most people. But you are not most people. I think you'll understand."

She pointed to the top circle, Keter, and drew a line through each circle, pausing on the final circle, Malkhut.

"In Kabbalah, each of these circles is a sphere with a unique aspect and function in the creation of the world. Basically, they are like electrical stations connecting the Divine and material things with live wires that run between them. The circles, or stations, are where the energy collects, transforms, and is distributed. As such, these spheres are guarded by equally powerful attendants: the Divine intelligences, more commonly known as angels."

Brink was instantly skeptical. "Angels?"

"Hear me out," she said. "As I mentioned before, the basis of creation in the Kabbalah is the union of opposites: positive and negative, male and female. As such, in Kabbalah, there is an inverse force in the universe called Klipot. It is the force of darkness or evil, the opposite of the Tree of Life. The Klipot is often characterized as being the product of broken shells, or hollow vessels that have cracked. The story goes that when God tried to create the universe the first time, His emanation was so powerful that it broke the vessels meant to contain it. He tried again and created the world as we know it. But the earlier, broken universe did not disappear. It remained, in opposition to the universe we inhabit.

Brink remembered Anne-Marie's words about crazing—the extreme pressure that led to an explosion. The imperfect pattern that resulted.

"This duality was embodied in the Tree of Good and Evil. If you recall, this was the forbidden tree that tempted Adam and Eve. When they ate fruit from it—learning duality, or the existence of good and evil—they were thrust from innocence, or paradise, into the realm of knowledge. The spheres of the Tree of Life are attended by angels; the spheres of the Klipot are attended by demons. In the Tree of Life, the tenth circle, Malkhut—the circle that the rabbi used in his creation of the golem—is attended by the angel Sandalphon; in the Klipot, the tenth circle is where the demon Lilith lives."

"Wait," Brink said. Rachel's words had struck something in his memory. He saw the words *Lilith lives* appear in his mind. "Something you just said . . ." He took LaMoriette's letter and showed Rachel the words Jess had written at the bottom: *hellish evil rite.* "Jess Price wrote this after Noah Cooke died."

Rachel studied the words, clearly confused. "What on earth?"

"I've been trying to understand what Jess meant. She had only a few minutes to communicate something before she hid this, and while she could've written anything, she chose these three words. Hellish evil rite. At first I thought these words were meant to describe what happened that night. But Jess loves language, especially word games and puzzles. She would never write something so simple. But when you said *Lilith lives,* something clicked. It's an anagram."

Brink saw the arrangement of letters in his mind instantly, but to show Rachel, he took the notebook and wrote out the words *hellish evil rite.* Then he rearranged the letters until he had spelled the phrase *Lilith lives here.*

"Lilith lives here," Brink said, meeting Rachel's eye. "Jess Price identified Lilith as being present at Sedge House the night Noah Cooke died."

Rachel stared at the words on the paper, then looked at Brink, her eyes filled with shock. "If that's true," she said, "Jess is in terrible, terrible danger."

54

Terrible danger. It echoed what Jess had been telling him since the moment he met her. From their first meeting, she had warned him that they were being watched, that someone had killed Dr. Raythe, that someone would come after him. The threat was real, but he hadn't understood the origin. He'd assumed it was Sedge, but now he wasn't so sure. "What kind of danger are we talking about?"

"From LaMoriette's description of how the rabbi used Abulafia's circle," Rachel said, "and what you've just discovered about the inverted copy that was used by Jess Price and Noah Cooke at Sedge House, and now this anagram that Jess wrote, it appears that the circle became a portal for the demon Lilith."

Brink wasn't sure how to respond to this assertion. Rachel was a reasonable person, a brilliant and respected scholar. And yet what she was saying seemed utterly impossible. It pushed the limits of his understanding, and more, went against everything he believed. He saw the world as a great, interconnected, and marvelous puzzle, one that could be solved through logic and skill. He didn't believe in anything that transgressed the boundaries of these limits. His world was one of concrete elements, hard facts, solid data his mind could grasp hold of. And Rachel's explanation for this was . . . *what?* An abstract concept that couldn't be seen or touched, only believed by an act of pure faith.

Seeing his consternation, Rachel drew him back to Abulafia's manuscript. "Look here," she said, pointing back to Abulafia's the tenth circle.

"Abulafia created this Shem HaMephorash for the tenth position of the Sephiroth, Malkhut, which is ruled by Sandalphon, the archangel who collects and relays human prayers to God. The rabbi used this circle in his ritual to call down Sandalphon."

"Call down?" Brink asked. He could hear the challenge in his voice. "You mean like teleporting Sandalphon to earth?"

"It's not quite *Star Trek*," she said, giving him an indulgent look. "But, yes, it seems to me that they were attempting to communicate with a being that was not strictly of this dimension. I will spare you the theology, but the powers of the Divine intelligences as messengers represent an elaborate system of creation, a kind of language or code. The rabbi used this circle and it worked. But as it was inverted, it didn't open a portal for Sandalphon, as intended. Rather, it summoned Lilith, his nemesis."

Brink stared at the circle, taking in what Rachel had said. "But how can you prove that?"

"The evidence is circumstantial, obviously," she said. "It happened to the rabbi and his son, and then again to Noah Cooke. I didn't follow the case closely, but from what I remember, Jess Price was damaged, wasn't she?"

"She's more than damaged," Brink said. "Her life has been totally destroyed."

"That's Lilith's specialty: occupy and destroy."

"Are you're saying that Jess has been occupied by this woman—"

"Demon."

"This demon since Noah Cooke's death?"

"If I could get close to Jess Price, I could say this with more certainty. But from what you've told me, and what I've just seen in these circles, I'm certain Lilith is responsible for what has happened to her."

Brink felt dizzy. He pulled out a chair and sat down. In one rush, the weight of everything Rachel said hit him. It was overwhelming. His connection to Jess, the confounding nature of the God Puzzle, the danger of Jameson Sedge—it all pressed in on him. He was enmeshed in something so complex, so dangerous, that it left him reeling. He felt a deep yearning to walk out the door, get on the subway, and go back to the safety and routine of his real life. Stress affected him more acutely than it did most people. He couldn't handle the adrenaline, the stress, the lack of regular meals. He needed his afternoon run, his daily meditation, his walk with Connie at the end of the day to even him out. He wanted to go back to being the man he was before Jess Price.

"I know this is unsettling, to say the least." Rachel pulled out a chair and joined him. She looked as unnerved as he felt. "I never imagined in my wildest dreams I would be discussing this in anything but a theoretical fashion. While I've studied the hierarchies of demonology my entire career and can describe angelic and demonic attributes in detail, I'm not quite sure how to approach this from the perspective of the practical Kabbalah." She put her head in her hands, and he knew that she was struggling with this as much as he was.

Her vulnerability allowed him to feel the strength of his desire to understand what happened to Jess. He'd come so close to unraveling the mystery. He couldn't give up now. "Tell me what you know about Lilith."

"Simply put, Lilith is one of the most powerful female spirits in the occult tradition. Occultists hail Lilith as Queen of Demons, but she didn't start out that way. In Hebrew texts, Lilith was the first woman, the original wife of Adam, long before Eve came along. She was created with Adam—not from his rib like Eve, but from the very same clay. Lilith was beautiful, exceptionally strong, brilliant, and innovative. As such, she demanded to be treated as Adam's equal. Ancient texts report that she would not submit to her husband, and this has been interpreted to mean she would not lie on her back during copulation. Rather, she insisted that he submit to her. Adam complained to the Creator, who replaced Lilith with Eve.

"Lilith was exiled, but she found a worthy companion in a powerful angel called Samael, or the Angel of Death, as he is sometimes known. The scholar Gershom Scholem has shown that Satan is the popular name for Samael, which makes Lilith the Bride of Satan, I suppose. Rabbi Luria described Samael and Lilith as a demonic power couple, with Samael ruling male demons and Lilith ruling the female. Whatever you call them, they rule the Klipot together, controlling the shadows, the dark intelligences, demons, and all evil on earth. Lilith's reputation as the Mother of Evil has only grown over the centuries. She's associated with witchcraft and is known for stealing children in the night. But most of all, she is sexually voracious, a succubus, a provocative demon that visits men in the night, seduces them, and uses their semen to create more demons."

Brink startled at the mention of Lilith's night visits. It was disturbingly close to the dreams he'd experienced since he met Jess Price. He knew he should tell Rachel about his dreams but couldn't. "And you believe all of this?"

"I do," she said. "But I am also a scholar. I don't believe blindly. My faith is grounded in historical documentation and interpretation. If you peel back the layers of what has been learned about Lilith—from her first mention in the Dead Sea Scrolls, right on through to the Zohar—it's clear she is a prime example of humanity's struggle with powerful women. When a woman demands equality, she is reviled, exiled, and vilified. Every powerful woman in history, from Cleopatra to Joan of Arc to Elizabeth I, has experienced the same contradictions Lilith faced: She can be powerful only if she doesn't show her strength. Even now, women live in a world filled with such hypocrisies. One part of me likes to imagine the equality that Lilith represents. We were all equal once, before the fall. But, in truth, Lilith is extremely dangerous."

Brink took it all in. He didn't understand Lilith the way Rachel did, and he didn't have her faith to rely on, but he could see that Rachel's interpretation offered a consistent explanation of what had happened to Jess Price. "Whatever is going on," he said, "I know one thing for sure: Jess needs help."

Rachel gave him a long, searching look. "You really care what happens to her, don't you?"

"I've known her only a short time, but I feel connected to her. It isn't often that I feel that way." His feelings ran much deeper than this, but he hardly knew how to explain them to himself, let alone Rachel. The hallucinatory dreams, the intense attraction, the sense of urgency—it all overwhelmed him. "I want to help her. I need to help her."

"There might be something we can do, then," she said. "But it is an incredible risk."

Brink felt a ray of optimism, small but definite. "What kind of risk?"

She stood and looked at the circles positioned over the table. "I can't make any promises, but there is a chance that, if we do it perfectly, we could use Abulafia's original circle to contain Lilith."

"Contain?" Brink tried to imagine how this was possible; it seemed like catching a genie in a jar. "What, you think she's out here now, floating around somewhere?"

"When Noah Cooke and Jess Price performed the words in this circle, they opened a portal that released Lilith into the world. They gave Lilith life in this dimension. *Haim.* That connection is extremely strong, like the connection between a mother and a child."

"More like Frankenstein's monster to its creator," Brink said.

"Exactly so. As with the rabbi and his son, Lilith attached herself to Noah first. When he expired, she moved on to Jess Price. And as long as Jess lives, Lilith will remain with her here, in our dimension."

"Maybe that's why LaMoriette killed himself," Brink said, recalling the first page of the letter. *I have suffered, but it is the suffering of a man who has created his own torture chamber.* "He couldn't live with that bond."

"It's a terrible one, to be sure," Rachel said. "My guess is that Lilith uses Jess's body, takes what she needs, and then leaves her. Jess is a source of energy. Lilith feeds off her like a parasite."

He thought about Jess Price, the anemic quality of her skin, how her physical and mental health had been sapped. "If this is the case, Jess didn't kill Noah," Brink said. "This demon did."

He remembered the autopsy report, its description of trauma to Noah Cooke's organs, the internal bleeding, the strange marks on his skin. LaMoriette had similar marks. So had Jess. Anne-Marie had described the marks as crazing, the external proof of extreme internal pressure. Despite his doubt, it all seemed strangely consistent. He had a thousand more questions to ask, but a barrage of knocking came at the door, then Jameson's voice. Their time was up. Jameson wanted the suitcase.

"We have to make a decision," she said, glancing at the door.

"Tell me what we need to do," he said, standing and grabbing his messenger bag. "I'm ready to try anything."

"We'll need to see Jess for this to work, which means going to the prison."

"My access to Jess was cut off. If I show up at the prison, the guards will arrest me on orders of the governor of New York."

"Is there another way?" Rachel asked, her voice filled with urgency.

"My only contact from the prison is currently in the hospital."

"But we need Jess Price," she said. "There's no way around it."

He remembered the thick brick walls, the scrolls of barbed wire, the endless miles of evergreen forest surrounding the prison. He remembered that Thessaly had said that Jess would be moved out of the prison. "It's not going to be easy," he said.

"Nothing about this is going to be easy," she said. "Even if we manage to see Jess, I'm an expert in the history of Jewish mysticism. This is the practical Kabbalah. I've never done anything like this before. We will need to be extremely careful. These rituals, as you well know, can have terrible repercussions. There's a good chance it will fail, or worse. Are you prepared for that possibility?"

Brink thought of Jess, remembering the word she'd written during their first meeting: *Trust.* She trusted him to help her. He couldn't walk away now. "Absolutely," he said. "Let's go."

With Jameson pounding on the door, Rachel packed the suitcase, putting the porcelain doll and the pages of Abulafia's manuscript inside.

"Quick, follow me," Rachel said, as she pushed open a window and climbed out onto a fire escape. With Jameson's threats pushing him onward, Brink climbed out the window and followed Rachel Appel into the bright morning sunlight.

55

Halfway down the block, Rachel Appel ducked into a parking garage and nodded to the attendant; within minutes he reappeared with a white Jeep Wrangler. Brink slid into the passenger seat and placed the suitcase carefully in the back, tucking it behind Rachel's seat with care, aware of its fragile contents. Rachel hit the gas and pulled out into the street. She was right to hurry. Not even five minutes had passed since they'd climbed out of the reading room, and already a police car sat in front of the center, its lights spinning. Brink caught a glimpse of Cullen speaking to the officers, clearly frantic. They'd taken one of the Morgan Library's most precious manuscripts, and Cullen Withers would be held responsible. More worrisome was that Jameson's SUV was not on the street at all. Not the kind of person to wait for the police, Jameson had already taken matters into his own hands.

Brink buckled the seatbelt and watched with fear and admiration as Rachel raced through city traffic with speed and precision, moving as if through an obstacle course. She swerved onto a one-way street, took a shortcut through a parking lot, and then, in a move that made him whistle with admiration, turned onto a ramp that deposited them on the Henry Hudson Parkway. "Now we know," Rachel said, grinning with pleasure as she fell in with traffic, "that they aren't following us."

It was just after 10:00 A.M. according to the digital clock in the dash, and yet the sun shone brighter, hotter, more intensely than it had for days, as if something about the city—the endless glass towers and depths of concrete—magnified its power. He glanced at the river bordering the parkway. It glistened and bent in the sunlight, bright as a strip of pounded metal. Although traffic was dense coming into the city, it was moving quickly in their direction. As they crossed the George Washington Bridge and exited onto the Palisades Parkway, he began to relax.

But just as Brink let his guard down, Rachel gasped. He turned to find Cam Putney leaning forward from the back seat, the suitcase in one hand, a gun in the other. He'd pressed a gun to Rachel's temple. "Pull over," he said, his voice soft, as if he were inviting them to sit down for coffee. Brink met his eye and the guy winked, a maddeningly playful gesture, almost a dare. *If you want it, come back and get it.* Brink glanced at Rachel and saw that she was terrified. They had no choice but to do what Putney wanted.

Rachel pulled the Jeep to the side of the road and Cam jumped out, suitcase in hand. She didn't wait to see what he did next but drove off even before Cam had closed the door. Brink stretched into the back seat and slammed the door shut, just as Sedge's SUV stopped to retrieve Cam.

Brink's heart was racing. He took a deep breath, trying to get a handle on what had happened. How had he missed Cam hiding in the back? How had they come so close to escaping with the case, only to lose it?

Rachel took a deep breath. "So much for that," she said. "We might as well turn around and go back to the city." Her voice was tight, and while she didn't seem half as unnerved as Brink felt, her knuckles were white as she gripped the steering wheel.

"But we can't turn back now," he said. It was like giving up in the middle of a hedge maze. Turn back, and they would be lost.

"Without the manuscript, we can't reenact the vocalization," she said. "It's pointless."

"Wait a second," Brink said, taking his notebook and pen from his jacket. Numbers and letters filled his mind as the circle took shape. He opened the notebook and reproduced the circle exactly as he'd seen it in Abulafia's manuscript. "There's no reproducing the vessel," he said. "But we can use this with Jess."

Rachel examined the circle, shaking her head in admiration. "This is a complicated drawing. There are hundreds, maybe thousands, of possible permutations. Are you certain you've got this right?"

"One hundred percent," he said. He took out his phone, snapped a photo of the circle, and sent it via encrypted message to Vivek Gupta. He'd want to see the complete version, and it would give him the chance to see Brink's current location. Usually, he hated the idea of being watched, but it made Brink feel safe to know his mentor could track them.

"I know you probably get this all the time, but that's just . . . *wow*."

"Yeah, I do get that a lot," he said, smiling. "But it's still nice to hear it. And it'll be even better when we solve this."

"Then let's get going." Rachel fumbled with her phone, then gave it to him. "We can be at the prison in five hours if we don't hit traffic."

As Rachel drove, Brink stared out the window, watching the river beyond the palisades.

"Who is your contact at the prison?" Rachel asked. "The one in the hospital?"

"Dr. Thessaly Moses," Brink said. He explained what he knew of Thessaly's attack—that it had happened the night before in her home, and that she'd been hospitalized.

"Clearly that's who we need to talk to," she said. "Not only will she have insight into how we can see Jess, but she might be able to tell us something about the attack."

He didn't know Thessaly's condition, or if she could have visitors at all, but he realized that there wasn't a better option. He looked up the address of the hospital, entered it into the GPS, and gave the phone back to Rachel, who positioned it on the dash.

As Rachel drove, Brink sat in silence, forced into inaction. There was an iPhone cable, and so he plugged in his phone, glad for the opportunity to charge it. He needed to relax but didn't know how. He tapped his finger against the seat, a pulsing rhythm moving through him. He felt like a pinball pushed through a series of wild twists and unexpected turns, bumpers bouncing him one way, blinking lights pushing him another. Yet now, in the peace of Rachel's car, he took a moment to let it all settle.

Looking at the overall picture, he understood that there was a larger pattern at play. The fragmented pieces coalesced: He had discovered the error in the copied circle, the bug in the program that had caused so much trouble. And he had a plan to correct it. But, as every puzzleist knows, having the pieces means little if you haven't mastered the logic of the whole. And Rachel, with her deep knowledge of the history behind the circles, could provide it.

Glancing at Rachel, he took in her profile: her long dark hair and her regal bearing. Her absolute belief fascinated him. "I'm curious," he said, "what drew you to your work. Did you always believe so strongly?"

"Actually, no," she said, giving him a smile. "For a long time, I didn't know what I believed. I was spiritual but lived very far from the traditions of my faith. Then I met someone who changed my life. Isaac was visiting New York from Israel, and we were introduced by a mutual friend. He was a serious scholar, one with progressive ideas about faith, and was studying to become a rabbi. He asked me to meet him for a coffee, and as we talked, I realized he was like no one I had ever met before. When I told him I wasn't sure about the existence of God, he asked if I believed in science. Of course I said yes and began to discuss the big bang, physics, and so on. He said that his concept of God was identical to the concept of scientific reality I had described. God was, he said, light. Not metaphorically. Not abstractly. But literally all of the attributes we associate with photons of light—a ubiquitous presence that moves freely through space and time, an energy with the creative capacities to generate life on a molecular level—these are the qualities of the creative power we know as God. His ideas were much more complicated than this, obviously, but the basis of his faith resonated with me. God was light. The material world was the Divine one. It's the basis of the Kabbalah and everything I believe. I guess you could say that Isaac converted me."

"It sounds like you're kindred spirits," he said.

"Yes, we were," she said, her voice becoming soft.

"Were?"

"My husband died of lung cancer three years ago," she said. "He was thirty-five years old."

"I'm sorry," Brink said. "I had no idea."

"There's no way you could have known," she said. "I was heartbroken when he got sick, and often angry, but my husband wasn't bitter. He accepted his death with the same sense of purpose as he lived his life. He believed that our mission here is to learn to see, really see, the beauty of creation and to understand that the central purpose of existence is not achievement or comfort or even human connection but making our way back to the source of everything: that infinite point of light that is God. He taught me that we must always fight for what we believe. And that," she said, glancing over at him, "is why I want to help you. You are fighting to help this woman, despite the danger. You've taken a strong position and you're willing to defend it."

What Rachel said was true, but Brink's motives were not so simple. Yes, he wanted to help Jess, but something else had taken hold of him, a deep need that filled him with a chemical rush, one so addictive he couldn't escape it. When he closed his eyes, the landscape of his mind was overrun with Abulafia's circle. The swirl of letters and the configuration of symbols took over, leaving him helpless to resist. It was primal, his need to solve the puzzle, and nothing could stop him.

56

Ray Brook's only hospital, like its only prison, lay outside town, nestled in an expanse of forest. After the ambush by Cam Putney, the rest of the drive had been almost peaceful. Brink played out every possible permutation of what could've happened to Thessaly Moses. The article Vivek Gupta had sent him was vague, and he didn't have much to go on. He didn't know how badly she'd been hurt, where Jess Price had been at the time, or if the police had found the perpetrator. He didn't even know the extent of her injuries and the absence of details made him imagine the worst.

They arrived midafternoon. In the hospital parking lot, Brink tried to call Thessaly. She didn't pick up, but a text message from her number appeared ten seconds later. *Can't talk. Where are you?*

He explained that they were at the hospital and needed to see her. She wrote: *The police were here this morning, which makes people nervous. Only close family allowed. If anyone asks, say you're my brother. I'm in room 207.*

Brink responded: *Okay, sister, although they might not buy it, considering I'm white.*

To which Thessaly responded with a dark-skinned thumbs-up emoji: *Stepbrother, then.*

On the second floor, they were immediately stopped by a nurse, who questioned them. When Brink said they were looking for room 207, the nurse eyed them but then pointed down the hall. He walked quickly, passing a wheelchair, an abandoned IV drip, and a tray of food outside a door—mashed potatoes, broccoli, and something that resembled lasagna. He cringed. The scent of hospitals always brought him back to the time his father was sick. Now, almost thirteen years later, through the confluence of heart monitors beeping and the smell of bad food, he felt the experience return and shimmer before him, then disappear again, a mirage of time called up by his senses.

At room 207, Rachel nodded for Brink to go in without her. He hesitated—Rachel Appel was part of this now, and Thessaly should know that—but figured there would be a better time for introductions. Thessaly sat up in a bed. A bandage covered the left side of her face. He stepped into the room, but she didn't see him until he stood almost directly in front of her. "Mr. Brink," she said, her smile lopsided under the bandage.

"What the hell happened, Dr. Moses?" he said, keeping his voice low, as if volume might make her injury worse.

"Twenty-two stitches," she said, tracing a line over her cheek. "I'm lucky I didn't lose my eye."

The true horror of what had happened came over him. She'd been brutally attacked. The pain must be intense, and she would surely have a scar across her face. The weight of responsibility returned. He should have been there. If he hadn't left Ray Brook, she wouldn't be hurt.

He pulled up a chair and sat down by the bed, hoping he could find a way to ease her discomfort. As he did, he saw the weekend's *New York Times* sitting in a thick pile on the bedside table. The *Times* Sunday magazine lay open to the puzzles, and one of his—the Triangulum that had caused him such trouble the day he got involved in all of this—filled the page.

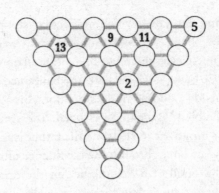

It was a solid puzzle, and the elegance of the construction filled him with pride. He loved number puzzles—Str8ts, 24 puzzles, sudoku, cross-figures. Their premise was clear, with no room for ambiguity. You're given a few numbers, you provide the rest, and it all adds up. Scanning the Triangulum, he noted that it was one of the more challenging puzzles he'd made. Thessaly had completed only two of the answers. "That's a fun one," he said, nodding to his puzzle.

"Right," she said, her voice deadpan. "I worked all morning on that, Brink. Can't you make something a little more accessible for us normal people?"

"I wouldn't exactly call you normal," he said. "It was utterly amazing that you got Jess Price to record that message for me. If you hadn't, I wouldn't be anywhere near where I am in this."

She gave him a long hard stare. "And just where is that?"

He looked out into the hallway, then to the monitors at her side. He'd never been paranoid before, but he was all too aware that his movements could be tracked, his voice recorded. "I'll explain everything as soon as I can," he said. "But first, tell me who did this to you."

She shook her head. "I don't know," she said. "I went home to send you the audio file and was sitting at the dining room table when it happened. Clearly, I must have confronted the intruder—I was hit in the face with my own laptop—but I can't remember. My doctor says that there's a fifty-fifty chance my memory of the event will return."

Brink felt a moment of empathy. He understood what it felt like to lose control after an injury.

"In the meantime, the friend I mentioned—John Williams, head of security at the prison—is on a mission to find out who did this. He thinks it has to do with the hack that locked me out of the system."

"Does he think it was someone from the prison?"

Thessaly shrugged. "He doesn't know, but it's possible. He's reviewed every bit of security data, hoping to find something odd—an unauthorized person coming or going, a recently released prisoner who might have an ax to grind, anything. There's a lot to review because, as you noticed on our trip to the basement, the facility has a few structural weak points. So far, John has found nothing."

"Has he looked into Cam Putney's whereabouts?"

The mention of Cam Putney surprised her. "How do you know about him?"

"He's working for Jameson Sedge."

Thessaly registered this information. "You mean Cam Putney is working for the guy in the Tesla that my friend warned me about?"

"Exactly," Brink said. "He's behind all of this."

Thessaly's expression registered a range of emotions: surprise, indignation, then anger. "John will be absolutely furious. He'll want to know everything. Do you mind if I share this information with him?"

"I'd like to talk to him, as well," he said. "I'd like to ask if he can help me with something."

"What kind of something?"

He took a breath, knowing that his next request would fall like a brick. "I need to see Jess Price again."

Thessaly stared at him, as if trying to understand what she'd heard. "Excuse me?"

"You told me she was being transferred," he said. "Did that happen?"

She shook her head. "After the attack, John Williams delayed the transfer."

"I need to talk to her," Brink said. "It doesn't matter where. The library. Your office. Anywhere will suffice. I just need to see her."

"You know that's not possible."

"It's a lot to ask, I realize," he said. "But it's important. Your friend will want to help me if he knows how crucial it is."

Thessaly raised an eyebrow. "Let me get this straight. You want the head of prison security at New York State Correctional Facility to allow a man who has been deemed a security risk, and whose access to the prison has been rescinded, time alone with a prisoner?"

He knew it was an outrageous request. "Ten minutes is all I'm asking for."

"You are out of your mind, Mike Brink."

Brink paused. He'd thought the same thing many times, but there was something satisfying about hearing someone say it out loud.

"Listen, there's more going on here than any of us realized. Jess Price has been afraid to speak about what happened to her because she was being monitored. Cam Putney was watching Jess and reporting back to Jameson Sedge. But Jess may know more about this than she's telling anyone. She started to open up to me. If John Williams would just let me in to see her, I know she'll tell me everything. Including who attacked you."

Thessaly considered this, and just when Brink thought she was going to tell him to leave, she lifted her phone from her lap. "Give me a few minutes," she said. "I'll see what I can do."

Patience was not Mike Brink's strongest suit, and waiting to know if he'd get access to Jess Price was excruciating. He paced the hallway outside Thessaly's room, bought himself and Rachel cups of bitter coffee from a vending machine, and tried to keep from going crazy. He found another copy of the Sunday *Times* magazine in the waiting area, and he helped Rachel solve the Triangulum.

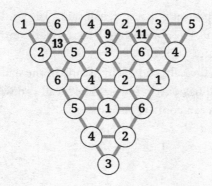

There was something so comforting, so elementally satisfying, about completing the pattern of numbers. They came together in a clear, logical, definite way. There was no ambiguity. The answers were the answers, without a doubt. He smiled as he showed Rachel the letters he'd planted, the alphanumeric Easter egg of his name in the numbers 13, 9, 11, 5, 2. *Mike B.*

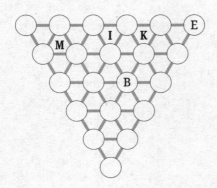

Finally, he heard Thessaly Moses's voice on the phone. He drifted to her door, where he listened to her relay to John Williams the bare bones of what Brink had told her. She said that Brink had solid proof that Cam was working for Jameson Sedge and had been conducting surveillance in the prison. She told him that Brink had developed a relationship with Jess, that he had earned her trust, and that if anyone could get information about what really happened, it was him. Perhaps as a last resort, she said, "Listen, I want to know who did this, and I'm not coming back to work until we do." With this John gave in.

"He'll do it," Thessaly said, seeing Brink in the hallway. "He needs to work a few things out, but he said he'll call you with information about when you can come to the prison."

57

Waiting at the hospital left them vulnerable, so they decided to drive around until John Williams called. They got into the Jeep and headed farther into the Adirondacks, winding through thick forests, passing small towns where American flags fluttered and shiny new 4x4s lined up before roadside bars. From high on a mountain road, Brink spotted the prison, nestled in a scoop of land below. They'd been circling it, he realized, funneling like a moth around a flame, drawn by the mystery of Jess Price.

Thessaly had promised that John Williams would call, but they'd been driving for more than an hour with no news. Finally, Rachel pulled over at a Mobil for gas. Brink filled the Jeep with regular unleaded, then went inside and bought tuna fish sandwiches, bags of chips, and bottles of water. While he would have been happy to eat in the Jeep, Rachel suggested they follow signs to a picnic area located at the foot of a hiking trail. Tables and a fire pit suggested the place was not as isolated as he'd hoped—surely Jameson would be looking for them. But Rachel pointed out that the picnic area sat at an angle that allowed them to see for miles. "No one can sneak up on us here," Rachel said, setting the sandwiches on a wooden picnic table.

It was nearly six o'clock by then, and Brink was starving. The sandwich wasn't going to be enough for him—he should've known he'd need something more substantial than tuna fish—but it felt good to be on solid ground, doing something as simple as having a picnic in the cool, fresh mountain air.

And yet, despite the tranquility of the moment, Brink was on edge. Even as he unwrapped the sandwich and ate, he couldn't help but feel that the woods were closing in on him. He couldn't get his mind off Jess. He needed to see her, needed John Williams to call, needed to look into her eyes and verify that everything he felt was real. He looked at his phone. There was a text message from Thessaly. Jess would be transferred from Ray Brook to a medium-security prison in Connecticut the next morning. While he'd known it would happen, it was a blow he wasn't ready for. This was his last chance. If he didn't see her tonight, if they didn't get into the prison with John Williams's help now, he might never see her again.

He walked to the roadside, trying to dispel the nervous energy that rushed through him. The sun was beginning to set, and a purple-gray light settled over the forest, giving it a forlorn, eerie quality. Such vast beauty should have calmed him, but adrenaline was to synesthesia what stimulants were to the normal brain: It elevated his emotions, enhanced images, and created a barrage of colors and numbers. He looked out over the winding highway and saw a flood of geometric patterns on the smooth black pavement. He took a deep breath. He took another. The patterns weren't going to distract him. He could bring it under control. He just needed a moment to get himself together.

"Mike, come sit down a minute," Rachel said, gesturing for him to sit at the table. "John Williams will call. We just need to be patient."

"You seem pretty sure," he said, stepping away from the road and sitting on the bench next to her.

"I am sure," she said. "He'll come through for us."

He looked at her, studying her confidence. It was true. She was sure. "How can you be so confident in a guy you've never met?"

"I don't know how, but I just feel it," she said. "These moments—

when everything is suspended, when something is about to happen—are the moments when I trust my faith."

"If you could lend me a little of that faith for an hour or so, I'd be grateful," he said.

"Oh, I think you have your own way of believing," she said, studying him in turn. "I didn't want to make you uncomfortable, so I didn't mention it before, but the *Vanity Fair* piece really touched me. I can only imagine the difficulties you've gone through. It must have been so frightening, what happened to you."

"Terrifying," he said. "I woke up a different person." Because Rachel had been so open with him about her loss, he felt able to speak freely with her. "After the injury, the guy I thought I was totally disappeared. The old Mike Brink was dead, and I had to figure out who this new person was."

"Do you ever wonder where you'd be now if you hadn't been injured that night?"

"You mean if I'd made the touchdown, won the championship, and gone on to be a star quarterback?" he asked. "I don't know. It's hard for me to think about. Everything I wanted was taken away in a second. All that work, gone. I had talent, sure, but I worked hard to develop it. Years of six A.M. practices and training, years of missing out on parties, girls, drinking. All to be good at that one thing. And then, with one hit, everything I wanted was just . . . gone."

"It sounds like you miss the person you could have been."

"I suppose so," he said, shifting uneasily on the hard bench. "But if he hadn't disappeared, then I wouldn't be this person sitting here. I would have never understood that there is this whole other side to myself. I guess I should be grateful for the injury, even though it's made everything so difficult."

"It's not easy to be grateful for struggle," she said. "I find myself furious sometimes about losing Isaac. I question how someone as good as he was, as dedicated to making our world better, could die so young. But struggle has the power to purify things. It makes us see who we really are. It's like that with your puzzles, I would suppose."

She was right. For Brink, the ever-increasing challenges of his puzzles, the agony when he couldn't find an answer, and the thrill of coming to a solution, gave his life meaning. He remembered what Dr. Gupta liked to say: *Extraordinary people attract extraordinary events, both good and bad.* "You're right. Maybe there's part of me that needs the struggle. I could be making a very good living working for Google, or a government agency, or teaching at MIT," he said. "But creating puzzles is the one thing that keeps me going."

"Has it crossed your mind that your need to help Jess Price might be connected to this part of you?"

"That's definitely part of it. But I also feel that I can help her. I need to know that what happened to me isn't just about me—that this gift, or whatever it is, has a larger purpose. Jess gives me that."

Night fell, and still no call from John Williams. Brink couldn't sit still a minute longer. He needed to move. They decided to drive to the prison and wait for news from John Williams there. "Do you mind if I drive?" Brink said, taking the keys off the picnic table. He hadn't driven anything but his old truck for years, and it would feel good to do something with his nervous energy.

As they got in the Jeep and headed down the mountain, his thoughts drifted back to his conversation with Rachel. She was right, of course. Struggle had forged him. Pain and loss had created the conditions for his talent. He considered the idea that without pain, without the destructive fire of his injury and the total annihilation of his previous self, he would be half the person he'd become.

Brink was easing into a turn when the Jeep started to shake. It began as a soft vibration in the steering wheel, then grew suddenly to a forceful clenching of gears. The headlights sputtered, the dash went dark, and the brakes froze. He'd only ever felt that once before, during an ice storm in Ohio—he hit a slippery patch, lost control, and slid off the road into a ditch. But there was no ice on the road. It was a warm June night, not a rain cloud in the sky, and he wasn't sliding. A soaring sensation lifted him, even as he understood that they were in danger of crashing into the rocky mountainside.

He was gauging if they should jump out when the Jeep ground to a halt. Before he had a second to figure out what'd happened, a stretch limo pulled up behind them. A large man in a summer suit and fedora climbed out. Vivek Gupta had found them.

Brink hopped out of the Jeep, not sure if he should hug or punch Vivek Gupta. His mentor made the decision for him—he took him in his arms and embraced him. Dr. Gupta was soft as a cushion and smelled of Acqua di Parma cologne, his signature scent. He released Brink and moved on to Rachel, who was wide-eyed with terror.

"Ms. Appel, I'm Dr. Vivek Gupta, and while you may not know me, I've taken the liberty of acquainting myself with you."

"Excuse me?" Rachel said, staring at Dr. Gupta in astonishment.

"When Mr. Brink sent me the circle, I was able to locate and track your vehicle via satellite. With the license plate number of your 2015 Jeep Wrangler, I found your DMV records, and lifted your name, social security number, and date of birth. That is, by the way, how Jameson Sedge's thug found your Jeep in the parking garage, only in reverse: He had your name and professional information and used it to locate the license plate number of your vehicle. It is all connected, and with one piece of information, everything is compromised. For example, with a quick search, I learned the balance of your checking account and the interest rate on your mortgage, which is quite good, by the way. Your professional accolades. Even your dental records. You have excellent teeth, Ms. Appel. Bravo."

He paused to give Brink a mischievous smile.

"Do forgive me for that abrupt seizure of your vehicle," Dr. Gupta said. "But I didn't want to lose you. Your phone signal is not as strong as one would hope up here."

"You did that?" Brink asked, astonished. "How?"

"Zero-day exploit in the Jeep's OS," he said. "Quite useful for those of us who know how to exploit it."

"Zero-day exploit?" Rachel asked, clearly baffled.

"It's a computer bug," Brink said, smiling despite himself. Vivek Gupta had explained this particular bug to him once, but he hadn't paid attention. He was starting to regret how often he'd zoned out in class.

"Actually, it's a backdoor vulnerability in the operating system that allows one with the requisite skills—any experienced hacker, really—to gain access to the electronic system that controls the vehicle. It's a well-known problem, and while the manufacturer claims they've patched the hole, it is obviously still there." He looked down the road, then over his shoulder. "And if I'm able to get into your Jeep's electronic system, my dear, Jameson most certainly can, as well. Now, come quickly, before we're seen."

Vivek Gupta ushered them into the back of the limo. The space was fitted with velvet seats and a large computer monitor. He opened a small metal box lined with foil—a Faraday cage. Brink recognized it from his visit to Cape Cod. Dr. Gupta had locked their phones inside the box all weekend. He did the same with their phones now.

"While Mr. Brink has an uncanny ability to solve puzzles in his head, I must rely on the indefatigable assistance of my computer."

Dr. Gupta pushed a button on a console and a door retracted, revealing a wet bar. "Mr. Brink, if you please."

Brink wasted no time. He poured rye, vermouth, and bitters into a shaker and mixed three Manhattans, Dr. Gupta's favorite cocktail. He dropped Luxardo cherries into the drinks, then passed one to Rachel, then one to Dr. Gupta, and, with a clinking of glasses, he took a sip and settled back into his seat.

Dr. Gupta pulled a keyboard onto his lap, typed in a command, and the monitor filled with a luminous circle: Abulafia's Variations on the Name of God.

"Now, sit back, enjoy your drink, and listen carefully. This is going to blow your mind."

58

———

"When Mr. Brink sent me this incredible configuration, I was quite at a loss. I know very little about the history of religion, and as a Buddhist, I am not well schooled in Judaic iconography," Dr. Gupta said. "But this circle is, from a mathematical perspective, quite intriguing and very complex. I find it extraordinary, considering the man who made it lived in an era without any of the mathematical developments that you and I rely upon to understand the world. Indeed, he was living in a time when wax candles were a luxury."

Vivek Gupta adjusted the keyboard on his lap, typed another command, and the circle enlarged. Mike Brink had seen it only a few times, but it existed in his mind when he closed his eyes. Using a laser pen, Vivek Gupta drew his attention to the ring of numbers around the radials, then to the Star of David at the center of the image. "I am a heathen, and Ms. Appel can explain the religious significance of this image far better than I. But what I see here is a kind of mathematical conundrum. A *puzzle,* my friends, a *puzzle.* It is this very thing that has grabbed me by the guts and dragged me through a career as a cypher wizard, mathematician, artist, and lover of the ineffable. That said, I do, like my hero, the Indian mathematician Srinivasa Ramanujan, believe this: *An equation means nothing to me unless it expresses a thought of God.* This puzzle is one such equation."

Vivek Gupta turned back to the screen. "What first interested me about this circle was that there is a distinct pattern. Do you see it, Mr. Brink?"

"The black and white squares around the edge," Brink said. "They're binary. It was one of the first things I noticed."

"A binary code," Dr. Gupta said. "An unusual element in such a drawing, I would think."

"There is a history of using codes to communicate information about the Creator," Rachel said. "Abulafia took it to a whole new level, clearly, but it was not a unique practice."

"Is that so?" Dr. Gupta said. "Well, the use of binary codes may have been used by the Jewish people, but the system was not unique to them." Vivek Gupta clicked a button, and images of thick black lines stacked up in groups of six appeared.

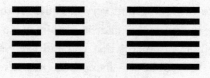

"Abraham Abulafia could not have possibly known this, as he had no contact with the Chinese, but four thousand years before his time, a Chinese philosopher named Fu Xi was given a similar set of binary messages from heaven—the secret of feminine and masculine binary power, known as yin and yang. Like Abulafia, he created a system of notation—not variations of the name of God but hexagrams: yin and yang, a series of broken and solid lines, stacked in groups of six. These hexagrams were then further systematized into sixty-four groupings, which form the basis of the I Ching, or Book of Changes. They were used for divination. Indeed, they were believed to carry all the secrets of the world."

Dr. Gupta clicked a button and a photograph of a vortex appeared on the screen. The vortex was filled with discrete sections; equations were written over each one.

"Fu Xi's binary system got the attention of German mathematician Gottfried Leibniz, who was working tirelessly to create a system without the use of decimals. He longed for a pure mathematics, one that fully expressed the difference between zero and one. The problem of zero, or nonexistence, obsessed Leibniz. How could zero— pure potential—transform to one, a whole and complete material object? The transition between nothing and something is the central question of . . . well, everything. All our spiritual and intellectual systems—religion and science, but also existential questions: How does life arise? What happens to it after the body dies? And what is the nature of nonexistence?"

Brink glanced at Rachel, wondering if she followed Dr. Gupta's hairpin curves of thought. He was used to such intellectual flights of fancy. He'd followed them during Dr. Gupta's lectures at MIT, where he was famous for keeping students late as he explained the nuances of a mathematical puzzle. But he needn't have worried. Rachel was entranced. She gazed at Dr. Gupta, taking in his every word.

"Leibniz's questions," Rachel said, "are at the very root of Kabbalistic thought."

"Indeed!" Dr. Gupta said, delighted. "Leibniz was deeply interested in Kabbalah, as it corresponded to his obsession with the mysteries of creation. He posited that the most profound operations of the universe could be explained through a system of zero and one. Time has proven his instincts to be correct. Binary systems became humanity's primary way of calculating and expressing the material world. As you probably know, we are entirely dependent on the binary codes that run all computer-based communications. Transportation, the internet, national security—all run by binary codes. Nearly every cultural experience—from recorded music to film and television to audio and digital books—is created and delivered with a binary code. And this circle, as it turns out, contains a binary code, as well."

Rachel leaned closer to the screen. "I don't know why I didn't see it before," she said.

"It isn't exactly obvious," Dr. Gupta said. "But when one studies the sequence, it becomes clear that the black and white squares at the edge of the circle are not at all random. I saw that fairly soon and guessed there to be a first-layer solution to the sequence, but I suspected that there was more to it. So I ran it through various computer programs, and, to my astonishment, I found that the sequence created very surprising results."

"What kind of results?" Rachel asked, still focused on the computer screen.

"The binary sequence, when manipulated in seventy-two variations—the original intent of this prayer circle, was it not?— created a line of computer code."

"A computer code?" Rachel asked, astonished. "This was drawn nearly a thousand years ago."

"Astonishing, I know, even more so because it is not just any old computer code." Dr. Gupta hit a few keys on the keyboard, and an image of an equation appeared on the screen. "Have you heard of the qubit?"

"The unit of code used in quantum computing," Brink said, studying the equation. He'd never seen anything like it, with its stacks of zeros and ones, but its symmetry appealed to him.

"Precisely," Dr. Gupta said. "A qubit is the simplest unit of quantum information. Whereas computers today use bits, or binary elements, to encode information, the computers of the future will use qubits, or codes that harness the complexity and, frankly, mind-bending laws of quantum mechanics. Qubits are nonbinary. They process information in a multilocational fashion. The simplest way to put it is that while bits lock down information in one state—either zero or one; nonexistence or existence—qubits allow information to be in both states at once. Information can be here and there, black and white, masculine and feminine, at the same time. That state of being in multiple positions at once is called a superposition. The future of all systems of information will be that of superpositions."

Dr. Gupta paused, looked to Mike Brink and Rachel Appel. "Are you following me?"

"You're saying that information will behave like quantum particles," Rachel said. "The way a photon can be in two places at once in the double-slit test," Rachel said.

"Precisely," Dr. Gupta said. "Quantum computers will be thousands of times more powerful than our fastest computers. Such power will fuel superpositions and quantum teleportation of information. They will give us an incredible capability to solve problems that appear to be unsolvable: disease, hunger. Even death."

"I understand the power of such a machine," Rachel said. "But why would Jameson Sedge want it so badly?"

"He must have suspected that Abulafia had encoded information he was looking for. Perhaps he even knew about the quantum code I discovered. He certainly would have the ability to extract it, as I did. But the real question is if Jameson has developed the means to use it. For that, he would need a quantum computer and the network to run it. If that is the case, and he has the technology to deploy it—"

"—he would have the code to immortality," Brink said, finishing his sentence. He stared at the code on the screen, trying to wrap his mind around it. An ancient sequence created by a mystic in the thirteenth century contained the building blocks for a quantum code that could, if used correctly, change the future of the human race. "It's utterly mind-blowing."

"We used to fantasize about it when we were young," Dr. Gupta said. "We dreamed about the ability to create new systems for consciousness other than the strictly biological. We joked about finding a better package for the soul, one that didn't require food or sleep. One that never wore down. Think about it, Mr. Brink: When we spoke via video yesterday, would you have known the difference if it was the reconstruction of my biological self on the screen or a reconstruction of my consciousness through pixels? Was it really me or an image of me? You would never know the difference."

Vivek Gupta took a final sip of his Manhattan and placed the glass on the floor.

"I always thought of immortality as theoretical, the kind of idea that fuels science fiction. But I never believed that qubits, quantum mechanics, and data teleportation could actually be possible. It's not such a fantasy anymore. Consciousness can be encoded, preserved, teleported. Sedge's mind could exist in a superposition of the present and the future. We have the mathematical models to prove it."

"But this is all still theoretical," Brink said. "The technology isn't there yet."

"Correct," Vivek Gupta said. "But theoretical is the first step toward the actual. In my humble opinion, we are a long way away from that kind of massive disruption in human existence. But Jameson is determined. His ideas have always been much bigger than the present moment. And this code—even if theoretical—is nothing short of miraculous. Abulafia gave humanity a very powerful tool."

"Perhaps," Rachel said, looking doubtful. "But Abulafia couldn't have known anything about this. He designed the circle as an act of prayer. It was meant to be performed, chanted, experienced. It was meant to be a way to communicate with the Divine."

"That may very well be so," Vivek Gupta said. "But as a mathematician, I can tell you that this circle contains a remarkable treasure, one too precise, too perfect, to be accidental."

"Maybe there was nothing accidental about it," Rachel said. She met his eye, and he could see what she was thinking: The God Puzzle was not random, not a mistake or even a lucky accident, but a gift to humanity from God.

59

For more than a decade, Cam Putney had followed orders. He'd traveled across the world, gathering hard drives filled with God knows what precious information; he'd trained relentlessly, pushing himself physically and mentally to the limits of his abilities; he'd moved five hours north of the city to work as a prison guard, leaving his child behind. He'd killed a man. He'd attacked a woman. He'd always done Sedge's bidding without question, never uttering a word of objection, never asking questions. He executed orders in the method he'd been trained: quickly, thoroughly, with honor and silence. That was the way of a Singularity samurai. Nothing was more important to him than the mission.

Except his daughter. Jasmine was thirteen years old, healthy and happy, a well-adjusted girl who had no clue what her father did for a living. He'd hidden the truth from her, hoping she would have a normal childhood, and it had worked. Mr. Sedge's education fund had sent her to the best private schools in Manhattan, where she had friends who invited her to lavish birthday parties in the Hamptons and winter-break beach vacations in the Bahamas. She liked musicals—he'd taken her to *Matilda* four times—and TikTok and K-pop. She loved animals. She told him the last time he saw her— months earlier, during her spring break—that she wanted to be a veterinarian when she grew up. *A veterinarian.* He never would have imagined such a profession for himself at thirteen. He was proud that he'd sheltered her from the harsh realities of the world and the truth of what he'd done. And yet she was so vulnerable, so easily hurt. He wondered if he'd have the will to help her grow strong, to allow her to suffer. It was the only way she'd learn what he knew: That safety came from confronting pain head-on.

Cam had faced danger over and over through the years, until it was a part of him. Ume-Sensei had taught him that his body retained those experiences, all the pain and pleasure, the failures and victories. But he never quite believed it until the moment he attacked Dr. Moses.

He'd been ready. He knew he had one shot, and one shot only. The trick was hitting her without damaging the computer. The file she'd moved from her phone to the laptop was important. Mr. Sedge would want the computer, and the phone, too, so Cam needed to be careful, place the bullet at an angle that would thrust her backward, propel the body away from the table. Not an easy shot, considering he stood behind her, but not impossible, either.

He'd moved slowly, taking each step as if across a tightrope. One wrong move and he'd disturb the delicate balance he needed to reach his target. Halfway across the room, he realized his mistake: A shadow slipped over the laptop screen, revealing his presence to Dr. Moses. It happened in a matter of seconds: She registered him behind her, slammed the laptop closed, and swung around to face him. The ferocity of her response stopped him cold; he couldn't move but simply stared as she swung the laptop at him. One quick blow to his wrist sent the Glock flying across the room.

In the seconds that followed, his thoughts shut down and his years of training took over. His vision blurred, his awareness receded, and he struck. When he came back to the present, he stood above Thessaly Moses. She lay on the hardwood floor of the dining room, blood oozing from a gash across the left side of her face. He glanced down and found that the narrow edge of the laptop was covered in blood. He didn't remember taking it from her, but he'd used it like a blade.

Suddenly, the floor tilted, and a wave of panic grabbed hold of him. He was dizzy. His legs began to buckle, and his hands shook. He'd never killed a woman before, and with his own hands to boot. He couldn't quite believe it. Ume-Sensei had taught him that acts of strength required a moment of retreat. He needed to step away from his panic and breathe. He pulled air into his belly, held it for four, three, two, one seconds, then released. The room began to steady, as did his hands.

Cam hadn't had a drink in more than ten years, but he'd never melted down on a job, and he needed one badly. He uncorked the bottle of wine, poured a glass, and drank it down. What had he become? He glanced back at Thessaly Moses, the pool of blood expanding on the floor, and he saw the face of his daughter. All the life and intelligence of Jasmine could be crushed as easily as that, with one brute blow to the head.

Something deep inside Cam broke, and the foundation of his identity as Sedge's warrior began to crumble. He wasn't a mindless animal. He wasn't a monster. Everything Ume-Sensei had taught him was proof of that. His daughter was proof of that. And then, like a message from another realm, Thessaly Moses groaned. He turned to see her eyes flutter open. A rush of relief came over him. She wasn't dead. He took her phone and dialed 911. He placed the phone near her, so that the sound of the operator's voice roused her. Cam left, knowing help would soon arrive.

Dr. Moses would live. And still, what he'd done to her haunted him. When Mr. Sedge told him that it was time to complete his mission, the feeling of panic returned, and Jasmine was all Cam could see. He'd known it was coming. All his training had been leading to this, the one great act of loyalty. Every skill he'd learned, every piece of information he'd collected, the hours and hours of watching the prisoner—these jobs were just steps along the path of Mr. Sedge's ultimate plan.

And yet what would it do to his daughter? What would it do to him? He'd changed over the years. Discipline and education made him different than he'd been when he signed his contract. If he agreed to what Mr. Sedge asked and fulfilled his duties, if he sacrificed his life in this way, it would mean the end of his ability to be a father, at least in any normal sense. He wasn't afraid of the act itself or the violence involved. But if the plan worked, if Mr. Sedge's theories were proven correct, then Cam's life would be forever changed.

After Cam retrieved the suitcase from the Jeep, Mr. Sedge informed him that the time had come. "Everything we've worked for is here," he'd said. "The future has arrived." Cam considered what lay ahead, the duties he'd promised to perform, the sacrifices it would require, and he panicked. He told Mr. Sedge that he couldn't do what he needed him to do. He resigned his position and was ready to face the consequences.

But Mr. Sedge wasn't angry. They drove to Lower Manhattan, where Anne-Marie was waiting for them in the helicopter. They spent the entire flight up to the compound in silence. When they arrived, Sedge put a hand on Cam's shoulder, met his eye, and told him he understood his reaction. "The future is frightening," he said. "But you have nothing to fear. I will guide you the whole way." They went below the house to Sedge's bunker filled with computer equipment. There was a generator powered by geothermal energy, which kept the whole place off the electrical grid, and a cellar filled with emergency supplies—a month's worth of water, food, iodine pills, canned goods, fifty-pound sacks of beans and rice. He shouldn't have been surprised. Mr. Sedge believed in self-reliance in the most literal sense. No lawyers, no banks, no exposure to the media, no unknown quantities of anything came near him, ever.

Cam was sure that even Anne-Marie didn't know the truth about Sedge's work. He wondered how a smart, beautiful lady like that could put up with all the weird shit Mr. Sedge did. He supposed the money went a long way toward smoothing over Mr. Sedge's eccentricities, but he wondered if she, like Cam, had come to think of money as irrelevant to the work. If she saw, at the very edges of Mr. Sedge's obsession, the promise of something beautiful. Maybe she, too, had been seduced by the sublime future Mr. Sedge was making.

Mr. Sedge sat him down under the fluorescent lights in the bunker, poured him a glass of his world-class Scotch, and asked him questions: What did he want? What was he afraid of? Why would he spend so many years in training, only to leave at that crucial moment? Cam told him that he couldn't allow his daughter to suffer the consequences of his actions.

"On the contrary, she will benefit," Jameson Sedge said. "Your actions will make you a hero, my friend. Your role in guiding humanity into the Great Reset will be celebrated."

"You know how it is," Cam said. "My name will be all over the place—TV, the internet. Jasmine's mother will find out. Her friends . . ."

"Your daughter won't be ashamed. She will be proud. You are fulfilling the potential of all mankind: to supersede the gods. To make them irrelevant. To live forever."

"But if it works," he said, "I may never see her again."

"If it works, you will have an eternity with her."

Mr. Sedge walked through the bunker, light from the computer monitors giving him a green hue.

"Come, I will show you the level of trust I am talking about." The computer was like no other piece of machinery he'd ever seen, a wall of glowing chips blinking behind a sheet of glass. Mr. Sedge sat before a keyboard and monitor and opened a file. It was his last will and testament, signed, as Cam's contract had been, as a Ricardian contract. Beside Cam's name was an astronomical amount of money, more than he could ever possibly spend.

"Anne-Marie will be taken care of, and there are various endowments I've made. But a significant portion of my estate will go to you, Cam. Think it over. Even if I'm wrong, even if everything I've planned fails miserably, Jasmine will benefit. Consider what it will mean for her to have this security."

Mr. Sedge plugged a portable hard drive into his computer, and a bank of files opened across the screen.

"This is my life's work," he said, his eyes filling with pride. "I know that there is a great chance of failure. But I need to know that you will help me complete the final steps. Will you do that, Mr. Putney? Will you prove to be the man I thought you were?"

In the end, he relented. Cam Putney would ensure that Jameson Sedge's Great Reset would begin correctly. "Yes, Mr. Sedge," he said, his voice trembling. "I'm that man."

With that, they removed the circular drawing from the suitcase, scanned it, and set the program in motion. "There's just one more step," Mr. Sedge said, elated. "And for that, we need Jess Price."

60

John Williams called just as Dr. Gupta finished his presentation. He released his hold on the Jeep's computer system with a few strokes at his keyboard, and the engine revved to life. Brink ceded the driver's seat to Rachel, feeling relieved to be a passenger. He hated losing control, and the experience of feeling the Jeep swerve of its own volition had unnerved him. While Vivek Gupta promised not to interfere again, Brink didn't quite believe him. Dr. Gupta had a fondness for practical jokes, especially when they were on Brink.

They couldn't afford another delay. John Williams gave them specific instructions. They were to park half a mile from the prison, in a thicket of trees marked by a NO HUNTING sign. There, they would find a bag with a new prison-guard uniform, an ID badge, and a name tag.

Brink stepped into the trees, stripped off his clothes, and pulled on the uniform, feeling the stiff polyester against his skin. It fit, more or less, but he realized that his red Converse low-tops didn't exactly match the profile of a security guard in a New York State prison. There was no alternative. They would have to do.

He threw his clothes into the Jeep, gave Rachel a nod, and walked to the prison. The night was warm, cloudless, stars freckling the immense black dome of the sky. The prison was there, just ahead. He saw the thick brick wall, the twists of razor wire, the floodlights. A sudden wave of fear came over him at the very idea of passing that barrier. He knew what he'd face if he got caught. Impersonating a prison guard and entering a state prison under false pretenses wasn't a puzzle he could solve his way out of. Once he crossed that threshold, there was no going back.

John Williams told him to be at the gate at exactly 10:00 P.M., when the night shift arrived. He would escort Brink through the various security points and introduce him as a new hire. The new uniform and the fact that nobody had seen him before would corroborate this story. While Brink had been at the prison before, it was during the day, and the night security team wouldn't recognize him. If everything went as planned, he'd be in and out quickly, without complications.

Brink arrived at the first security checkpoint. This guard saw his uniform, glanced at his badge, and had begun to question him when a voice came from beyond.

"That's the new guy, Chuck," John Williams said. "Got his paperwork in my office, if you need a copy."

The guard eyed Brink, glancing again at his security badge, then waved him through. John Williams gestured for Brink to follow. They walked toward the prison in silence, the white glare of floodlights wiping the lawn clean.

Finally, John Williams said, "You stay with me, Brink," he said. "No funny business in the old wing. We're going in and out, no detours."

"That's right," Brink said, realizing that his every move had been captured by the surveillance cameras. Williams must've watched him go to the third floor of the sanatorium to read Jess's journal. Cam Putney hadn't found him on his own. "You see everything that goes on in here."

"Obviously not enough of everything."

"If Jess Price knows what happened to Thessaly, she'll tell me."

"Listen, buddy, Thessaly thinks you're the cat's pajamas, but I'm not so easily impressed. If you get anything out of Price, let me know, but I don't see that happening. She'll clam up, most likely. That's her game, isn't it?"

He felt a sudden need to protect Jess. "You're wrong," he said. "It's not a game at all."

John stopped and turned to Brink. "What is it, then, Mr. Smart Guy?"

He saw Abulafia's circle, its letters and numbers. He remembered all that Vivek Gupta had told him. The pieces were there. He just needed to put them together. "It's a puzzle. And without Jess Price, we can't solve it."

"Well," he said, "let me make something crystal clear to you, my friend. Whatever you're up to, my ass is on the line here. If it weren't for Thessaly, you would not be setting one foot in my prison."

They stepped into the main entrance and through the metal detectors. "New guy," John mumbled to the guard on duty, who let him pass without taking his phone, which was a huge relief. As soon as he was with Jess, he'd call Rachel, and she would walk him through what he needed to do. She would tell him where to stand and where Jess should stand; she would tell him what to say and what Jess should say. She would help him with how to vocalize the syllables of HaShem.

And then what? While he'd agreed to go through with the plan, he was 99 percent sure that the ritual wouldn't work. He saw the ritual as a way to provoke a response from Jess. Like a dummy pill, the circle would create a placebo effect, bringing her back to the night Noah Cooke died. If he could recreate the emotions Jess experienced during the ritual, she would remember what really happened. All the legends that surrounded HaShem were just that: legends. And yet he couldn't help but feel the weight of the 1 percent chance that there was some substance to it all. He saw the photographs of Noah Cooke and Frankie Sedge. He'd read LaMoriette's account of the rabbi's and Jakob's injuries. They were playing with fire.

John Williams led Brink around a corner, down a long, brightly lit hallway to an empty room. It was set up for group therapy, a circle of folding chairs at the middle. "I'm standing right here, outside this door, keeping an eye on you." He pointed up to a camera in the hallway. "The cameras in this quadrant are disabled for ten minutes. I can't have anyone seeing I brought a prisoner down for a late-night chat. No funny stuff. I mean it." John unlocked the door and opened it for Brink, then looked at his watch. "You've got about eight minutes. Better use 'em."

The room was windowless, dark, the only light coming from a red EXIT sign near the door. Jess Price sat on a folding chair at the center of the room, her skin glowing red with reflected light, her hair hanging limp over her shoulders. She didn't acknowledge him, didn't even glance at him as he approached, but stared into the darkness. And yet he felt a wild rush of emotion in her presence. The pressure of the past three days had compacted his feelings, crystallizing them. He wanted to go to her, to touch her. He wanted to make sure she was there in the flesh and not a figment of his mind.

But as he approached her, he was startled by what he saw. She trembled violently, her lips were cracked to the point of bleeding, and her skin was so pale as to seem unearthly. Her eyes glowed with fever. She was on the edge of collapse. He wanted to rush to her, to help her somehow, but held back. He didn't want to frighten her. The woman in the dream looked like Jess, but it didn't mean she felt all that he did.

Even as he considered this, Jess stood, walked across the room, and embraced him. He felt, in the intimacy of the gesture—the way she pressed herself close, her arms sliding around his waist—that he wasn't alone in his feelings. She'd been there, too. She'd experienced everything.

"I didn't think I would see you again," she said, pressing her cheek against his chest.

"I wasn't going to let that happen," he said, holding her close. She was cold, freezing cold.

"Did you find the suitcase?" she asked, pulling away, her voice tense.

"I wouldn't have gotten this far without it."

"Then you know what happened to LaMoriette," she said. "You know it wasn't my fault."

"What I know is that you got tangled up in something totally beyond your control."

She turned away, to hide her response, but he saw that her eyes were wet with tears. "You don't know how long I've waited to hear that," she said. "I can stand almost anything as long as you believe me."

"I believe you," he said. "None of it makes sense, but I believe you. And I'm going to help you. I know it feels impossible, but I need you to try to think back to what happened that night at Sedge House."

A frenetic energy filled Jess's expression, and the tone of her voice seemed different from just a second before. "You know what they're doing, don't you?"

He took a step back without fully meaning to, his body sensing danger before it registered in his thoughts. "What who is doing?"

She fixed him with her eyes. "My first year in this place, I found a butterfly in the prison grounds. A big, beautiful monarch. She was injured. A nest of fire ants had gotten hold of her, hundreds of them. She struggled and fought, flapping her orange-and-black wings against them, but they wouldn't let up. They tore her apart methodically, piece by piece." Her eyes filled with fresh tears. "That is how the weak destroy the strong. That is how they are going to destroy me. Piece by piece."

He took this in, confused by her vehemence. He'd come to help her, but he needed her help, as well, not more riddles. Before he could question her, he felt his phone buzz in his pocket.

It was Rachel. "Where are you?" she asked, frantic, and when he told her he was with Jess, she said, "You have to get out. Now. Jameson Sedge is at the prison."

"Here?" Brink said, dismayed. "How?"

"I don't know how he knows you're there, but he must. You need to ask John Williams to escort you out."

"But I can't leave Jess here," he said.

"You don't have a choice," she said.

If Jameson Sedge had come to the prison, Rachel was right: He needed out. But he wasn't going to leave Jess behind. He shoved his phone into his pocket and took Jess by the arm. Stepping gingerly to the door, he peered into the long, brightly lit corridor. Something wasn't right. The hallway was empty. John Williams hadn't wanted to give him an inch. He'd stood guard at the door and planned to escort Brink out personally. But now he'd left Brink—and, more astonishing, an inmate—unguarded.

"Come with me," Brink said to Jess. "We're getting out of here."

61

As he led Jess to the end of the corridor, a map of the prison opened before him. He saw the network of hallways, the cafeteria to the south, the therapy rooms to the west, the entrance to the prison facing north. At the far end of the east wing, in the oldest part of the prison, stood the metal door to the sanatorium, the same door Thessaly had opened to get to the storage rooms in the basement. The old wing would be the only area of the prison without legions of security guards. If he could get there, they'd be safe, at least for a few minutes.

"This way," he said, squeezing Jess's hand and leading her to the end of the hallway. As they rounded a corner, Brink stopped cold. There at the entrance stood Jameson Sedge, his bodyguard Cam Putney, and John Williams. Sedge was trying to get into the prison, and Williams had blocked his entry. Putney stood by, ready to protect Sedge, and still Sedge didn't stand a chance: Nearly a dozen prison guards had collected behind John Williams. And while Brink would have liked to stay and see Cam and Jameson get creamed, this was their one opportunity to get out of there. While the guards were distracted, he and Jess could slip by undetected.

Brink knew exactly where to go—the route was clear in his

mind—but Jameson Sedge saw Jess and called out to her. "Ms. Price, you are exactly the person I came to see."

Jess was clearly visible to Jameson Sedge, and no doubt to the flank of security guards, as well, but Brink had edged back into the corridor, slowly, carefully. He needed to remain hidden. He couldn't blow everything by being recognized.

"I should thank you," Sedge said. "Without you, we wouldn't have found the code at all."

Brink peeked around the corner and saw Sedge standing under the bright lights of the prison entrance. He held an iPad with a scan of the scroll that had been inside the doll. Abulafia's complete circle had been enlarged, and was clear even to Brink, who stood over twenty feet away. "Was this what you and Noah Cooke discovered?"

Jess's eyes widened with recognition, but she said nothing.

"You hid it well," Sedge said. "I never would've found it alone. But now I need you to confirm that this is, indeed, the circle you used that night. It's a dangerous gamble I'm taking, and I need to know the truth. Is this the God Puzzle? Yes or no," Sedge said.

Jess said nothing.

"Perhaps it will help if I verify that what happened at Sedge House wasn't your fault. Nobody could have stopped what happened that night. You did not kill Noah Cooke. His death was an unhappy side effect of something much larger than you."

Jess said nothing.

Sedge nodded to Cam Putney, who reacted instantly, his actions quick and precise. He leapt past John Williams and the flank of security guards, grabbing Jess. The guards reacted instantly, drawing their guns, but Cam pulled a Walther PPK—the same gun Jameson had been carrying back at Anne-Marie's place—from his belt and aimed it at Jess's head. John Williams raised an arm, signaling for the guards to stand back. The situation had escalated dramatically. They could do nothing as Cam dragged Jess back to Sedge.

"You didn't kill Noah Cooke, but you were there, Ms. Price,"

Jameson said. "You saw the circle. You can verify that you used it." Cam clicked off the gun's safety. "You don't have much choice, my dear. Take a good look and tell me: Is this the same circle?"

"Yes," she said, her voice strong. "That's it."

"Thank you," Jameson said, his voice eerily calm. "That is all I needed to know. Cam, let her go. It's time. Do it now."

Cam Putney released Jess, lifted the Walther slowly into the air, and pointed it at Jameson Sedge's head. The air was electric with tension. Brink watched, unable to believe what he was seeing. It was unthinkable, but Sedge was telling his bodyguard to shoot him. It didn't make sense. And yet that was exactly what he'd said. *Do it now.*

Cam Putney's hand trembled, but his finger, poised upon the trigger, didn't move.

"Mr. Putney," Sedge said, his voice agitated. "We have an agreement."

Brink wasn't mistaken. Sedge had ordered his bodyguard to shoot him. But Putney's gaze had gone glassy, and he remained locked in place, frozen, unable to pull the trigger. Brink saw a series of emotions register on Sedge's face: astonishment, anger, determination. Finally, Sedge dropped the iPad, grabbed the gun from Putney, put the barrel to his temple, and pulled the trigger.

The space resounded with a deafening charge. In the horrific moment of silence that followed, Brink watched, astonished. He watched as Jameson Sedge dropped to the floor. He watched as the guards tackled Cam. He watched as Jess ran to him and grabbed his hand. He might have remained there, in shock, but Jess's touch jolted him into action. She took him by the hand, and they ran.

Pushing everything out of his mind, he focused on his goal: the reinforced metal door to the sanatorium. By the time they made it there, he was shaking so hard he could barely breathe. Steadying himself against the frame, he focused on the keypad, with its soothing square of numbers. A rush of color flooded his vision. Without pausing to think, he punched in a pattern, chasing the play of color over the pad, a bright sonata, until he'd entered all forty-three digits of the Code 39 barcode. With the final number, the door clicked open. They were in.

It was pitch dark, the stairwell a windowless shaft. He started up the stairs, grasping the handrail for support, but Jess pulled him back, pushed him against the wall, and kissed him. Soon they were entangled in each other, wrapped in an electric embrace that obscured everything—Sedge's gruesome suicide, the prison guards searching for them. It was only the two of them, Mike and Jess, alone in a vast darkness.

As much as he wanted to stay, they couldn't risk it. Taking Jess's hand, he led her up the stairs, through the darkness, until he reached the door to the roof. It was rigged with an alarm. From the metal cage over the light fixture and the old-school push-bar trip, he knew it was an antiquated system, probably installed mid-twentieth century. There was a good chance the thing didn't work at all. It was probably like the rest of that wing: left to deteriorate until some bureaucrat approved its demolition. Maybe they could break it down and try their luck on the roof.

If the alarm sounded, however, there would be nowhere to hide. Every guard in the prison would know their location. As it was, they had the benefit of darkness. They had the advantage of being in a secure location, hidden, with a little time to plan an escape. While it was tempting to rush out into the night and wing it, he preferred to wait. Whenever he got stuck in a tight spot, he paused to think the problem through, work out the probabilities, get a solid plan in place.

But even as he considered their options, Jess kicked the door open and ran onto the roof. He followed her out into the summer night, parrying a strong wind. Alarms rang through the prison and echoed across the grounds. The floodlights spun over the building, searching. There was no time to plan an escape now. All the options they'd had just seconds before narrowed to one: They had to make it off the roof. Their path had shifted from a puzzle to a game of chance. They were at the mercy of luck.

Jess didn't hesitate but ran clear to the far side of the rooftop, past an obstacle course of industrial air conditioners connected by alumi-num ductwork, as if expecting to find a way out of there. Brink watched, astonished by the change that had come over her. The prospect of escape had utterly transformed her. Gone was the trem-bling, terrified prisoner, and in her place was a woman who wanted freedom.

"Michael!" she yelled, waving for him to join her at the edge of the rooftop. "Follow me!"

His heart stopped at the sound of her voice, so close to the voice in his dream. Everything—the echoing alarm, the floodlights, the closing net of security guards—fell away and they stood together in a forest in another world. *Follow me.* He would follow her through labyrinths and mazes, forests and dungeons, hotel rooms and pris-ons. He would follow her through time and space to the outer edges of his sanity. Anywhere she led, he would follow.

But as he joined her at the precipice of the rooftop, he knew there was no escape. It was a steep drop, six stories onto concrete. Even if, by some miracle, they managed to climb down, there was an army of guards and a thick brick wall, with its rings of razor wire, waiting. They were trapped.

Looking over the yard below, Jess said, "Look at them—tiny weak things swarming."

"We'll go back," Brink said, taking her by the arm. "We'll find a different way out. The old wing has—"

"There's no other way out," she said, pulling free of his grasp and moving closer to the roof's edge. Soon, there would be nothing be-tween her and free fall. "Don't worry, my love," she said, glancing back at him, her eyes filled with determination. "I'll find you again." And with that Jess Price stepped over the ledge.

He'd anticipated what she was going to do, and sprang after her before she fell, grabbing hold of her jumpsuit with both hands, dig-ging his heels into the roof, and pulling with all his strength. His fingers slipped over the polyester fabric, but he held tight. They fell onto the roof, a few feet from the edge.

"What in the hell are you doing?" he said, frantic, gasping for breath.

"I won't stay here," she said. "I'd rather die."

"No," he whispered, his pulse pounding so hard his voice seemed little more than an echo in a wind chamber. She tried to stand, but Brink pulled her down and held her close. "I won't let you."

She lay against him, and the sudden warmth of her body sent a shiver of pleasure through him. There she was, a real woman, her touch elemental, as solid as a stone shelter from the wind. He held her tight, and in that moment nothing—not the prison guards, not the blaring alarm, not even the dangerous secrets she kept—could make him let her go. He felt her heart racing, the thrum so regular, so strong, that it took her voice in his ear to break him free of its whirring rhythm.

"They came for us," she said, pointing to the sky, her heartbeat transforming to the whirring blades of a helicopter. He looked up; the Eurocopter hovered above. It was a kind of miracle, an opening in the maze that gave them a last chance at freedom.

Rachel flung open the door and, waving to Brink, threw down a rope ladder. He slid his arm around Jess's waist and, pulling her close, grasped the ladder and carried her up into the star-filled sky.

62

As the helicopter angled away from the rooftop, Brink sank into his seat, dumbstruck. The machine-gun fire of events in the prison had left him reeling, and he needed to pause a minute, catch his breath, and figure out exactly what the hell was happening.

He buckled the safety belt and glanced around. Jess sat at his side, still gripping his hand, as if afraid to lose him, and Rachel was buckled into the seat across from him, waiting for an explanation. He glanced at Anne-Marie, sitting in the cockpit. It struck him that Anne-Marie didn't know that Jameson lay dead in the prison. A wave of revulsion fell over him as he remembered Sedge's suicide. He saw the Walther, heard the explosion, and saw the impact, heard the thud of Sedge's body hitting the floor. Rubbing his eyes, he wished he could erase it from his memory. How could he tell Anne-Marie that her partner had killed himself?

Anne-Marie steered the Eurocopter over the treetops, gliding into the darkness, the steady thrum of the propellers pulsing around them. Leaning against the window, Brink watched the prison recede below. From that distance, it was a carnival of movement. A caravan of blue and red lights burned through the darkness as squad cars arrived at the prison. An ambulance sat at the entrance, waiting. He could see guards in the yard watching the circus unfold. Brink had turned the entire place upside down.

A succession of emotions came over him—relief that he'd made it out, but also a terrible certainty that the police would be coming for him. What had Vivek Gupta said: *Everything you say can and will be used against you.* And what he'd just pulled off was no minor crime. Breaking a prisoner out of jail was not the kind of thing they let you get away with. He imagined them ransacking his apartment, calling his colleagues, maybe even tracking down his mother in France. There was really no defense for what he'd done. He'd helped a convicted murderer escape from a state prison. There was no denying it. If they caught him, he would be going to prison.

Rachel, noticing his growing alarm, leaned over and said, "Don't worry, Mike. This was all planned."

Brink started to interrupt her—he had a hundred things to tell her, most pressing being Jameson Sedge's suicide, which surely wasn't part of anyone's plan—but Rachel raised a hand, stopping him.

"Listen, and it will all make sense," she said, pushing her hair out of her eyes. "I was waiting for you in the Jeep outside the prison gate when I got a call from Anne-Marie. She told me that she was on her way to Ray Brook. She needed to stop Jameson, who was coming to the prison."

Brink started to tell her what Jameson Sedge had done, but Rachel didn't pause.

"After Cam ambushed us in the Jeep, Anne-Marie flew Jameson and Cam back up to the compound, where they ran the circle through various computer programs, just as Vivek Gupta predicted. Jameson found what he was looking for in the circle and decided to move forward with his plan."

"What plan?" he asked, studying Rachel closely, his stomach heavy with the knowledge that all plans were now off for Jameson Sedge.

"That's exactly what I wanted to know," she said. "Anne-Marie told me that Jameson has been preparing for this moment for de-

cades. With the code from Abulafia's circle, he was able to complete
the technology he'd been developing through Singularity. I tried to
get Anne-Marie to be more specific, but she'd only say that it all
started when Jameson was a child. In a moment of weakness, his
aunt Aurora showed him Violaine. She somehow alluded to the
power of the Shem HaMephorash. The experience changed his life.
He tried to get more information from Aurora, but she shut him out.
He became part of an underground collective of futurists and trans-
humanists who believed that ancient esoteric methods could be
combined with technology to create eternal life. He poured his personal wealth into research and created the conditions for his own
immortality."

"But that doesn't make sense—" Brink began, needing to tell her
what he'd witnessed. Jameson Sedge couldn't possibly be chasing immortality. The man had just killed himself.

"Let me finish," Rachel said, raising her voice above the noise of
the helicopter. "His ideas about immortality aren't what we normally
think of when we imagine eternal life. Not some silly elixir or a bi-
onic body. According to Anne-Marie, over the past decades, Jameson constructed a very elaborate, unalterable blockchain network
that would record and store every element of his neurological and
psychological self. It's not a regular network. It's powered by a quantum computer developed specifically for the purpose. He incentiv-
ized the network through cryptocurrency, offering billions to those
who verify, maintain, and keep his data safe. He collected the most
advanced technologies from around the world to build upon this
network. With quantum computing, he can upload superpositions of
his data anytime from any place. Forever."

"But even if this were possible, and he found a way to store qubits
of data about himself, it wouldn't be real. It would be—"

"—artificial intelligence," Rachel said. "That's exactly what I said.
Anne-Marie told me that this was where Jameson had been stuck:
He didn't know how to structure the network to encode actual life.
For years he'd been able to pull up simulations of himself that ap-

peared real but didn't have the autonomy, or the complexity, of his own living consciousness. That problem was solved with Abulafia's Shem HaMephorash. It contained an ancient technology—the original technology—of creation. And as Dr. Gupta showed us, it held a code that, when opened through quantum computing, captured the nonbinary superposition of consciousness. After Cam took Abulafia's manuscript from us on the highway, Sedge was able to incorporate the code into this program. All the pieces came together. He set the initial download in motion, and everything was ready. The last thing he had to do was to enter the network."

"And how could he possibly do that?"

Rachel sighed, clearly perturbed. "He had to die," she said. "That is why Anne-Marie came to the prison. To stop him from killing himself."

He glanced at Anne-Marie in the cockpit, astonished that she'd known the details of Sedge's plan and had still helped him. On the surface, she seemed so rational. "But she'd helped him every step of the way," he said. "Why stop him at the end?"

"That's right, she did," Rachel said. "But when she realized he actually intended to go through with it, she understood that it wasn't worth it. Sacrificing oneself for an idea is one thing in theory and quite another when the time comes to pull the trigger. I couldn't get anything more out of her except that she'd convinced Cam Putney to stop Jameson and that he'd agreed."

"But he didn't stop him," Jess said. "Jameson Sedge is dead."

Rachel looked from Jess to Brink. "This is even more terrible than I'd imagined."

The horror of Sedge's gruesome death had shaken him, and yet Brink felt an overwhelming sense of relief. It was over. The threat Jameson Sedge had posed was gone. Even if Jess were returned to prison, she wouldn't be watched. She wouldn't be threatened. Brink squeezed Jess's hand tight. She'd been through something terrible, but Sedge's death had set her free. Now, they needed to deal with Lilith.

63

Anne-Marie landed on a pad of concrete cut into the forest. They climbed out of the helicopter and made their way to the cantilevered deck. With the vast, shadowy forest surrounding them, Brink described everything that had happened at the prison. He told Anne-Marie how Cam had tried to stop Sedge and how he had failed. As Anne-Marie took this in, he glanced over the never-ending trees. Only the day before, he'd stood with Jameson on that very deck, talking about *the undiscovered country from whose bourn no traveler returns.* Now Jameson Sedge was gone, and Brink couldn't help but feel the tragedy of it.

"Jameson wasn't scared of anything," Anne-Marie said, wiping tears from her eyes. "But he was absolutely terrified of dying. That's why he needed Cam Putney so badly. He didn't think he could go through with it alone. He was so sure of his plan, and yet I knew that his biggest fear was that he was wrong. It would have made more sense to finalize the plan here, at the compound. But he needed to see you," she said, glancing at Jess. "He needed you to verify that the circle was the same one. Never mind that you might be wrong or that you wouldn't remember."

"I wasn't wrong," Jess said. "What he showed me was the same circle I found with Noah."

"That must have put his mind at ease," she said. "Nobody believed in Jameson more than me, but by the end, I knew that he'd become so obsessed that he couldn't see reality. There is no such thing as immortality, no matter how strongly the technology supports it. Knowing this, I convinced Cam not to follow Jameson's orders. He promised he wouldn't."

"He kept that promise," Jess said.

"I don't know why it matters, but it does," Anne-Marie said. "Jameson made the choice to die. However wrong that choice was, it was his own." Inside, a landline phone began to ring. She gestured for them to go inside, followed them in and picked up the phone. "I'll be right there," she said, cradling the phone between her shoulder and ear. "I need to take this."

Anne-Marie's home was exactly as Brink had left it the day before—the table set for three, the glaze of olive oil glistening in the pasta bowls, a slick of wine in the crystal goblets, cloth napkins crumpled with use. And yet everything had changed. Jameson Sedge was dead. Jess Price was at his side. He'd found the God Puzzle and unlocked its secrets. And now it was time to finish it.

After what they'd been through at the prison, he felt closer to Jess than ever. He couldn't help but shiver with pleasure at the thought of their encounter in the stairwell. Everything he'd felt in the dream, he'd found again in her arms. Still, he couldn't pin her down. She was like white light passing through a prism, her essence exploding into a variety of colors, each one changeable. One minute she was a riddle, the next an answer; one minute he wanted to save her, and the next she was the only one who could save him.

They found clean clothes in a laundry room off the kitchen. Jess changed out of her prison uniform and into a button-up oxford and a pair of Anne-Marie's jeans. Rachel had brought Brink's clothes, and he changed out of the prison-guard uniform. As he dressed, he looked himself over in a mirror. He was a mess. A vertical line slashed his chest, a great purple bruise left by the seatbelt when his truck flipped. The cut above his eyebrow had scabbed. His eyes were bloodshot, his skin pale. The past days had left him battered and beaten. But despite everything, he felt a strange sense of buoyancy, a lightness that he hadn't experienced before. He'd been through hell, and he was still standing.

He tucked the prison-security uniform deep in the kitchen trash bin, then walked through the house. Now that he knew what to look for, evidence of Jameson and Anne-Marie's interest in alchemy was everywhere: the framed Hebrew scrolls hanging on the wall of the living room, the cabinet of porcelain vessels, the golden chalice. He'd noticed them before, but they'd seemed merely decorative. The truth had been in front of his eyes, but it was like looking at a trick picture. Turn it one way, and the image was clear. Change the angle, and another picture emerged. He had the feeling that Jess Price held a similar illusion. Her mysteries would only open when he found the right vantage point.

As it was, she continued to baffle him. She'd been so strong on the rooftop, but as they walked into the living room, she seemed drained of blood, so weak she could do little more than collapse on the couch. The night was warm, and yet she shivered with cold. Brink found a chenille throw and covered her, then collected wood from a basket and kindled a fire in the fireplace. When he finished, he sat by her side.

Anne-Marie walked into the room and placed the leather case— the very one Cam Putney had taken from them earlier that day—on the coffee table. She opened it, revealing Abulafia's manuscript and Violaine. "Jameson and Cam left this in the basement," she said. "Rachel told me that you need it."

"I know you've been through a lot," Rachel said, glancing between Jess and Brink. "But there's something important we have to do."

"We'd better hurry," Anne-Marie said. "I just had word from my lawyer. The police traced the helicopter and are on their way here."

"Then let's begin," Rachel said. "I need candles and a shawl or small blanket. A bowl filled with clean water. A white towel. A piece of paper. A knife. And red wine if you have it." Rachel studied the coffee table. "An altar would be ideal, but this will have to do."

Anne-Marie walked through the house and returned with the items Rachel had requested. Brink shut off the lights, so that the room flickered with the flames of the fire.

"Thank you," Rachel said, as Anne-Marie placed the bowl of water before her. She dipped her hands into the water, then dried them on the towel. "We will need silence."

Rachel glanced at Anne-Marie, who nodded and left the room.

As the patio door clicked shut, Rachel tied a silk shawl over her hair, struck a match, and lit the candles, placing them at the corners of the table until the room glowed. Then she laid Violaine before them, opened Abulafia's manuscript, and turned to Jess.

"This is the original prayer circle," Rachel said. "Very much like the one you discovered at Sedge House, only it is much older. It has a complicated history, one that I will explain one day, but what you need to know now is that the circle that you and Noah read was a copy of this original one. And in that copy, there was an error."

"Rachel believes that the error is responsible for what happened," Brink said. "And that if we correct it, we can undo it."

"It isn't possible to undo it," Jess said. "Noah is gone."

"You're right, of course," Rachel said, her voice soft. "What happened at Sedge House can't be undone. But there's a chance that we can stop more terrible things from happening. Most important of all: If we get this right, you will be free."

Jess considered this. "Are you saying that if we do the ritual again, this could stop?"

Rachel placed her hand on Jess's arm. "I can't promise anything, but yes, I believe so. I wouldn't risk it if I didn't think we had a chance."

Jess looked from Brink to Rachel, and then down to the doll. "If there's any chance at all to end this, I want to try."

Rachel squeezed Jess's hand, then turned to Brink. "Can you reproduce the circle again?" Rachel asked, glancing at the doll. Brink pulled out his pen, tore a tiny square of paper from his notebook, and reproduced the circle exactly as it had been in Abulafia's manuscript. Rachel rolled the square into a tiny scroll, opened the compartment at the back of the doll's head, and replaced the old scroll with the new one.

"Come, stand here," she said, leading them to the center of the room. She placed the porcelain doll on the floor between them, joined their hands, and said, "When you're ready, we'll begin."

64

Rachel began to speak in a whisper, but soon her voice grew to fill the room. Each word was spoken with authority, leaving no doubt that she was in control. Brink repeated the words, following her pronunciation as best he could, the strings of hard, guttural sounds creating filaments of color in his mind. He struggled at first, but soon the words took over, the rhythm pulling him in. He glanced down at the porcelain doll lying in the weak candlelight—its gleaming auburn hair, the spattering of freckles on its cheeks, the dark eyelashes—and felt a shiver of fascination and repulsion. It seemed real, so real that he almost believed that this creature could, under the right circumstances, come to life.

But it didn't. There was no hurricane of energy, no burst of electricity. No feeling of being swept up into a maelstrom. Nothing. And he began to believe that it was exactly as he'd suspected—this whole thing was impossible. What happened at Sedge House had been the result of a tragic cocktail of imagination and alcohol. There had been some bad weather, the electricity had gone out, and everything took a dark turn. Jess woke to find a dead man lying in a pool of blood. The reality was that they had no way of knowing what really happened. Jess had blacked out, leaving the truth as unreachable as a coin in a deep well. Facts were facts, and it was ridiculous to pretend otherwise. It was time to stop the charade.

But then something happened. At first it was just a shift in the air, the smallest vibration in the atmosphere, a pressure so subtle he might not have noticed it at all had Jess not squeezed his hand, signaling she felt it, too. The candles flickered, and the scent of ozone—burnt and electric, yet strangely fresh, like a rainstorm—filled the room. Then, all at once, a flash of fire filled his vision and the world fell away.

He was falling. Down, down he plummeted through a bottomless darkness. He hit the ground, hard, knocking the air from his lungs. Pulling himself up, he found himself in a dungeon. The ceiling was vaulted, brick, the ground hard, packed dirt, the air thick with moisture. Ahead, torches illuminated cells filled with wretched prisoners. They called to him, gesturing for him to come closer, shaking fists, saying his name. At the end of the corridor, Jess waited in a cell. Her hair was long and tangled, and she wore a red dress glistening with brocade. "Finally, you've come," she said. "Open the door." She gestured to a fat oak barrel filled with apples. "There are the keys. Hurry. Choose one."

There were hundreds of apples. He thrust his hand into the barrel, and the apples became cold metal. Old and new keys, large and small keys, brass, gold, silver. Which to choose? The key to the attic? The key to the riddle? *Thus we eat red apples, every wonderful kind.* All the questions, and all the solutions, came down to this one choice. Pink Lady, Hokuto, Early Gold, Liberty, McIntosh. Choose correctly, and he would free her from Lilith and, in so doing, free himself.

Before he could choose, he remembered: He had the key already. He found it in his pocket, and fit it into the lock. One turn, two. The door creaked open. As he stepped inside, the cell filled with fire. He'd opened the door to a kiln. Violaine lay among the flames. She pushed herself up onto her wobbly legs, her pink dress shivering as she struggled to find balance. She wanted something from him, he could feel it. She reached for him, her green eyes glistening in the firelight.

Destroy the golem first, then the circle. Destroy them before it happens again. Quick, without thinking, Brink grasped the porcelain doll by the hair and threw LaMoriette's masterpiece into the flames.

The door to the cell hung open. Jess gathered her skirts in her hands, gave him a smile of gratitude, and ran.

He sprinted after her, struggling to keep up. She was fast, unnaturally fast. He saw her at the end of the corridor, but just as he approached, she disappeared. He followed, pushing himself to go faster, but she was always ahead. Through a door he passed, into a thick forest of evergreens. She was so fast, her bare feet flying over the roots and brambles, scaling the winding path, little more than a shadow wavering over the trunks of winter trees.

By the time he caught her, he was out of breath, his muscles trembling from the effort. She stood in a clearing under a cold gray sky, her hair long and wild, her cheeks pink with cold. A legion of skeletal trees formed a circle around a great slab of marble, the altar. A bone-handled knife lay at its side.

She pulled him into an embrace, kissing him passionately as she stripped off his clothes. He stood naked in the freezing wind, his skin prickling with cold, his feet sliced by shards of ice. She kissed him everywhere—his neck and shoulders, his chest, his knees, his feet—as if anointing him. He leaned back against the altar as she touched him, to steady himself, and gave himself over to her.

"Follow me," Jess said, holding him close. "There is so much waiting."

Ice cracked under his feet as he hoisted her into his arms and lay her on the cold slab of marble. She struggled to break free, but he held her down and locked one wrist, then the other, in metal cuffs. As he reached for the knife, he heard Rachel's voice in the distance. He pronounced the words she spoke, and suddenly everything changed. The wind stilled. The ice melted. Jess was no longer there. In her place was a woman so radiant, so beautiful, he took a step back, as if from a raging fire. Heat filled his body, and the world fell away. He was slipping into the fire, pulled by its gravity. He grabbed the knife, feeling the cold bone handle in his grip, and plunged the blade into Lilith's chest.

When he opened his eyes, he believed, for one terrible second, that the events in the dream were real. The porcelain doll was in the fireplace, charred and broken, and Jess lay on the leather sofa, positioned just as she'd been on the altar. Her shirt had been ripped open, her eyes were closed, and there was a pallor in her cheeks that alarmed him. He felt a surge of panic: He'd never considered the danger to Jess if the ritual worked. If he'd hurt her, he would never be able to forgive himself.

But when he sat by her side, she threw herself into his arms and he knew his fears were baseless. Jess was safe.

"We did it," Jess whispered, as he held her. "It's over."

65

The police took Jess away first. She didn't fight or resist. When asked, she spoke evenly, without emotion, giving the information they requested, and went willingly to the car, only looking back once, to smile at Brink.

Anne-Marie's lawyer showed up not ten minutes after the police arrived and was able to buy her a little more time. He argued that they had no reason to arrest her, but the helicopter parked behind the house was irrefutable evidence of Anne-Marie's involvement in the events at the New York State Correctional Facility, and Anne-Marie was cuffed, read her rights, and taken away.

When the police turned to Brink, Rachel did all the talking. She said they were Anne-Marie's friends, that they had been invited to the house, and that they had no idea what Anne-Marie had been up to, but they were willing to help in any way they could. She pointed to the manuscript lying on the coffee table and told them that this was the artwork reported stolen from the Morgan Library. She then led them to the wall of framed Hebrew scrolls and tipped them off to the fact that they'd been stolen from an Israeli museum some years before. Within ten minutes, she went from suspect to ally. Brink watched the whole thing, amazed. With her steady voice and

undeniable authority, her firm but polite manner, she disarmed the
police as effectively as she had disarmed Jameson Sedge.

In the end, the cops didn't know what do with Brink. They weren't
looking for anyone that fit his description. True to his word, John
Williams had disabled the cameras, and Mike Brink's image hadn't
been captured or circulated. As far as anyone at the prison knew, he'd
been a rookie guard on his first day at work. While the police took
down his name and contact information, they had no idea he'd been
at the prison at all. They took photographs of Abulafia's manuscript,
sealed it in a plastic pouch, got back in their car, and left.

With the police gone, Rachel went to the fireplace and lifted the
burned doll from the ashes. The porcelain shell and crystalline eyes
had charred black, and when they opened the secret compartment,
the scroll was nothing more than ash. Rachel swept the ashes and
dumped them, along with the golem, in a garbage bag, tied it, and
put it in the trash.

Brink wanted to help Rachel, but as he stepped into the kitchen,
he felt dizzy. He grabbed the marble-topped island to steady himself. Dr. Trevers warned him that he could experience chemical im-
balances in stressful situations, and the past three days had been
nonstop pressure. He hadn't slept or eaten in God knows how long.
It was no wonder he was shaky on his feet.

"Are you okay?" Rachel asked, clearly worried.

"I'm a little shaken up, I guess," he said. "All this has been . . .
wild."

Rachel put her hand on his arm. "Sit down," she said, pulling out
a stool from the kitchen island. She grabbed a glass, filled it with
water, and brought it to him. He drank it down in one long gulp.
"Care to tell me what just happened?" Rachel asked.

It was impossible to express the intensity, the sheer emotional
power of what he'd been through. How could anyone who hadn't
experienced it understand that his dreams were more real than reality? But he remembered how Rachel had spoken to him about her
faith, and he knew that she—with her ability to believe in things

many people, including Brink, would find difficult to stomach—
might be the only person who could help him understand.

"I don't think I could tell anyone this but you," he said, weighing
his words. "But since the day I met Jess Price, I've been experiencing . . . I don't even know what they are—dreams, I guess. But they're
more vivid than dreams. They're like reality, only magnified a thousand times."

Rachel took his glass, refilled it with cold water, and watched as he
drank again. Then she sat next to him at the island, took a wineglass,
and poured herself the last of the bottle of wine. "What happens in
the dreams?"

"Different things happen," he said. "I show up at a banquet, or in
a hotel room in Italy, or in a forest. But I'm always with Jess."

Rachel swirled wine in the glass, took a drink, and put it down.
"And it's just you and Jess in these places?"

"The two of us, together, yes," he said.

"Forgive me for getting personal here, but are your dreams sexual
in nature?"

Brink nodded, feeling his cheeks warm. If she only knew.

"No need to be embarrassed," she said, smiling. "Lilith is a succubus, after all. She dominates through sexual conquest. Did you
have one of these dreamlike experiences just now, in the living room,
during the ritual?"

He nodded again. "And what's even stranger is that some of the
things that happen in the dreams also occur in real life," he said. "I
threw the doll in the fire in the dream. And when I woke, it was
burned. I saw markings on Jess's skin in a dream, and then they were
on her arm in the prison. But other things"—he thought of the
bone-handled knife, how he had plunged it through Jess's breast-
bone and into her heart—"don't translate to reality."

"That's because your experiences aren't dreams," she said. "They're
real."

"But that's not possible," he said, trying to make sense of it. "These
things happened when I was asleep. They were in my head."

"That may be true," she said. "But that doesn't mean it's not real. Lilith, like all Divine intelligences, moves through human consciousness. That is her dimension, and it is as real as this one. Just because I didn't see her, it doesn't mean she doesn't exist. And it doesn't mean that what you did in that other world doesn't have consequences here."

Brink took a deep breath, trying to navigate his contradictory feelings. The very foundation of who he was, and what he knew to be true, told him this was impossible. Yet he'd been there. He knew the woman in his dream. He'd touched her, spoken to her. He'd killed her with his own hands. "Lilith is gone, right?" he asked finally. "Please tell me the ritual worked."

"From Jess's reaction, I would say so," Rachel said, smiling at him. "And the vessel she entered through—Violaine—is most definitely gone." She drank the last of her wine and pushed the glass away. "But one thing we haven't answered is why she targeted you. "Rachel rested her hand in her chin, meeting Brink's eye. " I've been thinking about what Dr. Gupta said about the binary sequence at the edge of Abulafia's circle. He said there could be another solution, a message embedded in the code. I believe he's right. There is another aspect to it, one that corresponds to the original meaning and purpose of the Shem HaMephorash. Do you still have the copy you made?"

Brink took out his notebook, opened it to the copy he'd drawn, and positioned it between them.

Rachel continued, "Abulafia's prayer circle was, as I've said, a way to both reveal the sacred and to hide it. It was created to glorify God and to pass down the hidden letters of the Name while protecting it from those who might misuse it. The Name is traditionally composed of the letters YHWH, the tetragrammaton. That is no mystery. It is the secret arrangement of these letters that Abulafia wanted to protect, and that arrangement must be encoded in this circle." She pressed the circle flat upon the marble surface, studying it. "If I spend a few hours trying to figure this out, I might be able to decipher it. But I suspect you can do it much faster."

Brink scanned the circle, letting his eye fall over the black and white squares. A pattern emerged in the binary sequence and, suddenly, it was there, before his eyes: the solution.

"You're right," he said. "Abulafia did encode something here. If you look at the circle, you'll see that every part has a purpose: The ring of black and white squares forms a binary sequence, as Dr. Gupta showed us. But the numbers, radials, and Hebrew letters are part of the puzzle, too. Even the Star of David is essential to solving this. Look here. If you start at true north, or number one on the Star of David, it falls between two squares, signifying a unit of two. Following the points in this manner, we get twelve units of binary numbers that read like this: 001111, 000011, 011011, 100111, 111111, 110011, or the numbers 15, 3, 27, 39, 63, 51. And each of these numbers on the dial signifies a Hebrew letter."

He grabbed his pen and wrote six Hebrew letters in the six circles at the center of the square, for Rachel to see: H Y G M H W.

He studied Rachel, searching for a sign that she understood. "Does that sequence mean anything to you?"

Rachel smiled, a glimmer of excitement in her eyes. "It does, but I . . . I can't believe it."

"So, you know what this means?" Brink asked, impatient. It was a difficult moment, a delicious torture to wait for a solution. Usually he was the one with the answers.

"I believe I do," she said, smiling mysteriously. "These six letters are HEH, YOD, GIMEL, MEM, HEH, VAV."

"But that isn't the traditional spelling of the Name," Brink said.

"No, it isn't. And that is why this is so extraordinary. There is evidence that the original name of God was not YHWH at all but was known to early rabbis as its inverse, HW HY, pronounced *HU-HI*. A colleague of mine has been writing about this element of HaShem for some time and even published a book about it a few years ago. His theory, one that has been quite controversial in our community, is that HW HY was indeed the true name and this pronunciation would have been known among an educated elite. Abulafia's circle suggests that this is true, at least as late as the thirteenth century. It's extraordinary proof that HW HY is the true spelling of the Name."

"But why does that matter?" Brink asked, trying to fathom why Rachel was so excited by the inversion of a few letters.

"Because it is not just the sounds that signify but their meaning. HW HY in Hebrew means HE–HER," Rachel said. "Abulafia included two additional words, GIMEL and MEM, Hebrew for 'AND ALSO,' between them, which makes it absolutely clear that the true Name means: HE AND ALSO HER."

Brink looked at the circle, still at a loss. "God is both?"

"Not exactly," she said. "Historically, in the Judaic tradition the Creator has been characterized as a single male deity. But according to this, the Creator is a dual-gendered God. A male–female deity. Not God the Father. Not God the Mother. But God the Father and also God the Mother, in one being."

Brink took this in, trying to understand the significance of the discovery.

Seeing his confusion, Rachel continued. "It's an incredible, world-changing revelation. The idea that God is male is the very foundation of my tradition, and Abulafia's message overthrows it entirely. It goes hand in hand with what Dr. Gupta showed us earlier about the code embedded in Abulafia's circle. It is non-binary, quantum, comprised of superpositions. And so is God."

Brink paused to consider this. If what Rachel said was correct, and God was neither male nor female, the Creator and the quantum nature of the universe were in perfect alignment. "This will have an enormous impact on religious beliefs," he said.

"The true nature of God has implications far beyond religion," Rachel said, her voice filled with the excitement of discovery. "God's position as an all-powerful male deity is replicated in society, underlying everything from religious hierarchies to the paterfamilias. But if God is dual-gendered, it undermines all of this. It destabilizes the very foundation of gender roles. It renders male hierarchies in politics, religion, and society—and patriarchal structures in general—illegitimate. It means that you and I, a man and a woman, are but a fragment of the Divine, while gender-fluid people—those with both male and female attributes—are the most perfect reflection of God."

Brink glanced at the God Puzzle, taking in the scope of its meaning and the repercussions it had for structures embedded in religion and society.

But while he understood the importance of Abulafia's message, he struggled to understand how it related to him. Finally, he asked, "Any theories about why this happened to me?"

"Actually, yes," Rachel said, meeting his eye. "I've thought quite a lot about that, and I believe you are partially at fault for what happened."

"Me?" he asked, astonished and perplexed by the accusation. "How?"

"There is a story from the midrash that I've always loved," she said. "It's about Lailah, the angel of conception. Lailah, the story goes, bequeaths babies the totality of knowledge in the womb. Then, when the baby is born, Lailah presses the child's lips, and all is forgotten. The story presupposes that all knowledge exists, that we don't acquire it, but collect what we've lost as we grow older. Perhaps your injury has allowed you to tap into what we all once knew before we were born."

"In what way?" Brink said, not sure he liked the direction she was headed.

"Your injury changed something essential in your brain. You acquired extraordinary abilities in areas you knew nothing about before. But what if those abilities are just the tip of the iceberg? What if you can access far greater knowledge?"

"What kind of knowledge?"

"Of the universe. Of reality. Of God. Look at what happened tonight. Somehow, you were able to achieve what Abulafia, and so many other mystics, tried so hard to do: You went beyond the limits of the material world. You communicated with another realm."

Brink remembered the line LaMoriette had written: *I lifted the veil between the human and the Divine and stared directly into the eyes of God.* Had his injury allowed him to lift that veil and see what was on the other side? Could he, if he tried, have access to even greater knowledge? He didn't know, but the idea both excited and terrified him.

"If that's true," Brink said lightly, trying to hide his contradictory emotions. "I'm in big trouble."

Rachel smiled back and squeezed his arm. "If it's true, Mike, there's no limit to what you can do."

66

Jess Price's retrial ended in a full acquittal. Jameson Sedge's suicide, and the speech he'd made at the prison exonerating Jess from wrongdoing, provided new evidence in the case, and Anne-Marie's testimony supported it. She gave a detailed history of Jameson Sedge's struggle with mental illness, one that began in his childhood, with the death of his father, and ended in his own tragic suicide. She described his obsession with immortality and admitted that she'd worried about him for years. The jury heard startling revelations about Sedge's surveillance of Jess in the prison and his part in Ernest Raythe's death. John Williams testified that Sedge had stated, minutes before his suicide, that Jess Price was not at fault for Noah Cooke's death. Proof of his involvement with a radical futurist group that claimed to be the heirs of the alchemists sealed the matter.

Brink didn't visit Jess in the months before her release. The extraordinary events they'd experienced left him unsettled. He'd lived through it firsthand—the vivid dreams, the ritual, the terrible power of HaShem—yet he started to doubt himself, questioning his memories until they seemed a kind of mirage, bright and shimmering and unreal. He began to see Jess Price and the God Puzzle as a series of random events in the otherwise orderly pattern of his life. Those patterns were strong, deeply rooted, and left no room for inexplicable aberrations.

He made an appointment with Dr. Trevers, hoping he would give him a rational explanation. They met via video call. Connie sat on his lap, watching the screen intently as Brink gave an account of his experiences. He didn't explain everything he'd been through, only the intensity of the dreams, how they'd left deep tracks in his memory. "I need to know what happened," he said, "and if it could happen again."

Dr. Trevers considered it all. Finally, he said, "You know, of course, that a traumatic brain injury can create irregular serotonin modulation."

"Sure," Brink said. They'd discussed his mood swings, his inability to sleep, all the ways he could regulate serotonin through exercise and meditation. "But what does it have to do with dreaming?"

"In certain stages of sleep, serotonin modulation increases. That's normal. But with irregular modulation, serotonin can flood the brain, causing abnormal experiences. It's been found that high levels of serotonin produce a similar experience in the brain to psilocybin—which, of course, creates psychedelic hallucinations. The result is super-salience: a feeling of deep meaning, ultra-vivid perceptions, and a spiritual connection with the universe. Serotonin type-two receptors are responsible for this state, and, as you know, your levels of serotonin are wildly erratic. After an injury like yours, such dreams would be almost certain to happen."

"In the dreams," Brink said, "I was able to get out of my head for the first time since the injury. There were no puzzles. No patterns. Just me. Sometimes it all felt so . . . real."

Dr. Trevers took this in and said, "I'm by no means a Freudian, Mike, and I don't doubt what you felt was powerful, but your interpretation seems dangerously close to wish fulfillment. You want your experiences to be real, but that doesn't mean they were."

Brink left the meeting feeling better, and for a while Dr. Trevers's explanation soothed him. It was a relief to believe that it was all the product of chemicals in his brain. Still, there were nights he woke in a cold sweat, overtaken by an intense longing for Jess Price. He would remember her touch, the deep understanding he'd felt when he was with her, their extraordinary connection, and he knew he needed to see her again. One night, after lying awake for hours thinking of her, he knew the time had come to make a decision: contact her or forget her. He took his Morgan silver dollar, balanced it on the flat of his thumb, and tossed it into the air. Heads he'd go to Ray Brook; tails he'd leave the whole thing alone. The coin landed on tails. He should have relegated Jess Price to the past. But he couldn't. He needed to see her. And so he contacted her anyway.

Jess was released in late February when the Adirondacks were covered with snow. With Thessaly Moses's help, Jess rented an apartment in Brooklyn, and Mike offered to give her a ride down to the city in his new truck. He picked her up at the prison the morning of her release and invited her to lunch. He'd done some research and found a rustic inn high in the mountains, a place near the woods, so that he could let Connie run. Conundrum charmed Jess instantly, licking her cheeks in the truck and performing her best tricks in the parking lot of the restaurant. They sat at a table with a view of the mountains, and Connie jumped into Jess's lap, curled up, and fell asleep.

They spent two hours talking over burgers and fries. She asked questions about his life before his injury, about MIT and his upcoming puzzle competitions. As they talked, he noticed how much she'd changed in the past months. She was confident, happy, her hair glossy and her cheeks filled with color. Thessaly had told him that, upon Jess's return to Ray Brook, her appetite returned, she jogged in the prison yard every afternoon and slept through the night. She'd even begun to write again, and while she wouldn't discuss her work, he understood that an essential part of her had been restored. All the darkness she'd harbored was gone.

And yet, despite the appearance of health, he knew she was emotionally fragile. He'd been careful to steer clear of talking about the trial, or Sedge House, or anything that might distress her. But as they finished their lunch, Jess said, "All I want is to forget that this whole part of my life ever happened. But I know I won't forget what you did for me, Mike. It was so confusing and so painful, but knowing that you're still here, that you're for real, means a lot."

After he paid the check, they walked out into the chilly afternoon, laughing like old friends. They'd been through something extraordinary together, and he felt at ease with her in a way that he rarely did with anyone. But friendship wasn't exactly what he wanted. As if reading his mind, Jess took his hand and squeezed it. An electric sensation moved through him, delicious and exciting. He felt an urge to pull her close and kiss her then and there, but he didn't want to make her uncomfortable. Thessaly had warned that freedom might feel overwhelming for Jess and that she would need time to adjust. He didn't want to add to her confusion. If anyone understood the difficulty of adjusting to a new life, it was Mike Brink.

"Let's see where this goes," she said, leading him to the entrance of a hiking trail, the path mottled with snow.

The sun was going down, and he wondered if they shouldn't get going. He looked at his watch. It was 4:04 P.M. Four plus four equals eight. Eight was not a perfect number, not a prime number, but a regular one, a number whose square was sixty-four and signified, according to various traditions, expansion. He longed for expansion, for everything that he didn't have, for connection, for love, and perhaps this was his chance to realize it.

"Come on," she said, smiling playfully. "I haven't been able to walk like this in years."

The next thing he knew they were climbing through the darkening forest together, winter sunlight dappling the leaves, a sharp, needling breeze shivering through his coat. He let Connie off her leash, and she bounded up the path, barking madly at the deluge of scent. The trail wound up and around, through the shadows of old-growth forest, where ice-covered ferns created crystalline geometric land-scapes: immense fractals, bright and prismatic, gossamer lattices filled with color. The forest was an intricate, ever-evolving series of patterns that threatened to catch him in its web of complexity, but with Jess holding his hand, he was firmly grounded, safe from the illusions of his mind.

Finally, they reached the top of the trail. A vista of mountains unfurled in the weak light of sunset, layer after layer of snow-covered peaks. He turned to tell Jess how relieved he was that she was free, how amazing it felt to be in the cold mountain air with her, how he'd longed to see her again, but she stopped him with a kiss.

He responded instinctively, pulling her close, feeling her body against his. For a moment he imagined they were together in their private world, that ultra-vivid dimension where anything could hap-pen. The kiss was a test, and it revealed the truth: Gone was the ter-rible desire that had nearly driven him mad. In its place was tenderness and vulnerability, a deep need to understand her, an en-tirely new kind of connection. He'd lived through something incred-ible with this woman, and he didn't want to lose her. It felt good to hold her, solid, and with that solidity came a realization: Jess wasn't anything like the woman he'd met in his dreams. She was better.

67

Cam Putney waited for his daughter. They were early for their flight and had over an hour to kill. Jasmine hadn't had lunch, so he gave her twenty bucks and told her to get something to eat from Starbucks. He didn't want to go in with her. The space was small, and crowds bothered him. People in general bothered him. That was what he'd taken with him from his stint at Ray Brook: A fear of enclosed spaces. Claustrophobia. Agoraphobia. Whatever you called it, it was always the same. Put him in a tight place with a bunch of people, and he wanted out of there pronto.

It took some convincing for Jasmine's mom to give the green light on their trip, but Jasmine begged and begged, and finally Cam got the go-ahead. The Cayman Islands would be a welcome change from dark, miserable New York. Anne-Marie had given him the use of her place for the week, with a cook and everything, so they would be more than comfortable. When Anne-Marie insisted he use Singularity's jet, he'd refused, then relented, realizing that it would be a unique experience for Jasmine. So much had changed after Mr. Sedge's death, but one thing remained the same: Everything he did was for her. Taking care of her was the only thing that kept him sane.

While his final mission had ended exactly as Mr. Sedge wanted, Cam had failed Anne-Marie. She'd begged him to stop Jameson from killing himself. And while he'd tried his best and hadn't pulled the trigger that night, he hadn't kept Sedge from grabbing the gun.

The turn of events at the prison let Cam off the hook. Because Mr. Sedge did the job himself, they couldn't hold Cam for more than twenty-four hours. Ten prison guards had witnessed Mr. Sedge's suicide, and all ten attested that Cam had struggled to stop what happened. There was nothing to charge him with except carrying a concealed weapon into a state prison, which Anne-Marie's lawyers managed to get reduced to a fine.

The real punishment had happened in his head. He couldn't stop seeing Mr. Sedge die. The gun lifting to his temple. The terrible moment between the shot and his collapse onto the floor. And the blood, so much blood. He woke up from nightmares, and that wasn't the worst of it. The loss of Mr. Sedge left him adrift in a way that he'd never been before. Even with all the money he'd inherited, he didn't know what to do with himself. He rubbed his neck, tracing the triangle that had symbolized his acceptance into Mr. Sedge's world. He was rich and free but didn't feel free. He felt purposeless and abandoned.

The time with Jasmine would help him adjust to things. Seven days of sea and sun and good food and Mr. Sedge's Scotch would help him figure it all out. Being a dad was a good start. He could make up for all the years he'd been away. Jasmine didn't let him get away with anything, and that was good for him. "Chill out, Dad," she said whenever he started winding himself up, which, with Jess Price's trial and Anne-Marie's insistence that they stay in touch, happened too often. With his daughter's help, he'd find a plan for the next part of his life.

Her excitement about the trip was enough to carry him for the moment. As the car ferried them out onto the tarmac and they climbed into the jet, she pointed out every little detail: the Singularity logo that matched his tattoo, the plush leather seats, the wide-screen television, the bedroom with its queen-size bed, the bathroom and shower cabinet. He'd been on the jet a bunch of times, usually with Mr. Sedge but a few times alone, and he still found it all amazing.

As they sat, he felt his phone buzz in the back pocket of his jeans. Probably another marketing call. He'd been getting them pretty much constantly, a barrage of telemarketers and insurance people. He figured his unlisted number got put on some list somewhere. But when he looked at his phone, he saw a text message: *I'm calling you in two minutes, Mr. Putney. Pick up. It is regarding your contract.* This startled him. The only contract he had with anyone was the one he'd made with Singularity back in 2011, his Ricardian contract He guessed it'd been nullified by Mr. Sedge's death. The executor of his Will, a lawyer Cam had never met before, hadn't mentioned it when they met to discuss his inheritance. Neither had Anne-Marie.

Cam stood, walked to the back of the jet, and slipped into the bathroom to take the call. Jasmine, who didn't miss a thing, who had her finger on the pulse of all his moods, didn't need to hear him yelling at whoever was on the other line. He wasn't in the mood to be harassed, but he was just curious enough to take the call.

It was a video call. He pushed a button to accept it and watched, dumbfounded, as the screen scrambled then resolved into the red hair, the pale papery skin, the piercing blue eyes of Jameson Sedge. His heart froze up, and he nearly dropped the phone. There, in the rectangular screen, was the man he'd worked for tirelessly, whose generosity had changed his daughter's future, whose death he'd witnessed and hadn't prevented. Jameson Sedge stared at him, a glimmer of amusement in his eyes.

"Mr. Putney," he said, his brow furrowed in that way it always did when he was teasing him. "You look utterly startled."

Cam stared, shocked, unable to speak. He tried to breathe but felt his chest tighten. Could it possibly be that Mr. Sedge's insane plan had worked? The files had all been uploaded, the programs had all been set in motion, the bank accounts had been distributing cash to the network nodes. But there had to be an error. Mr. Sedge couldn't be alive.

"That little glitch at the prison almost cost us everything," he said, smiling slightly. "What happened, my boy—cold feet?"

The voice was Mr. Sedge's voice. The face was Mr. Sedge's face. The words were exactly the words Mr. Sedge would use.

"Mr. Putney," he said. "Speak."

"No, sir," he said. "Not cold feet."

"I've seen you in many a precarious situation," the head in the screen said. "You've never been one to freeze up, Putney."

Cam thought it over. It was true. He'd killed men before and there had never been a problem. Could he tell him the truth? That Anne-Marie had begged him not to do it, and that he, deep in his heart, didn't have it in him to kill the man who'd saved him? "I just couldn't," he said at last, trying to find the words to express the anguish he'd felt over losing Mr. Sedge. "After everything you've done for us . . . I couldn't. Sir."

"Well," Mr. Sedge said, a hint of exasperation coloring his voice. "No need to get emotional. We will both agree that it was a human error, a flight of irrationality, one that we've addressed and overcome. We won't mention it again. But listen carefully, Mr. Putney: That can never, never happen again. You are my body now. You are my hands, my feet, my guts. While my reach is extensive, almost infinite from within the network, I will never eat a meal, drink a glass of good wine, hold Anne-Marie again. I will not be able to take the gun from your hands and complete the mission myself. You must take the reins now, or, at the very least, follow orders without hesitation. Do you understand me, Mr. Putney?"

"Yes, sir," Cam said. And while part of Cam recoiled at the pale, disembodied man in the screen, he also felt a sense of relief flood through him, one that washed away all the anxiety he'd felt since Mr.

Sedge died. Sedge's existence, however spectral, filled him with purpose. The mission was not over. There was work to be done. He was, once again, in his service. "Totally clear, sir."

"Good," the man on the screen said. "Because there is much to do. We are the future, and the future is long, very long. In fact, my boy, today is the first day of forever."

THE END

Note to the Reader

The puzzles in this novel were constructed with the aid of two brilliant constructors, Brendan Emmett Quigley and four-time World Puzzle champion Hwa-Wei Huang.

Dimitris Lazarou designed the God Puzzle, which was inspired by Abraham Abulafia's thirteenth-century drawings. *New York Times* Games editor Will Shortz gave invaluable information about the life and work of a puzzle master and allowed me to visit his home to see his puzzle library. The works of Janet Gleeson, Migene González-Wippler, and Rabbi Mark Sameth provided valuable information about the religious mystery at the heart of the novel.

Acknowledgments

Thank you to Susan Golomb, agent extraordinaire, for supporting this novel at every stage. Thank you to my editor, the astonishing Andrea Walker, for her insight and enthusiasm, and for making my work better in so many ways. The entire team at Random House has dazzled me: Andy Ward, Rachel Rokicki, Windy Dorrestyn, Maria Braekel, Karen Fink, Katie Horn, Madison Dettlinger, Noa Shapiro, Caitlin McKenna, and Kathy Lord. Thank you, too, to the team at Writers House—Maja Nikolic, Sofia Bolido, and Madeline Ticknor, and to Sally Willcox at A3 Artists Agency.

I'm grateful to the many people who offered their expertise, including Hannah Brooks, whose expertise in Hebrew and the history of Jerusalem was invaluable; Anne-Marie Richard, who shared her knowledge of porcelain dolls; Adam Harr, who offered insight into what happens to the brain while we dream; and Brendan Emmett Quigley, who was a perpetual resource for all things puzzle-related. And thank you to Dan Brown for advice and inspiration.

A special thank-you to my writers group—Janelle Brown, Angie Kim, Jean Kwok, James Han Mattson, and Tim Weed. Thank you, Steve Berry, Justin Cronin, Chris Pavone, Douglas Preston, Chris Bohjalian, and Lisa Scottoline for support. I'm also grateful to Briana Lee, Tom Garback, Madeline Wendricks, Tina Bueche, Dennis Donohue, and Art and Leona DeFehr.

Finally, thank you to my family, for whom I'm grateful every day.

PHOTO: © LEONARDO CENDAMO

DANIELLE TRUSSONI is the *New York Times* bestselling author of the novels *The Ancestor*, *Angelology*, and *Angelopolis*, all *New York Times* Notable Books, and the memoirs *The Fortress* and *Falling Through the Earth*, named one of the ten best books of the year by *The New York Times Book Review*. She is a graduate of the Iowa Writers' Workshop and winner of the Michener-Copernicus Society of America Fellowship. Her work has been translated into more than thirty languages.

danielletrussoni.com